"Your field peo⸺ ⸺ ⸺g on, know the people ⸺ ⸺ language, the terrain, friend from foe ... I don't mind improvising when a situation calls for it, but I have to have something to improvise with."

"We have a copy of Bellna's memories and personality," Dameron answered my argument. "Once it's impressed on your mind it will act like a reference library, telling you how to deal with the people you meet, whether or not Bellna knows them, how she usually acts with them if she does know them, and what would and would not be in character for her. It does more than studying her for years would, and was taken only recently, which means it's up-to-date ... If we're going to move on this, we'll have to do it soon."

I said at last, drawling the way he'd drawled earlier, "Just remember: if I get killed I'll never speak to you again."

MIND GUEST

Sharon Green

A Diana Santee Spaceways Novel

DAW BOOKS, INC.
DONALD A. WOLLHEIM, PUBLISHER

1633 Broadway, New York, NY 10019

DAW Collectors' Book No. 601

DEDICATION

For Vel dePowell, who will one day be my
personal accountant—when I can afford her.

First Printing, November 1984

1 2 3 4 5 6 7 8 9

PRINTED IN U.S.A.

CHAPTER 1

Waking up began as a struggle, the sort you strain against with all your strength and get absolutely nowhere with. I strained and struggled and found nothing but fog to fight, but by the time I reached the groaning stage the fog was beginning to lift. I became aware of what *I* entailed, then felt the hum that touched deeply but lightly in my bones. I knew the hum should mean something, but I was still too deep in the fog to know what.

It took a lot of effort to turn to my left side and open my eyes, and I couldn't remember why the effort was necessary. All I saw was a small room, plain metal walls, built-in drawers, and nothing else. All behind a thin but unbreakable mesh of monostrand, the sort used in spaceships to protect sleepers from the sudden loss of gravity.

Spaceship.

I had to be on a ship, but where was I going? Was the assignment finished *already*? Assignment. What assignment? What the hell was going on? I put a hand to my head as if that would stop the spasms going on inside it,

but there was still too much fog. Raising my arm seemed
to be a signal for the fog to close in again, and that
turned the switch off on my struggling.

The next time my eyes opened, the fog was all gone.
I saw the top of the bunk section, the monostrand safety
net closing the only open side, felt the throb that meant
live but unfiring engines. I was in a ship, all right, but
this time I knew all about it. The assignment I'd been
so worried over even when I didn't remember anything
about it *hadn't* been finished, not unless you count getting grabbed as finishing it. I'd walked right into
Radman's waiting arms, just as if I were responding to
an invitation he'd sent out. I sat up carefully on the
bunk, trying not to bash my thick head on the metal
above, disgusted with myself and impatient with the
dizziness the last of the drug caused. Radman had used
cryosol, and there was no knowing how long it had kept
me under.

I ran my hands through my tangled hair as I sat
cross-legged, giving myself a couple of minutes to take
inventory before pressing on to the harder job of getting
out of the bunk. My entire body felt heavy and without
strength, probably a combination reaction from the drug
and the length of time I'd been unconscious, but I
didn't hurt anymore. My clothes were long gone, cut
away at Radman's direction while he stood and grinned
and drooled, and naturally not replaced. He'd pretended
to be delighted that it was a female Special Agent who
had been sent after him, but his delight had switched to
panic when one of his men had gotten careless enough
to let me almost get one leg free. There were only five
of them there besides Radman himself, and those aren't
very comfortable odds against a hyper-A. The nickname means High Percentage Risk Agent, and isn't
handed out to every male with big muscles or every

female with a pretty smile. Radman had never heard the nickname, but he didn't have to. He'd heard about Special Agents, and believed enough of what he'd heard to be very, very careful.

I unhooked the monostrand mesh and swung my legs over the side of the bunk, then stood up. I was feeling steadier than I thought I would, but a couple of twinges flashed here and there, an unpleasant tail-end reminder of Radman's reaction to my "attempted escape." After I'd been chained with no more than a single link's space between wrists and ankles, Radman had spent some time kicking me around—literally. Experience had probably taught him how much pain he could give without actually breaking anything important, and he'd put that knowledge to work. By the time he'd worked off the heavy sweat he'd felt at the thought of my getting loose I was sure he'd cracked a couple of ribs at the very least, but I'd been wrong. Nothing had scraped together inside when a couple of Radman's men had carried me to a metal-framed cot and had shifted the chains on me to create the ever-popular spread-eagled look. Radman had gotten hot from the fun he'd had knocking me around, and wanted to spend some time working *that* off. I have a high pain threshold, but happily not that high; it didn't take long before his second-stage battering put me out. Which was a damned good thing. If I'd still been conscious when it came time for him to let rip I would have spit in his face, and I'd been in no shape to stand what would have come from *that* little gesture.

The small cabin opened onto a somewhat larger common room, from which it was possible to reach the rest of the ship. All the lights were set at daylight normal, but I ignored the brightness in the common room the way I had in the cabin and made my way to the tiny galley. I took a long drink of water while the ship thawed and heated a synth-egg sandwich for me, then sat and ate it while a second was being done. Cryosol slows your bodily processes while it keeps you unconscious, but that just means you won't starve to death before you wake up. It doesn't mean you can afford to forget to grab at least a quick bite once you're up and around again, despite the fact that you're not feeling very hungry. People have been known to die from the oversight, and it would have been rude of me to die so quickly and thereby spoil all of Radman's carefully laid plans.

When the second sandwich was ready I took it with me to the control room. Radman had had a lot of fun telling me all about what he intended doing, but even knowing what to expect didn't stop the flutter of panic I felt at sight of all that red on the pilot's console. Most pilots equate blinking red with the pumping of lifeblood out of a major artery, and I was no different. It took an effort to keep from running closer and quickly slapping switches, but since I knew how useless slapping switches would be I could walk forward slowly until I stood behind the pilot's chair.

The acceleration and deceleration switches had been cut off flush with the console, giving the check-off computer hysterics, and the emergency rocket toggle was also gone. The life-support system, meteor deflectors, view screens and communicator were still on the green, but that meant nothing. Radman had preset the view from the forward view screen, and the location computer was running a continuous "no information" blank tape, showing that I'd left human-inhabited space long behind me. Just for the hell of it I checked the number of inches of blank tape, multiplied by the standard rounded figure supplied in the front of every ephemeris, then took a long, slow bite of my sandwich. At the time of calculation I'd already been in an area of space that would not be explored for a minimum of two hundred standard years, with each second passing sending me farther and farther away. I'd be able to watch where I was going, Radman had said, live comfortably and eat well while I thought about ways of coming back, but there'd be no coming back. By going after him I'd earned a free, unending vacation trip, and he was going to see that I got what I'd earned. I could still hear his heavy, brutal laughter as the cryosol was hypo-sprayed into my bloodstream, and I looked down to see that I'd unconsciously crushed the sandwich to slop in one hand. I turned and left the control room then, and went to get a cup of coffee and another sandwich.

I set up a loose schedule for living in the days that followed, but still spent a lot of time reviewing and re-reviewing the moves I'd made in going after Radman. I'd expected to see what I'd done wrong rather quickly, but time passed and as far as I could see I hadn't done *anything* wrong. Nothing I'd done would have told Radman I was coming after him, but I'd still found him waiting for me. I usually had to go heavy on the exercising after coming to that conclusion, even though I knew intense rage was a waste of time and energy. The position I'd been forced into wasn't condusive to sane calm and logical thinking.

I must have been about two months on my way to nowhere when I finally decided I'd had enough of sitting around and doing nothing. Aside from the fact that there wasn't much I *could* do, most of my hesitation had come from that terrible human disease called wishful thinking. Being fully adult and more realistic than most hadn't stopped me from hoping that Starman Courageous and his loyal crew would somehow stumble across me, save me from the fate worse than death that had been imposed on me, and quickly return me to hearth and home. It took me that two months to admit that I *was* the proud possessor of a fate worse than death, and that Starman Courageous, every broad-shouldered and wide-chested inch of him, was too busy saving slender helpless-female types on tri-v to show up. If anything was going to be done, I was the one who would have to do it.

I took one last cigarette with my feet propped up, grabbed a quick shower, then found an adjusting tool and headed for the control room. I knew almost nothing about transbar electronics, but I was faced with the choice of tinkering and possibly killing myself fast, or leaving it alone and continuing on until I went crazy. Being a loner I hadn't found the two months totally unbearable, but two months wasn't two years or twenty. If I didn't do something, I was sealed into what would eventually become my tomb, and sitting around waiting for the inevitable wasn't my usual style.

The controls had been damaged at the pilot's console, which is usually a pretty permanent way of damaging them, but there was one remote chance. The transbar leads were tucked away in a box of their own, and if I could figure out which leads controlled what, I might be able to bypass the console. Only I was not an electrical engineer. My talents lie in other directions, and I've piloted many ships, but never had to fix any of them. I opened the panel that covered the leads, groaned at the nine million different colored wires, then took a deep breath and got started.

I'd found the leads that controlled the shower, the lights, and a dozen and a half unknown functions before it happened. I was tightening the last lead I'd loosened when the adjusting tool slipped, knocking out a lead in

the unexplored section. The loose lead swung down and
to the left, toward the bottom contact, but fouled on
another lead instead. There was a spray of pretty blue
sparks for about three seconds, then silence. I wondered
if I'd done anything serious, only to notice the new
flashing red light on the control console. I closed my
eyes for a minute then went to see what it was. It
turned out to be nothing much—the new blinking red
light was for the life support system.

After I carefully tossed the adjusting tool away, I sat
down in the pilot's seat. I would have done better using
spit and baling wire on the control console, the way
Starman Courageous would have, but it might have
taken me another two standard months to kill myself
with spit and baling wire. Why waste the time?

Then my eyes fell on the forward viewscreen, and I
stared hard. I hadn't bothered checking it for weeks,
but I should have taken a peek before starting on the
transbar leads—it would have saved some trouble. The
ship had blundered into the middle of a star system,
cutting across the orbital path of at least one of the
planets. I could tell this easily by the sight of the
good-sized moon I was heading for, but I couldn't tell
by eye whether or not I'd hit it. My hand went toward
the computer outlet automatically, but I pulled it back
before asking for the data. If the ship was going to hit,
it would hit. There was nothing I could do about it one
way or the other, and if I hit I wouldn't have to worry
about the new ringing in my ears. My tinkering with
the transbar leads had done something to the air pressure,
and I hadn't the faintest idea of how to undo it. I sat
back in the seat and simply watched the moon.

Six hours later, I was a lot closer to the moon and a
lot closer to upchucking. The on-again, off-again ringing in my ears was making me dizzy and nauseated, but

C H A P T E R 2

Waking up was downright luxurious. I was lying belly down and I stretched in comfort and yawned, wondering why the bunk felt so soft, then groaned when I realized it was probably a malfunction in the gravity control. I buried my face in the softness, knowing damned well that there was almost nothing I could do about it, then lay very still. The gentle fragrance coming from what I was lying on was nothing like the paper bed linen I'd used so long, and it was also nothing like anything I'd ever encountered before. There was dark all around me, the familiar dark I always slept in, but even in the dark there was something different about my surroundings.

I moved my fingers over whatever it was I was lying on, getting the impression of a soft and very rich-feeling fur. There was no pillow under my face, just the fur, and stretching my arms out limited the size of the fur whatever to little more than the width of a double bed. I was closer to the edge on the right, so I hung my right arm over it and found that the floor was no more than twelve inches below me—and also covered with what felt like fur. None of what was happening made any sense: was I dreaming—or just plain crazy?

I shifted over onto my back, in the process making another unsettling discovery. I knew I had no clothes on, but I'd had the impression that I was covered with something like a light blanket. Now I could feel there was a warmth on me, from shoulder height down to past my toes, but the warmth wasn't coming from anything as banal as a cover. All at once I began feeling annoyed, knowing damned well that by rights I ought to be scared stiff, but the whole thing was too stupid to be scary. When someone puts you in the dark to terrify you, they don't give you fur to lie on, and they don't make sure you're snuggly warm. I brushed my loose hair away from my face and made up my mind, then sat up slowly, holding one hand above my head to see if there was anything over me.

As soon as I was sitting straight, there was no longer any need to hold my hand up. A light had begun glowing from somewhere, starting very faint and low, then brightening to a good level. I took a deep breath and let it out slowly, fairly sure—or at least hoping—that there was a photocell or some equivalent involved.

The room that had just come to view was no more than twelve by twelve, having very few things in it. There was a small round metallic shape next to the bed-couch I was lying on, an amorphous blob that might have been a chair, and nothing else. I looked down at the bed-couch under me, expecting to see fur, but saw nothing but cloth. Granted, it was a silvery-gray cloth that looked better than any other cloth I'd ever seen, but it was still just cloth. The couch-bed was a low platform, an eight foot by seven foot oblong, raised slightly at the end that was against the wall, and seemingly upholstered. I shifted around a little, noticing that the warmth I'd felt earlier was fading, then decided to ask the major question: where the hell could I possibly be? It was fairly obvious that the proximity alarm *had* meant another ship, but where had they come from, and who were they? And while I was listing interesting questions, it would be smart to include, why? Someone had gone to more than a little trouble intercepting my ship, had managed to pull me out of it alive—and then had neatly tucked me into beddy-bye before disappearing from view. I'm normally grateful for any help I get in saving my neck, but I'd learned to be skeptical as well.

The warmth was entirely gone, so I put my feet out to the fur-cloth floor and stood up, looking around again. The floor-fur was a deep green, setting off the light salmon-colored wall panels, the panels themselves being very plain. Each three foot section of wall was separated from the others by a panel line, and there must have been a door there somewhere, but I couldn't spot it just then. I also saw no windows—which didn't mean there weren't any—but the far wall had something square on it. I moved closer, trying to figure out what the square might be. It was a light, slightly flickering gold in color, and could have been anything from an observation screen or window to an example of the art of tomorrow. I felt the urge to touch it, but pulled back suddenly. I was old enough to know better than to touch strange, unexplained objects; I'd had enough of waking up in odd places for a while.

"I see you've taken it upon yourself to leave your bed," an annoyed male voice said from behind me. "Are you sure you're feeling well enough?"

The unexpectedness of the voice startled me, that and the fact it was using an unknown language that I somehow understood perfectly. I turned slowly and took the time to prepare myself for whatever might be standing behind me, but the whole thing was a giant let-down. The only thing standing behind me, well to the right, was a mild-looking little man, round-cheeked and slightly pot-bellied, wearing a dark gold, one-piece outfit that could have been a uniform. The outfit had patches here and there, supporting the uniform theory, and the little man wasn't looking at all pleased with me. The entire scene had a very unreal quality to it, as if it would all turn out to be someone's idea of a practical joke, but I dismissed that thought fast and smiled my friendliest smile.

"How sweet of you to be concerned about me," I purred, moving a step or two closer to him. "I'm feeling just fine now, and I'll bet I have *you* to thank for it. I can see in your eyes that you're a very—*special*—sort of man."

His blue eyes didn't get any darker, but his chest swelled and his face settled into a prissy look of satisfaction.

"I did very little more than see to your comfort, my dear," he said smoothly. "And yet you may rest assured that had anything been seriously wrong with you, I would have seen to it to the best of my ability. We're rather isolated out here, but our medical facilities can't be bettered anywhere."

I let my smile warm slightly, mainly to cover the fact that I was still moving slowly toward him, and said, "I *knew* I was right about you, but I'm just a little confused. You mentioned your medical facilities here, but you didn't say where 'here' was. Can you tell me where I am?"

The satisfaction shifted to a frown, and the little man peered at me.

"This is an observation outpost of our Absari Con-

federacy," he answered sharply. "The planet is called
Tildor by its natives. Hadn't you any idea you were in
our neighborhood? The area happens to be proscribed."

I stopped where I was, about five feet from my
visitor, determined not to show how off balance I suddenly was. Not only hadn't I known that the area was
proscribed, I'd never even heard of proscribed areas,
not to mention something called the "Absari Confederacy." Things were back to being unreal again, but
there was one thing I knew for a rock-hard fact: if my
Federation had ever had contact with an Absari Confederacy, I would have heard about it. My not having
heard about them meant we'd never contacted them,
and I was back to wandering in the dark, searching for a
candle.

The little man was still watching me closely, so I
decided to use some of the confusion I felt to my own
advantage.

"I must have gone farther astray than I thought," I
breathed weakly, putting my hand to my head. "I haven't
the faintest idea of how I got here."

"But, my dear girl, where were you going?" he asked,
stepping closer to me with professional concern. "And
where did you start from? Surely no one would have
allowed someone with such meager knowledge of star
locations to travel about alone?"

We were no more than three feet apart, and that was
just about right for what I was going to have to do.
He'd already asked three questions I couldn't possibly
answer, and I also couldn't afford to wait around until
those questions came from a more official source. I had
to get out of there as fast as possible, without leaving
anyone behind who could begin yelling before I was
well out of reach.

I had stiffened the fingers of my right hand and was

just lifting the arm, when a section of the wall panel directly behind the little man slid aside, showing a second male visitor. This one was a good deal larger than the first, much taller and with much broader shoulders and no pot-belly, wearing the same sort of one-piece uniform that the little man wore, but his was a cobalt blue, with the patches in different places. His dark eyes gave me a slow, frank stare of appraisal, and he must have been pleased with what he saw—his rugged face creased into a grin, and he stopped next to the little man, his eyes still on me.

"How's our patient doing, Landren?" he asked in the sort of deep voice one would expect. "Is she up to having visitors yet?"

The little man had glanced at the newcomer, but his attention was still on me.

"She's still a bit shaky, Commander," he answered with what was becoming a familiar frown. "But there seems to be something odd going on here. You specifically told me she was alone, but why would such a helpless young woman be traveling alone? And another thing . . ."

"You're perfectly right, Landren," the man addressed as Commander interrupted. "I'm sure there are many things to discuss, but this isn't the time for it. The young lady and I are going to have a chat now, and I'd appreciate it if you would have someone bring a tray of edibles to us. You and I can have a talk later."

I stood casually where I was, making sure my muscles were relaxed in spite of the fact that the bigger man hadn't taken his dark eyes off me and now stood between me and my erstwhile target. The little man was annoyed all over again, not knowing how close he had come to the end of every annoyance, but there seemed to be little he could do. He nodded once, angrily, and drew himself up.

"Very well, Commander," he grudged to the larger man's back. "We'll discuss the matter later. And I'll speak to one of your team members about the rest of it."

He looked at me with what was probably supposed to have been a smile, bowed stiffly, then turned and walked out. The man who now stood and studied me with folded arms and sharp, intelligent eyes was nothing like the first man and would not be as easy to handle, but he would still have to be handled one way or another. I'd done a lot of bluffing in my professional life, but never in a situation where I didn't even know what I was supposed to be bluffing about. The man's eyes kept moving over me, as though he were looking for some sign of embarrassment on my part due to the fact that he was dressed and I wasn't, but he wasn't likely to find one. I'd been born and raised on one of the only two nudist planets in the Federation, and standing around raw had never bothered me. I looked away from the man, extended my left arm for inspection, then rubbed at an invisible spot with a small frown and a whole lot of concentration. I heard the sound of a snort of amusement, then the big man shifted slightly where he stood.

"You're really very good, girl," he commented in that deep voice. "If I didn't know better, I'd swear you were as innocent as you look."

The comment did nothing for my peace of mind, but I smiled at him with polite interest.

"I don't understand, Commander," I said, putting just a touch of confusion into my tone. "Am I supposed to be guilty of something?"

The question made the man smile again, then he laughed aloud.

"All right, I give up," he conceded with a chuckle. "I'd better stop trying to shake that calm of yours before I push you into trying something violent. I'll start off by telling you that I already know you're not native to our Confederacy, so you can relax as far as that goes. If you'll join me out on the terrace, we can both relax and discuss the rest of it."

He stood not three feet away from me, grinning informally but in no way off guard, and I didn't know what the hell to do. Insisting you know something as a fact when all you do is suspect is such an old trick that lots of people have forgotten about it. If he was telling the truth, the fact that I wasn't in a jail cell was an encouraging sign, but then I reminded myself that iron bars do not a prison make.

"I hate to seem dense, Commander, but I'm afraid I have very little idea of what you're talking about," I drawled. "Suppose you add a few details to what you've already said, and then maybe I'll be able to hold up my end of the conversation."

He studied me again, then he nodded.

"Considering your position, I can't blame you for being cautious," he conceded. "Maybe it would be better if we both knew what was happening." He moved to his right, no more than five or six steps, then touched one of the salmon-colored wall panels. A thin, horizontal section of the wall snapped out, knee height from the floor, and the Commander sat himself down on it.

"All right, from the beginning," he said, leaning back against the wall in his bench seat. "As soon as we looked at your ship, we knew you were not from one of the member planets of the Confederacy. By 'we' I mean my second in command and myself. He and I are the only ones who know about you, which is why Landren was so confused."

He stretched his legs out and crossed his ankles, frowning slightly in concentration. "The Absari Confederacy has known about your Federation for some twenty standard years now, but the knowledge hasn't been spread about. One of our scout ships netted a primitive rocket, calculated the direction from which it had come, then backtracked on it. When they began picking up communicator signals, they turned back and reported to Absar Central, and we've been tip-toeing around the edges of your volume of space ever since. We're nearly to the point of introducing ourselves, but things like that take time." His eyes came back to me, and the grin was starting again. "If I were going to execute you as an undesirable alien, it would have been done by now, so how about calling a truce and having something to eat with me? I'll feel like a fool if I have to call a bodyguard before I can relax with you in arm's reach."

This time I studied him and his grin, weighing my options. I could trust him and take my chances or wipe him and take my chances, but either way it would be a risk. The way he moved and held himself said a lot about his ability, and the lack of fat on his well muscled body said he had very little need of a bodyguard. I would have backed my own ability against his no matter what he knew, but even if I did best him and then managed to find my way to a ship without running afoul of anyone else, which way did I point the ship? Which quadrant had I come in from? I took a strand of my hair to chew on, and the Commander's grin widened.

"You look as though you're having trouble making up your mind," he observed, moving his back away from the wall to lean one elbow on a broad thigh. "Suppose I add this as support for being reasonable: you must have a lot of questions you'd like answered, and I'll be glad to answer them—as well as fill you in on what you said when I questioned you. You were unconscious at the time, so you're hardly likely to remember it by yourself."

I continued to stare at him for a second, then smiled, as did he. He was trying to bribe me with my own curiosity, and that made me feel better about him. A man who understands bribery *can't* be all bad.

"All right, Commander, you've got me," I laughed, shaking my head at him. "Curiosity always has been my fatal flaw, and I've got a question that's been bothering me since that other man first opened his mouth. I feel as though I'm speaking my own language, but what I'm speaking and hearing isn't my own language. I mean, I'm pretty sure it isn't my own language, even though I'm thinking in it, too. Does that make any sense, or do I have a lump on the head to account for it?"

"You're perfectly all right," he chuckled, getting to his feet and hiding the seat. "You had to have a language lesson before I could question you, and there was no reason to take it back again once you had it."

I could have spent a lot of time thinking about their methods of teaching languages to people who were unconscious, but the Commander had moved another two feet to his right and had put his hand on the wall again. A panel popped open, revealing a footed jumpsuit, and he pulled it out then closed the panel again. The jumpsuit looked like the uniform he was wearing—aside from being dark green in color and having no patches— and it also looked like it might fit me.

"You'd better put this on," he said, tossing me the suit with what looked like regret on his face. "We usually wear clothing of some sort around here, and there's no sense in getting people curious."

As soon as I had the suit, he turned away from me and walked over to that shimmering golden square on the wall. He brushed his fingers along the upper right side of it, and I blinked as it began lengthening and widening as though it were made of syngel. The former square kept changing until it was about seven feet high and four feet wide, then he seemed to be satisfied. It still shimmered goldenly, but now it was a doorway, showing a hazy view of green skies and yellow sunshine above a wide, carved wood balcony. The big man took time out from staring through the doorway to glance at me, and I realized I'd just been standing there holding the suit in my hand, so I began getting into it. It didn't take more than a minute, which made the timing just right.

"Ah—here's the food," the big man observed, causing me to look around.

The panel door had slid aside again, and this time it was a really oversized male who entered pushing a cart. He was bigger and wider—and younger—than the Commander, with brown hair and eyes and a broad, square face, and he wore the same uniform outfit, only in a deep red. He pushed the cart—which had no wheels but some sort of runners—through the golden haze and out onto the terrace, then came back through the golden doorway without it. He nodded to Commander whoever, sent a wink in my direction, then left again without a word. When the panel had slid closed behind his broad back, I looked over toward the Commander again and commented, "Now I know why that doorway is so high. I'm glad to see he's friendly."

"That's Leandor, head of my special section," the Commander supplied, looking toward the now empty doorway. "He must have heard about our visitor and decided to get a look at her to break up the boredom. Waiting on tables isn't what he was trained for."

"How about discussing what he *was* trained for," I

suggested with a bright smile. "As an easy lead-in to all those questions you're going to answer for me."

"You sound as though you think I won't be answering any questions," he said with an injured air of innocence. "You do have my word, you know, and I consider my word a solemn oath. Let's take a look and see what Leandor brought."

He headed out through the golden haze with a half-swallowed grin on his face, leaving me no option but to ignore my annoyance and follow him. It was pretty obvious he intended running our interview to suit himself, and it didn't yet suit him to get down to cases.

As I passed through the golden haze, I felt a light tingling sensation, the same sort of tingling you feel when moving through a light grade force shield. Once I was through it, I noticed immediately that the quality of the air was different. Inside the air was fresh and clean, but fresh and clean in the way of having been laundered through a recirculator; outside was the fresh and clean of true outdoors, with a lot of that just-born feeling of recent rain. I took a deep, sweet breath of it, knowing how lucky I was to be able to breath air like that again, then looked around.

The green sky was early-afternoon light, lacking the too-bright glare of morning. The yellow sunshine covered everything, and in some strange way made the ten foot, carved wood balcony a very dark brown. The wood gleamed as though it were polished, intricate designs following themselves around the entire area of it. Commander who-sis was busy at the tray, so I walked to the thigh-high balcony rail, leaned one hand on it, and looked over.

Below the balcony was miles of unoccupied air, falling away dizzily to medium-sized foothills a long way down. If there was anything on the ground far below I couldn't see it, but there didn't seem to be anything anywhere—just miles and miles of emptiness. That first little man had said we were in an outpost, and I wondered briefly what sort of an outpost it could be.

I turned away from the balcony rail to see that the Commander had transferred a number of thin, oblong dishes to a wide block of pure white stone that was obviously going to be our table, so I left the rail and joined him. There were matching white stone benches to sit on, so I lowered myself and rested an elbow on the table.

"Question number one which requires a detailed response," I announced, watching the big man as he paused over uncovering a dish to glance at me. "What do I call you when I get tired of 'Commander'?"

The question was obviously an acceptable one, and the wary look faded from his eyes as he bowed.

"I am Commander Arlent Selam Delrah Garmar Hantal Queltes Dameron," he answered, pronouncing the names slowly and distinctly. "Please call me Dameron."

"That's what I get for asking for detail," I sighed, shaking my head. "If you hadn't added that last, I might have gotten discouraged."

"I somehow doubt that," he laughed, seating himself on his own white bench. "And what would you like to be called?"

"Now, why should you have to ask my name?" I mused, keeping my eyes on him. "What about all that sleep talking I did?"

He smiled gently.

"I know that your name is," and suddenly his pronunciation became foreign, " 'Special Agent of the Federation Council Diana Santee,' but which of those names do you prefer being addressed by? We usually choose the one we like best, no matter what position it holds in the full title."

"Our familiar names are usually chosen for us," I answered with an air of faint disappointment. "My chosen name is Diana, and Diana had thought she'd caught you in a little bit of fast foot-shuffling. I'll just have to drown my sorrow at the mistake in some of that food which smells so delicious."

"Best idea I've heard yet," he agreed with what was becoming a usual grin, then started digging in. I went at it a little more cautiously, but didn't find any hidden caches of camouflaged ptomaine. Everything tasted as good as it smelled, which let me shift my eating to automatic while my mind paid attention to thinking.

For some reason, it appeared I had given my name and rank in Basic rather than in whatever I was speaking then. I didn't know enough about the situation to even begin to guess why, but could only hope I also hadn't gone into detail about my job. No matter what my position there turned out to be, they would watch a non-combatant a lot less carefully than they'd watch an experienced professional. And as large as I was, the man who had named himself Dameron was larger still, and obviously a fighting man. No matter what he had learned about me, it probably would not be enough to make him call that bodyguard he'd joked about earlier—and therein lay another advantage for me. His eyes came to me as I watched him chew, and I smiled in response to his smile, but we weren't smiling at the same thing.

After I'd eaten most of what had been put in front of me, I decided to get on with the question and answer game. I picked up the hexagonal glass of what had turned out to be a light, sparkling silver wine, sipped at it, then cleared my throat. When Dameron's dark eyes were on me, I put the glass down again.

"If you've regained part of your strength, I'd like to get on with our information exchange," I said, gesturing at all the empty dishes. "So far, all we've exchanged is our names, and that's not my idea of making headway."

"You do have a point," he sighed, looking regretfully at the leftovers but pushing his plate away anyway. "Go ahead and ask your questions."

"I've got the next one all ready," I said, leaning forward a little. "I was told that this is an outpost, but no one's said what sort of an outpost. Does your Confederacy have a colony here?"

Dameron poured himself more of the wine, then leaned to one side of his bench with a sigh.

"We have no colony here, but there *are* people who we protect—in a way," he said, sipping from his glass before waving a finger at me. "No, don't start looking at me like that, I'm *trying* to explain!"

He was annoyed at the expression on my face, but if that was his idea of explaining, he was bound to get even more annoyed. I kept my skepticism voiceless and leaned my forearm down to my own bench, and he continued with a vague gesture of his wine glass.

"We of the Absari Confederacy like to think of ourselves as civilized," he groped. "Being civilized, we feel it our duty to help those people in our area of space who haven't gotten as far as we have. We watch over them and lend an anonymous hand, easing them more quickly through certain standard steps of advancement. For instance, we supply various rulers with advisors who put a premium on intelligence and a gift for invention. When our assisted kingdoms begin to prosper, their neighbors copy the methods used to catch up, thereby spreading the idea painlessly. We also encourage force of arms—no sense helping a kingdom to prosperity just to see them lose it to the nearest strong man—but we don't supply any clues which will lead to the more advanced sorts of weaponry. They don't know about us, won't know about us unless a catastrophe happens, and we maintain a strict hands-off policy with anything that's really new. We won't try to change something we've never seen before; after all, how can we evaluate it?"

He paused at that point to swallow at his wine, and I sipped at my own, finally understanding why he'd had such a problem with his explanation. His Confederacy mixed into the affairs of non-member planets, and it's easy to misinterpret something like that, no matter what the motive behind it is. I took another sip of wine and smiled at him.

"I can understand why you're careful about something new. Have you come across many really new things?"

"Not many," he smiled back, relaxing a little. "But a few. As a matter of fact, this planet has a beauty of a poser that we've been trying to get to the bottom of since we got here. We try not to have our agents commit their full lives to a backward planet like this one, and we certainly don't allow families to settle here, but we may have to make an exception. The mystery is handed down in certain families only, and outsiders don't have a chance of getting anywhere near it. Something will have to be done, but I hope it's done after my time. It's bound to be involved and risky."

He stopped again, as though he'd already said whatever there was to say, and I shifted on the bench, my curiosity really aroused.

"Well?" I prompted, wondering if he'd ever remem-

ber to include details. "What is this fantastic mystery?
Don't tell me the secret is a secret?"

He looked down into his glass as he gently swirled
the light, silvery wine, and he seemed to be fascinated
with whatever he saw there.

"I'm sorry to say that the secret is just exactly that,"
he murmured. "I don't think you should be too overburdened with knowledge when you go back to your home
sector."

He was so off-hand and casual about it that I nearly
missed it. My arm, which was stretched out to put my
glass back on the table, froze to complete motionlessness,
and my jaw dropped down to where I was sitting.

"Do you mean to sit there and say that you're sending
me home?" I gasped, staring at him. "Why?"

The grin he'd been hiding came all the way out, and
he laughed aloud.

"Because, as I told you, we hope to make peaceful
contact with your people some day," he chuckled. "The
more friends we have there when the day comes, the
better off we'll be. I'm also personally convinced you'll
say nothing about us when you do get back."

I finished putting my glass on the table, then added
my forearms right in front of it.

"Oh, yes," I nodded with a grumble. "I'd almost
forgotten that unconscious conversation we had. Maybe
if you tell me what I said, I'll find it easier to believe
what *you're* saying."

"You'll believe it when you get there," he grinned,
then finished off his wine. "I found out that much about
you. You said you'd been sent away from your people
by someone who wanted to get rid of you before you
put him out of business. I gathered that the business
was illegal, and you're some sort of law enforcement
agent for your Federation."

His eyes were on me in a casual, mildly curious way, so I made sure to squirm uncomfortably and blush enough to be noticed.

"I'd already gotten the proof I needed, but I got careless," I confessed in an embarrassed voice. "Radman's a slaver, and that's too lucrative a business not to watch closely. My department would have known he was responsible for my disappearance, but the way he worked it, he would have come out as innocent as an infant if he were put to the Question. He would have been asked about my present physical whereabouts and condition, and he would have been able to answer in all honesty, 'I don't know'!"

The thought of it made me furious all over again, but I was careful not to show the feeling. Radman had seen to it that I would have been able to stay alive and healthy for years, and hadn't given a damn that during those years I most likely would have become a raving lunatic. The thought had been with me constantly during those two months aboard the ship, but now I was able to think about coming face to face with him again, now there was more than just the dream of it. The fingernails of my right hand scraped along the white stone of the table top, and I barely felt it.

I was brought back to my surroundings when Dameron rose from his bench and put his hand out to me.

"If you feel up to a short guided tour, we can check on your transportation home on the way," he smiled. "My second and I've been working on your ship in our free time, getting it back together, and the only thing we haven't done yet is reprogram your course computer. You know, you really did a job on that ship. I don't know how we managed to get you out of it alive."

"Personally," I said, getting to my feet, "I attribute it to my great mechanical ability, my unbelievable strength for survival—and more luck than any ten people see in a lifetime."

He chuckled his agreement and we left the terrace, but going back was an experience in itself. The terrace seemed to grow out of the mountainside, sheer gray rock stretching almost as far up as the ground below was down, and right in the center of the gray rock was a hazy golden doorway, through which the plain bedroom could be seen. When we were both back through the tingling haze, Dameron touched the side of the doorway again, and in a matter of moments the doorway was once again a square. I chewed at the inside of my lip as I stared, knowing that you give away how much you know by the questions you ask, but the terrace question was one I couldn't let slide. When Dameron began leading the way toward the sliding exit of the room, I made up my mind.

"The view from the terrace was magnificent," I said as normally as I could as I followed him to the door. "If that's what's outside these rooms, I'm surprised you can keep anyone indoors."

"I might have had a problem if that was what was there," he agreed, slowing as he left the room to let me catch up. "But it happens that those terraces are nowhere near this base—or this volume of space."

I tried not to frown. "That's not what I would call an informative answer," I protested, looking up at him as we walked. He chuckled at the irritation in my tone.

"I don't have many details to give you," he answered, sounding almost embarrassed. "The splinter terraces are something we use, but not because we understand them." He sighed a little and shook his head. "They were looking for a transportation breakthrough and found the Skytops instead. That's what we call those mountains, and I'm sure you saw why. We built a terrace and anchored it in the rock, then used it as a base for exploration. None of the exploration teams or subsequent searchers were ever heard from again."

His face was serious and his voice was quiet, the sort of quiet some people use when they speak of the uselessly dead. He'd stopped in the middle of the corridor and was staring down at the carpeting.

"Wherever that place is," he continued heavily, "all we know about it is that the constellations are totally unfamiliar—when we finally get to see them. The days are very long—some fifty standard hours' worth—and the nights correspond. Our people had survival equipment and communication equipment, but we still lost them—suddenly and without explanation. The searchers who went after them were lost too—at a different point. And there's the last thing to consider." His eyes came back up to me, holding mine as if daring me to dispute him. "Each time a new doorway is put into use, a new terrace has to be built. The terrace is always there after that, but a new doorway means a new terrace, and the view always seems to be the same. I don't know how many doorways are in use, but no one has ever seen more than the terrace he stood on. You're welcome to the information I have on the terraces, because they're something I would personally like to see explained. I had a friend on the first ex-team that was lost."

I nodded my head, understanding how he felt, and smiled faintly. "So they're called splinter terraces because someone feels they're parallel universes or some such. Do you put much stock in that?"

"Who knows?" He shrugged, starting to walk again. "It's always a possibility, no matter how odd it sounds. We use the terraces in bases like these to keep the personnel from developing claustrophobia, but that's all they're good for."

"You still haven't said what's outside," I reminded him, pacing him down the salmon-colored corridor on dark green carpeting. There were doorways on both sides of the corridor, and up ahead, about twenty-five feet in front of us, was an airtight door that looked dependable.

"Outside is nothing but airless moonscape," he answered. "This base is underground on Tildor's nearer moon. When the Tildorani achieve spaceflight we'll welcome them to the group, but we don't want to be discovered by them before then."

"Don't blame you a bit," I commented, looking around as I walked. The doors along the corridor were unmarked, but there were small, metal plates to the right and left of each door, each pair of plates having a symbol of some sort, the symbols on each door being different.

"This is our residential area," Dameron supplied in true tour-guide fashion. "We have to pass through the work area to reach the docking facilities, so you'll get to see most of the base. It's a typical base in most respects, but we find it comfortable."

I nodded again without commenting, and continued to look around. We passed through the airtight door into another corridor, making sure the door was properly sealed behind us, then paced the length of the corridor. The walls were a brisk electric blue here with bright rust carpeting on the floor—a combination which seemed to encourage bustle. People bustled out of one doorway and into another, not really rushing but certainly not taking their time, and through the open doorways I could see other people sitting at odd-looking cubes or standing near what must have been computer terminals. Everyone was busy, and Dameron gestured toward them.

"This is our work area, where everything gets done,"

he explained. "Detailed information about areas and people are constantly updated, reports are added to their proper places, supply lists are confirmed and filled, and place-on-planet profiles are developed for each of our team people. Knowing that an advisor-agent is about to take a trip helps me to keep our barbarian-agents from attacking his escort—and also gives the barbarian-agents a chance to keep a protective eye on him. I don't ever want to have to send a report to Absar Central telling them that half my field team just wiped out the other half. Reports like that aren't appreciated."

"That's one comment I can understand without details," I laughed, still looking around. Everything seemed so familiar and home-like that it was beginning to disturb me. I know that humanoid cultures at certain levels will be basically the same even if they begin light-years away from each other, but the base was so totally non-alien that I was finding it hard not to think of it as an extension of home. If I had had to learn their language the hard way it would have been easier remembering that they were strangers and still-possible enemies, but the ease of communication worked against my trained instincts. If I didn't find something really alien about these people, I might find myself in the trap of beginning to like them. Almost in desperation, I turned my head to Dameron.

"What are the people on the planet like?" I asked, hoping for something extreme.

"The Tildorani are just like you and me," he answered without hesitation, taking time out from inspecting his work force to glance at me. "The humanoid form seems to be a popular one, and base personnel always look like the natives they're Watchers for. You can never tell when some emergency will arise which will call for shuttling down most of us, and it's best to be prepared."

"You must have a large group of trained Watchers to be able to match every backward planet," I commented. "Even among humanoids there can be a broad enough spread of variations to make a noticeable difference."

"That poses no problem," he said, stopping where he was again. "We have a simple answer for that based on . . ."

There was a sudden shout of, "Dameron!" and we both turned to see a woman standing in a doorway on the righthand side of the corridor, about fifteen feet ahead of us. The woman was looking considerably upset, and Dameron didn't hesitate. He headed for her immediately at a trot, with me right behind him.

"I'm assuming that that was a shout of joy, Gemiral," he said as he reached the woman. "I left orders that there were to be no problems today."

"If this weren't so serious, I'd laugh myself silly over that," the woman snorted. "You'd better come in here and hear the latest."

Dameron frowned, but followed the woman back through the doorway she'd come out of. Being shy never pays, so I tagged along after them into what looked like a communications center. There were three men and two women seated at consoles, whisper mikes and ear discs in place, and one unoccupied console had a man standing next to it, a web-thin headset in his hand. He was big and dark-haired, wearing a uniform of a blue only slightly lighter than Dameron's, and he gave me a curious stare before turning his attention to the Commander.

"Is Leandor's team in trouble?" Cameron asked him, frowning.

"Nothing that simple," the big man answered, tossing

the headset gently onto the console he stood near. "Post five just called to warn us that Clero's up to something that will affect Bellna when she leaves for the capital to marry Prince Remo. They'll call back when they have all the details."

"I *knew* Clero would try something!" Dameron growled, smacking his open palm with a wide fist. "Just our luck that it took this long to find out what. We'd better have enough time to set up a counter-plan, or everything we've worked for will go right down the tubes."

"It'll be worse than that," the big man said, shaking his head. "We won't simply be back to square one, we'll be off the board entirely. If we lose Bellna, we have no one to replace her with."

"I know, I know," Dameron grumbled, gesturing a dismissal at the other man as he turned away from him. "It's Bellna or nothing, and Clero's trying to make it nothing. A lot he has to worry about, with five daughters to throw in the pot. If he loses one or two, he still has the others. Well, I'm not prepared to lose Bellna, and I won't lose her as long as I have enough information to plan with. Where the hell is post 5?"

He turned to stare at the silent console, his impatience willing it to come alive and tell him what he wanted to know, but it didn't respond. The men and women at the other consoles paid only partial attention to the displays in front of them, most of their concern directed toward the same spot Dameron stared at. The woman Gemiral had reclaimed her seat and headphones, but her presence wasn't doing any more than Dameron's stare. The only one who looked at all distracted was the large, dark-haired man, who leaned against Gemiral's console with folded arms, his eyes resting on me. I leaned back against the wall near the door and folded

my own arms, absorbing the casual stare without ac-
knowledging it. I didn't want anyone demanding to
know what I was doing there at least until I found out
what the flap was all about, which meant that near
invisibility was called for. I looked at nothing in particular and didn't make a sound, and happily there were no
demands coming my way.

My time sense isn't too inaccurate, but a wait like
that is hard to judge. Subjectively it felt like hours were
passing, but objectively it couldn't have been more than
fifteen or twenty minutes before the console began blinking a demanding orange. The woman Gemiral began
removing her headset, but Dameron gestured impatiently and stepped forward to flip a switch.

"I'm right here, Eavamon," he said to the now steady
orange light. "What have you got?"

"Not nearly enough," a thin voice answered, sounding impossibly distant. "We've discovered there's going
to be an attempt and we know approximately when
they'll hit, but exactly who will be doing the hitting and
what spot they've chosen is still Clero's secret. He's not
taking any chances on a leak."

"You'd better tell me everything you know," Dameron said with a frustrated look on his face. "It may still
be possible to do something."

"There's very little to it," the thin voice answered.
"Clero knows Bellna will be leaving for the capital soon,
and has arranged it so that she never gets there. It
would be harder for him if Havro planned on using his
own men as an escort, but his own men are too deep in
that fight on his western border. Grigon tells us that
mercenaries have been hired, and you know what mercenaries are like."

"Only too well," Dameron muttered, then turned his
head to the big man who stood not far from him.

"Valdon, how many men can we put together to be mercenaries if Havro's bunch turn out to be useless or bought?"

"None." The big man called Valdon shrugged. "All of you do. I don't expect to lose, but if I do, the turn is all Natha escapade in post 9's territory. With the number of barbarians in that area, pulling them out quickly is just about impossible. And forget about Leandor even before you ask. He's Healed, but he's nowhere ready to go back—if we ever intend seeing him again. But neither of you has heard the latest from the capital. Sardrin's message came in a little while ago."

"This time it had better be good news," Dameron said, suddenly looking more alert. "Is it anything we can use?"

"Only if you'd like Bellna to have a King's Escort," Valdon answered with a grin. "King Naro has sent the Escort to deliver the dowry gifts and collect his son's bride, and there are two hundred of them. Can you see Clero attacking a King's Escort of two hundred fighters?"

"Easily," came the miniature voice of Eavamon from the console, putting a damper on the pleased grins Dameron and Valdon were showing. "He'd need two or three times their number in attackers, but the game's worth it to him. When is the Escort due?"

"In a little less than a local week," Valdon supplied, exchanging looks with Dameron. "Sardrin would have told us about them as soon as they left, but King Naro insisted that his most trusted advisers join him in the pre-nuptial religious ceremonies that are expected of him. Sardrin thinks Naro wants him to come up with a way out of the need for ceremonies like that, and after going through one himself he's more than willing. Why did you ask about the Escort's ETA?"

"I was hoping they might be so close that Clero

would not have the time to find the number of men he needed," Eavamon answered, his sigh so clear it should have caused a flicker in the orange light. "Unfortunately that's more than enough time, especially if he has relay riders watching the capital, which I'm sure he does. He'll know they're coming and he'll be prepared."

"He may know they're coming, but if he doesn't care about them he *won't* be prepared," Dameron said, the words slow and thoughtful.

"Is that supposed to mean something?" the invisible Eavamon asked while Valdon gave Dameron a look that said the same thing.

"It means that Clero won't care about the Escort if he thinks Bellna has already left with mercenaries," Dameron said, his face and voice both announcing his grin. "He'll be too busy chasing the mercenary group to care about an Escort that miraculously missed them."

"With a decoy!" the Eavamon voice crowed, enjoying the idea as much as Dameron. "A decoy ought to be easy to arrange!"

"Not as easy as all that," Valdon said, taking his turn at wet-blanket throwing. "Don't forget about the Natha gatherings in 9's territory. How are we supposed to reach a suitable decoy?"

"You can't tell me *every* female fighter we have is in on that," Dameron protested, an edge of impatience to his voice. "Get busy and start checking, and give me some choices. With almost a week to work in we'll be able to pull this off, but only if we get going immediately. Eavamon, let me know if you hear anything else, no matter how insignificant it is, and start preparing the leak that will tell Clero Bellna has left secretly with mercenaries. Don't release it until I give you the word, but have it ready."

"Will do," Eavamon agreed, already sounding thoughtful. "I'll also get in touch with Grigon and have him begin preparing a way to keep Bellna away from those mercenaries and around for the Escort. He'll need the time."

"He probably will," Dameron said with a nod he seemed to think the absent Eavamon could see. "We'll call you if we need anything else, but right now it's up to us. Base out." He flipped off the orange light, then turned his head. "Valdon, get on that search fast. I want that information as soon as the files can be programmed."

He turned away from the console without seeing Valdon's preoccupied nod, the big man having already settled in front of what was probably a computer terminal. Dameron was heading for the door I was standing beside, deep in thought, and wouldn't have seen me even if I'd been dressed in flashing sun-sign. I had no interest in being left behind as a permanent wall post, so I accepted the risk of being run down and stepped directly in his path. The commander stopped short, frowned at me for a minute or two without recognition, then memory flashed briefly in his eyes. He took my arm and led me out of the room, then waited for the door to slide closed again behind us before giving me an apologetic look.

"I'm sorry that took so long, but we have a crisis," he said, trying hard to really look sorry. "At least you got to see something of the way we operate. Did you find it interesting?"

"Oh, yes, very," I nodded, keeping my tone solemn. "I get a real kick out of being in the true thick of things. You said my ship was this way?"

"Your ship," he echoed, not doing well with hiding his impatience at the thought of being distracted from his crisis. "That's right, we were going to your ship, weren't we?" I could almost see his mind going clickety-clickety-click behind his eyes, but he was obviously the type who considered business before visitors. He made up his mind fast, apparently feeling no guilt over the decision. "I can't take the time for that now," he admitted, giving me the bad news without flinching. "Once I have this problem squared away we can program your course computer, and I promise it will be the first thing I do."

"The first thing after a planetary week's worth of waiting?" I asked, trying not to sound as boorish as I was feeling. He and his people had saved my life—but I'd been looking forward to going *home*. "You won't mind my wandering around here alone and—amusing—myself?"

His expression changed at that, just the way I'd wanted it to, but the semi-panic he must have been feeling didn't push him in the direction I was hoping for. He pasted a friendly expression on his face, took my arm again, then started guiding me up the corridor in our original direction.

"You know, now that you mention it, I think it might interest you more if you knew exactly what we're in the middle of," he said, sounding as if he were selling magazines. "Let's get comfortable in my office, and I'll fill you in."

"There's an old saying about interesting times," I commented, not letting him hurry me as fast as he wanted to. "Suppose you give me your coordinates and the proper quadrant and I do my own programming?"

"You may remember what I said about not wanting you too overburdened with unnecessary information," he said, glancing down at me as he put a little more muscle into his hauling. "The coordinates of this base come under the heading of unnecessary."

"Suppose I offer to close my eyes?" I suggested, but

only to be annoying. Dameron would have to enter his
location in my ship's computer in order to program the
proper course back to the Federation, but he could
always build in an automatic forget order once destination was reached which would remove the information.
A program like that could not be tampered with without purging it completely or ruining it enough to be
useless; *telling* me the coordinates would negate the
entire effort. He snorted under his breath at my
suggestion, not even bothering to comment or refuse,
and we continued to the end of the corridor.

The last room on the left turned out to be Dameron's,
and the door slid aside to show a rust and blue combination that would have deafened me in a week if I'd had to
use it regularly. There was a squarish but comfortable-
looking chair standing to the right of a low block of
plastic or metal, what was probably a computer terminal to the right of the chair, and a couple of lump chairs
in front of the block-chair-terminal arrangement. All
around the walls were filled shelves, gaps here and there
allowing the hanging of various somethings including
very clear photographs of unpeopled landscapes. The
lighting level brightened up from dim as soon as we
entered, and Dameron guided me to the second lump
chair before trying to ease me down into it. I put my
right leg slightly behind me and locked the knee, assuming what was almost standard attack-defense stance, and
the good commander found he couldn't do much against
it. He would have had to knee me in the middle to get
me to bend, and he wasn't prepared to go quite that far.

"You'll find the background a lot more comfortable to
listen to if you do it sitting down," he said, turning
away as if leaving me erect had been his original idea.
"If nothing else, it will fill the time until—"

His words broke off as his attention was captured by

the supposed computer terminal, which was signaling for his attention. He hit a key that sent symbols of all sorts scurrying across the screen, giving him information that he absorbed as fast as it came. It took two or three minutes before he had it all, and then he flipped it back to blank while muttering under his breath.

"I take it the news wasn't particularly good," I observed, watching him drop into the squarish chair with a preoccupied look. "More headaches to add to the ones you already have?"

"Just an added dimension to the existing ones," he answered with a sigh, breaking out of the preoccupation. "It seems Valdon was right: every one of our female fighters is commited to post 9's territory, and we'd have to use a scoutship to reach them—if we knew exactly where they were. They're involved with the barbarians and the barbarians are on the move, and we can't just walk in there and politely ask to speak to one or two of our girls. We can't settle the crisis in Narella by creating a new one in Natha."

"You know, I've heard it said that the best way to think is to occupy your hands and attention with something that has nothing to do with your problem," I remarked, folding my arms as I looked down at him. "The subconscious gets it all settled for you, and you've accomplished two things instead of one."

"You don't give up, do you?" he rejoindered, amused. "This isn't the sort of problem my subconscious can do anything about. It may turn out to need something on the order of a miracle. Are you going to make me get a crick in my neck from looking up at you while I talk? These details take some telling."

I could see from the sparkle in his dark eyes that his amusement had increased, but I wasn't sharing any of it. He wasn't going to be working on my course computer unless I threatened his life, and probably not even then. He struck me as the sort who would die in his tracks rather than let himself be forced into something he'd decided against, even if the decision was temporary. I looked up at the blue ceiling in defeat as I shook my head, then turned to the lump chair I'd refused earlier. I'd listen to his damned story, then start working on him again once it was over.

"You have my neck's grateful appreciation," he chuckled as he watched me sit, trying not to sound *too* victorious. "I've also heard it said that you can solve a problem by explaining the situation to someone else aloud, so don't think of this as wasting time. Think of it as giving me some help in return for the help I'll be giving you."

He grinned outright at that, probably thinking he was backing me into a corner of guilt-riddled gratitude, but he had to be forgiven for the mistaken belief. He just didn't know me very well—but he would learn.

"The area we're primarily concerned with right now is called Narella, after Naro, its current king, the fourth in his line," Dameron began, leaning back comfortably in his squarish chair. "Narella is the most advanced country on this continent, and although we're not ignoring the other countries, this is where we're concentrating our efforts. Here's what the country looks like."

He reached over to tap a series of keys on his terminal, and suddenly the block of metal or plastic on his other side was no longer blank. The side facing me lit up to show a map of sorts, heavy lines surrounding an area that was divided up into six subareas of varying sizes.

"King Naro rules the country, but he has five princes governing different parts of it under him," Dameron continued, looking at the top of the block, which was out of my line of vision. "The eastern-most area is his own domain, and larger than any of the other five. His capital city Naridon is here, near the western border."

A black dot appeared on the map, roughly halfway between the northern and southern boundaries, just as Dameron put a finger on the top of the block in what would be the same place if he had a view of the map in front of him. The block seemed to be a repeater screen of middling complexity, and not the limited desk area I had originally guessed at.

"The political situation in Narella is no different from any other primitive area—and too many so-called civilized ones," the lecture went on. "Naro is a really good king, not terribly despotic, more fair-minded than you would expect, a crafty leader, a capable military commander, and a man willing to consider intelligent advice. He runs the country to suit himself, but he understands that the better off his people are, the more he can demand in taxes and levies. Despite the fact that Naro is making life profitable and pleasant for his princes as well as himself, some of them would prefer seeing another king on the throne, namely one of their number.

"The leader of the most well organized opposition is Prince Clero, a man we know more about than we care for. He's not nearly as intelligent as he thinks he is, has the support of the others through fear, and indulges in brutality just for the fun of it. Giving him advice is like spitting before you know what direction the wind is coming from: you only find out after you do it whether or not it was a good idea. He's a paranoid who suspects everyone of plotting against him, and we lost two agents before we were able to adopt a lower profile in his keep. His lands are here."

Black dots circled the second most westerly division as Dameron's finger moved around a section on the top of the block. Not counting the king's lands, the area was second largest of the rest, the section to the west of it being a third again its size.

"This Clero sounds like a real charmer," I said, studying the map. "Why don't you arrange for a fatal accident and be rid of him?"

"Have you ever tried to reach a paranoid in high position?" Dameron asked with a serious snort. "We might be able to justify a move like that to Absar Central, but even if we could we'd still have to be able to do it without using anything of our more advanced technology. If I authorized taking Clero out any other way, I'd spend the rest of my career on Absar, listing the thousand best reasons why I should have the same thing done to me. We're here to help these people by guiding them, not by taking them over."

"Then why are you working so hard against Clero?" I asked, raising my eyes to Dameron's face. "If you don't have the right to stop him by killing him, it could be argued that you don't have the right to stop him at all. Maybe he'd make a better king than Naro in spite of your opinions to the contrary."

"We're not discussing unsupported opinion," Dameron snapped, with a frown. He didn't realize I was needling him on purpose, playing devil's advocate to get even for the lecture he was forcing me to sit through. "We're discussing carefully documented evidence that supports the contention that Clero is a dangerous psychopath who would have the country in ruins in less than two years. Even if you dismissed everything else, his views on the slave trade should be enough to prove the point."

"The slave trade?" I echoed, suddenly seeing Radman's face flash across my mind. "He's a slaver?"

"Not directly, no," Dameron answered with a headshake, his face grim and his voice nearly a growl. "He just gives slaving his whole-hearted support, and patronizes the trade regularly and eagerly. He buys male slaves and works them to death without looking at them twice; he wouldn't care if it was his own grandfather who had been enslaved. Female slaves he looks at more than twice, especially the very young ones. Some of them have been sold to the slavers by their fathers, some were stolen when they weren't watched carefully enough; he never questions their origins when he buys them. After he buys them—well, they usually survive, but you'd be surprised how little that says. Use like that is hard enough on grown women; what it does to little girls is unspeakable, especially if he decides to train them to a life of it. That's one of his hobbies. Can you see it in his eyes?"

The map was suddenly replaced by a depth photo of a man, but Dameron's question was bitterness without meaning. The eyes that stared out at me were light-colored and laughing, set in a handsome face topped by sandy hair. The handsome face was wreathed in smiles, true delight and good-natured happiness clear in every line. If the man had been a politician women would have eagerly raised their babies for him to kiss, and fathers would have volunteered their teenage daughters to help him in his compaigning. It was the face of a man who loved life and loved people, a man who trusted and could be trusted—a man who, according to Dameron, was a sadistic psychopath.

"And Naro's above all that?" I asked after a minute of studying the mature, handsome face. "No hidden little twists he keeps out of the public eye?"

"Naro's a product of his culture," Dameron shrugged, tapping the terminal again. "He enjoys indulging himself with female slaves, but he knows the slave trade can get out of hand if it isn't kept under tight control. people beating the woods for stolen children aren't very productive, and a drop in productivity affects his tax collections. He's nothing if not practical, but what more can people ask for in a ruler?"

The face now projected in front of me was approximately the same age as Clero's, but there the similarity ended. Naro was dark-haired and dark-eyed, his features average and nondescript except for a faint and difficult to define air to competence and decisiveness. He also looked as though he would be harder to get along with than Clero, harder to talk to and harder to relate to.

"Why isn't Naro taking care of seeing to Clero?" I asked, looking up to see Dameron's eyes on me. "If he's as competent as you say, he ought to know who the opposition is."

"Naro does know who the opposition is," Dameron answered with a faint, humorless smile. "He knows all about the distant cousin of his who Clero uses as a front. As far as Clero goes, no one beyond the other princes involved—and ourselves—know what he's up to. And even if people were told about it, how many of them would believe it? Could you look Clero in the face and suspect him of anything underhanded? Being hard on slaves doesn't equate with planning treason. Everyone is hard on slaves."

"You do have a problem," I admitted, seeing that King Naro's face had been replaced with the map we'd been looking at. "And just what *is* Clero planning?"

"He's trying to reach the throne by the back door," Dameron said, his tone still annoyed. "King Naro's oldest son and heir, Remo, is seventeen, a ripe marriageable age. Clero has been trying to pair Remo up with one of his daughters, which would be the beginning of the end for Naro. Right after the marriage an accident could be arranged to settle Naro, and then Remo would become king. Remo's two brothers would then follow their father, after which it would be Remo's turn. With Clero's daughter a widowed queen and no other heir in sight, guess who could walk into the Regent's job—which would evolve into the kingship?"

"Why would a widowed queen need a regent?" was my next try, seriously curious. "Are Clero's daughters so incompetent they'd need a regent, or are they just so far under daddy's thumb they'd ask for him?"

"Neither," Dameron came back, a sudden amusement in his dark eyes. "Narella will never be ruled by a queen simply because women aren't competent enough to rule. They're shallow, flighty, empty-headed, unknowledgeable, too flatterable and totally helpless. Women are made for bedrooms and kitchens, not thronerooms."

"How would you like your arm broken in three places?" I asked mildly and pleasantly through a comfortable smile. "Afterward I can even give you the medical terminology for each of the breaks, which break came first, and a pretty good estimation of how long each will take to heal."

"Why do I get the feeling you're not really joking?" Dameron asked, his grin coming full out. "If I didn't know better I'd think you were angry with me, but that couldn't be. All I was doing was quoting the way Narellan men see the thing. Which, of course, has nothing to do with my own views."

"Oh, of course," I agreed with a sober nod. "Are they really all that backward?"

"Backward isn't the word," Dameron snorted, still somewhat amused. "If their women step out of line they beat them, without hesitation and without regret. A woman with a smart mouth would get it twice as fast, just to be sure she didn't make the same mistake a second time. If there's one thing those women give their men, it's obedience and respect."

"That's two things," I pointed out, giving him the ghost of a smile. "And there's a difference between respect and fear, a big difference. So Clero's daughter as a widowed queen would mean Clero as king, but you and your horde have a plan to stop him—if you can make it work right."

"It damned well *better* work right," Dameron growled. "The only way we could counter his move was to find another candidate for bride-to-be, which we did. Havro is another prince governing under Naro, his lands lying here, to the west of Clero's."

The dots ran around the most westerly section, the largest area after the king's, the one lying right next to Clero's, and then the map disappeared to show the face of a man. Obviously part of the age group shared by Naro and Clero, Prince Havro was a man with a broad, boyish face and bright red hair, blue eyes sharp with private amusement. He wasn't as distant as Naro or as handsome as Clero, but there was still something—involved—about him.

"Havro is a competent man, reliable enough to guard the country's western border from barbarian invasion, and intelligent enough to take suggestions when they make sense," Dameron said. "He considers ruling a responsibility rather than a right, and he has a daughter who is perfect for our purposes. Bellna has no sisters, but in any contest between her and Clero's three eligible girls, she might as well be considered quintuplets. She's prettier than Clero's three, smarter than they are, quick to learn, and eager to become the eventual queen of Narella. We maneuvered Bellna and Remo into a meeting at the capital—right after Remo'd had Clero's daughters presented to him. Our timing couldn't have been better."

The repeater screen first showed three girls ranging in age from fourteen to seventeen years, standing near a dark-haired, dark-eyed, very handsome young male. The male looked as though he would have been happy to drop through the floor, but from boredom more than anything else. The youngest girl was still a boy, straight up and down and with no hint of femininity even in her face. The second girl was clearly feminine, but too sweetly female and very delicate looking. The third and oldest was pretty, but the stiffness in her stance and the forced smile on her face said that nothing in life was likely to please her. All three wore long, complicated party gowns, well fitted and well made, but none of them looked *right* in the clothing.

And then the screen changed to a single girl standing near the boy, and I blinked at the extreme difference. This girl had lots of bright red hair and dancing blue eyes, a smile to make a man three days dead rise again, and a body that made *all* the previous three look like boys. The young male was grinning down at her, his eyes nearly a blur, his approval and interest so clear that anyone watching him would have to laugh softly. The girl returned his look with a cloaked arrogance and wordless challenge in her eyes that had probably made him quiver, and I laughed at that, too.

"Bellna is no more than about fifteen, but Remo considers that perfect," Dameron said, a chuckle in his voice. "His bride *has* to be from one of   incely families, and Clero's daughters are about average among the rest. Remo spoke to his father about his decision, got Naro's approval, then made the engagement formal. He's bright and able to make even unpleasant decisions quickly, and should make a good king when he succeeds his father."

"And his marrying Bellna should let him live long

enough to reach that point," I nodded. "I'm assuming that if Bellna ends up a widowed queen with all the rest of Remo's family gone, Havro rather than Clero would be tapped as Regent. What I'm wondering is, wouldn't that simply put Havro in the same spot as Naro and the others? If Clero can scratch a king and his sons, what's to keep him from doing it to another prince like himself?"

"That's a good question," Dameron said with a smile of approval. "You're right in all of your assumptions except for the one concerning worry about Havro. Havro and Clero are enemies of long standing, and while Havro isn't paranoid he also isn't foolish enough to let Clero or any of his friends or hirelings get anywhere near him. If we can keep Bellina safe until she marries Remo, Clero will be stopped cold until he can think of something else."

"Which brings you right back to the big if," I said, leaning back in the lump chair. "You can decoy Clero away *if* you can find a stand-in for Bellna. None of the women I've seen in this base looks much like her, but I suppose padding, make-up and a wig would take care of that. Why don't you use one of the gals you have here?"

"Because none of them are trained fighters," Dameron said, in a voice charged with frustration. "They've all had field experience to one degree or another, but whoever goes out as decoy has to expect to be the object of Clero's attempt at bloody murder. The Tildorani are still in the sword-swinging stage before gunpowder, but that only means that our decoy has to be able to handle a blade well enough so that she needn't depend on protection from someone else. Getting separated from outside protection can happen all too easily. Whoever does the decoy work not only has to look exactly like Bellna, she also has to be able to fight a whole lot better than that pretty little girl."

The block to Dameron's right reverted to its original picturelessness as Dameron tapped keys on his terminal, but I sat and frowned at it a minute before shifting my eyes back to the man.

"What do you mean, the decoy has to look exactly like Bellna?" I asked, watching him as he tapped at keys. "I can understand the need for fighting ability, but aren't you crowding your options a little by insisting on an exact look-alike? It could be years before you found anyone like that—if you ever did. I thought you said you had less than a week."

"I don't have to *find* someone who looks exactly like Bellna," Dameron said with a snort of faint amusement, still paying attention to his terminal. "The changes in facial structure and all will require only minor Healing, nothing major involved. Less than a week gives us more, than enough time for it—if we can find someone to change soon enough. If we didn't need that relationship with the barbarians so badly—"

His voice trailed off as the symbols of his terminal took his attention again, and I didn't say anything more to distract him, being too busy with my own thoughts. If I was understanding him correctly—and I didn't see how I could be mistaken—Dameron's people were able to change anyone to look like anyone else as easily as my people shuttled back and forth from planets to or-bital stations. The possibilities inherent in the process were endless and fascinating, especially in my line of work. If I could be changed to look like—oh, that young girl Bellna, for instance, I could get away with almost anything I tried. Rather than depending on my brown hair and eyes to let me melt into a crowd as camouflage, I could let red hair and blue eyes distract any male to the point where I could stalk a target, reach him, and then walk away without ever being suspected of anything nasty. No one would believe that a fifteen-year-old girl could be a Special Agent, and that would give me more of an edge than being female did. I crossed my legs as I watched pictures parading past my inner eye, and forgot all about Dameron.

At least until he made a sound of pleased surprise and turned away from his terminal. His face was lit with hopeful excitement, and he bounced out of his chair as if he had just shed ten years of heavy worry.

"The gods must be on our side in this one," he said through a grin as he headed for the door. "One of the gals from post nine is on her way in, and should be here any minute. You just relax where you are, girl. I won't be long."

By that time the door was already sliding closed behind him, so there wasn't much sense in trying to argue. I was annoyed at being left there to sit and twiddle when I could have been a good number of parsecs on my way back home, but there wasn't anything I could do about it until Dameron got back. I leaned back in the lump chair again and began sketching out a going-home campaign that would grab Dameron's attention by the throat and hold it long enough to get something done.

I had developed a line of attack with enough variables to cover almost any contingency and was ready to start fleshing it out with carefully chosen detail, when the door to the room slid open again. I thought it was Dameron coming back, but the figure walking through the opening belonged to the one who had been called Valdon. He had dark black hair and dark black eyes, and although he wasn't quite as big as the junior giant named Leandor, he didn't miss by much. He moved as lightly and with as much confidence as the leader of the field team had, which was usually unexpected in such big men. He hesitated very briefly when he saw me, as though he hadn't expected to find me there, then headed straight for Dameron's chair.

"Well, there you are again," he observed, sitting down and keying the terminal to life without taking his eyes off me. "I saw you earlier, with Dameron, in the communications room."

"Yes, I remember that," I observed back, keeping the answer neutral and uncommitted. I didn't know where this Valdon stood in the base, but the fewer people who knew about my origins, the better. It might be necessary for Dameron and his second to have all the details, but as far as I was concerned that was still two too many. Either one of them could, at any time, come up with a dozen great reasons for keeping me there a while longer, and the more people who knew about me, the better the chance that some mental lightbulbs would glow. Leaving the base amid tearful good-byes was preferable to fighting my way out of it, so a low profile was definitely a high priority.

The terminal beeped for attention, giving Valdon something else to stare at, but the distraction didn't last long. There were only three rows of symbols for him to glance at and respond to, and then his dark black eyes were on me again.

"How do you like our facilities?" he asked, as though just making conversation to while away the time. "The base is pretty standard, but we like to think we have better optionals than any other outpost in the Confederacy."

"I'm sure you do," I agreed in a sober way, leaving it to him to decide whether I was agreeing with his opinion or his conclusion. A faint shadow that might have been annoyance flickered in his eyes while he waited for

me to add to my four word statement, and when I
didn't he stirred in the squarish chair.

"We don't often get visitors like you, and I'm curious
about you," he admitted in a friendly, outgoing way.
"I'm assuming you're lost, and were heading somewhere else. Where were you going, and how long did it
take you to get here?"

He was playing it casual, asking his too-pointed questions and trying to keep his interested inspection of me
from becoming overly obvious. He seemed to be a man
who felt no discomfort from really looking at a woman,
but who had learned that many women flinched from
that sort of hunter's interest. I couldn't remember a
time when the thought of being hunted didn't amuse
and interest me more than bother me, but the opportunity was too good to miss.

"I—really don't remember," I answered only the last
of his questions, swallowing hard as I looked down at
my hands in my lap. I had quietly drawn my knees
together and was sitting as stiffly and primly as the
lump chair allowed. "How much longer do you think
Dameron will be?"

"Oh, I'm sure he'll be back any minute," Valdon's
voice rushed to reassure me, his tone a shade too jolly.
"How about something to drink while we're waiting?"

"Drink?" I echoed as if I'd never heard the word
before, and nearly panicked. I was letting it all fall apart
at once, as though my previous coolness had been no
more than a front I couldn't maintain any longer. Valdon
was a very handsome man, with the sort of masculine
features and mannerisms that too often flustered women
right into hysterics. If the way he shrugged meant
anything, he'd had to face that particular problem before and shouldn't be too hard to divert from detecting.

"Yes, a drink," he repeated with a pleasant smile. "As a matter of fact, I'll be glad to join you. What would you like?"

He started to get out of Dameron's chair, anxious to be doing something other than trying not to stare at me, but he'd asked another question that it wouldn't be safe to give a non-specific answer to. The man might be temporarily flustered, but he wasn't likely to be stupid; too many artful evasions would be bound to set him thinking. Instead of registering his question in any way I scrambled out of the lump chair and backed away from him in mute, wide-eyed fear, hoping I wasn't pushing the act too far. I fully expected to back out the door into the corridor, but found myself startled for real when the door didn't slide open behind me. I'd been wondering why Dameron had been so casual about leaving me unaccompanied and unwatched, and now I'd accidently gotten the answer. Being locked in annoyed the hell out of me, but for the sake of the performance I was putting on for Valdon, I couldn't let it show.

"This is ridiculous," Valdon muttered, straightening slowly out of the chair, seeming annoyed. "You're acting as though I'm about to attack you. My self-control is really a lot better than that—I haven't attacked a woman in months."

He grinned a very attractive grin to show he was just kidding, but I couldn't afford to chuckle in answer the way I wanted to. I gave him a sickly smile to show I was trying, and put a shaky hand to my hair.

"I know I'm being silly, but I can't help it," I said in a very small voice, sending him a pleading look. "The way you were looking at me, the way you talk—I'm just not used to it. Do you think you can go and see what's keeping Dameron?"

To say I was trying to get rid of him was an

understatement, and I was expecting him to be more than happy to go—but things didn't work out that way. A deeply frustrated expression flashed briefly across his face, and then he was looking apologetic.

"I already know what's keeping Dameron, and I'm afraid I have to stay here," he said, very sincere compassion clear in his tone. "I've got to keep an eye on the progress of certain of our projects until he gets back, and I've got to do it with this terminal. You don't mind sharing the room with me for that short a time, do you?"

He brought the grin back and made it really warm, trying to jolly me out of my upset and interest me by turning on the charm. The only problem with that was that in another minute we'd be back to chummy conversation and more questions, the avoidance of which was my original reason for starting that nonsense. I needed him gone or neutralized, and if I couldn't have one I'd have to settle for the other; it all depended on how gullible he was. I let my eyes begin filming over with tears, and plucked nervously at the one-piece suit I was wearing.

"But I'm afraid of you," I whispered, making sure my voice came out ragged. "I've never been this close to someone like you before, someone who has actually worked among uncivilized barbarians. You keep looking at me the way one of *them* would—I'm going to cry hard, I just know I am!"

I sniffled a little, finding it damned hard not to burst out laughing at the stricken look that replaced his well-practiced grin. Most men were sensible enough to ignore blackmail tears, but every now and then one would come along who turned to quivering jelly at the first choked sob and/or glisten of moisture. I was almost ashamed to go on taking advantage, but he'd had his chance to bail out and hadn't taken it. It was too bad, but business was business.

"Now, now, you don't really want to cry," he said, looking as though he wanted to come closer and put his manly arms around me—but didn't dare. "What if I promise not to look at you the way one of *them* would? That would make you feel better, wouldn't it?"

"I don't know," I sniffled, sounding absolutely forlorn. "Maybe—maybe—if you didn't look at me at all—"

"That's a good idea," he agreed with enthusiasm, turning completely around to look at me over his shoulder. "This is better, isn't it?"

"You're still looking at me," I pointed out with the same quiver in my voice. "And you're much too close. And you sound so—so—overawing."

"All right, all right, I'll take care of it," he said, *that* close to growling. I wasn't sure there *was* such a word as overawing, but he was still trying to keep me from being overawed. He turned his head completely away from me, stalked up to the wall directly behind Dameron's block-chair-terminal arrangement, then spoke to the wall.

"This had better do it for you," he said, making sure not to turn again. "I've never been very good at melting into polycrete."

"Oh, that's *perfect*," I gushed, with a slight grin. "If you can only stay like that until Dameron comes back, I'm sure I won't cry."

"You have no idea how much those words mean to me," he muttered, folding his arms across his chest to signal an end to the conversation that frightened me so much. I laughed without sound as I eased myself over to the second lump chair and then into it, finally stretching out to prop my feet on the block Dameron had done so much with. I would have put Valdon into the room's corner if I hadn't thought that would be pushing it, but seeing him standing in front of the wall like a naughty little boy was almost as good. If he hadn't been considering me a helpless little flutterhead of a female he never would have gone along with my insistances, so he deserved whatever he got for that as well as for being too nosy.

Another twenty minutes or so passed with Valdon shifting at the wall but doing no more than that, a pleasant silence surrounding us that let me go on with developing my campaign against Dameron. I was ready to pull my feet down if the terminal signaled for Valdon's attention, but the interruption never came and Valdon never turned. I was finding it hard to believe that a grown man could be put to a wall and kept there with such a pack of nonsense, but that's the way it went until the door to the room slid noiselessly aside and Dameron stepped in. He stopped in the doorway to stare first at Valdon and then at me, and a look of confusion settled on his broad features.

"What are you two doing?" he asked, sounding and looking bewildered.

"We were waiting for you to get back," I answered, looking up at him without moving even though Valdon turned immediately away from the wall. "You certainly took long enough."

"There was more involved than I thought there—I still don't understand." Dameron's bewilderment was about to turn into annoyance. "Why is Valdon standing near the wall all the way over there, while you're—what the hell is going on?"

"Nothing's going on," I assured him, putting my feet down and standing up to face him. Valdon was staring at me without saying a word, but I had more pressing matters to think about. "Why don't you and I take a little walk and see to that chore we were discussing earlier? It won't take long, and then you can concentrate on Narella without any distractions. And there are a few other very pertinent advantages I'll be glad to point out on the way. You might say it'll be an offer you can't refuse."

I gave him an impatient grimace, but before he could answer, another precinct was heard from.

"I could be mistaken, but it sounds as if you're over your bout of shyness," Valdon observed, his deep voice having intensified. "Or is it just those of us who have *really* worked with 'uncivilized barbarians' who make you want to cry?"

"I'm very unprejudiced," I said, looking over my shoulder at Valdon's annoyance. "If the situation calls for it, I'm willing to shed a few tears for anyone. Are you feeling cheated because I didn't make good on the threat?"

"She threatened you?" Dameron demanded of Valdon, still trying to figure out what was going on. "What did you do to her?"

"I—'overawed' her," Valdon answered dryly, as he stared at me. "I made her so nervous by the ferocious way I looked at her and talked to her that she almost had hysterics. I had to promise not to look at her again or say a word, just to keep her from fainting or throwing a crying fit."

"Hysterics," Dameron repeated in a flat voice. "Fainting and crying. Are we talking about the same female?"

I turned my head to Dameron to see that although his unfriendly stare was aimed at me, his faint air of ridicule was directed at Valdon. The big man's handsome face had darkened in response to Dameron's scoffing, but he hadn't added anything.

"I had to find *something* amusing to pass the time," I told Dameron's accusing stare in a hurt tone designed to let him know how unjust his accusation was. "It wasn't *my* idea to be left here unoccupied and ignored while you went trotting off to have fun. And I don't know what you're complaining about—no one got hurt, did they?"

I made my question as pointed as possible without being deliberately offensive; Dameron showed he got the point by straightening where he stood and sobering. I hadn't strung Valdon just for the fun of it, but if Dameron understood that the interlude could have been destructive rather than embarrassing, we didn't have to go into anything else. I wanted Dameron to see how much better off his base would be with me gone from it, and if his expression was anything to judge by, I wasn't far from getting what I wanted. Dameron opened his mouth, probably to agree to my suggestion of a walk, but the big hand suddenly wrapping around my right arm stopped any words from being said.

"So making me look like a fool was nothing more than an amusement for you," Valdon growled, tightening his grip to match the anger in his eyes. "You needed some entertainment to stave off boredom, and I was it. Did you find all the fun you were looking for? You weren't disappointed?"

"If you don't like being conned, try being less nosy," I told him, meeting his anger calmly. "Not everyone considers exchanging life histories the best of conversational topics. And don't feel too raw over being taken in. You aren't the first to fall for some line I happened to come up with, and you won't be the last. The best thing you can do right now is forget it—and let go of my arm."

"Or you'll cry?" he asked, still staring down at me. "Maybe a few tears would be the best thing that could happen to you after all—to see to it that I *am* the last one to fall for some line of yours. You had *your* fun; it would only be fair if I took *my* turn."

"Valdon," Dameron rumbled warningly from behind my left shoulder, but those deep black eyes gave no indication that the warning had been heard. They were locked to my face, watching for a reaction to the threat he'd made, waiting for the fainthearted regret he expected to set in. It was too bad I wouldn't be leaving there without trouble after all, but that's the way things went sometimes.

"You're entitled to make a stab at taking your turn," I agreed, then shot my arm forward and sideways fast against his fingers, which broke his hold on my arm. "Only don't expect me to stand here like a statue while you do. I don't expect to lose, but if I do the turn is all yours."

I set myself without being obvious about it, curious as to how good he was. The way he moved said he wasn't likely to be clumsy or awkward, and his size, handled as easily as he handled it, was a definite asset for him. If he didn't have a weak middle or a glass jaw I would have my hands full, and shortly thereafter the rest of me would match, with bruises if nothing else. Killing him was out, of course, for many reasons even beyond the one that said he had a right to try getting even. I usually followed the adage that counseled, "Never make enemies by accident, only on purpose," but that time I'd missed. If a few bruises were the price for reclaiming the slip, I'd pay the price and count myself lucky, there had been times when it had been higher. I watched the man in front of me carefully, waiting for his first move, but for some reason it didn't come. He just stood and frowned down at me, finally shaking his head.

"If you're expecting me to start a fist fight with you,

you can forget it," he said, his tone flat and final. "Despite your generous offer, I don't make a habit of fist-fighting with women—even when they deserve a good swatting at the very least. All you can expect from me is the swatting, but I'll choose my own time and place, thanks. I'm used to setting up my own schedules."

I watched him walk between Dameron and me and head for the door, and once it had closed behind him I couldn't help shaking my head the way he had.

"What in the name of the deep endless dark was he talking about?" I asked no one in particular, then looked at Dameron. "And what's a swatting?"

"He was trying to tell you that he doesn't beat up on women even when they're expecting him to," Dameron answered, leaning back against the wall by the door with folded arms. "How did all that happen to get started?"

"He came in and immediately began asking me all sorts of questions," I explained, still feeling the urge to shake my head. "I decided that it was enough for you and your second to know about me, and we didn't need baby to make three. I had the choice of telling him what to do with his questions and thereby starting a fight, or conning him and keeping it peaceful. Believe it or not, I decided to keep it peaceful."

"Do all of your people use the same definition of peaceful?" Dameron asked with a snort of amusement. "If they do, I can't wait until we're in full contact with them. And for your information, Valdon *is* my second in command. He wasn't there when I was questioning you—a small crisis had come up that needed seeing to—and he was probably trying to find out what he'd missed. Looks like he got more than he bargained for."

"He should have told me who he was," I said with a shrug, ready to dismiss the whole thing. "I usually use restraint when dealing with an ally. And speaking about dealing, now that your urgent errand is seen to, let's take that walk and do a little dealing of our own. I think I can safely say you owe it to your people to get me out of here as soon as possible."

"You may be right about that." He nodded, still sticking to his piece of wall. "But when you talk about my urgent errand having been seen to, don't start assuming it was seen to successfully. Flantoril, the post 9 fighter who just came in, can't do the job I need her for. The only reason she's back here is to be treated for the wounds she took in a recent fight; if she hadn't been brought back, she would have died. Healing will keep her alive, but only if she doesn't have to go through a second session of Healing to change her into Bellna. Humanoids from her home sector don't react well to too much Healing. Did you really intend trying to defend yourself against Valdon?"

"Why not?" I asked, surprised by the sudden, out-of-context question. "A small, harmless-looking man like him ought to be a cinch to take. What has that got to do with our visit to my course computer?"

"It has a lot to do with it," he said, finally coming away from the wall to stand himself in front of me. "When I saw you calmly accepting the possibility of a fight with a man most *men* would try to appease, it came to me to wonder how well you can handle a sword."

"No, you don't!" I said with an immediate headshake, holding one hand up toward him while the other turned into an automatic, unconscious fist. "As far as you're concerned, I don't even know what the word sword means. Your problems in Narella are none of my business, and I intend keeping it that way. If you'll just show me the blinking red sign reading 'Exit' I'll get out of your way and take care of my course computer myself."

"Without specific coordinate and quadrant data?" he asked very mildly, the dark eyes looking down at me faintly amused. "I'll bet you can handle a sword at least as well as one of my team girls."

"The couple of times I tried, I nearly cut my own foot off," I said, feeling absolutely no guilt over the lie as I met his gaze. "And as far as coordinates and quadrant data go, I'll take my chances without them. The same luck that got me here just might get me home again."

"That would be more miracle than luck," he snorted, still looking at me with those piercing eyes. "And don't you think you owe us more than a brisk 'thanks!' and a farewell wave? If not for us you'd be a stiff, blue corpse, riding an airless hulk into eternity."

"Very poetic," I applauded with a nod. "Not to mention graphic. Now, out of pure, soul-deep gratitude, I'm supposed to put my neck on the chopping block with an eager smile? What's the difference between dying in space and dying on a planet I have no business going near?"

"The more I talk to you and think about you, the more convinced I become that if anyone can survive, you're the one," he said. "It may have taken me awhile to put the whole picture together, but now that I have, you can't deny it."

"How about if I deny your sanity?" I came back, putting my fingers on my hips. "I don't know what you're thinking about, and I doubt very much if *you* do."

"I know exactly what I'm talking about," he chuckled, suddenly moving past me to his blocky chair. He sat, tapped a few keys on his terminal, got half a dozen symbols in answer, then turned all the way back to me. "I don't know why I didn't think of the question sooner, but it finally came to me to ask why you were put in a crippled ship and headed into the deep black."

He beamed at me with a possessiveness I'd noticed earlier, looking as though he'd made his point and was just waiting for me to acknowledge it. I have often found myself with my head in a noose, but I can honestly say I never helped put it there.

"You see a big secret in that?" I came back immediately, throwing in a shrug for good measure. "All I see is the caution of a man who knows what's good for him. My people knew what I was doing and who I was involved with; if they decided to bring Radman in and put him to the Question, he'd have to be able to say that the last time he saw me I was alive and healthy, and was still in that condition as far as he knew. That's why he made sure I had everything I needed to be comfortable."

"Very logical and neat," Dameron conceded, but his nod and smile showed nothing of concession. "The man did it to protect himself. But you did say he was a slaver, didn't you? Couldn't he just have added you to his inventory and been able to say the same thing? I can't imagine his having any trouble selling a woman with your—ah—obvious attributes, and I'm sure your Federation has too many planets for him to be afraid that your people might stumble across you. If he didn't arrange a set of chains and a private auction for you, there must have been a reason."

He paused again, still wearing that "gotcha" expression, clearly waiting for me to comment; being compassionate, I saw no reason to disappoint him.

"Yes?" I prompted, looking faintly interested. "And the reason was?"

"That he thought you had too good a chance to get

yourself out of any arrangement like that," he growled, suddenly annoyed that I was ignoring the way he was pinning me to the wall. "If an enemy who knew you went to such lengths to be safely rid of you, then you have to be more than just average at what you do. Now go ahead and make your denials."

"I have no denials to make," I shrugged, turning away from his dark-eyed stare to go and reclaim my old lump-chair. I slid into it and made myself comfortable, then looked at him again. "I see no reason to either confirm or deny anything you say. Just let me know when you get to the end of your lecture series and the testing is about to start. That's when I'd like to leave."

"Damn it, you can't refuse to do this job for me!" he snapped, leaning forward toward me to emphasize his words. "You needed rescuing and I need a decoy; you got what you needed, and now it's my turn!"

"I only got half of what I needed," I pointed out, resting my elbow on my thigh and my chin in my palm. "When it came time to discuss C & Q data, you were much too busy. If the kind of help that buys you is what you're looking for, I'll be glad to supply it. If not, you've got a problem."

"How would you like to spend the rest of this crisis time in irons?" he asked, growling again. "I promised to reprogram your course computer as soon as I find the time, and I will. I saved your life, and I'll see to it that you don't have to go searching for where you came from. What more do you want?"

"What more do you have?" I muttered, playing smart to cover the tiny, tingling doubts I was beginning to feel. I'd pushed Dameron as hard as I'd been able, expecting to see the iron fist flash out of the velvet glove, ready to do some fisting myself on my way out of there, but it hadn't happened. Instead of threatening me

Dameron was pleading, and not a word about holding back the information I needed! I leaned all the way back in the lump chair, silently cursing the roll of the dice. Coersion I can understand and cope with; frantic requests for help are harder to ignore.

"I think I can understand how you feel," I heard after a long minute, looking up to see softer, more compassionate eyes on me. "You're a long way from home and want to start back, without any twisting, dangerous side trips. In your place I'd feel the same, but Diana—I can't afford to put myself in your place. Too many lives are hanging in the balance, and I have no one else to turn to."

"I see you've finally remembered my name," I commented, despite his sober expression. "What if I still say no?"

"You mean, what will I do to get even?" he asked, looking straight at me for another five seconds before raising his eyes to the blue ceiling and folding his hands behind his head. "I could always string you up by the thumbs, but I'd have to wait until an overhead hook became available. Putting in new hooks always loses us some air. Once you're strung up I could light a fire under your bare feet, but the automatic extinguishers don't like open fires. Skinning you alive might do the trick, but. . . ."

"Okay, okay, enough," I interrupted, showing my palm to admit surrender before his list got to be 'phone book length. "If you were trying to tell me you're beyond that sort of thing, I got the point. The only thing I still don't know is what you're not beyond."

"I'm not beyond dickering, if that's what you meant," he answered, back to looking at me. "Motivation is important when it comes to survival, and saving your favorite neck isn't always enough. I've always found bonuses helpful."

"I don't expect to hang around long enough to spend a bonus," I snorted, dismissing the suggestion with a wave of my hand. "And survival has always been a good enough motivation for me on its own."

"Then you *are* experienced in handling dangerous situations," he said softly, a grin spreading across his face. I suppose something in my expression showed what I thought of his methods of data-gathering; he wiped the grin fast and leaned forward in his chair. "I wasn't digging for that, but I'm glad to have the reassurance—since you're not admitting or denying anything. What I meant to say was, the bonuses I offer aren't in the form of legal tender. I try to offer things that would not normally be for sale at any price."

"Like what?" I asked, more curious than hooked. I still couldn't generate much enthusiasm for the idea of working for him. I had things at home waiting to be done—like a recently scheduled second meeting with Radman the slaver.

"Oh, items like certain souvenirs," Dameron drawled, his grin back again. "The Tildorani have turned carving into a high art, but they aren't in a position to do any exporting. Some of my people are collectors, and wouldn't be able to pick, choose and carry off any of the better items without field team help. And then there are those who do more—personal—collecting, for any of a variety of reasons. Even if the reason happens to be vanity, all they have to do is collect the necessary number of points."

I could feel the hook being dangled more enticingly in front of me, but I couldn't make out the nature of the bait. I could see I was supposed to ask what points and what they bought, allowing ignorance and innocence to

draw me closer to the hidden barbs, but that wasn't my
first time at dickering. I glanced around, as though
unconsciously trying to check the time, a shadow of
impatience to the movement, and Dameron suddenly
lost his drawl.

"Not all of our people have original Absari blood," he
said. "Those who do substitution work—or decoy work,
if you'd like to put it like that—and have to be changed
here in the base, have the option of keeping the features
they've been given if they want them. Those team
members earn one point for each job, and it takes three
points to buy the option, but I won't ask the same price
of you. Do this job for me and Bellna's looks are yours
to keep or give back, whichever way you want it. She's
the most attractive humanoid female I've ever seen; if
she weren't, I would not have brought the point up.
You're pretty enough in your own right, girl, but Bellna's
one of those one-in-a-million special cases. Can you sit
there and tell me you're not tempted even a little?"

I sat there and didn't tell him anything at all. Truthfully I was far from unhappy with my own looks,
notwithstanding the fact that no one would ever consider me beautiful. How I looked was part of who I was
to *me*, and I was satisfied with the whole and not
particularly anxious to change it. The only thing that
kept me from refusing outright was that Dameron was
right: Bellna *was* spectacularly beautiful, and I remembered my earlier thoughts on the subject. If the change
would benefit my job and make life—and surviving—
easier, saying no could be the stupidest thing I'd ever
done. I grappled with the pros and cons as I brushed
my lips with a strand of hair, then focused on Dameron
again with one of the more cogent cons.

"You're asking an impossibility," I said, not terribly
unhappy with the conclusion. "Your field people know

all about what's going on, know the people involved, the language, the terrain, friend from foe. I'd have to be crazy to involve myself in a project with that many minuses on my side, as crazy as you are for suggesting it. I don't mind improvising when a situation calls for it, but I have to have *something* to improvise *with*."

"You have no idea how glad I am to hear that objection," Dameron said, his expression serious. "It means you're finally thinking about the project as something to be thought about, not just something to reject out of hand. But I'm equally as glad to say that your objection is invalid. How do you think my field people learn what they need to know? Do you think I can afford to have them waste desperately needed working time cramming discs of information or groping around blind until they learn what's what? They're given what they need to know just the way you were given our language, quickly and painlessly. We even have a tape of Bellna's *persona* for you."

"What do you mean, a 'tape' of her '*persona*'?" I interrupted the flow, trying to ignore the diminishing of my resolve. Dameron with his fascinating new ways of doing things was doing a lot better job of hooking me than the usual bonus he'd promised. When it comes to curiosity, cats have *nothing* on me.

"We have a copy of Bellna's memories and personality," Dameron said, really warming to his subject. "Once it's impressed on your mind it will act like a reference library, telling you how to deal with the people you meet, whether or not Bellna knows them, how she usually acts with them if she does know them, and what would and would not be in character for her. It does more than studying her for years would, and was taken only recently, which means it's up-to-date. Any more objections?"

"Give me a minute, and I'll think of *something*, I muttered, turning to stare at his impassive face. I was curious—perhaps too much so—but I was still reluctant. Telling myself that going home was the smarter move didn't help; I wanted to work with Dameron's techniques and find out how they did. Against that, a two-month trip filled with boredom didn't have a chance, especially when I might get home to find that someone else had settled Radman's hash in my absence. Something in the back of my head was telling me I was putting my foot in it clear up to the shoulder, but I've never been very good at taking advice to be sensible, even when the advice is my own. My fingers drummed on the arm of the lump chair with a monotonous sound, but Dameron didn't let it go on for long.

"Your minute's up," he announced, no real push in his voice. "If you need another one, by all means take it. I'd hate to have you think I'm rushing you into anything."

"That sounds like a suitable epitaph," I nodded, bringing my eyes back to him. " 'At least she wasn't rushed.' How far would I have to restrain my instincts for self-preservation?"

"Any time it's a choice between you or the other guy, I expect you to give me the time to think up a better epitaph than the one you just mentioned," he answered with a faint grin. "As long as you don't use Tildor as a private hunting preserve, you have everyone's blessing in staying alive. I'm still not trying to rush you, but my people will need some time to check your Healing tolerance and calibrate their doses and instrumentation. If we're going to move on this, we'll have to do it soon."

His eyes were calm and his big body was relaxed in the squarish chair, but two of his fingers rubbed against one another in a gesture I was sure he was unaware of. I stared at him another ten seconds, but only to add to his inner turmoil; I was sure he knew I couldn't resist his bait; that was why he'd dangled it.

"It really would never do to make your people do their calibration in a hurry," I said at last, drawling the way he'd drawled earlier. "Just remember: if I get killed, I'll never speak to you again."

He let out a whoop of victory and bounced out of his chair, leaned down to grab my wrists, then hauled me to my feet.

"We'll get right over there," he grinned, pounding me on the back in a happy, enthusiastic way. If I hadn't been in decent shape, his friendly approval would have done a lot toward flattening me. "Let's just—"

His words cut off as his terminal signaled for attention. He turned toward it and impatiently tapped a couple of keys, giving me the chance to flex the muscles in my shoulder that he'd been playing pat-a-cake on. Symbols appeared on the screen, and when Dameron saw them he muttered under his breath, then tapped another couple of keys.

"Post 7 needs help of some sort," he said, turning back to me and rubbing his broad face in frustration. "I want you turned over to the clinicians *now*, not after 7's endless explanations, but you can't go yourself. I'll have to send Valdon with you."

"Is that supposed to be reassurance or a threat?" I asked, letting Dameron take my arm and steer us both toward the door. "It does help in one way, I guess. With Valdon there, I won't have to look for any enemies among your clinicians."

"Valdon's not your enemy," Dameron said, a touch of annoyance in his voice as the door slid open in front of us. "He was trying to help you, and you made him look foolish. You can't blame him for being angry."

"Sure I can," I answered, looking up at him. "Before rushing in to help someone, it's smart to find out whether or not they need your help, and also whether or not they want it. Valdon strikes me as the sort who never bothers asking those questions when a female's involved, and that means he deserves whatever he gets. There *are* one or two of us who can take care of ourselves."

"He wasn't raised to look at it like that," Dameron said, heading us across the corridor, but more slowly. "He was taught to be courteous to and considerate of women, and that's what he is. He wasn't trying to insult you; he was just trying to keep you from being afraid of him. For some reason, a good number of women are uncomfortable around him."

"It's that hunter's look in his eyes," I said, stopping a couple of feet from the door Dameron was moving toward so that I could chuckle softly. "I knew it was something that gave him trouble, but it's not a trait he can change. So women run screaming from him, do they?"

"They don't run screaming from him," Dameron came back, trying to be stern, but he couldn't hold the look and meet my grin at the same time. He came up with his own chuckle and grin, then shook his head. "They start out being attracted to him, but as soon as he tries to return their interest, they suddenly remember appointments elsewhere. I didn't believe it happened to him all the time at home until it happened once out here. The field team girls don't usually react to him that way, but they're not in the base much."

"Poor baby," I commiserated, still laughing softly. "He leads a rough life. All right, I'll try not to be so hard on him. I'll give him as much elbow room as he gives me."

"That sounds fair enough," Dameron grinned, then

gestured toward the door in front of us. "He ought to be in there."

We started toward the door again and it slid open, showing an office just like Dameron's except for the presence of Valdon. The big man sat in his own squarish chair staring down at a complex map projected on his cube, but when he saw us he reached behind him to his terminal and keyed the cube blank again.

"Valdon, we have our decoy Bellna," Dameron announced, leaving me a couple of steps inside the doorway to walk closer to the other man alone. "I was about to take her to the clinicians, but post 7 called in, so you'll have to take her there for me. Tell them she's a native of a new associated world, so they need to calibrate her completely. And I want everything given to her at once, as quickly as her system can take it. We'll need all the time we can get for briefing and planning sessions."

"And for laying in a supply of hankies for her tears," Valdon said, barely glancing at me as he stood up. "Who would you like assigned to the job of holding her hand and wiping her nose?"

"Make it someone interesting," I said before Dameron could vocalize the annoyance on his face. "It would be a pleasant change to meet someone interesting around here."

"That's enough out of both of you," Dameron growled, glaring first at me and then at Valdon. "I don't have the time to referee the tiffs between two small children. You both have jobs to do, and I expect to see them done *without* bickering."

"I think you're making a mistake, but you're in charge." Valdon shrugged, turning his head to look straight at me. "If I'm wrong I'll apologize, but I don't think she can handle it. Odds are she's never touched a sword in her life."

"Well, I may not be all that capable, but I'm willing to learn," I purred, meeting his dark-eyed stare with a small smile. "Why don't you find us a couple of weapons and give me some lessons?"

"If you did that, you'd be the biggest fool I know," Dameron said, interrupting what would probably have been agreement from Valdon. "Can't you see she'd never have made the offer if she wasn't pretty damned good with a blade? You refused to give me a straight answer before, girl, but I want one now. How much experience have you had with swordplay?"

"Enough," I answered, looking at Dameron as I folded my arms. "If you have any doubts, I won't feel insulted if you withdraw your offer. There are other things I'd rather be doing."

"I'm not withdrawing anything," Dameron growled, annoyed at the way I'd answered him—or not answered him. "As I said before, I don't have the time for this. Valdon, get her over to the clinicians."

With that he stomped out of the room, barely giving the door time to slide out of his way. He seemed to do a lot of that, playing chicken with doors, and as sight of his back disappeared, I wondered what happened when he lost.

"It seems I have my orders," Valdon's deep voice came, and I turned my head back to see him staring at me. "You'd better be as good as you think you are. Tildor is no place for beginners."

"No one's as good as they think they are," I came back, noticing again how really attractive he was. He stood with wide arms crossed over a broad chest, lean-hipped, longish black hair a perfect match to the hunter's look in his unwavering, black-eyed stare. He was still annoyed with me, and would probably go on being annoyed if he was waiting for me to get flustered. It was too bad, really, but he just wasn't my type.

"At least that's one point in your favor," he granted, moving closer to look down at me with slightly less annoyance. "You're not a braggart. Talkers don't live very long on Tildor, and this project is too important to gamble on hot air."

"Approval at last," I sighed, folding my hands as I looked up at him adoringly. "I think I'm in love."

"Very funny," he growled, turning me away from him by the shoulders and pushing me toward the door. Valdon still didn't appreciate my sense of humor, and that was it as far as friendly conversation between us went, which was fine with me. I was a lot more interested in Dameron's procedures than in Valdon, and as the clinicians bustled me away from him, the last glance I got of his expression said that he knew it.

CHAPTER 3

I awoke on the furry couch-bed a second time, this time seeing a soft light glowing in the room, and this time knowing exactly where I was. I took a deep breath and found that I was braced for pain, but there was none. No pain, no discomfort, just a feeling of health and vitality and well-being. I hadn't expected the aftermath to be that easy, not after seeing the array of equipment the clinicians had had. I'd been weighed and measured and probed and scanned and practically turned inside out, and then I'd been put to sleep. That last step had taken longer than it should have, I was told, simply because my readings were different from everyone else's, different in a way difficult to measure. They'd had to do a lot of delicate recalibration before they were ready to start on me, and after all that build-up I'd missed the procedures themselves by being unconscious. I wasn't awake long enough or fully enough to be annoyed, but once I was I expected to be.

I sat up on the couch-bed and ran my fingers through my hair, wondering if my last thought made any sense at all. Despite the feeling of glowing good health I was also feeling faintly fuzzy around the edges, as though I'd just been roused out of a very deep sleep. The room light brightened to a point just short of eye-hurting, letting me look down at myself and the delicate pink, slim-strapped body suit someone had put on me. The clinicians must have thought my sense of modesty needed protecting, but all the suit's presence did was increase my annoyance. I never slept in anything, and if they'd had the good sense to ask first—

The argumentative train of thought was ended completely by the appearance of a thick lock of hair falling over my left shoulder. It wasn't as though that was the first time it had ever happened, but the lock of hair was *red*! I grabbed more hair and brought it around to see it, and *it* was red, too! The excitement rising in me said I may have accepted Dameron's procedures intellectually, but emotionally I hadn't believed they could do it. I put my hands to my face, trying to detect differences, but didn't know my own features well enough that way to make anything out. What I needed was a mirror.

I stood up fast and looked around, but all the salmon and green room held was what it had held before: the couch-bed, the round thing next to it, and a lump chair. I was about to go storming out into the corridor yelling for Dameron, but the need to search the salmon-colored panels for the one that was the door brought me up short. Dameron had done so much with the wall panels that it would be stupid of me not to try them first. I strode over and began touching them here and there, finding absolutely nothing until my fingers slid over an invisible, yielding patch. A door popped open to my left, allowing access to a narrow space between the walls—and on the back of the door was a full-length mirror.

Looking into the mirror was something of a shock.

Have you ever had your hair cut or styled in a way totally different from the way you usually wear it? Do you remember your first conviction that the face you stared at wasn't your own—and that it would take a while to get used to your new image? My eyes found Bellna staring back at me, her face even more beautiful than the photo had shown it to be, her blue eyes sparkling with life and an impish delight, her bright red hair falling in thick cascades around her face and shoulders. My face and shoulders. I shook my head, trying to break away from the sense of unreality, finding myself even more confused when the image in the mirror did the same.

Okay, let's bring this back down to earth, I told myself firmly, straightening myself and the mirror image at the same time. That's what you look like now, and you'd better get used to it. Have you ever seen a complexion that flawless? Such perfectly arched eyebrows? Such real, true beauty? You know you haven't, and now it's yours; how about getting started on using it?

I let a smile come through and the mirror face glowed with warmth and invitation, so softly sensual that the smile suddenly disappeared and the wide blue eyes widened even farther. A smile on that face was a devastating weapon, one I'd be smart to take it easy with. I didn't want to spend my time on Tildor fighting off rape attempts, especially since Bellna's face went so well with my body and hers. The girl and I were almost equally well-endowed, the only major changes intended having been to lighten my skin to a red-head's shade, and change all of my bodily hair to match hers. Luckily, Bellna was a big girl, only about two inches less than my own height, which meant it hadn't been necessary to shorten me. The clinicians had discussed the point at some length, and practical considerations had dictated their final decision. My reflexes and sense of balance were adjusted to my body as it was; shortening me would throw off that adjustment, possibly fatally if I couldn't readjust before I had to defend myself from serious attack. It would be a lot simpler putting me in flat-heeled boots rather than the high-heeled ones Bellna wore, thereby adjusting the height difference painlessly. I moved my body slowly in the mirror, glad it was more recognizable than my face even if it *was* covered by that ridiculous bodysuit. The pink of it went terribly with my hair, and I saw my new face frown as the thought came that the thing was much too revealing and immodest. Whoever had put me in it should have been whipped for the insult, to do such a thing to someone such as I! How dare they treat me so, as though I were a peasant girl or a slave! Who would dare!

"What's the matter, don't you like it?" a voice came suddenly from behind me, and I whirled around while blinking back clouds of highly incensed anger. Valdon stood just inside the door to the corridor, still too close to let it slide closed again behind him. He'd come in with no more announcement than I ever got, and I was getting tired of the intrusion.

"Next time, you'd better figure out some way of letting me know you're out there," I said, only somewhat distracted by the sweet, girlish tones I'd produced that just had to be Bellna's voice. "I value my privacy, and have been known to go to some lengths to ensure it."

"You can worry about your privacy once this is all over," he countered, taking a few steps forward and folding his arms across his chest. "In case it hasn't come through to you yet, I'm part of this project too, but in a position just a little higher than yours. Now, what were you doing a minute ago?"

He stood there in front of the now-closed door, that unwavering stare coming straight at me, and I suddenly realized something else about him. It wasn't only a hunter who looked out from his eyes, it was also a man who was used to dominating everything and everyone around him. I hadn't seen that look often before, but I was bright enough to recognize it—and human enough to resent it. I didn't work for Valdon no matter what opinions he had to the contrary, and it was time he knew it.

"None of your damned business what I was doing a minute ago," I answered, turning back to the mirror. "You managed to find your way in here, so now let's see if you can remember the way out. If I decide I need you for something, I'll send someone to rattle your cage."

I shook my head to move the hair back from my face, seeing, in reflection, the way Valdon's jaw tightened in anger, the look in his dark eyes hardening even further. He unfolded his arms and straightened to full height, then started coming toward me.

"Now, you listen to me, you little—" he began, his right hand outstretched to wrap around my arm again, yet that was far too much. No one had the authority to touch my person, least of all boorish louts such as he. I turned somewhat back to him, my right side toward his reaching one, struck upward with my arm against his to raise it, then kicked sideways into his ribs, twisting my hip into the kick. The churl grunted aloud with pain as he bent forward, his arms wrapped about himself, and then he leaned upon one knee, seeking with eyes closed to recover what breath he might. I had swiftly taken myself back a pace or two, well prepared to continue should he show signs of further foolishness, but then came an interruption.

"*Now* what are you two doing?" Dameron demanded from the doorway, frowning at Valdon and me. I shook my head hard as I relaxed from the standard attack-defense position I'd taken, and Valdon raised himself to his feet, though obviously still in pain. He took a deep breath, wincing as he did so, then made for the door as Dameron moved to one side.

"Nothing but a small difference of opinion," he muttered as he passed Dameron. "I'll see you later."

Dameron leaned out to watch Valdon disappear up the corridor, then came back in to turn his sudden confusion toward me.

"I don't understand any of this," he protested, a plaintive note in his tone. "What happened between you two this time, and where is he going? There's a briefing scheduled for you in a little while, and I wanted him there."

I moved my hand over the panel, closing up the mirror again, then gave my attention to finding the closet that had been used the last time. When I did find it and found that it had been used again, I pulled out the jumpsuit that had been neatly hung back in place. As I began getting into the suit, I shrugged in answer to Dameron's question.

"I don't know where he's going," I said over my shoulder, predictably adding to Dameron's confusion. "And it's just the way he said. A small difference of opinion."

Dameron shook his head without comment, not terribly satisfied with my answer, but I wasn't very happy with it myself. I was trying to figure out what had made me act the way I had, but the crystal-clear reasons of a few minutes earlier had somehow clouded to total irrelevance. No matter how annoyed I got, I wasn't in the habit of assaulting people who weren't bent on offering me harm. Getting physical rarely does more than cause hard feelings or create awkward, unexplainable bodies. I'd struck out at Valdon without warning or excuse, and the action bothered me more than any possible consequences. It wasn't *like* me to do something like that, and I'd have to be careful to watch myself closely in the future. I closed the jumpsuit with a stroke of my hand, then went with Dameron to his briefing.

The scoutship settled to the ground in the deep black of the woods, making no more sound than a leaf settling the same way. The night sky was dark with racing clouds, and we nestled in the darkness, showing no lights of our own. The hull of the small scout ship was clear all about the pilot and me, but nothing could be seen through it from the outside. The pilot's instrument board glowed a steady, unexcited blue, and he and I sat in silence, waiting for the agent who was supposed to rendezvous with us.

The past few base days had been dull tripled and squared, filled with nothing but briefing sessions. Right from the very first, the impressed memories I'd been given had made the briefings a bore, going over and over again points I already knew. I kept getting the urge to explode and walk out, but I overrode that feeling. I've been invited to many briefing sessions, but I've never purposely missed one and I never will. When your life can depend on some insignificant little point some bore grinds out, you learn to listen with full attention. I was told about the political and geographical twistings and forkings, given a list of friend and foe, filled in on plans, hopes and wishful thinking. I was a fairly good improviser and hadn't been caught off-balance too many times, so I wasn't worrying about the operation, but that didn't mean I had no worries.

I'd been silently examining my inner self, and what I'd noticed about my attitudes and reactions had not only not gone away, it had begun to spread, coloring my thinking when I wasn't consciously willing it not to. When someone warned me to watch out for this or that possibility, I experienced a very strong desire to laugh at him and tell him just how good I was. That part of it scared me more than the presence of a knife at my throat would have; thinking you're the best and smartest around is the first step toward a messy ending. Over and over I caught myself mentally strutting around, discounting advice even before I'd heard it, minimizing the plottings of opponents. I kept telling myself that it was only a slight aberration, a weird reaction from having been alone so long, thinking myself finished, and then suddenly finding myself saved. Relief can do strange things to people, and as soon as the shock or whatever it was passed, I'd be my old, practical self again. I told that to myself often, and hoped that I wasn't conning myself.

The woods around us were thick and old, the black shadow-leaves swaying in a rhythm that had been known forever. I couldn't feel what was moving them, but I could see its passage, and I recalled what the woods were like during the daylight hours, when I had ridden them with my escort. My escort had been large, of course, as befitted a princess, and they had been ever alert to keep harm from me. My ladies had disliked riding the woods as often as I did, finding the experience uncomfortable in the extreme, therefore did I ever insist upon their accompanying me. It was necessary to teach them that my needs and desires were all-important, theirs nothing but ignorable whim. Once, to punish them for daring to beg to be excused, I picnicked for a very long time with the captain of my guard, allowing

all of my escort the time to carry my three ladies off
into the woods. I knew they and the others of my ladies
had been taken into the woods before by certain members of my escort, yet never had all of them taken only
three. I felt the punishment would do well for them,
and when they were later returned to me, tears staining
their cheeks, I considered the matter properly seen to.
Thereafter they recalled that I was a princess and they
were not. It was a—

I broke off the thought fast and shook my head,
forcing the rambling back from wherever it had come.
Bellna's own neighborhood seemed to have triggered
her memories, and it wasn't taking me long to discover
that I didn't like her very much. I moved around in my
seat, ignoring the questioning look I was getting from
the pilot, and that reminded me of the other questioning
looks I'd been getting lately—or maybe "questionable"
would be a better word. Not long after the briefings
had started, Valdon had shown up and put himself in a
quiet corner, listening but not contributing. No one had
questioned his presence so I couldn't very well object,
but he'd spent most of his time staring at me with no
expression on his face. Normal staring doesn't bother
me a bit, but there was something about his stare that
rubbed me the wrong way, something behind it that
primed me like a high explosive. I gritted my teeth and
stuck it out during the briefings, but made sure to be
nowhere near him afterward. The new, touchy part of
me felt satisfaction over what I had done to him and
was more than willing to have me do it again, but there
was no sense in adding complications. Dameron was
trying to minimize possible trouble spots in the operation,
and I had decided to try doing the same.

Although nothing but a sprinkling of stars relieved
the darkness outside, the planetary time wasn't all that

late. Just then I was waiting to be collected by one of
the resident agents of Tildor, who would escort me—or,
rather, the Princess Bellna—to a hunting lodge not far
from Havro's keep. The lodge was sometimes used by
certain of Havro's guests, but just then it would be
empty. The agent and I would spend the night, and in
the morning my secret mercenary escort would pick me
up. No one knew about this secret leave-taking but
Prince Clero and his cronies, who had been told soon
enough to target their plans against my traveling group,
but not soon enough to send riders against the lodge. I'd
be able to get one night's uninterrupted sleep before the
fun began, and after that it would be catch as catch can.

I sighed as I thought about the plans that had been
made for after the attack. They all hinged on whether
or not I was still breathing, of course, but assuming I
was, I was to dump my escort and then head south.
Once I had put a lot of emptiness between me and other
people a scout ship would pick me up, guided in by the
beacon that had been implanted somewhere in my body.
Just where that beacon was I had no idea; there wasn't a
mark or scar on me. As a matter of fact, one or two
scars that I'd had for a while had also disappeared
without a trace, all of it due to the process known as
Healing. I wanted to spend a lot of time thinking about
that, but in the middle of Dameron's precious project I
couldn't spare the attention. Once it was over, though . . .

The pilot next to me had been helping me watch the
darkness, but he'd been using his instruments instead of
his eyesight. He stiffened suddenly just before I caught
a hint of movement about twenty-five feet from where
we sat, but the stiffness left him almost immediately
and his hand relaxed away from his sidearm. His panel
light glowed a cool blue, telling us my date had arrived.

Four dark, cloaked figures came up to the scouter,

one slightly ahead of the other three, all of them waiting for the pilot to activate the access release. When the panel next to my right arm slid aside I gathered my cape together, then climbed out into the night. The figure closest to the scouter took my arm to help me down, then all five of us moved back about ten feet from the scouter and watched it rise soundlessly into the air, gliding higher and higher, becoming harder and harder to see. In no more than seconds it had blended with the dark gray clouds sliding through the skies, totally gone from mere mortal senses. I took a deep breath to drown the sudden, childish feeling of abandonment I was abruptly filled with, and only then discovered that the hand that had taken my arm hadn't let go again. I tugged slightly to show that I was ready to be turned loose, but the hand on my arm only tightened.

"Have no fear, you will not be harmed," a gruff, impatient voice came from the shadow figure beside me, speaking the Tildorani language. "These—ah—guardsmen—and I will escort you to your destination, Princess. During this short journey, we require no converse from you."

It wasn't hard to tell that I'd just been ordered to keep quiet, or that the other three men were Absari agents posing as Tildorani. The Bellna memories I'd been given identified the voice as belonging to Grigon, Prince Havro's chief adviser, but the tone and sense of command weren't part of those memories. Grigon usually used smoothly professional calm on Bellna, and I couldn't see any reason to change that.

"Converse is unnecessary when issuing commands, Grigon," I told him coldly, resisting the pull that was trying to take me deeper into the surrounding trees. "You and these others may indeed escort me, yet only in the manner befitting my station. Release my arm, and begin such actions at once."

"Your station during the longer journey before you remains as yet undetermined," the Grigon-shadow growled, obviously displeased with my retort. "Should it be necessary for the exalted Princess Bellna to adopt the actions and mannerisms of a peasant girl to escape her father's enemies, it is best that she be fully prepared to do so. This walk will begin to prepare her."

His grip tightened even more on my arm, and then I was yanked along so hard I nearly went down from the pull. I felt outrage and shock that a servant like Grigon would act that way with me, then impatiently pushed those feelings aside. The reaction was Bellna's rather than mine, just as most of my previous speech had been. I wasn't used to keeping the new set of memories and personality from affecting my own, and the lack had already begun making trouble. I can't say I enjoyed the way Grigon was manhandling me through the windy dark, but getting up on a high horse wasn't the way to stop it. His dialogue had told me we were in enemy territory and had to watch what we said, so it was hardly the place to teach him the right way to greet a fellow conspirator. It would be smarter to wait until we got where we were going and could talk freely—even though ignoring the annoyance was hard. I got a left-handed grip on the cape and long-skirted dress I was wearing, got them out of the way of the hurried steps being forced on me, and just followed quietly—if not meekly—along.

It took at least twenty minutes to reach our destination. Grigon started out at a good clip that had me almost running beside him, but we weren't following a road or even a trail. Continuing on like that in the dark would have run us into a tree or a ground depression in no

time, and the man knew it. He slowed almost at once
and gestured one of the other three into leading our
little parade, giving him the job of traversing the terrain
before we set our dainty boots on it. The chosen one
took over the job of point without comment, leaving the
other two to follow along behind. We moved a little
faster then, but not so fast that I had trouble keeping
up. I hate wearing skirts, most especially long skirts,
but awkward or not, that's what I had to work with. All
Tildorani women dressed that way, even underage princesses who had been given their way much too often in
life.

The wind whipped all our capes around, and the dark
was so deep under the trees that we wouldn't have been
able to see the moons even if there hadn't been clouds. I
didn't know we had reached where we were going until I
saw the small clearing we had entered, and looked around
the side of the big man in front of me to see the large,
wooden two-story we were approaching. Bellna had
never been to the hunting lodge, and I could feel the
sense of reserved curiosity that sight of it brought to the
part that was her. She knew that her father had used it
and for that reason it was somewhat acceptable, but
other than that it was much too low-class to suit her
tastes. Although I hadn't exactly been raised in a barn
myself, her attitude made me want to shake my head.
Snobs have their place in life, I suppose, and I'm just being
short-sighted in not being able to see where.

A dark shadow stepped into sight on the other side of
the clearing, grew an arm to gesture with, then melted
back into the trees it had come from. Grigon did nothing to acknowledge the go-ahead signal; he spoke, instead,
to the three men with us.

"The lodge remains secure," he said, his gruff voice
low enough to carry no farther than the men around us.

"I will take the girl inside and remain to instruct her. For you, the others do not exist. Guard us as though you were alone."

The three gave no vocal agreement, but there was no doubt they'd follow orders. Two of them moved away from us toward the sides of the lodge as Grigon pulled me toward the wide porch that fronted the place, and by the time we reached the door the two were gone from sight and hearing. The third had let us pass him and then had followed, but once he reached the steps leading up to the porch he stopped and turned around, his back to the lodge as he faced outward. I caught a glimpse of a sheathed sword as he turned to take his post, and then Grigon had pulled me through the door he had opened, into the dimly lit interior. The door was closed again with a firm click, and at long last my arm was released from capture. I took the opportunity to rub it as I looked around, squinting only a little at the increased light as Grigon turned the lamp higher.

The word "rustic" must have been coined for the room we stood in. The log walls were well made and properly sealed, but were totally undecorated except for the bows and spears hanging on two of them, mostly around the two closed doors. A big stone fireplace dominated another of the walls, with four heavy, hand-made chairs standing not far from the crackling blaze someone had started on its hearth. The only wall that wasn't bare was the front one containing windows; heavy brown drapes covered them so that they couldn't be seen from inside. The wooden floors were as bare as most of the walls, but the whole place was neat and entirely lacking that empty, untenanted feel that seldom-used places usually had. I unhooked my cape and began to slide it off my shoulders, already feeling the difference the fire made after the cool of the night; as I did so, the man called Grigon stopped prowling around and came over to give me the benefit of his expertise.

"There was no need whatsoever for you to attempt so superior a manner," he said, unhooking his own cape and pulling it off as he glared at me. He was a tall man with a thin face and a perpetually stooped look, wearing black pants and boots and a wide-sleeved, plain white shirt. "You were commanded to silence, and silent you should have remained. Such behavior was unprofessional and the height of stupidity. It will not be forgotten."

"How good of you to greet me so warmly," I drawled, hanging my cape over my left arm with a comradely smile. He was still using the Tildorani tongue, so I did the same. "Your graciousness will be a great comfort to me during my sojourn here."

"Your manner remains entirely unacceptable," he growled, a faint flush of anger tinging his smooth-shaven cheeks. "It is neither the youthful imperiousness of the princess, nor the carefully respectful response of a peasant girl. Do you think yourself in the midst of a female group-sewing, that you behave so? Do you seek to nullify our careful planning?"

"It is scarcely possible for me to nullify your superior planning from this room," I came back, finding it impossible to keep the dryness from my voice. "I would, however, appreciate being informed concerning the reason for your having twice referred to the possibility of my being presented as a peasant girl. I was given the impression in base that I was to be the Princess Bellna alone."

"Guard your unthinking tongue!" he snapped, the look in his dark eyes sharpening. "Though this lodge is secure, you are not again to refer to 'base'! Also, it is not for you to question what role you will play! Should we think it necessary that you be disguised as a peasant, you will obey our orders without question—if such a difficult undertaking is not beyond your abilities! You stand dressed in the clothing of a princess; remove it and show me the peasant girl I may require."

His voice had grown cold and haughty, a Tildorani male giving orders to a lowly female. My temper flared in response to his attitude, but my own reactions were sweet calm compared to the outrage coming from the Bellna personality. No one spoke to a princess like that, and she wasn't about to stand for it.

"How dare you!" I found myself hissing, fists clenched as I leaned forward toward the man not far from me. "Is it now that you will overstep yourself, peasantish servant? Am I now to be able to speak to my father, giving him proof of your lack of respect for me? Till now he has laughingly dismissed my protests; there will be little laughter caused by *this!* Show me to my rooms at once, and perhaps you will retain your head when your manhood has been taken!"

I looked coldly upon the wretch, seeing his frown and the first signs of apprehension. Surely did he know that my words had not been idle, yet rather than attempt apology he abruptly straightened from the stoop that had ever been a part of him, strode across the distance separating us, then grasped my arms. He shook me with strength, shocking me with such unbelievable behavior, and I didn't know what the hell was going on.

"Snap out of it!" Grigon ordered, clear worry in his eyes as he shook me again. "That's the second time you've done it, and this time I'm sure. Cut it out!"

"Cut what out?" I growled, raising both fists in front of me and then snapping them outward to break his hold. He had shifted to base language, and that seemed to be adding to my confusion. "What the hell are you talking about?"

"I'm talking about that speech you just gave me," he answered, his eyes narrowed as he looked at me. He seemed both larger and younger now that he'd dropped his role—and a lot less belligerent. "Bellna has resented Grigon's influence over her father for a long time, and she and he have had more than one venomous exchange like that. That wasn't you pretending to be Bellna; that was Bellna herself."

"Don't be ridiculous," I scoffed, picking up my cape and then looking around for some place other than the floor to put it down. "Just because I don't have the hang of using her *persona* yet doesn't mean there's anything strange going on. Once I get a little practice in, her personality won't jump out every time she gets upset."

"You're missing the point," he said, his touch on my arm bringing my eyes back to his sober face. "I don't know where you got the idea that practice has anything to do with it, but her personality isn't supposed to jump out at all. It's an unliving, unaware reference file, not another person inside your head to be fought with. Does Dameron know about this?"

I stared at him for a minute without answering, feeling even more confused, then finally shook my head.

"How can Dameron know about it when *I* don't know about it?" I asked, searching his face for signs that he was putting me on. "Are you trying to tell me that impression isn't supposed to work this way? That this sort of thing—whatever it is—has never happened to anyone else?"

"Not until now." He took a deep breath as he looked away from me, let it out slowly, then brought his eyes back. "It's a good thing I had a communicator installed here, just in case. I'd better call Dameron."

"And tell him what?" I demanded, stopping Grigon as he began turning away from me. "That we scrap the whole project because of one minor unexpected complication? A suggestion like that is guaranteed to make him love you forever."

"One *minor* complication?" he echoed, outrage thick in his tone. "You've got a living, thinking Bellna sharing your head and body, taking over whenever she pleases, and you call that *minor*? Has anyone ever told you you have a gift for understatement?"

"She doesn't take over whenever she pleases," I denied sourly, deciding I might as well hang onto the damned cape for a while. "She's been able to take over to a small extent because I didn't know she wasn't supposed to be able to. From now on I'll make sure I stay permanently in the driver's seat."

"Oh, sure you will," he agreed with heavy sarcasm, turning all the way back to me and folding his arms. "You'll have no trouble at all in making a fifteen-year-old brat do things your way while Clero's men close in from all sides. They won't distract you from matching wills with her, and she won't distract you from keeping yourself unspitted. It's done all the time."

"If it isn't done all the time, how do *you* know how hard it will be?" I countered, getting more and more annoyed at his pessimism. "And I thought this project was a top-priority, die-before-failing necessity. Someone listening to you would think you were *looking* for a reason to call it off."

I was trying to put him on the defensive, trying to take his mind off the single track it had been clinging to, but the man was no child or beginner. Instead of getting insulted or trying to justify his position, he let his eyes grow cold.

"You're right about this being a top-priority project,"

he said, staring down at me. "The part you're wrong about is thinking we'd throw away the life of one of our own people just to see our purpose accomplished. I know Dameron picked you because he thought you had a much better than even chance of surviving this mess; I also know he'll want to hear my reasons for thinking you won't survive. Want to bet he *will* love me forever?"

He stared at me for a minute after that, giving me a chance to make the sucker bet if I was foolish enough to do so, but I knew better than to waste the effort. The Absari base commander would side with *him*, not with me. After the minute he unfolded his arms and began to turn away again, but I couldn't let him go through with it.

"Grigon, don't call Dameron," I sighed, giving up my previous attempts to buffalo him. "You don't have to tell me he'll cancel the project. I know he will."

"Don't you think he should?" the man called Grigon asked, his tone more reasonable than argumentative. "I can't imagine what could have gone wrong with the impression, but it's bound to make your role five times more difficult, if not downright impossible. Your wanting to go with it tells me you're probably a suicide buff."

"Sorry, but suicide's not my thing," I denied, shifting that stupid cape to my other arm. "I'm on the inside with this problem, and I'm telling you that it honestly doesn't feel as terrible as you're describing it. I've never walked away from an assignment already committed to in my entire career, not unless there were reasons a lot more compelling than some stray thoughts in my head. Just how positive are you that your guess is better than mine?"

He hesitated visibly then, considering my question, but logic was on *my* side. No one can be an expert on something that's never happened before, and Grigon couldn't pretend that he was.

"I can't possibly be positive, and you know it," he said, ending the brief pause, annoyance back in his voice and eyes. "What makes you so sure that *you* have the way of it? If you find out I'm right with your last living thought, do you intend sending your spirit back to let me say I told you so? I won't find it nearly as satisfying as you seem to think I will."

"Why do you insist on seeing me dead?" I demanded, trying to ignore the severe adult-to-child overtones that kept escaping his control. "You said yourself that Dameron would not have sent me if he didn't think I could handle it. I'd like to know what makes you believe I can't."

"Maybe it's the fact that I know this world and I don't know you," he said, rubbing his face with one hand, the vexation in his voice stronger. "We've got to settle this one way or the other *tonight*, before we commit to this project too far to back out if it becomes necessary. Come with me."

He turned and strode to the left-hand door, threw it open, then waited for me to follow as he'd ordered. When I got there and looked past him I saw a dim, narrow back hall with two more closed doors straight ahead, and a heavy staircase to the left. I wondered why my guide had stopped at the threshold rather than leading the way through, but he didn't leave me wondering long.

"Take those stairs to the next floor and go to the last room along the hall," he said, gesturing briefly with one hand. "I'll be there as soon as I report your safe arrival, and then we can discuss the problem until we both know where we stand."

I hesitated very briefly, trying to think of a diplo-

matic way of offering to go with him while he reported
my "arrival," but there didn't seem to be one. Anything
I said would translate out as not trusting him—which
was exactly the way I felt but was not an attitude
calculated to make him think more kindly about my
chances of continuing with the project. The only thing I
could do was give him the chance to blow the whistle
behind my back—and hope I'd raised enough doubt in
his mind to keep him from doing no more than think
about it. I craned my neck around a little more, using
sightseeing to account for my silence, then nodded as I
glanced at him.

"Up to the second floor, then down to the end," I
agreed, using my free hand to get a grip on the long
skirt that would have tripped me on those stairs. "See
you there."

I walked to the stairs and began climbing them without looking back, not even pausing when I heard the
soft click of the door being closed. There was no guarantee Grigon was on the outside of the closed door, and
I'd already cut him loose in my mind. Taking him out
of the game entirely would have been the only way of
stopping him from reporting anything he pleased, and I
wasn't willing to do that. The Lord of Luck had been
good to me in my time, and the only way to repay him
is to trust him completely when none of your own
efforts will do the trick.

The door at the end of the hall was not door but
doors. Two beautifully carved doors stood quietly in
the half-lit shadow of a single wall candle, and opening
one of them showed me a room that banished all thoughts
of rustic. A fire danced and crackled in the large marble
fireplace to the left of the doors, an occasional spark
jumping out to the wide stone apron in front of it.
Beyond the apron was a single well-padded chair stand-

ing on the beginnings of a room-wide, deep-napped carpet in what seemed to be wine-red. All the wall space in the room was covered with heavy cloth hangings, and ahead and to the right was an enormous bed, cano-pied and curtained in the same dark red, with another, lighter color showing faintly inside the curtains. Gold thread picked out Prince Havro's emblem on the front curtain, a large circle enclosing a snarling, clawing isphalgor standing on an intricately embroidered rendi-tion of the three letters of Havro's family name. I could feel Bellna's recognition of her father's insignia, but it came as something of a shock to realize that she couldn't read the letters. Women on Tildor were kept illiterate as a matter of course, and even Bellna's position as prin-cess hadn't saved her from the darkness. The back-ground information I'd been given let me read as well as any Tildorani male, but that was a point I'd have to keep firmly in mind. No matter who I was on that planet, if the character was female it would have to forget how to read.

I closed the door behind me and moved farther into the room, seeing a large, beautifully carved wardrobe and matching bench standing to the right of the bed. I finally got rid of the cape by dumping it on the bench, then walked over to the wide carved screen of wood that had been set up to the right of the wardrobe. There was faint candlelight trickling out around its edges that made me curious, but stepping behind it fed me a jolt of shock from the Bellna presence. The area behind the screen was all mirrored, wall and screen alike, and thick, soft fur pelts covered the more sedate wine-red carpeting. The area was a slave nook, and if I'd both-ered looking for them among the furs, I probably could have found the chains. Bellna was sputtering indig-nantly in my head, upset not so much by the discovery of her father's play nest as by having to look at something that free, high-born women were usually sheltered from. Everyone knew what men used female slaves for, but that didn't mean it was something a well-bred woman would want to look at!

Idly wondering if Grigon had lit the candle, I turned my head to one of the mirrors and stared at the red-headed reflection there, consciously swallowing down the indignation and forcing it away from me. There was no expression on the beautiful face, but it took a minute or two for the tension to leave the well-rounded figure dressed all in dark blue. The effort necessary to push the Bellna presence to the back of my mind hadn't been excessive, but a faint doubt came to dance around lightly on my nerve ends. Was I just being stubborn by insisting that I could handle the role? Was I endangering everyone involved—as well as the project itself—by not going straight back to base? Was Grigon right in thinking that I couldn't fight Bellna and Clero's men both at the same time? The hell of it was he *could* be right, but there was no way of telling until the time came. Did I take the chance and go on with it, or did I opt for the cautious point of view and head on back?

A look of disgust formed on the face I was staring at, but the Bellna presence had nothing to do with it. I was the one who felt the disgust, and entirely with myself. The thought of something having gone wrong with the impression didn't frighten me, not when I could regain control so easily. I'd been in a lot hotter water that time I'd been fed an illegal zombie drug, and hadn't been able to throw it off. The problem was that I still didn't really want to be there, and my devious mind was digging for a way out that would free me from my commitment to Dameron without my having to renege. Could Dameron find someone to replace me in time to keep the project going? No. Did I take the job on without coercion and promise to see it through? Yes. Then how about cutting out the emoting and breast-beating—*and* the needling of your co-workers—and getting serious about this? I looked sternly at the mirror image that was me and held the stare for a minute, then let a faint grin come through. My sense of right hadn't let me allow Grigon to send me back without an argument, but my escape reflex had almost had me ready to accept the easy out he wanted to hand me. I'd accept the challenge instead, and *still* make it home in time to vote.

"You look very much at home in there," a voice came, filled with faint amusement. "Except for the clothes, of course. You'll have to get rid of those."

"I wouldn't dream of ursurping my host's right to initiate all actions," I laughed, turning to look at Grigon. "After you, my lord."

"You picked a hell of a time to be gracious," Grigon grinned, stepping back from the end of the screen. "Come on out here and let's get acquainted."

I followed him back out to the middle of the room, then stood watching as he walked to the chair in front of the fire and lowered himself into it. Aside from the bench in front of the wardrobe and the bed it was the only place to sit, but I wasn't given my choice of the two other locations. Grigon moved the chair so that he could see me more easily, then gestured me closer.

"I've been thinking about our problem, and I believe I've come up with a way to settle it," he said, making himself comfortable as he looked up at me. "It all depends on how determined you are that I'm wrong and you're right."

"I'm very determined," I said, folding my arms as I looked down at him. "Does your solution have anything to do with making me stand up until I fall over?"

"In a manner of speaking it does," he said, a flicker of annoyance showing in his eyes. "Since you seem to have slept through all the briefing sessions you were given, let me repeat the point I thought I'd made when you first got here: if you keep wise-cracking the way you've been doing, you'll either outline yourself as a complete stranger and foreigner, or end up tied to a whipping stand. You won't find either possibility enjoyable, and the rest of us are far from eager to join you. Do you think you can get it through your head that you're putting *our* necks on the block right along with yours?"

"I'm fully aware of the fact that flip doesn't go over well on this world," I said, feeling none of the guilt he was trying to feed me—and trying not to feel the annoyance. "If I'd known that wise-cracking in this lodge would put you and the others in jeopardy, I wouldn't have done it. Please accept my apology, and also my assurance that it won't happen again."

"You're still not funny," he growled, letting his eyes go cold as he looked at me. "The only way I can judge how you'll act out there is by seeing how you do in here—and so far you're not making it. It doesn't matter whether anyone else can hear you. *I* can hear you."

"I didn't know I was being tested," I shrugged, still not very impressed but finally seeing his point. "If you want to evaluate the role I'll be playing that's another story, but bear in mind that Bellna would not allow herself to be kept standing like this. Once I settle into her, you'll have to vacate that chair."

"Bellna might not be the only role you'll be playing," he said, comfortably crossing his legs as he ignored my last comment. "If you find yourself on your own you may have to switch to being the peasant girl we discussed earlier—with nothing of Bellna showing. Do you know how a peasant girl on this world acts?"

"Certainly," I answered, ignoring the ripple of outrage coming from the Bellna presence. "Do you want the peasant girl instead of Bellna?"

"I want them both," he answered flatly, locking eyes with me. "Bellna first and then the peasant, and I want it all to be you. You'll take your cue from the way I speak to you, and then act accordingly. If Remo hadn't made his and Bellna's engagement official while she was still in the Capital, I wouldn't have been able to test you as far as I think necessary."

"I don't understand," I frowned, also not understanding the sudden gleam in his dark eyes. "What has that got to do with anything?"

"You should know more about that than I do," he said, grinning faintly as he got out of the chair. "When Remo made the engagement official he was entitled to take Bellna to bed—which he did, at almost breakneck speed. She's not a virgin any longer, which means you can be put through the role of peasant. Peasant girls are given to men as soon as they stop looking like boys."

I had to work at ignoring the flurry of embarrassment coming from Bellna, but got some help at it from the part of my mind that houses nasty suspicions. Grigon was still grinning at me, and that put a sharper edge on it.

"Is this test the solution you came up with?" I asked, still holding his eyes. "Set me into a convenient role, and then indulge in a little rape? How nice that your safety can be confirmed so pleasantly."

"I thought well of the idea," he said, and then his grin hardened. "And whatever *you* think about it, you'll still go along with it if you want a piece of this project. If you can keep Bellna from taking over while you're

being treated as a peasant, I'll agree that you'll be able
to do it at any time. If you're going to lose the argument,
which is the better time: while you're being raped, or
while you're being attacked?"

He stared down at me, waiting to see if I would back
away from the deal or continue arguing, but I couldn't
really do either. The son of a joy girl was right, no
matter what his motivations were. If I couldn't handle
it, we were better off finding out right then.

"A pity you didn't opt for the attack instead of the
rape," I commented, brushing at the skirt of my dress.
"Let's get this over with. I'm going to need whatever
sleep I can grab."

"One must admire your self-confidence," he retorted,
moving to my left, away from the fire. "Are you always
so sure that things will work out the way you want
them to?"

"I can only judge from past experience." I shrugged,
turning my head to look at him. "Since things usually
do work out the way I want them to, it's only reasonable
to expect they'll continue on like that."

"For your sake, I hope they will," he said, and then
his face suddenly took on a supercilious look. "My lady
Princess," he said in broad, clipped Rimilian, sketching
a stiff bow. "Pray be seated and rest yourself the while I
fetch refreshments."

"Fetch them quickly, Ruthor," I answered in Bellna's
pettish private tones, recognizing the character Grigon
was imitating. Prince Ruthor was one of Clero's sons,
and he'd been ardently courting Bellna, probably at his
father's urging, before Prince Remo came on the scene.
"The journey here has positively exhausted me, and I
must look an absolute hag."

"Such a thing would be an impossibility," Ruthor-
Grigon protested distantly as I sat in the oversized

chair. He had gone to one of the draped walls and parted the drape to expose a good stock of drinkables, his back to me as he messed and clinked. I ran my palms over the very soft leather of the chair arms, making myself comfortable while I had the chance. Grigon was trying to disarm me—and the Bellna presence as well—by evoking Ruthor, who was hardly the most capable of Clero's sons. If Ruthor got very, very lucky, he might one day qualify for the honor of dropping the last letter of his name, but Bellna didn't think he'd make it and her memories forced me to agree with her. He was a stiff-necked snob who always acted in the precisely correct manner, never speaking out of turn, never seeking a corner where he might take me in his arms as Remo had. . . .

"Your drink, my lady Princess," Grigon-Ruthor announced from right in front of me, his arm extended with a tiny, delicate glass held carefully between his fingers. I took the glass without thanking him, treating him like a servant the way Bellna always did, privately cursing myself up, down and sideways. I'd almost let it happen again—no, it had already started happening again, and the only thing that had pulled me out of it was Grigon's interruption. I'd let my mind wander and Bellna had immediately started to come out. Damn it! If I didn't do any better than that, I *deserved* to be sent back!

"You dislike the drink?" Grigon-Ruthor's voice came, and I looked up to see him staring down at me, a cool, distant smile on his face. "Perhaps you would care for something less—potent?"

"I am perfectly capable of drinking anything *you* choose, Ruthor," I answered, bristling with insult. "I am scarcely the child you seem to think me!"

"I see you as no less than perfect, my lady Princess," he answered with another bow. "I recall now that it was your father the Prince who commanded that you abstain. Forgive my poor memory, and allow me to dispose of that for you."

He plucked the tiny glass out of my hand and turned away with it, carrying it back to the hidden niche it came from. I let myself sputter and oh! just the way Bellna would have done, all the while wondering what Grigon was up to. I wouldn't have minded swallowing that drink, but I hadn't been given the chance to do more than look at it. I pinned my fellow conspirator with an accusing stare as he came back toward me, and he betrayed a well-practiced chuckle.

"Your pout is the most attractive that I have ever seen," he said, stopping in front of me. "Should you wish it, my lady Princess, you may climb into my lap and have a sip from my glass. Surely your father the Prince would have no objection to a single sip."

"How dare you speak to me so—so—patronizingly!" I gasped, fighting both to be Bellna and not be her. "As you clearly think me a child, Ruthor, you may leave me at once!"

I got to my feet and stood with chin raised high, projecting all the outraged indignation I could feel Bellna putting out. My doing what she was feeling was like living an echo, but managing it wasn't as hard as I'd thought it would be at first. I seemed to be getting the hang of it, and that made me feel a good deal better.

"Ah, but I shall not leave you," Grigon-Ruthor purred, taking a step closer to me. "And now that I think on it, you seem to be someone other than the Princess. You wear her clothing, yet you are clearly not she. *Who are you?*"

His question, coming as suddenly as it did, was more than a little startling. Bellna recoiled in shock from a Ruthor she had never seen before, but that was only on the inside, where Grigon's careful stare couldn't see it. Outwardly I took my cue as I was supposed to, and looked down nervously at my hands.

"I am no one, Lord," I whispered, making sure my voice trembled. "A poor peasant girl, wishing no more than to know the feel of her mistress' clothing upon her skin. I would not have stolen the things. . . ."

"A likely tale!" Grigon snorted, his voice still cold. "Let me see you."

His hand came to my chin and raised my face, letting me see the gleam in his dark eyes. I cringed back without moving out of his negligent grasp, a trick I'd learned some years earlier, and he chuckled his appreciation of the gesture.

"Now that I've caught you, I believe I shall make use of you," he said, moving his hand from under my chin to touch my face. "Have you the ability to serve me properly, girl?"

"I—I am not much used, Lord," I whispered, borrowing some of Bellna's wide-eyed, disbelieving fear. "I will serve as best I may . . ."

"You will serve better than that," he said, his tone dry. "You may be very sure I will see to it. Come and put yourself in my lap now."

He moved past me to reclaim the chair, then looked up as he sipped from the wineglass he held. He'd given himself three or four times what he'd given me, and was even getting to drink some of it. Being careful not to jiggle his arm I climbed into his lap, feeling as ridiculous as I always did in a situation like that. Grigon was a big man, but I'm not what might be described as a little girl. Behind my eyes Bellna was beginning to come out of the shock she'd felt, heavy coils of outrage forming, almost ready to explode. I took a good grip on the rather large reserve of singlemindedness I come equipped with, and tried to ignore her.

"I shall now allow you the sip of wine I promised earlier," Grigon said, his supercilious Ruthor-tones increasing in patronizing-load. I reached for the glass he held out toward me, but he shook his head. "Both hands, if you please, little peasant. I should dislike having the contents of this glass emptied upon me. You have my word that I would dislike it a very great deal."

The hardened glint in his eyes told me that he would undoubtedly use an excuse like that to beat me, and a beating was one thing I couldn't risk. I didn't yet have an experienced-enough hold on the Bellna presence to believe I could hold her back during the infliction of pain; I could finally see that what I'd done to Valdon *must* have been because of the faulty impression. If Grigon hurt me and I loosened his teeth in revenge it would be satisfying, but it would also lose me the game.

"Now for the sip," Grigon directed once I had the glass in both hands. He watched carefully as I took a single, undersized swallow, but didn't see anything of Bellna's sputtering rage. Her intense feelings of humiliation poured through me, bringing a trembling to my hands, but the trembling was perfectly in character. The swallow of wine would awe and impress a real peasant, who would hardly be expected to know the vintage was just backward enough to keep it from being considered really good. My throat swallowed and my hands trembled, but Grigon didn't take the glass when I offered it back to him.

"You may hold that for me for the moment," he said, putting one hand on my skirt-covered leg and looking down at my boots. "I am unaccustomed to seeing one of your station draped about so. We will first remove those, and then perhaps have another sip of wine."

His hands went to the lacings on my boot, and Bellna was again shocked as well as scandalized. She was too young and inexperienced to understand the smirking pleasure Grigon was showing in his role of Ruthor; after all, all he was doing was taking off her—*my*—boots. It was an action fit for a servant. I sighed to myself, thinking about groaning as well; how would she react once she began to understand?

Grigon unlaced my boots slowly, drew them off one at a time, then reached out to take the wine glass from me. He had raised the bottom of my skirt to my knees to reach the lacings, and hadn't lowered it again after the boots were gone. He sipped at his wine as he ran one palm over my now bare calf, and anyone who could have heard the racket in my head would have thought he was running his hand over my naked body. Although outraged, I did not pull the skirt back down, but couldn't keep from shifting a little in the presence of Bellna's furious embarrassment.

"A wench who blushes!" Grigon-Ruthor chuckled, his warm, broad hand still moving slowly over my leg. "How delightful I find you, my young innocent. Your times at use must have been few indeed. Take the glass and hold it, but do not drink. Such youth and innocence must not be wasted in a drunken stupor."

I took the glass with two hands again, finding the very real amusement in his eyes as difficult to bear as Bellna's raving. I wasn't the blushing type, but apparently Bellna was. I had enough time to be grateful that Grigon didn't know me better, and then all I could do was gasp and try not to spill the wine. Grigon-Ruthor was sliding his palm up under the skirt and along my leg to my thigh, and Bellna was just about jumping out of her—*my*—skin.

"You have not been given my permission to be quite

as shy as that, little peasant," Grigon said, his hand having paused in its upward movement. "Unlock your muscles, and do not attempt to refuse me again. You are aware, are you not, that you are mine to do with as I please?"

"Yes, Lord," I whispered, forcing my knees apart against tremendous resistance. I had never before had to fight to control my own body in quite the same way, and the sweat breaking out all over me under the dress was adding to the mad I was beginning to feel. That was *my* body, damn it, and no one else had the right to try to run it! I held the wine glass carefully, forced my knees apart with mental teeth clenched, and thought I could feel some of the strength in the Bellna ravings fade a little.

"Ah, you seek to please me," Grigon-Ruthor said, the supercilious smile back in place. "I do indeed find myself pleased, for I mean to see if I may know how many men you have served before me."

I had a sudden, horrible premonition that he knew something I didn't, but I wouldn't have had the time to ask about it even if the question would have been in character. His hand slid quickly up between my thighs before I could utter a sound, and the next instant I was gasping in my own disbelief and trying to move away from him. His other hand in the middle of my back kept me from moving that way, and the glass of wine I held kept me from flying up toward the ceiling.

"Why, you are scarcely removed from the state of virginity," he laughed, watching my face as I closed my eyes and trembled. "I would be very much surprised if there has been more than a single man who has tasted you. And I must say how thoughtful I consider you, to have refrained from wearing the undergarments of a lady when you donned the outer garments. Such a lack would show your true origins to any man who touched you."

The half-growl in his voice was more accusation than approval, but at that point I really didn't care. I hadn't worn the heavy, uncomfortable underwear simply because I hadn't expected anyone to be checking for their presence; the fact that *he* was checking was the least of my worries. I'd been told I'd be matched to Bellna, but I hadn't expected to be matched to the extent of being turned into the next thing to a virgin! My own reflexive urge to push his hand away stumbled into Bellna's desperate need, the two flowed together, and it was all I could do to keep from really defending myself. I kept my eyes closed tight and trembled from the effort to do no more than that, and Ruthor's chuckle sounded again.

"How strong an appeal I find in the innocent," he said, the faint slur in his voice pointing up the interest of an apprentice sadist. "You may release the wine now, and when I am done with it we will continue."

I opened my eyes to an awareness of the fact that he had been trying to take the wine glass back from me, but hadn't been able to get my hands to release their hold. I surrendered the glass to his smirk without argument, despite the fact that I would have been willing to fight him for it. Backward or not I could have used that wine, which was probably his reason for refusing it to me. If I won the game it would be without help, especially the sort that would steady my jangled nerve-endings and numb my perceptions to a certain degree. Under normal conditions I preferred keeping a clear head during a job, but on that job a clear head was the one thing I wouldn't have no matter how little I drank. I took a deep breath against the clamor still raging in my skull, pretending I didn't see the way Grigon-Ruthor was staring at me over his glass rim, reflecting that it was a good thing I'd opted for being an "innocent" peasant girl. Being inexperienced can excuse a lot of blunders, but it was also helping me cover my fight against Bellna. Her time with Remo had been the sort of frustratingly distasteful experience very sheltered women often have during their first taste of sex. Remo had been too eager to arouse her properly before going for his good time, and by the time she was past the fear and pain of his attack and just beginning to feel something else, he was already through with her. There hadn't been more than that one bout between them, and Bellna, childlike, expected all subsequent experiences to be like the first. No one had told her any differently, and I had already discovered that although I could hear her thoughts, none of mine reached her. The fear that underlay her shock and outrage was worse than those other two emotions and I swallowed hard, trying to get rid of the taste of it.

"Do you anticipate my continued attention, child?" Grigon-Ruthor asked, finishing off the last of his wine and tossing the glass away. "You seem unsettled and unsure, yet this cannot be so. You are eager to serve and please me, are you not?"

"Yes, Lord," I whispered, wishing he would get on with it rather than dragging it out the way he was doing. "I am eager to serve and please you."

"As you should be," he said, the smugness in his voice setting my teeth on edge. "It is the place of peasant girls to be eager to serve their betters, and yet there are times when reluctance and inexperience are a good deal more—warming—than eager anticipation. If I were to release you from the need to give me service, would you find yourself filled with gratitude toward me?"

I blinked at the faintly smiling indulgence on his face,

wondering what he was up to, wondering if he meant what he said. Was he really going to let me off?"

"Lord, I would be grateful for whatever attention was given me by you," I whispered, deciding to play it as safe as possible. "If I were to be left untouched, however, I would be. . . ."

"Deeply disappointed," he interrupted, nodding with world-weary acceptance, knowing damned well that that wasn't what I'd been about to say. "I have no other recourse then than to complete what was begun. Ah me, how difficult it is at times to see to one's duty as a lord. Come and lay your head upon my chest, child, and we will see to your lusts as well as we may."

His hand forced me down against him, my cheek to his shoulder, the disappointment welling up from inside me bringing actual tears to my eyes. Even as I fought against being overwhelmed I cursed silently, finally understanding that his little act of supposed generosity had been designed to reach Bellna rather than me. He was trying to force her reactions out into the open, beyond my control, to a place where he could see them and recognize them for what they were. If I had been silly enough to believe him myself he might have gotten what he wanted, but I'm not what could be described as a trusting soul. I'd hoped he'd meant what he'd said, but I hadn't believed it; the little girl inside my head *had* believed, and I couldn't escape paying the price for her gullibility. Bellna didn't know what was going on, but she certainly knew she wanted no more of it.

Grigon's shirt was a semi-soft linen, undoubtedly the best material available to those who were above the level of peasant but below the level of nobility. I found a faint, musky, masculine odor and concentrated on that, trying to keep my attention away from where my antagonist's free hand had returned. Bellna wanted to

kick and scream and fight and throw herself around, but
the peasant I was supposed to be would never be allowed that kind of theatrics. Grigon had taken to indulging in a bout of slow teasing, and after a few minutes of
his silent indulgence, I made another unpleasant discovery. It had been a long time since I'd last seen to my
sexual needs, and although my body had been made to
match Bellna's, my reactions to things like Grigon's
teasing were strictly my own. It came to me that this
time the bastard was after *me*, but there was less I could
do about it than when he'd dug for Bellna's reactions.
I'd been able to keep her from taking over when *she'd*
been the victim, but keeping control was going to be
harder with me on the hot seat. I squirmed involuntarily at the picture those thought-words evoked, and immediately regretted it. Grigon-Ruthor laughed softly
and increased his efforts, the predator immediately attacking at the scent of blood. He was going to get me
one way or the other, and he damned well knew it.

It didn't take long before I was hanging onto the back
of his shirt with trembling fists, my face against his
shoulder, my eyes closed again. I had to remember not
to let Bellna take over, remember not to break the role
of peasant girl, and remember not to react the way an
experienced woman would, all while being subjected to
the close attention of a man who knew his way around a
woman's body a hell of a lot better than any Tildorani
would have. I was somehow managing to do everything
I had to, but only if you don't count breathing normally
as part of everything. I may be fairly capable in my
chosen line of work, but I'm still human; I wanted to
stroke Grigon's body the way he stroked mine, kiss his
face softly to tell him I was ready to move on to better
things. I wanted to begin opening his shirt as he ran his
hands over me—but that wasn't what *he* wanted, or

Bellna either. She didn't understand the strange feelings assaulting her, and she feared them; Grigon understood only too well, and wasn't about to let up.

"You may begin to undo the clothing of a lady,'" he said in Ruthor's lazy tones, making no effort to hide the growing slur in his voice. "Should the sight of your body please me, you may well find yourself ravaged without mercy."

I almost gasped at the throbbing wave of fear coursing through me, finding it necessary to sit still for a brief moment before pushing away from his chest. Grigon was now conducting an attack on two fronts, trying to prod Bellna and me both at the same time. If I wanted what I needed, and also wanted to keep from breaking my role I had to listen to him, but if I did as he said Bellna would surely become even more violent than she had been. She knew he was hardly likely to *dis*like her body, and the panic was already beginning to set in. I forced myself to raise my hands to the buttons on the front of my dress, feeling my cheeks flame with Bellna's embarrassment, finding it impossible to sit still in the face of Grigon's toying, biting my lip to show the consternation of a very young peasant girl. I felt as though I were three people and briefly, dizzyingly, couldn't remember which of the three was supposed to show. The buttons fought my fingers the way everything on that planet was fighting me, and hot, fat tears began to roll down my cheek, courtesy of Bellna's fright and misery.

"Does your clumsiness distress you, little one?" Grigon-Ruthor asked with oh-so-much concern in his voice, finally taking his hand away from me. "You attempt to obey me, yet find yourself unable to do so. It is clear I must assist you."

His hands came to mine to push them gently away,

and then he tackled the buttons. He wet his lips with pleased anticipation as he undid them, but his expression changed abruptly when the opened buttons showed nothing but the silken underdress I hadn't been able to get out of wearing. He was so obviously disappointed that nothing sexy showed that his expression was downright comical. Under normal circumstances I might have smiled to myself and saved the snicker for a private time, but those circumstances were far from normal. Bellna was a little girl, and so was the peasant girl of my role; the two of them combined and giggled aloud in relief.

"You dare to laugh at me?" Grigon-Ruthor thundered, his frown widening my eyes above the hand I'd hastily clapped over my mouth. "You dare to find amusement in the doings of your lord?"

I was about to assure him very sincerely that I hadn't been laughing, and especially not at him, when he interrupted the intention in the most direct way possible. His hands took the blue velvet dress I was wearing and ripped it open, then did the same to the white silk underdress. Bellna's shock coursed through me as he threw me off his lap to the floor, the disbelief intensifying as I hit hard. I'd been able to cushion the jolt a little by using my hands, but the ruined material of dress and underdress had been pushed down onto my arms, tying me into what was left of once-elegant clothing. My left hip got the worst of it, but one benefit came out of the unpleasant episode: the presence in my mind was so shocked that it went speechless and motionless, leaving me free to show appropriate fear and repentance when Grigon-Ruthor went down to one knee and pulled me back toward him.

"Insolence is punished as ever it will be, girl," he told me coldly, half-kneeling above me. "Do you continue to feel amusement?"

"I feel only the desire to serve you, Lord!" I quavered, looking up at him with none of the growl I felt inside me. I wanted to serve him, all right, but that sort of serving would have to wait—until I won.

"You need not fear," he said, reaching out to touch one of my now-exposed breasts. "You will do exactly that. Get to your feet."

He stood straight and watched me struggle around until I could rise, holding the pieces of dress and underdress to keep them from falling off me. I knew he wanted me stripped, but he wanted it done at his own pace, and wouldn't appreciate being anticipated. When I was standing in front of him he reached out and ripped everything the rest of the way, then stepped back a pace to study me.

"Unexpected largesse," he murmured, looking at me with the most intrusive stare he could manage. "More than I had anticipated—yet without the hint of a blush. Are you other than the innocent I thought you to be?"

"I am frightened, Lord," I whispered, cursing myself for forgetting such an important detail. I had expected Bellna's embarrassment to do the job for me, and when it didn't I hadn't been bright enough to take over. "If you wish it I will attempt to do other than feel fear, and yet. . . ."

"Still your tongue," he interrupted irritably, gesturing with one hand. "I want no further words from you. Rid yourself of those rags, and take yourself to my bed."

I got my wrists loose from the dress sleeves and let the "rags" fall to the floor, then let my hesitation and reluctance show as I hurried toward the curtained bed. Despite the fact that I knew I'd never sleep without a good deal of soothing, I *did* feel reluctant at the thought of sharing Grigon's bed. He wasn't likely to do anything for me without indulging in a little more torture first, and whatever he did do would be tempered by the way I'd been changed to match Bellna. I wasn't afraid of the man, but wary wouldn't be a word too far from the mark.

Grigon waited until I'd parted the curtains, groped to find the covers, then slipped under them before following me over. I was just beginning to feel safe and snug in the darkness when the curtains were jerked aside as far as they would go, and Grigon's darkened form moved toward the head of the bed. I heard him reaching around, then heard a rattle and a scrape. A spark flared bright in the darkness, catching immediately on the slim piece of wood it had flared near, and from that slim piece of wood a candle on the narrow shelf above the bed was lit. Grigon blew out the flame on the piece of wood and set it back in its place, and then he was ready for other things.

"I dislike being unable to see what I am about," he said, moving back to the curtain opening at the side of the bed. "Were you given permission to hide yourself beneath those covers?"

"No, Lord," I whispered, throwing the covers away as though they were hot. "I meant no disobedience, Lord. I ask your forgiveness, Lord. . . ."

"Enough," he said, pulling his shirt out of his pants and then hauling it off over his head. "I had thought it clear that I wished no more of your chatter. I see you must be silenced by other means."

I watched him pull his boots off and then tackle his pants, his broad, hair-covered chest more of a distraction than it should have been. He had something else in mind for me, something I was not likely to enjoy, but my mind insisted on watching him with wide-eyed interest as he got down to the buff. He was certainly well made as a man, a fact sitting in his lap had only hinted at. His degree of arousal would have had some men pawing at the ground and demanding to get on with working it off, but Grigon acted as though he had all the time in the world. He tossed his pants to one side with a careless gesture, smiled faintly when he saw my eyes on him, then moved closer to stand over me.

"You will lie flat so that I may examine you at my leisure," he said in his Ruthor voice, leaning down to shove me partway across the bed so that he might climb in himself. The bed linen wasn't linen but silk, and he had seen to it that I'd warmed a place for him. "Should I hear a single sound from you, you will be punished. Have I made myself clear?"

I bobbed my head spasmodically, giving him a wide-eyed stare filled with the apprehension of innocence. Bellna was bewildered in the shock she was still suffering from and so was my role character; I, unfortunately, could now guess at what he was up to. He sat next to me where I lay and looked down at me, the faint smile on his face touched with a hint of true amusement as his big hand came to stroke gently at my middle. I'd never be able to take his "examination" without making some kind of a sound, not in the face of the sort of expertise he'd shown earlier. He was going to use that as an excuse to "punish" me, but maybe being forewarned would be enough to let me hold out. His stroking right hand came to slide over my breast, two of his fingers catching the nipple between them and squeezing gently; I was able to keep the gasp from coming out even though my mouth opened, but I quickly changed my mind. Being forewarned wasn't going to do me a damn bit of good, at least as far as holding out went. Maybe I could do something with it afterward.

Surprisingly enough, "afterward" took a while to arrive.

Grigon worked on me slowly and deliberately, rekindling the blaze he had started earlier and building on it. His hands and lips went everywhere, touching, tasting, arousing, driving me more insane with every minute that passed. I held the light blue silk clenched in my fists as I twisted and writhed, barely aware of the still-frightened child behind my eyes, totally consumed by the needs of my body. I felt his hands like metal on my thighs, holding them apart and raising me from the bed; I felt his breath, blown gently from between his lips; when his tongue touched me I threw my head back and screamed, completely beyond thinking and caring. That was what Grigon had been waiting for, of course, and the open-handed slap that made my ears ring brought me back and told me I'd lost the round.

"Again you disobey!" Grigon-Ruthor snarled, his second slap blurring my vision and bringing tears to my eyes. "Go and fetch my belt, at once!"

Teary-eyed and trembling I backed away from him, then slid off the bed to do as he'd ordered. Control! I told myself with held-off desperation, feeling the blubbering fear pour through me as I groped in the shadows on my knees for Grigon's belt. It was lying half covered by his pants, as though it had been set in place in anticipation of use, which of course it had been. I picked up the soft but heavy leather in trembling hands and held it to me, still not knowing whether or not I could go through with it. I had a thing about being beaten that stemmed from a very unpleasant experience during one of my assignments, and I didn't know whether or not I could hold still for being beaten by Grigon. I rose to my feet again, still clutching the belt, and hurried back to the bed through the chill of the room. One way or another, my question was about to be answered.

Grigon-Ruthor sat waiting for me on the bed, the

small candle above throwing shadows all about as I climbed over his legs. The tears were still running down my cheeks as I reached the belt out toward him with both hands, and for a minute his eyes met mine. That I knew he was going to beat me must have been clear to see; as he took the belt a peculiar expression flickered across his face. He glanced at the trembling in my hands, the hopelessness my face must have been covered with, the roundness of defeat in my shoulders, and suddenly there was a different decision in his eyes.

"Such youthful innocence," he murmured, reaching a hand out to touch my face. "That there are men who find pleasure in destroying such freshness and beauty has never failed to infuriate me. I am no longer able to continue with this. Come to my arms, child."

I watched him throw the belt away but didn't really understand, not until he had taken me in his arms and raised my face for his kiss. He had spoken in his own voice, not that of Ruthor, and the game seemed to be over. I say seemed to be because he was still speaking in the Tildorani tongue, and he had begun to caress me again. I tested his truthfulness with a small moan and got nothing but a murmur in response, but the burning in my cheeks where he had slapped me worked to keep me skeptical. I might have won the game already, but there was no sense in not making sure.

Grigon's kiss was long and tender, and by the time it was over I lay in his arms with both of us horizontal rather than vertical. His hands moved over me with a gentleness that surprised and startled the guest behind my eyes, and did something more than that: it also aroused her. How that could be possible I hadn't the faintest idea, but if a glandular emotion like anger or embarrassment was possible for her, why not arousal? The only possibility I could think of was that she was using *my* body as an emotion-receptor, and with her diminished fear came awareness of other sensations. Whatever it was, I was suddenly gripped by arousal out of control, the sort that's usually channeled and used through knowledge and experience to heighten enjoyment. I clutched Grigon's back convulsively, pressing myself up against him, hearing his chuckle as he pressed me flat to the bed. Bellna was ready to get on with it and so was he, and once again I was in the minority. I tried to push away her presence but it surged all around me, raw with power, impossible to control. My knees separated of their own accord, the baldest invitation possible, and Grigon wasn't slow to accept. He positioned himself between my thighs, gathered me to him, then smothered me with a kiss as he surged forward into me.

If not for that kiss it would have been all over right then and there. Aroused or not, Bellna was suddenly afraid, and she tried to cry out when Grigon entered me. From my point of view the sensation was unbelievable; Grigon felt as though he were twice the size he actually was. Bellna, unused to that sensation under any circumstances, tried to fight her way free and then panicked when she couldn't. Panic for her happily consisted of withdrawal from control, and I was back where I was supposed to be when Grigon raised his head.

"Does something disturb you, little one?" he asked, kissing my face gently as he smoothed my hair back. "It was my impression that you attempted to speak."

"I—am merely overwhelmed," I got out, trying to gather up all the ends Bellna had dropped, before he decided something was peculiar. "I had not anticipated such size and strength from you. Perhaps you would allow me to see to your needs in another manner?"

"My sympathy and understanding are yours, wench, yet this may not be," he answered, his words nearly a murmur as his hips began to move slowly. "I cannot bring myself to abandon the exquisite tightness of you which, though it now disturbs you, will only be aided and lessened by my presence. You have obeyed me well till now; will you continue to do so?"

"Am I now permitted disobedience if that is my wish?" I asked, nearly gasping the words. His movement was making his presence even more unbelievable, and I didn't know how long I could stand it.

"No," he said with a merry grin, gathering me to him again. "I would indeed be a fool were I to permit such a thing. Perhaps afterward."

He lost interest in conversation then, and it occurred to me that I had another afterward to look forward to. Grigon's performance was considerate as far as rape usually goes, but considerate or not it was still rape. With that in mind I forced myself to concentrate on what he was doing rather than ignoring it, and began to help him—in my own way. A woman who knows what she's doing can either extend a man's performance or force it into termination, and Grigon had been holding back a longer time than was usual. I know he was looking forward to a leisurely ride, but I've had training from an adept of Saccarion, and he couldn't resist my muscle movement. With teeth gritted he tried to hold back, fighting the urge for release with non-movement, but he didn't have a chance. He climaxed uncontrollably, his hands on my shoulders, and then he withdrew to lay down beside me and breathe deeply for a minute or two. I stirred where I lay, well aware of the fact that *my* needs hadn't been seen to, but I'd rather have to use a lot of self-control and cold showers than submit to rape.

"I apologize for the brevity of the entertainment," Grigon said at last, rolling onto his side to put his hand on my middle again. I was surprised to see that he didn't understand what had been done to him, but it did save me some trouble. "We will proceed to your suggestion of alternate amusement, and then will return for a second and longer encounter of intimate enjoyment, eh? Let us. . . ."

"Forget it," I interrupted, switching back to base language as I pushed his hand away and sat up. "You've had enough fun for one night at my expense. Let's discuss whether or not I've passed the test."

"You're a hard woman," he sighed, following my example as to language. Other than that he turned to his back again, tucked his hands behind his head, and looked up at me. "As far as the test goes, I'm not the one to ask about it. How did it go from your end?"

"It wasn't as simple as I thought it would be," I admitted, running both hands through my hair while my elbows rested on my knees. "Isn't there some way to get rid of her so I can get on with this project in peace?"

"Not without going back home," he said, watching me closely without moving. "I'll call Dameron and arrange for retrieval."

"Forget it," I repeated, giving him a sour glance. "As far as the project goes, nothing has changed. If I don't go, there's no one waiting to be sent in my place. I'll have to manage just as I am."

"Manage to do what?" he asked, keeping his tone level. "Get yourself killed? The men on this world don't fool around. If your—alternate personality comes out at the wrong time, you probably won't have the chance to repair the damage. It's too much of a risk."

"Breathing in and out is a risk," I countered. "And you forget one thing: I'm supposed to *be* Bellna. If I slip *as Bellna*, there's not much harm done. After it's all over, I'll just have to stay away from people until I'm picked up. I've lived off the land before; I won't starve or trip over something with teeth and claws."

"I still don't like it," he said, finally sitting up straight and folding his legs in front of him. "There are so many things that can go wrong that we didn't dare ask the computer to list them; it would still be working on the question. What if you *can't* avoid being among people? What if you *do* trip over something with teeth and claws? What if you run afoul of something we haven't even thought of? I keep getting visions of you lying half under a bush, awash in your own blood, complete vacancy behind those pretty blue eyes. I don't think I could shrug off being partly responsible for the death of a young girl with everything to live for."

I could see him fairly well in the flickering candlelight, and he wasn't joking or being sarcastic. He really felt concern for me—but for the strangest reason.

"You're not by any chance thinking of me as being as young as I look, are you?" I asked suddenly, bringing a flash of startlement to his eyes. "*Bellna* is this young and innocent and helpless; I'm not. Putting me half under a bush, awash in my own blood, has been tried before any number of times. It didn't work then, and it's not guaranteed to work now. If you don't believe that, I'll be glad to prove it by tossing you into the fireplace. Just say the word."

"I think I can get along well enough without your kind offer," he answered, a faint smile just beginning to curve his lips. "I'm not that easy to toss into a fireplace, but I'm willing to stipulate the fact that you're competent. The only question is, are you competent enough to overcome the handicap you have? Will you be able to handle it no matter what the situation?"

"Well, I can think of one situation when I may not be able to handle it," I said, deciding to try some calculated misdirection. "I'm glad you didn't try beating me with that belt; I don't know if I could have kept control of myself."

"You think you would have lost control to Bellna?" he asked with a frown. "Because of a beating? What makes you think she would have dominated you at a time like that?"

"I'm not talking about her dominating me," I said, shaking my head as I lay back down and stretched out. "In fact, it has nothing to do with Bellna. *I'm* the one with an aversion to being beaten, and I've been known to be somewhat—harsh with people who try it. I had a run-in with a heavy whip once, and the passage of time hasn't done much to make me forget it."

"Harsh," he echoed, a strange expression on his face as he looked down at me. "Your eyes turn soulless when you say that. I've never had a heavy whip used on me, but I can imagine what it must be like. Tell me what was done to you."

"It's impossible to imagine what it's like without experiencing it," I said, unable to keep the—harshness out of my tone even though I looked away from him. "As far as the rest of it goes, I'd rather not discuss it."

"You're trembling," he said, his hand suddenly on my arm. "Of course we don't have to discuss it if you don't want to. Are you all right?"

I turned my head back to him and nodded without speaking. I always trembled when I thought about that one particular incident, and not just from anger. Anyone who thinks they would react differently and more bravely is invited to try it for themselves.

"You shouldn't have much to worry about on that score at least," Grigon said, moving his other hand to stroke my hair. "Most men on this world would rather bed a female than beat her, especially one who looks like Bellna. Your peasant girl role was good enough to mollify anyone who wasn't actively bent on harming Bellna; if you run into the other kind, you're free to defend yourself. If you were able to keep me from seeing such deep-seated emotions when you brought my belt, you should be able to retain control at other times. I feel considerably better about this now."

"I'm glad to hear that," I said, producing a smile to match the one he was wearing. "With that in mind, I think I ought to get some sleep now. Tomorrow will be a busy day."

"Uh, yes, tomorrow," he agreed, suddenly looking more reluctant than friendly or approving. "I suppose you *will* need your rest. Are you sure there isn't anything else you need—that I could help you with?"

"Don't tell me you're *asking*," I said with brows high, raising up on one elbow toward him. "What happened to the demands and orders?"

"They go with the other characters," he said, showing a grin. "In my own *persona*, I don't indulge in rape unless I have to. And that 'have to' refers to professional necessity, not last-ditch desperation. If you tell me to walk away, it won't be the first time I've done it."

"Then I don't have to feel guilty about making you do it again," I said, lying back down. "Good night."

"That value judgment is open to debate," he sighed, taking his hands away from me. "Merely expressed as a wish to be granted, however, I offer the same back to you. Sleep well."

I waited until he had gotten off the bed and had started for his clothes before calling him back. I'd been curious to see if he really meant what he'd said about leaving, and at that point there was no doubt. Although rape tends to turn me stubborn, free agreement on all sides is another matter entirely—and his abruptly terminated performance earlier had gotten me curious about how he would do under other circumstances. He came back to the bed with a soft laugh, took me in his arms, then proceeded to make my struggle with Bellna less of a struggle. My invisible guest was losing both her fear and her reluctance, but her overenthusiasm was something left to be worked on. I had a very pleasant time— but Bellna loved it.

CHAPTER 4

I awoke when the automatic sensing system I've developed over the years told me I was no longer alone in the room. I could hear soft, whispered conversation, and could see the sudden glow of a just-lit candle through my slitted eyes. Whoever the intruders were, they certainly weren't trying to sneak up on me; a second candle cut the dimness, and another whisper joined the others. The last whisper overrode the first two sharply, and there was a brief period of silence during which I could see three long-skirted figures moving across the carpeting in front of the fireplace. A fourth skirted form passed behind the first three to the hearth, set wood in it, then worked briefly to get a fire going. While this was being accomplished the first three opened a large box, pawed through its hidden contents, then began arguing in very low tones. All four of the intruders were female, and Bellna's thoughts indicated they were servants. I hadn't been told to expect any servants, but then I hadn't been told much of anything. They seemed to be trying very hard not to wake me up, and the chill in the room's air did well to convince me that staying where I was was probably my best course of action. I yawned silently, snuggled down farther under the covers, and continued with my best course of action.

I wasn't sleepy enough to fall asleep again, but the comfort of the warmed silk cradling my body set my mind to drifting. It was highly unlikely that the four women were anything other than the servants Bellna thought them, and that meant my last-ditch effort with Grigon the night before hadn't worn off the way I'd been afraid it might. He'd been very attentive and considerate while making love to me, but most mature men have no trouble separating bed time from thinking time. If he hadn't downchecked me for the project, it meant that he really had been convinced by the story I'd told him. Not that the story wasn't true. There are an uncounted number of times when truth will do more for you than lying; the catch is in knowing when one of those times has come by.

I felt a contented purr in my mind, and realized that Bellna was also thinking about Grigon. He was talented enough to satisfy almost any woman, but especially one with Bellna's limited experience. She'd lost control almost from the first moment he'd entered me, but I'd been able to ignore her until Grigon began trotting out various facets of his talent. There are certain things no woman alive can ignore, especially if she starts out aroused. Grigon had the advantage over me the second time, and he wasn't shy about pushing for all he was worth. I'd felt my control slipping, fought to regain it, then realized that I couldn't fight. My awareness was sliding into Bellna's, the two of them running together, the resulting consciousness completely bound to the man who was laughing softly as he watched me. Grigon obviously knew total surrender when he saw it; the rest of our time together had been filled with pleasure, but

I'd had no say in any part of it. I'd felt nothing but
satisfaction at the time, but looking back on it was
somewhat embarrassing, just as Bellna's girlish memories were. My feeling the way she did had caused the
bonding between us, but was that any better than having her assume control? The resulting personality didn't
do things the way I did; it might be best if I tried to
avoid—

"Forgive me, Highness, yet I must awaken you," a
soft voice interrupted my thoughts, coming from right
beside the bed. I opened my eyes to see a young girl,
her hands held nervously before her, no more of her
expression visible than the tremor in her voice. I was
basing my guess as to her age on the sound of her voice,
but when she stepped back and turned enough so that
the candlelight touched most of her face, I saw I was
right.

"Inform the Princess that her coach and escort have
already arrived," a stage-whisper came from one of the
other three. "We must hasten if we are not to anger the
captain."

"You need have fear of angering none save me," I
interrupted with Bellna-huffiness, sitting up while making sure I held the covers modestly over myself. "Who
is this captain you speak of, and how dare he make
demands of me?"

"Captain Fallan is the leader of your mercenary escort,
Highness," the quavering answer came, this time directly from the girl who had whispered before. She
stood with the other two not far from the fireplace, and
all four of them looked nervous and uncomfortable.
"Though he uttered no words of demand, we were
instructed to ready you as quickly as possible. It would
be foolish to ignore such instructions, for mercenaries

are known to have little patience, most especially captains of mercenaries."

The girl stopped to breathe after getting all that out in a rush, the other three nodding their heads in agreement. All four of them were young, no more than sixteen at the most, and all of them were clearly peasants. They wore long print skirts made from some cheap material, low-cut blouses that had once been white, had solid-colored shawls tied around their hips out of the way, and were barefoot. Bellna didn't know any of them, and couldn't understand why they were there. The female servants who usually looked after her were trained ladies' maids, efficient, genteel—and quietly obedient.

"We were brought here by Captain Fallan for the express purpose of assisting you to readiness," the girl next to the bed said, drawing my eyes back to her. "We had best do so immediately."

"Had we really," I murmured, letting Bellna's annoyance touch me. "Have you ever before been privileged to serve a Princess?" They all shook their heads, looking confused, and I nodded. "I thought not. You have much to learn before you will be acceptable. Bring me a wrap."

None of the four was terribly pleased with my attitude, and I could see they were having difficulty remembering and accepting my higher social position. If I'd been older than they it would have been easier all around, but I wasn't older and I may even have been younger. One of the two who hadn't spoken yet, a pretty redhead with a good figure, went to the large box I'd seen them open earlier and pulled out a long, tie-around dress. The tie-around was the wrap I'd asked for, and when she brought it to the bed I threw the covers aside, stood up, and let her put it around me.

"You may bring beverages and foods to break my

fast," I informed them haughtily as I tied the tie-around. "When I have finished my repast, you may then dress me."

The two who had done all the talking so far began sputtering as a prelude to arguing, but I wasn't listening to anything I didn't want to hear. I moved between the heavy curtain and the bed, found the lighter arrangement Grigon had used the night before, lit the candle, then went back to jerk the drapes closed in the faces of my new servants. They were half outraged and half frightened, but I didn't think they'd make the mistake of outright disobedience. They may not have liked it, but I *was* a princess.

I spent some time behind the curtain making use of the room's chamber pot in private, then went out to find that two of the four girls, the two talkative ones, were gone. The other two glanced at me uncomfortably, but kept quiet as I went to the chair in front of the fire and sat down. Their disapproval was as loud as shouting, but as long as they didn't say anything out loud Bellna was satisfied, which meant that I was satisfied. I was more eager to get going than to stop for a meal, but letting myself be rushed wouldn't have been in character. Bellna was used to doing things *her* way, so obnoxious was the way I would have to play it.

It didn't take long for the two girls to get back, and they didn't look happy. One of them carried a tray and the other opened the door for her, and the two of them hurried over to where I was sitting.

"Captain Fallan sends his compliments, Princess," the second one said while the first, the one who had been nearest the bed, put the tray across the arms of the chair I sat in. "He wishes you a hearty repast, yet asks that you partake of it as quickly as possible. Dawn approaches swiftly, and it is best that we be on our way before then."

"He swore when he heard you had not yet dressed," the girl who had carried the tray blurted, her face pale in the candlelight. She had brown hair, just as the second girl did, but looked fractionally younger. "Had it been I he swore at, I would not have been able to cease trembling. His anger grows as his patience thins."

"And yet the word he sent was most courteous," I pointed out, lifting the thick wedge of bread smeared with what looked like butter. "He may swear as he wishes in the presence of peasants, yet would my father have his tongue out were he to do the same before *me*. He will wait as long as necessary, for it is in *my* service that he moves. Was the lord Grigon as displeased as he?"

"The lord spoke no word in our presence, yet did he seem touched by annoyance," the girl answered, glancing at her friends. They weren't used to seeing a female get away with murder when dealing with men, and they weren't sure whether or not they liked it.

"The lord Grigon will also survive," I said with a sniff, then tackled the fried meat and boiled oats on my plate. The meal was a quick, slapped-together affair that Bellna didn't care for, but rather than refuse to touch it, I simply showed distaste while slowly shoveling it in. I *did* have to get the show on the road, and could intelligently delay things only so long. The four girls stood around watching me, the oddest expressions on their faces, their annoyance growing when they realized I was ignoring them just as much as I was ignoring the men.

Even the slowest meal has to come to an end, and the girls were all ready for me when I indicated that the wooden tray could be taken. I'd spent a small amount of time privately admiring the intricately carved bone that

was used in place of wood or metal plates, and could
finally understand Dameron's reference to collectors.
The bone plate would have fit well into my own collection of rare and beautiful things, but there was no way
for me to get it out of there. The only practical solution
would be to come back for it once all the excitement
was over, but that time was a long way off. I had to live
through everything in between first, and that might
turn out to be easier said than done.

Once the tray was taken, I had to let myself be
dressed. I would have preferred doing it alone, without
help, but that would have been out of character. The
underwear I had managed to avoid in the base was the
first thing produced, to Bellna's satisfaction and the
girls' amusement. The bottom part fit tight down to
below my knees, was drawn closed at my waist, and
was made up of frilly layers of lace. The top part was a
short-sleeved, waist-long jacket with lacings in front,
made of silk without frilly layers, as confining as a
straitjacket with the lacings closed. Raising my arms so
that the underdress could be put on me wasn't the easy
gesture it should have been, setting me to wonder how I
was supposed to fight in that rig. A light blue dress had
been supplied to take the place of the dark blue one
Grigon had torn, and then I was urged into the chair so
that my boots could be put on and laced. My underwear came to just about the top of the boots, and with
the long sleeved, high-collared dress, I was covered all
over. Bellna considered that the only decent way to
appear in public, but I couldn't help wishing there was
some way to be *in*decent yet stay in character. The
blazing fire was making me sweat, and outdoors would
hardly be better. The nights grew cool around there,
but the days were pleasantly warm.

After my hair had been combed to Bellna's satisfaction,

I led the way out of the room. It was useful being able to leave some of the small details to the Bellna presence, but I had to be careful not to do it too often. Something like that could get to be a habit, and habits like that I didn't need. The girls followed after me down the stairs, trying not to step on my skirts in their hurry, even more upset that I was still taking my time. At the bottom of the stairs the redhead, who was carrying my cape, squeezed past me and got to the door to the outer room first, then held it open. I knew she was telling the men I'd finally gotten there, and when I reached the doorway I found two sets of eyes on me.

Grigon stood in the same conservative dark trousers and white shirt he had worn the day before, stoop-shouldered and narrow-faced, his faint air of disapproval covered by the small bow he performed. As far as being the center of attention, though, he could have been jumping up and down and waving his arms and he still wouldn't have made it. The second man dominated the room completely, despite the fact that he was doing nothing but standing there. He was taller and broader than Grigon, brown-haired and brown-eyed, square-faced and almost handsome in his ugliness. His pants and knee-length boots were black, but his shirt was a bright, blazing red, telling everyone who looked at him that he was a mercenary. The long neck-scarf he wore was a light blue, showing that he was employed by Prince Havro, whose main color was light blue. My information told me his neck scarf was black when he was unemployed, and also that the length of it proclaimed him captain of his group. His left hand rested on the hilt of a plain, workmanlike sword, which was sheathed in a well-worn brown leather scabbard belted around his waist; his eyes, piercingly direct and without any trace of backwardness, rested only on me. Bellna fluttered in my mind at the impact of those eyes, impressed despite herself, sharing the sense of excitement that crackled among the four girls behind me like static electricity. Fallan was the sort of man whose attention most females tried to attract; it seemed only fair to let him know where he stood with *me*.

"I hope, Lieutenant, that you and your men are prepared to depart," I told his stare as I moved briskly into the center of the room. "The journey before us is lengthy, and there is little sense in standing about here."

"In standing about here," he echoed in a deep voice, watching without expression as I approached him. "*You* are concerned as to whether or not *we* are prepared to depart?"

"My Princess, allow me to present the leader of your escort," Grigon hastily interposed as Fallan began drawing himself up to the explosion point. "This is *Captain* Fallan, leader of twenty, engaged by your father the Prince to protect you from his enemies at all costs. Where your safety is concerned, the Captain has been authorized to speak with your father's voice. I feel quite sure, Captain, that my Princess will afford you full cooperation."

"I will be pleased to give the—Captain, did you say, Grigon?—the Captain's planned itinerary my personal attention," I answered as I adjusted the sleeves and skirt of my dress, not looking directly at either of the men. "It will undoubtedly be acceptable with only the most minor corrections."

Grigon looked as if he wanted to close his eyes in pain, and the four girls behind me gasped in shock; Fallan, surprisingly, showed amusement rather than anger.

"My—itinerary—has already received the approval of your father, Princess," he said with the smallest bow it's possible for the human body to perform. "It is therefore unnecessary for you to concern yourself with the matter, save in compliance. As sufficient time has already been wasted in awaiting your appearance, you may now take yourself to the coach which stands without. My men and I seek to complete our commission before we have attained too great an age to attempt others after it."

"How dare you!" I gasped, using only a small part of Bellna's shocked indignation at the way he'd spoken to me. "Perhaps it has escaped your notice that you address someone other than a peasant, Captain! I assure you my father will hear of your impertinence!"

"Your father has already heard of my impertinence," Fallan grinned, moving a step closer to me. "It is undoubtedly the reason I was given this commission. You may inform his Highness that all proceeds apace, Lord Grigon."

"It will be my pleasure to do so, Captain," Grigon agreed with the ghost of a smile on his narrow face. "Now, if I may have a moment alone with the Princess before your departure. . . ."

"You may not," Fallan said, a finality in his voice as his big hand wrapped around my arm. "The Princess has expended more moments than her share; yours must unfortunately replace one of them. This moment is the one we depart."

Grigon's mouth opened in protest, his faint amusement gone, but he wasn't given a chance to get any words out. Fallan was already hustling me toward the door, his pace and effort easy enough to pretend to be assistance, his grip solid enough to really give me no choice. Bellna was having a screaming fit in my head, furious over the way Fallan was treating me, but I glanced back at Grigon feeling disturbed. My fellow agent had clearly wanted to tell me something, and was just as clearly not going to get the chance. I sputtered indignantly at Fallan just to stay in character, but inwardly I was cursing at him in a way that probably would have shocked him if I'd done it aloud. Missing inside information was hazardous to the health in my line of work, and I was missing it because of Fallan.

Apparently the information Grigon had wasn't important enough to cause him to make a fuss over Fallan's decision. I heard him trailing along behind with the four girls as I was taken through the door into the early dawn. At the foot of the porch steps was a large, ornate carriage, light blue trimmed with gold, Prince Havro's sigil on the door facing us, six brown vair harnessed to the front of it. Vair were tall, doe-eyed draft animals, four-legged and soft-coated, maned and tailed and usually even-tempered. Fallan's twenty were also mounted on vair, though not at the time we left the lodge. Right then they were standing around looking bored, but when they saw us they immediately perked up.

"Your four wenches must accompany you in the coach," Fallan told me as I hastily lifted my skirts to keep from tripping down the steps. "I lack sufficient vair to mount them among my men, and would not wish the distraction even had I the vair. They will ride with you."

"They are not mine, therefore may they be left behind!" I snapped, annoyed at the way he was treating me, but even more frustrated by his suggestion. When Clero's men caught up with that coach, I wanted to be the only one in it. If attackers become confused about who the target is, they tend to wipe out everyone in sight just to be on the safe side.

"They will not be left behind," he answered, more interested in reaching for the handle of the coach door than in arguing with me. "It is necessary that they accompany you, and they shall do so. Allow me to assist you into the coach."

His hand on my arm forced me up the narrow steps and into the coach, letting me go only when I made the obvious choice between standing up all bent over and sitting down on the right-hand seat. The seething Bellna was doing bubbled through my mind and body, involving me more than a little. Fallan was making an occasional, casual attempt to treat me with the respect a princess was supposed to be given, but only if the attempt didn't put him out any. I pulled angrily at my skirt to straighten it under me, fighting off the urge to tell Fallan exactly what I thought of him—in terms guaranteed to make him come after me. A boot in the face would teach him to watch his mouth when he spoke to me, not to mention how personally pleasant I would find—

I shook my head hard, making sure that line of thought was cut off cold. Bellna's frothing was beginning to affect my annoyance, and I couldn't let that happen. I needed Fallen to help me spring Clero's trap, and even if I didn't, beating up on him would be somewhat out of character. I could sit there and scowl at the back of his head, but that was all I had better do.

At Fallan's gesture the four girls hurried to the coach, then climbed inside wearing harried expressions. They weren't about to disobey Fallan and *not* enter the coach, but my very obvious displeasure was making them uneasy. The first three to scramble inside made sure to take the opposite seat, as far from me as possible, but that left the fourth one, the redhead, out in the cold—or at least out of a seat. There just wasn't any more room on the other side, and I was sitting in the middle of my seat. Another man had come up to join Fallan at the coach door, this one wearing a light blue neck scarf of lieutenant's length, and when the redhead hesitated, half in and half out of the coach, he decided to take advantage of the situation.

"Should there be no room for this one, Captain, I will gladly take her with me," he said with a grin, then slid his hand up under her cheap print skirt. "Her presence will pass the time quite pleasantly."

The girl gasped and reddened when the mercenary's hand reached its target, but she still had nowhere to go. Her left arm clutched my cape to her body as both mercenaries laughed, and then her widened eyes closed in misery. She couldn't climb in and she couldn't climb out, and Bellna was smugly pleased to see her like that. What happened to peasants was of no concern to a princess, the two men were enjoying the girl's discomfort, and even the other three peasant girls were snickering to themselves. No one felt the least amount of pity for the victim caught in the middle, but I've never been bright about things like that. I reached out and took the girl's right arm, hauled her past me to the seat to my right, then turned my head toward Fallan.

"I had thought grown men would be more difficult to divert from their duty," I observed in Bellna's sleekest, nastiest tone. "Apparently, my father's enemies will need do no more than dangle some pleasant wench before you, and you will be theirs. I now see the necessity for the presence of *these* peasants: to allow you to retain memory of your commission."

The second man was as pretty-handsome as Fallan was ugly, and he hadn't liked the way I'd taken his toy away. My speech turned his frown into a scowl, but before he could vocalize his displeasure, Fallan's big hand was on his shoulder.

"It is long past time to depart, Ralnor," Fallan said in a strangely even tone, his eyes unmoving from my face.

"Have the men mount up." He waited for Ralnor to move away with a curt nod, then closed the coach door with a slam. "As for you, Missy," he continued in a lower tone, looking up at me through the window, "Princess or no, injured sensibilities or no, you had best learn to curb your tongue. Should I find it necessary to remonstrate with you for impertinence as your father has given me leave to do, you will find the occasion less than pleasant."

With that he turned and walked behind the coach, undoubtedly to get his vair, leaving me to cope with the painful resonance of Bellna's shock. My uninvited guest was finding it impossible to believe that her father would have given Fallan permission to keep her in line, and was scandalized at the mere suggestion that he had. For my own part I was fairly certain Fallan was exaggerating if not lying outright, a possibility supported by the uncertain look on Grigon's face. The Absari agent was still standing on the lodge porch, watching the goings-on but not joining them; when he saw me looking at him his expression turned determined and he started down the steps, but he was too late. Fallan shouted an order, another voice echoed it, and the coach lurched briskly away from the lodge.

"I cannot fathom the reason you have placed yourself in jeopardy for me," a faint voice said from my right. "You are a Princess and I am no one."

I turned my head to see the red-haired girl, backed as far away from me on the seat as she could get, still clutching my cape, vast confusion in her big blue eyes. At the same time I became aware of the fact that the other three girls were also staring at me, all of them practically shouting that I'd stepped out of character. They weren't far wrong, but I didn't want them to go on believing it.

"I, placed in jeopardy?" I asked with brows raised high, pulling my skirt away from the redhead as though she might contaminate it. "You speak foolishly, girl, for you know not what you say. Think you that lout toyed with *you*? As you say, you are less than nothing and I am a princess. To put hands upon the servant of a princess is to offer insult to the princess herself, and that I shall not allow. That fool of a captain is now aware of it."

"And yet he promised you punishment," the girl whispered, still hugging my cape. "You cannot know what punishment is at the hands of one such as he."

"Nor shall I know," I smirked, waving the point away with one hand. "He attempts to frighten me with child's tales which I shall not, of course, believe. Have no fear, girl. You stand beneath *my* protection."

I turned my attention to the forest we rode through, pretending I didn't see the looks exchanged among the three girls opposite me. They were now probably considering me no more than a pompous brat, which was just the way I wanted it. When the attack came, their first thought would be to put as much distance between me and them as possible—which just might keep them alive.

It didn't take long before our party reached a wide road through the woods, and shortly thereafter the real boredom began. Although the day was beginning to be pretty, there's just so much you can get out of forests and fields and more forests. My mercenary escort rode all around the coach, their neck scarves streaming out behind them, their eyes constantly in motion in all directions. The four girls in the coach untied their shawls from around their waists and retied them around their shoulders against the early morning chill, then began discussing in low tones the various mercenaries they could see from the coach, possibly to take their minds off how cold they still were. In all the layers of clothes I'd been stuffed into, cold was the least of my worries; once the sun came up for real, I'd be sweating like a metal bucket filled with ice. I moved in discomfort, silently cursing the way my layered underwear made it feel as if I were sitting on something lumpy. Only chains could have tied me tighter than those clothes, and I didn't like the feeling. I stared out of the window on my left morosely, trying to block out the giggling of the peasant girls, and suddenly a beautiful red bird flashed out of the trees, pacing us with lazy wingbeats for a moment before turning away back to the forest. I watched the bird until it disappeared, delighting in its beauty and freedom, not realizing that I was being watched just as closely until I noticed Fallan. The mercenary captain rode his vair not five feet from the coach, and when he saw my eyes on him he urged his mount closer.

"I had not known you had a smile of such beauty, Princess," he said, looking at me in a way that made Bellna shiver in my mind. "A pity it is so often displaced by a pout."

He grinned then and sent his vair on ahead and out of sight, leaving behind a deep silence in the coach. All four of the girls were staring at me wide-eyed, their faces reflecting the thrilled excitement Bellna was sending racing through my bloodstream. Fallan had actually shown a faint interest in me, and Bellna was almost ready to consider it a promise of undying love. All of the girls, Bellna included, were beginning to have a crush on the big mercenary, and I felt like groaning. I hadn't had a crush on a man since I'd seen Starman Courageous without his chest pads and girdle; and wasn't about to be caught up in the nonsense. As far as I was concerned Fallan was nothing more than a pain in the rump, and on that point I *would* make the decision stick. I turned back to stare out the window again, ignoring an urge to lean out and look ahead that *wasn't* mine, and worked at sticking to my resolve.

The motion of the coach put me to sleep for a while, but I was awake again when we reached the inn. We'd only been on the road for a few hours, and at first I didn't understand why we were stopping. It took a minute before I realized that Tildorani ate four meals a day rather than three, and it was time for the second meal. I wasn't particularly hungry, but I was too bored not to be looking forward to the stop.

The inn was a large, three-story yellow and white house with a high wall and gate, a stable not far from the house, and a wide entrance court. Stable boys hurried over to help with the mercenaries' mounts, and Fallan himself came to hand me out of the coach. His touch on my arm was deferential rather than demanding, and combined with the same look he had given me earlier it was enough to turn Bellna shy with fluster. I, however, hadn't forgotten how pushy he'd been at the lodge; when I climbed out of the coach I made sure to come down right on his foot. The instep is a high pain target, which took care of the half-amused, half-interested look he'd been wearing.

"Oh, how clumsy of me!" I exclaimed immediately, as he closed his eyes and flinched. "I do hope you will forgive me, Captain."

"Certainly, Princess," he got out through his teeth, then looked at me with a lot less friendliness. "Had the misstep not been an accident, it would certainly have been punished. As it *was* an accident, it will certainly be forgiven."

"How fortunate, then, that it *was* an accident," I said with a pleasant smile, ignoring the fact that he had told me he suspected it wasn't. "Shall we enter the inn now?"

"As soon as I am able to walk again," he muttered, turning back to the coach to gesture the four girls out. They came out one at a time, making sure to touch the ground nowhere near Fallan's feet, and the way they loosened their shawls reminded me how uncomfortable *I* was. It wasn't Fallan's fault that I'd been closed into layer after layer of straitjacket, but having gotten some of my own back from him even raised my spirits about that.

"This way, Princess," Fallan directed, and led off all alone toward the inn. I followed after him, the girls followed after me, and the rest of Fallan's men completed the parade. The only one to hurry was Fallan's lieutenant, Ralnor, who hustled a little to catch up to Fallan before the mercenary captain reached the inn. The two of them paused in the doorway, blocking the parade, and I realized they were checking out the interior before letting me walk in. It seemed like a sensible idea, even though Clero's men shouldn't have had the time to get there yet. But then, Fallan and his men didn't know about the timetable we'd established, and I wasn't about to tell them.

The appearance of the inn turned out to be acceptable. Fallan and Ralnor moved farther inside and then stepped apart, making an aisle for me to walk through. I used the aisle casually, showing nothing of the upset the Bellna presence felt over what I'd done to Fallan. It was almost like looking out at the world through two sets of eyes, one mine and the other—well, mine also but strangely different. One way Fallan looked big and roughly attractive and annoyingly in the way, the other he was an overpoweringly attractive man of violence and sex appeal. It wasn't too difficult keeping the two views separated, but it still felt strange.

The inside of the inn was cozy, in a rustic, backward way. The ground floor seemed to be all one room, except for a part at the back separated by a wall and door, which probably hid the cooking facilities. Most of the back wall was taken up by a fireplace, filled at the moment with nothing but fresh, unburned logs. The numerous windows streaming sunlight were uncurtained, and the animal-fat wall lamps were unlit. More than a dozen travelers sat about at trestle tables of various sizes, and every one of them turned to stare when we made our entrance. A short, thin man came out of the door in the far wall, started when he saw us, then hurried over.

"Forgive me for not having known of your presence sooner, Captain," he said to Fallan with a few absent-minded bows, his eyes glued to me with a glitter. "May I be of service to you?"

"The Princess honors your house in order to dine," Fallan answered, his voice cold and dangerous. "It were best that you not disappoint her expectations."

"The Princess!" the small man gasped, utterly de-lighted. "Highness, my house is yours! Pray enter and be seated!"

This time the bowing was for me, along with the stares of everyone in the room. Considering the fact that Fallan was supposed to be protecting me, he was being awfully generous with information as to who I was. Most nobles traveled around on Tildor *without* telling people who they were; that was why the innkeeper had addressed himself to Fallan; he hadn't expected to be told who I was. As a decoy for the real princess it didn't matter much to *me*, but Fallan wasn't supposed to know

I was a decoy. I frowned as I followed the innkeeper across the floor and tried to catch Fallan's eye, but the big mercenary seemed to be avoiding looking in my direction.

The innkeeper led us all the way to the left, to a corner area standing apart from the rest of the room. The tables there were crafted rather than thrown together, short lengths of white cloth covered them, and four or five big, well-carved chairs stood together in a corner. My host hurried over to one of the chairs, dragged it to the head of the largest table, tossed aside the plain chair standing there, then bowed to me again.

"Your seat, Highness," he burbled, thrilled with the entire situation. "Allow me to assist you."

"*I* will assist her," Fallan said, totally untouched by the way the small man's face fell. "*You* may return to your hearth and have our meal prepared. Those three wenches are to be fed in your kitchens; the fourth will remain here to serve the Princess. My lieutenant and some of my men will accompany you."

Ralnor moved two steps off to wait for the innkeeper, who looked nervous rather than insulted. Fallan's lieutenant would be there to make sure there was nothing added to our meal that shouldn't be added, and if something aroused his suspicions he might not take the time to ask questions. The innkeeper nodded his head in resignation, bowed to me again, then led Ralnor and his four mercenaries and the three dark-haired girls toward the door in the far wall. The only one of the girls left was the redhead, and she looked nervous for some odd reason. I went to the ornate chair and took my place, then watched Fallan seat himself to my right, his back to the wall our table stood near. His men arranged themselves very obtrusively around us, and Fallan turned to glance at the still standing redhead.

"Place yourself behind the Princess and to her left, where you may serve her without intrusion," Fallan directed, stretching out comfortably in his chair. "Yon inn wenches will serve no more than my men and I."

The girl turned her head to see the three inn girls who were hurrying toward us, two of them carrying wooden trays filled with metal goblets for the men, one of them with a silver tray and a single, intricately wrought gold-colored goblet. The goblet probably *was* gold, but even though the redhead quickly rounded the back of my chair to take it from the inn girl, the thing never reached me.

"The Princess does not take wine at such an early hour of the day," Fallan announced, stopping both girls in their tracks. "Return that goblet, and fetch a pot of andilla."

The inn girl, looking frightened, sketched a fast curtsy and headed back the way she came, leaving the redhead to step back behind my chair. Bellna didn't understand what was going on any more than I did, which made it my option to comment.

"How thoughtful of you to look after my wants so carefully, Captain," I commented, finally bringing those eyes directly to me. "And how clever of you to be aware of them without consulting me."

"My commission demands both thoughtfulness and cleverness, Princess," Fallan answered with a faint grin, accepting a copper-colored goblet from one of the inn girls. "You will find that I shall not shirk my duty."

"Ah, you are aware, then, of your duty." I nodded in approval, then looked at him with exaggerated sweetness. "Would you, in that event, be so kind as to explain it to *me*? It has seemed, till now, that the demands of duty have escaped you entirely."

A small gasp came from behind my chair, echoed in

some part by the Bellna presence. Both Bellna and the
redhead thought I was pushing it with Fallan, something neither one of them would have done. I *was*
pushing it, but I had to find out what he was up to.

"Appearances are often deceiving, Princess," Fallan
answered with an impassive drawl. "One often finds it
necessary to see the last of a series of actions before the
first of those actions is clarified. Now comes your andilla."

Which ended the discussion. The inn girl with the
silver tray was back, this time bringing a beautifully
designed ceramic pitcher and mug, the pitcher presum-
ably filled with the warm, chocolatey drink called andilla.
The redhead stepped out from behind my chair, took
the mug and pitcher from the tray, poured me a mugful
of andilla, then disappeared behind my chair again. I
still didn't know what Fallan was up to, still didn't
understand why the redhead had to serve me instead of
one of the inn girls, and didn't want any part of the
andilla. I could see faint wisps of steam rising from the
mug, and didn't much care for chocolate drinks even
when they were cold. I tugged at the high collar of my
dress and moved in annoyance in the big chair, but that
did me as much good as questioning Fallan had. It was
fairly clear that the meal stop would *not* be a particularly pleasant one.

My guess didn't prove to be entirely wrong. The men
had their wine poured for them, and then the food
began coming. Omelets and light soups and thin cuts of
meat, lightly fried fowl and vegetables and fresh-baked
bread, and all of it was brought to me first. During an
assignment I usually believe in eating whenever I can,
knowing the next chance I get might be a long time
in coming, but that was pushing it even for me. I tasted
all of the dishes out of curiosity, finding them under-
seasoned but otherwise acceptable, then spent some time

watching everyone else eat. Fallan's men did their eating standing up, and Fallan, although seated, spent as much time as they did looking around. Their goblets were refilled almost as soon as they emptied them, but none of them was drinking at all hard. Most mercenaries drank wine the way other people drink water, or at least that was what Bellna believed; true or not true, I could see they were watching their intake. It gave me the impression they were expecting trouble, and that set me to wondering what they knew that I didn't. Clero's men could show up at any time, but Fallan and company shouldn't have known that.

Our meal was just about over when the trouble happened. It was nothing more than a simple scuffle, but it drew the attention of Fallan himself. Two men seated on the other side of the room, merchants or landed gentry by their clothing, tried to come over to my table for some reason or other. Fallan's men barred their way, telling them to go back to their own table, but the two strangers disagreed. Hard words followed, swords came half out of scabbards, and Fallan, with a snapped order to the redhead to stay behind my chair, got up and joined the party. Once he got there the two men forgot about swords and tried bluster, but it was clear to everyone in the room that the argument was over. Fallan wasn't the leader of his men because someone had appointed him to the job, and both of the strangers wilted visibly under his stare. I leaned back in my chair again, disappointed to a large degree that the argument wasn't the prelude to the attack I was waiting for. That attack would put my neck on the line, but it would also give me the chance to get off that planet. Dameron's so-important job was beginning to bore me, and boredom was more dangerous than attack. It made the most alert careless, the fastest sluggish, the brightest uncaring; boredom had killed more agents than weapons and ambush, and I didn't want *my* name added to the list. It didn't help that Bellna was even more bored than I was; that sort of reaction doesn't need reinforcement.

I suppose I could say that what I did next was an attempt to end the boredom, and to a great extent it would be true. The real truth is that when I get bored, I also get an irresistible urge to liven things up. I've had trouble because of that particular urge, but nothing that I didn't consider well worth the fun involved. I didn't often indulge the urge during an assignment, but when I saw Fallan watching his men as they escorted the two intruders back to their table on the other side of the inn, the idea came to me all at once. His goblet stood to my right, still half filled with wine, and it didn't take very long to empty it—down my throat. For a very young wine it wasn't bad, but drinking it was only half of what I had in mind. The other half was refilling the goblet to its previous level with the andilla I hadn't touched, the andilla I'd been given because of Fallan. It seemed only fair to return the favor—and then see what developed. The Bellna presence giggled nervously as I sat back again, but was too delighted with what she'd— *I'd*—done to really regret it. The boredom was taken care of, and that was what counted.

No more than another couple of minutes passed before Fallan came back to my side of the table. He stopped behind his chair but didn't sit, instead looking around before glancing at me.

"It is more than time that we continued on, Princess," he said, absently reaching for the goblet he'd left unemptied. "There has already been one incident, and the next may be less easily seen to. It seems I was ill-advised to announce your identity so openly."

No, don't tell me! I responded, but only to myself as

I stared up at him in silence. He was noticing the obvious pretty damned late, but somehow he seemed more satisfied than contrite. He was still up to something, but questioning him would have been a waste of breath. I sat instead and watched him raise his goblet to his lips as he continued to look around, saw him take a good, healthy swallow—then watched straight-faced as he spit out the unexpected drink. Andilla isn't bad when it's warm; cold, it tastes very much like unwashed armpits. Half a dozen men at a nearby table laughed uproariously, obviously having seen what I'd done and eagerly awaiting the trap to close. Fallan wiped his mouth with the back of his hand as his eyes moved to me, and Bellna was suddenly all out of giggles.

"I would know the meaning of this—gift, Princess," he ground out, the expression on his face and the blaze in his eyes enough to replace the recent laughter at the nearby table with immediate silence. "Has it some significance which eludes me?"

"I merely sought to emulate *your* actions, Captain," I answered in the most innocent tone I could manage, at the same time rising from my chair. "Your anticipation of my wishes was enviable, so much so that I attempted the same for you. Have I failed so dismally, then?"

He stared at me briefly without answering, returned the goblet to the table with a thud, then came closer to take my arm.

"Had you truly sought to anticipate my wishes, you would have bared your bottom, *Princess*," he growled very low, his hand closing a bit more on my arm. "Another doing such as this, and I will make the effort for you. For that you have my word."

"Why, Captain, whatever do you mean?" I asked, oddly feeling the fear Bellna experienced coursing through my body. Fallan's threat had panicked her, but I knew better. If he had been going to do anything it would have been in the heat of anger, not after he'd had a chance to cool down. Bellna the princess was safe from Fallan the mercenary.

He growled again at my very innocent lack of understanding, but this time wordlessly as he began to guide me away from the table by the arm he held. If Clero's men took long enough finding me, I'd have Fallan-baiting down to an exact science. It was obvious the man could threaten me as much as he liked, but rousting me around by one arm was as much as he could *do*. The game should keep me from getting bored again, and should also go some distance toward diverting Bellna from the way she was reacting to Fallan. The presence in my head was sending ripples of excitement through me, more strongly than she had done earlier, a little-girl-crush reaction to Fallan's being so close. I raised the bottom of my dress with my left hand and tried to ignore those feelings; *would* have ignored them even if they were my own. The only thing infatuation can do for you on an assignment is end your life rather abruptly.

It wasn't long before the four girls and I were in the coach, the men were mounted, and we were on our way again. I kept my eyes open and my mind intent on the scenery we passed, but a couple of hours went by and no one jumped out of the shrubbery or fields to attack us. It seemed strange that Clero's men weren't all over us yet, but they might have had some delay we hadn't counted on. I was trying to calculate the *latest* time for them to reach me, when the coach began slowing down. There wasn't much around, just the road through a forested area, with no inn or other building in sight. Being the suspicious sort, I immediately began to wonder, but we left the road and came to a full stop and no one came by to mention what was going on. Fallan's men dismounted and began messing with something ahead of the coach, where I couldn't see it. I craned around half out of the window for a minute or two, got absolutely nowhere, then noticed that Fallan was on his way over to me. He had dismounted along with his men, and when he reached the coach he pulled open the door next to me.

"The next point on our itinerary has been reached, Princess," he said, grinning faintly as he held his hand out. "You must now leave the coach for a few moments."

"Must I, indeed?" I murmured, making no effort to take the offered hand. "And for what reason would I do such an otherwise unnecessary thing?"

"For the reason that you are told to do so," he answered, all friendliness gone as he reached in and took my arm. "We may not halt here long, else it shall be noticed. We shall make haste, and then we shall once again be on our way."

Being pulled out of a coach is not the same as being pushed into one; if Fallan hadn't taken me around the waist as soon as I was in reach and lifted me out to set me on the ground, I probably would have tripped over those idiotically long skirts. Bellna was confused and frightened and flustered and outraged all at once, a reaction I found dizzy-making on top of my own reactions. I don't like being dragged around and told what to do without explanation or reason, and if it happens I tend to grow short-tempered. If I hadn't been on assignment, Fallan would have had a serious problem; since I *was* on assignment, there was almost nothing I could do to show my annoyance. As soon as he let go of me I fought those stupid skirts out of the way, then kicked him hard right in the shins.

"How *dare* you treat me in so cavalier a manner!" I

hissed, showing the fury Bellna would have shown if it had been anyone other than Fallan manhandling her. "When my father hears of this, your company will be disbanded and you yourself ended horribly! Men will shudder at your fate, and women will grow faint! You will be. . . ."

"Silence!" Fallan roared, interrupting me just as I was really getting rolling. He'd flinched faintly when I'd kicked him, but aside from that he showed no reaction to my girlish attack at all. What was getting him angry was all the threatening I was doing, which, spite and all, was pure Bellna.

"I will not be silent!" I huffed, ready to climb back on the high horse he'd shouted me off of, but Fallan wasn't about to give me the chance to remount.

"You *will* be silent," he growled, looking down at me as he rested his left hand on his sword hilt. "You will also obey me, for I mean to see you safely to your destination in the most effective manner. We not go to the tent which has been erected to protect your sensibilities. Should you attempt to disobey me, your sensibilities will be sorely bruised. Leave that coach, you wenches, and follow us quickly."

He took my arm then, and began leading me toward the vair at the front of the coach at a pace faster than I could manage without half running. At that point I could see the medium-sized green tent that had been put up among the trees, a tent that blended into the greens and browns all around us. Fallan's men were all very busy away from the tent they'd put up, but it wasn't hard to tell they were watching closely to see what would happen. I was more than curious myself about what was going on, but sputtering indignantly was what the role called for right then, and I was stuck with it. I squeaked in outrage as I was hustled firmly toward that green tent, and couldn't even enjoy the faint breeze that tickled its way through the trees.

It would have been dark inside the tent without the small lamp that hung on the far wall. Fallan pulled me inside and released me with a small push, then turned to watch the four peasant girls hurry in behind him. Bellna was storming back and forth inside my head, half furiously injured dignity, half flashes of romantic fantasizing; one minute she wanted to see Fallan executed by her father's soldiers, the next she wanted Fallan to throw the peasant girls out, tear her clothes off, and make violent love to her. I shook my head hard, trying to push away the ringing in my ears and the faint flashes of golden haze in front of my eyes, but didn't get anywhere until I turned to see Fallan right behind me. He'd pulled closed the tent flap behind the last of the girls, and all five of them were staring at me. Bellna froze in mid-tantrum, suddenly convinced that something horribly final was about to happen, causing me to take an involuntary step back from the big mercenary.

"You need have no fear, Princess," Fallan said at once, his deep voice unusually gentle and reassuring. He stayed right where he was, his thumbs hooked into his swordbelt, his eyes on me with more concern than I would have expected.

"A princess feels no fear," I answered, the quaver in my voice all Bellna's doing. "Murder me if you will, yet know that my father shall avenge me. And I shall die as a princess should, with head held high."

I flinched inwardly as I raised my chin to match the words forced on me by the Bellna presence, but I wasn't the only one to consider my speech of bravery more ridiculous than dramatic. The four peasant girls snickered among themselves and Fallan closed his eyes with a deep sigh, both reactions startling Bellna enough to let me grab a corner of control again. Bellna's fear and my own suspicions had let the presence in my mind take the reins for a while, but no more than a short struggle got them back for me. I thought about wiping my damp forehead on the back of my sleeve, then rejected the idea. It wasn't something Bellna would do, and it was too close in the tent for anyone to wonder why I might be sweating.

"There is to be no murder, girl," Fallan said with thick patience, speaking slowly and clearly. "I have brought you within this tent so that you might give up your clothing with the privacy due your station."

"Give up my clothing?" I echoed as I stared at him, every bit as confused and dumbfounded as my mind-guest. "For what reason am I to give up my clothing?"

"For the reason of your safety," Fallan answered, still heavy-voiced with patience. "The enemies of your father must be expected to know that you travel now to your nuptials, and must also be expected to attempt some manner of interference. Should they descend upon us, there will be no easy victim for their blades—or, shall we say, no proper victim. The princess will not stand in her own shadow."

He ignored the way I was staring at him, totally speechless, and turned to gesture at the redhead. She left the others and approached him, and they both met my stare.

"This wench has been sold by her father into slavery," Fallan explained, putting one big hand on the shoulder of the girl who now stood in front of him. "The Lord Grigon purchased her before she might be given over to the training of a slave, and she has been given this vow: should she comport herself in so adequate a manner that the enemies of the Prince believe her to be you, and should she survive whatever attempts are made against her, she will be given her freedom once more, and adequate gold to assure her retention of that freedom. You must now take her clothing as she takes yours, and quickly, so that the journey might continue. I will, of course, await you without the tent."

So that was why the girl had hovered around me in the inn! To learn the way a princess behaved in public! I was still staring at Fallan in disbelief as I tried to figure out where Grigon fit into all of that, but the big mercenary began turning away before even the faintest hint came through. I still didn't understand what they were all up to, but one point I was crystal clear on: Fallan was trying to replace a decoy with a decoy!

"Hold, Captain!" I said, stopping him before he could head for the tent flap, not about to stand still for that nonsense. "My clothing will remain in its proper place—with *me!*"

Fallan turned back to me impatiently, but this time the jump was mine.

"Do you think me craven enough to set another to die in my place?" I demanded, making no effort to keep the outrage from my voice. "My father is a Prince who will never hide fearfully from his enemies; his daughter may do no less."

There was no way I was going to let that little girl be set up for the slaughter, no matter how eager they'd made her to give it a shot. Her eyes were wide and pleasing as she looked at me, begging me to let her take her chances, but she didn't know what she was asking. Even I had no guarantees about surviving, and if she had even half the training I did, I'd eat that tent. Without salt.

"Do you think my company so incompetent that her death is sure to be?" Fallan demanded in turn, but gently. "Attackers, should they come, will find no easy access to her, for that you have my word. It is our intention that she shall survive—as shall you. Remove the clothing."

"Never," I answered in as final a way as possible, meeting his eyes to let him know I meant it. Under other circumstances the idea of hanging on doggedly to clothes I would have loved to be rid of would have been funny; under those circumstances, funny didn't enter into it.

"Then there is nothing for it save that I do the thing for you," Fallan said, with the same finality. "Should this be other than that which you wish, your own efforts must be made upon the moment."

Slowly he began to close the four or five steps between us, the calm expression in his eyes saying he sympathized with my stand but had no intentions of letting me keep to it. I felt a flash of burning hot resentment behind my eyes, the sort that comes from someone who isn't used to not getting her own way, and quickly wiped away the annoyance *I* was feeling. If my reactions merged with Bellna's *I* would be the loser, and if I was stupid enough to forget that, I deserved whatever I got. I didn't like having Fallan telling me what to do, but there was more freedom of option in *that* situation than in having Bellna take over. Fallan was two steps closer and just beginning to reach a hand out when the grip of my control over myself stopped slipping enough for me to raise the bottom of my skirts and try to make a break for it.

Fallan stood between me and the tent flap, but there was enough room in the dim tent for a lot of dodging and fancy footwork. I ran three full steps to the left then dodged right, avoiding Fallan's grab by a wish and the rustle of skirts. The mercenary cursed in a low voice at the miss, but I was already past him and on the way to

the tent flap. The four peasant girls "eeked" and gasped
and drew back from the chase but, unfortunately for
me, in the wrong direction. They clumped up in front
of the flap I needed to get out of the tent, and Fallan
was too close behind me to let me take the time I
needed to plow through the girls. I moved to my left
again and darted away, and again Fallan cursed when
his hand closed on empty air. He was faster than a man
his size had the right to be, and Bellna was silent and
shocked inside my head. She'd expected to be able to
get away from him easily, and now that she—I—hadn't,
she was starting to get worried.

I led Fallan around the tent, avoiding half of his grabs
by sheer luck, trying to work my way back toward the
tent flap, but this time from the right. From that
direction, along the front wall, the four girls ought to
scatter to the left, away from the flap, giving me clear
running room. Fallan tried cornering me against the
side wall we were near, watched carefully as I bobbed
back and forth in front of him, saw the feint I made to
my right, then lunged to my left, where he thought I
was going. To his disgust I continued on to my right,
turning the feint into real motion, and blasted at top
speed right toward the flap. I was so covered with sweat
that it rolled down my forehead to burn my eyes, but I
couldn't let that stop me. Once I was outside I would
lose Fallan and his friends fast, backtrack to the inn
we'd stopped at, then burst hysterically in, telling everyone that my escort had tried to assassinate me. That
would keep Fallan away if he managed to follow, and
also spread the word with the departing travelers as to
where the Princess Bellna could be found. If Clero's
men didn't show up after *that*, I would throw in the
towel.

The four girls squeaked again, and began scattering

like a flock of ducks in hunting season. I took a chance and swiped at my eyes with the back of my sleeve, trying to clear my vision, and because of that didn't see the slim leg stretched out directly in my path. I did notice it, though, as soon as I tripped over it, tried to recover, and didn't quite make it. The grassy ground the tent had been pitched over came up to knock the wind out of me, but as soon as I could I started to roll, silly enough to think I still had a chance. I'd forgotten about those stupid skirts again, and Fallan was on me before I could fight them out of my way.

"No, no, you will not again take to your heels," Fallan panted as I struggled to avoid his reaching hands and scramble to my feet. "Timely assistance has brought you down, and I will see that you remain so."

As his hands closed on my wrists I felt Bellna's panic, and an instant later my own panic joined hers. She was flowing toward my store of unarmed aggressive techniques, determined to use them on Fallan the way I'd used one of them on Valdon! If that didn't send everything sky high nothing would, and instead of having just Fallan to struggle with, I found myself in a double fight. Fallan forced my arms away from between us and pinned my body with his, drawing a scream of rage from Bellna and an increase in her struggles. I say *her* struggles because I'd lost that much control, finding myself dragged along as most of my power of denial covered the one file of information I couldn't afford to let Bellna have. My body writhed and twisted on the ground, my feet kicking the way my mind kicked, and then the Lord of Luck came to my rescue again. Bellna's struggles had brought Fallan's arm close to my face, and by timing the effort I was able to make my teeth close on that arm. Fallan bellowed and pulled away as Bellna froze again in fear, and then I was all alone and back in control—just in time for Fallan's open-handed slap. My ears rang from that slap and my cheek flamed hotter than the stifling air of the tent, but at least those parts were mine again. I saw Fallan raise his arm for another slap and cringed back in true Bellna style, but that seemed to make the mercenary change his mind.

"There has been more than enough of this foolishness," he growled, lowering his arm without swinging at me a second time. "Remove her from this clothing at once."

He pulled me into a sitting position, locked one fist in my hair, then moved as far to my left as he could, to be out of the way of the three dark-haired girls. The three girls had come on the run at his growl, but the fourth, the redhead, just stood to one side and watched me. Her young, pretty face showed no signs of triumph or smug satisfaction, but her light eyes were filled with trembling determination. She was the one who had tripped me, of course, and all for the privilege of being set up as a target. I suddenly realized how much freedom meant to her, and looked away in resignation. To prefer death to lifelong slavery was a philosophy I could identify with, even if it did make my job that much harder.

The three girls near me started unlacing my boots, their heads down to cover their amusement at my discomfort. Having your boots unlaced is no big thing, but that wasn't the way Bellna looked at it. She knew that after the boots the rest of my things would be taken, and was also overly aware of Fallen beside me, his big hand tight in my hair. She and I would be stripped naked in front of Fallan, and although I couldn't have cared less, Bellna was still young enough and innocent enough to feel the hot-glowing flash of embarrassment. I didn't need a mirror to know I was blushing like a failure light on a pilot's board, and to say I was uncomfortable would be the understatement of the week. I had control and I would keep it, but that didn't mean I wasn't paying the price.

Both of my boots were pulled off at just about the same time, and then the girls came away from my feet to tackle the light blue dress. Trying to push them away accomplished no more than making two of the girls each take one of my arms, leaving the third free to work on the dress. I struggled ineffectively as it was opened and then pulled off first my arms and then down past my legs, and couldn't help struggling even harder when the underdress was lifted up. That *couldn't* be slipped off around my feet, and the girls needed Fallan's help to get it free. His arm around my waist held me relatively still while my arms windmilled and my hands tried to hang onto the underdress, but the three girls pulled it off and tossed it away out of my reach.

"My, my, what lovely, delicate, feminine underthings," Fallan drawled over my shoulder, obviously looking at the lower part of my underwear. "Had I known what beauty lay beneath those skirts, I well might have contrived to see it the sooner."

The three girls added their giggles to Fallan's chuckle, and I couldn't hold back the mortified wail that came from Bellna. I was burning up with the humiliation flaming through me, but swinging my arms back in an attempt to hit Fallan did me no good at all. He caught my wrists and held them behind me, clearing the way for one of the girls to reach to the lacings on my underbodice, at the same time looking over my shoulder to watch the process with grinning interest. Fallan was getting even for everything I'd done to him, and at that point I would have done my damnedest to take him apart if I could have gotten loose, but I couldn't get loose. I could only pull at his hands on my wrists as I sat with legs straight out in front of me, and watch myself being stripped.

The grinning girl undoing the lacings moved as slowly as possible, trying to increase my misery and Fallan's interest. As the bodice opened wider and wider, I became aware of how close Fallan's face was to mine; inside my mind Bellna shivered, and all at once she was fantasizing. In her fantasy Fallan reached one hand over my far shoulder, slipped it inside the half opened bodice, squeezed slowly and with infinite relish, then went on to make violent love to her. I would have thought she'd had enough of violence, but some girls are never satisfied. I suffered in silence as Bellna fantasized and the dark-haired girl took her time opening the lacings, but at least fantasy didn't turn into reality. The real Fallan kept his hands to himself, satisfying his thirst for revenge with no more than words.

"Those breasts could do with a bit of sun," he observed, his tone thoughtful and faintly critical as the bodice was pushed all the way open. "A bit less confinement might also increase their size."

The girls near me giggled again, enjoying Fallan's putdown, and Bellna was too wrapped up in her daydreaming to notice. That left the option to me again, and I didn't mind taking it up.

"Your disapproval of my form devastates me, Captain," I said, turning my head to look at his very near profile. "How fortunate I am that it is another I must please, and not you."

"Fortunate, indeed," he drawled, turning his head to look me in the eye. "I am not a man to be easily pleased, as many a wench has already learned."

"Some men do come rather late to their manhood," I allowed with a compassionate smile. "Have patience,

Captain, and do not despair. One day you, too, will be
pleased as easily as other men."

The girls around me flinched in silent pain, staring
wide-eyed at the thunder my deliberate misinterpreta-
tion of Fallan's meaning put in the big mercenary's
eyes. I was skating close to the edge by insulting him
that way, but he couldn't say he hadn't asked for it.
Besides, life without risk is no more than existence.

"How good of you to be concerned regarding my
manhood, Princess," he said at last, obviously trying to
control the rasp in his voice as well as the look in his
eyes. "It must be of considerable interest to you, to
cause so great a concern."

The girls tried to giggle at his comeback, but the
laughter came off rather flat, just like Fallan's try. But
he *was* trying, which meant he hoped to learn the game;
could I do less than attempt to teach it to him?

"Alas, Captain, I find it beyond me to aspire to one
such as you," I sighed, trying hard to keep the drawl out
of my tone. "I am resigned to having no more than that
which I already possess, meager as that position is."

"Resigned," he echoed, studying me thoughtfully and
with considerably less anger than I had expected. "I
find it difficult to believe, Princess, that one such as you
finds it necessary to be resigned to any matter whatsoever.
Though the pink of embarrassment remains in your
cheeks, still do you strive to give me blow for blow in
defense against attack. Were you a boy and of the
proper background, I would take you in my company
and teach you the weapons of a man. However, as you
are not a boy—and therefore in need of learning the
benefits of maidenly silence—I fear I must further bruise
your sensibilities."

A lighthearted grin lit up his ugly face as he said that,
and I didn't even have the time to wonder what he was

up to. He turned my wrists loose so suddenly I was
startled, pulled the underbodice off in one sharp motion,
then had me around the waist before I could even begin
to react. Bellna's wail sounded in my head as Fallan
threw me face down on the ground, put his knee in my
back, and pulled open the tie at my waist. He was
doing it by the numbers, the bastard, and the last
number was to begin working off the lace-layered undies,
as slowly as the girl had unlaced the bodice, letting his
palms touch my flesh only very briefly and once in a
long while. I screamed with the unbearable outrage and
unbearable desire Bellna was sending through me, kicking and struggling as if I really expected to get loose,
silently cursing Fallan for playing the game his own
way. Using his own rules there was no way he could
lose, which was, of course, the whole point.

"And so much for the last of the clothing of a Princess,"
Fallan said, drawing off the lace undies from my legs
and tossing them away. "When once you have dressed
again, Missy, you will be no more than a servant to a
Princess. You need not be concerned over recalling such
a novel position; I have already seen to the matter to
assure your memory of the thing. Hurry now, wenches,
and assist the new Princess in dressing."

The three girls who had been helping Fallan turned
immediately to the redhead, who was already beginning
to get out of her clothes. Fallan's knee continued to keep
me face down in the dirt and grass, which was playing
hell with my struggle to stay in control. Bellna was
terribly aware of how close Fallan was, while she lay
there stark naked. I could feel the heat all over my body
from her embarrassment, and could also feel her out-of-
control arousal. She kept expecting Fallan to touch her
in some way, preferably intimately, but the redhead
was hurriedly laced and stuffed into my sweaty clothes

and nothing like that happened. I tried to make myself aware of how good it felt being out of clothing, but Bellna's sense of humiliation was too strong to overcome. I squirmed under Fallan's knee in silent protest, inwardly cursing Fallan *and* Bellna, but it wasn't what one might consider an effective effort.

When the girls began lacing up my boots on the redhead, Fallan's weight was suddenly gone from my back. My own first reaction was to get to my feet, but Bellna's feelings were stronger than mine and they dragged mine along. On the ground Bellna had some small amount of modesty protection; upright there would be nothing more than what my hands could cover, which wasn't much. A thin, golden haze began obscuring my vision, and I discovered I had lost the battle for control when I tried to move and nothing happened. A flash of frustrated anger touched me, whirling in with the other emotions storming around inside me.

"You may now arise and begin dressing, Missy," Fallan spoke from behind me, a casual pat on my horribly bare bottom coming just before the sound of his rising. "It will take no more than a moment for you to do so, I know, for I mean to remain here and direct you."

"You cannot!" I wailed, mortified at the thought of being arrayed so openly before him. "And how may I dress when that—that—peasant has been given my clothing?"

"That is the princess you speak of, girl, and *you* no more than the peasant," the brute replied, a chuckle to be heard in his vile tone. His hand took my arm and forced me to my feet despite my protests, despite the enormity of such a thing. I searched within me for the new knowledge which would cause him harm for the thing he dared, yet it was covered and kept from me by some means. Instead of finding myself able to chastise him, I was able to do no more than stand with my hands before me, knowing the concealment pitifully inadequate, trembling at the amusement which took him. Deep in my heart I knew I would not find myself able to struggle if he were to step forward and take me in his arms, yet he made no attempt to do so. There were none to halt him there, and none who would dare speak of it were he to thrust himself within me, yet he made no attempt to do so.

"That tinge of red does you no justice, girl," the beast chuckled, sending his gaze to touch every part of me. "Were you not red-haired it would perhaps be attractive, but as you are— Best you dress quickly."

I had no wish to don the crude trappings of a peasant, yet how might I refuse to cover myself against the stare of the brute? The skirt brought me was a plum print, the badly made bodice a thin once-white, the heavy shawl dyed an uneven green. Additional insult was given me in that none of the servants brought to furnish service to *me* lifted even a single hand in assistance. Out of necessity, then, I covered my own body, and when the shawl was tied about my waist the mercenary Fallan stepped closer to look down upon me.

"The lines of your body are more easily seen through clothing such as that," he murmured, a glint in the dark of his eyes. "Best you stay close to me when you are without the coach, else I may not be able to answer for your safety. Men are no more than men, most considering peasant girls theirs for the taking. None will pause to ask if you are indeed a peasant."

He turned from me then to gesture the others from the tent, and then it was me back in control again and not Bellna. I was startled that she'd given up so abruptly, without anything like a struggle, but while I was taking a deep breath and tightening my grip on the control, I found her quaking back in a corner of my mind. Fallan had frightened her badly when he'd told her how men would react to her, and her imagination was picturing her being raped by men without number, none of them Fallan. She wanted Fallan so badly my body burned with the need, but she didn't want any part of a gang rape by strangers. I can't say how relieved I was that she looked at it like that, but it's amusing only to think about afterward. At the time the only consideration involved was that if she *had* liked the idea, it would have been *my* body taking the punishment.

Fallan lifted the tent flap and let the "princess" and her servants leave the tent first, then pushed me out after them with a hand in the middle of my back. He came out right behind me, calling to his men to get the tent folded and put away even as he followed us to the coach. The redhead was trying not to move stiffly in her new finery, but the weight of it was already beginning to get to her. She moved her head in discomfort, trying to loosen her collar and let in some of the fresh forest air, and Fallan passed me in two strides to catch up to her.

"You must not hold yourself so timidly," he instructed her, his voice gentle and supportive as he looked down at her. "You must be as bold and arrogant as the true princess is, for now you are she. Think of the gold you will have when this chore is done, and think of the awe and respect which will be yours when you return among your people. Think also of the insult which you may give others, without fear of reprisal; you should, by now, be well schooled in that subject at the very least."

All four of the girls giggled at the dryness in Fallan's voice, knowing exactly who the butt of his humor was. I knew it too, but right then I couldn't have cared less; I was too busy backing away from the coach, just about ready to make a break for it. No matter how good Fallan was, he'd never catch me once I was into the woods, and then I could finish up that assignment the right way. I backed up another step, then another, almost ready to turn—and backed right into a hard, male body.

"You mistake your direction, wench," a voice came from the body I'd backed into, causing me to turn my head fast. The mercenary Ralnor stood there, the one who was Fallan's lieutenant, a faint grin of amusement on his handsome face. His hand came up to take my arm in a deliberately heavy grip and Bellna, remembering what the man had done to the redhead, began quaking even harder in her corner.

"Should there be a mistake, it is certainly on your part," I told him, fighting hard to keep from growling as Bellna's shivering had a tendency to make me do. "Remove your hand from my arm, and do so immediately."

"What occurs here?" Fallan demanded, coming up behind me in time to see the grin disappear from Ralnor's face. Fallan's lieutenant was no longer amused, and that suited me just fine.

"Captain, I caught the wench attempting to take herself off," Ralnor said with a growl of his own, his hand tightening even more on my arm. "Allow me to punish her for you."

His pretty eyes looked at me with a hardness that was supposed to be intimidating; instead of feeling intimidated, all I wanted to do was offer him his best shot. Unfortunately, the role I was committed to didn't even let me pull my arm free of his hand; the only weapon I could use was words.

"As you realize you must ask permission before offering me harm, you must also realize what will befall you should you attempt the deed under any circumstances," I said in my coldest tone, holding his eyes the way Bellna would have if she were a little older and more mature. "It has clearly slipped your mind to whom you give insult, Lieutenant. Were I you, I would retract that insult."

"And yet you are not I, *wench*," Ralnor answered through his teeth, tightening his grip again to the point where I winced against the pain. "No wench, neither peasant nor princess, may speak to me as you do. Such insolence demands a reckoning, and I shall. . . ."

"Do naught," Fallan interrupted, wrapping his hand around Ralnor's wrist and pulling his fingers away from my arm. "Do you forget the oath we have sworn, Ralnor? Do you forget the cautions we were given? You declared yourself able to withstand even the haughtiest of princesses. Were you mistaken in the judgment of your strength?"

"Perhaps . . . merely in my capacity for patience, Captain," the other man grudged, backing down as gracefully as his still-present anger would allow. "I had not meant to approach the wench after the earlier words exchanged between us, and did not; it was I who was approached, and in an unexpected manner. I will now take myself elsewhere, where I will not place our company in jeopardy."

He gave me a last glare then turned and walked off, heading toward a group of men tending their vair. I rubbed at my arm where his grip had probably left fingerprints, wondering exactly why I'd gotten into an argument with the man, and Fallan turned from watching Ralnor's receding back to look down at me with less than friendliness.

"Such a thing will *not* occur again, Missy," he growled,

with a look in his eyes that made Ralnor's glare a smile
by comparison. "That my men and I are pledged to
your safety does not mean you may address us as you
please. Had Ralnor less control of his own temper, that
overbearing temper *you* display would surely have been
properly trimmed. Let me see your arm."

I'd thought I'd been doing my rubbing surreptitiously,
but eagle-eye Fallan had spotted it anyway. He pushed
my other hand away and took my arm with such unexpected gentleness that for once I was more surprised
than Bellna. Just below the short sleeve of my new
blouse angry red fingermarks could be seen, a couple of
which were bound to turn into bruises. Fallan inspected
the arm and marks with no expression on his face, then
raised his gaze to mine again.

"I regret that skin so fair and soft must know the
results of a man's anger," he said, looking much too
deeply into my eyes. "The fault is mine, for I should
not have let you move from my side. Where did you
think to go other than to the coach?"

"I w-wished to avail my-myself of the bushes here-
about," I stuttered, sounding and feeling like a little girl
whose arm was still being held by the man she was
beginning to be terribly in love with. Bellna's throbbing
was racing all through me, showing she didn't have to
be in control to make me act like an idiot. I could feel
Fallan's warmth through my arm where his big hand
touched me, could see how he looked at my body
through the thin cloth covering it, could taste how
badly my arousal wanted satisfaction from him. With
all that against me I found it impossible not to tremble,
and a faint grin lightened the near-ugliness of his face.

"You should have spoken to me of the need," he said,
taking my hand instead of my arm. "It would have been

my pleasure to escort you to the privacy which is yours by right. As I shall do now. Follow me, wench."

Bellna fluttered again, thrilled with the way he called me "wench," and I discovered that the story I'd come up with on the spur of the moment wasn't just a story any longer. I really did need some bushes, and maybe then I'd be able to reclaim the rest of my bodily functions. I let Fallan guide me to a ring of greenery to one side of the clearing, discovered there was no way of sneaking out again without someone noticing, did what I had to, then let him take me back to the coach again. The bushes offer was made to the four girls and accepted by them, giving me the faint hope that I'd be left alone by the coach, but no such luck. Fallan stayed with me while the girls guided themselves, and when they came back he helped the "princess" in first.

"And now the rest of you may enter," he said, giving the others a hand before he turned to me. "When the next inn is reached, Missy, you and the other wenches will take yourselves to the kitchens, as was previously done. The princess will be served by the inn girls, allowing her servants a time of rest. I trust there will be no confusion as to which place is yours."

"I am well aware of which place is mine," I answered with a pout, trying hard to shove Bellna's reactions away from me. "Equally am I aware that that place has been taken from me. Which of the others will serve me in the kitchens?"

"None will serve you in the kitchens," Fallan answered with something of a sigh as he leaned one hand against the coach above my head. "You will be required to serve yourself, and my men and I as well. You are to be a peasant wench, and convincingly, else shall I be forced to punish you soundly. Far better a strapping at my hands, than a sword in the throat from those who seek your life. Your safety will be assured—at whatever cost."

His eyes said he'd just given me his word, but that was all he was giving me; rather than letting me have the time to argue, he hustled me up the steps into the coach, and slammed the door on me. I was able to climb over all the legs and get to my seat on the far side before the coach moved off again, but the lurching start shifted me over toward the redhead. She looked at me distantly and gathered her skirts closer to her, making sure the peasant didn't dirty them by being too near them, and the other three girls giggled in appreciation. The red-head had picked up the necessary attitudes of Tildorani nobility, and was practicing them on me in the same way I'd done with her. Bellna was huffing inside my head, ready to be insulted, but I had other things to think about. I moved all the way over to my side of the seat, ignored the giggling, whispering girls, and brooded at the forest flowing past.

Right at that moment, I couldn't decide whether Bellna or Fallan was my biggest problem. Fallan was alternating between threats and sweet-talking, a tactic designed to put a young girl off balance and keep her that way. Bellna was reacting just the way Fallan wanted her to, and her unbridled reactions were throwing *me* off balance. As I sat and stared at the forest the road wound through, my unwelcome guest was sighing and thinking about the way Fallan had treated her. Treated me. Hell, treated both of us. He hadn't liked the way I'd argued with Ralnor, but the marks on my arm had seemed to really bother him. Bellna's reactions to his small kindnesses were making me begin to like Fallan the mercenary, and I couldn't afford to like him. I was on an assignment that would undoubtedly produce a whole lot of dead bodies all around me, and I couldn't afford to find myself in the position of having liked one of them. The sort of emotions evoked at a time like that are not conducive to survival.

I sighed and shifted my bare feet on the floorboards of the coach, feeling the repugnance Bellna felt at the sensation. She had never been made to go barefoot before in her entire life, and her over-awareness of the state was enough to divert part of her attention from thoughts of Fallan. It annoyed her that that indignity had been forced on her by Fallan himself, but she was ready to forgive him—grudgingly—if he continued to act as though she might be important to him in some way. I wondered about that, about why he was concerning himself so directly with the young girl in his charge, but could only guess when it came to drawing conclusions. It wasn't likely that he was seriously interested in her, not when she was a princess already promised in marriage to the crown prince of Narella. Attachments like that were formed only in fiction; real-life, practical men knew better, and if nothing else, Fallan seemed practical. He was probably only trying to make life easier on himself by having Bellna too starry-eyed to give him a hard time. Or too wide-eyed by his threats, the latest of which had done exactly that to her. He had said he would beat me if I didn't act like the peasant I was supposed to be, but somehow I still didn't believe him. It wasn't the sort of thing a mercenary could get away with, even in the name of protection. Fallan was probably hoping that if he said it calmly and seriously enough, Bellna the child would believe it. Unfortunately for him he wasn't dealing with Bellna, and I didn't like the arrangements he'd made with the redhead. I leaned back on the coach seat and closed my eyes on the decision that I'd have to push the good captain a little more, and sabotage his plans if at all possible. I was the one getting paid to take the risks; the idea of over-protecting a decoy was absurd.

The distance to the next inn wasn't far enough to let me do more than grab a catnap. When the captain of Bellna's mercenaries came to hand her out of the coach, all of us, including the new princess, were given a surprise. The man wearing the captain's neck scarf was Ralnor, and he was the picture of courtesy to the redhead. Fallan, now a lieutenant, gathered the rest of us "girls" together, and herded us along after his captain and our princess. The rest of the mercenaries took up their places around and behind us, and we repeated our parade to the inn. After Ralnor and Fallan checked out the interior we went inside, were immediately noticed by the tall, slightly pot-bellied man who was the innkeeper, then went through the same revelation scene we had at the previous inn. I'd decided to wait for the grand announcement before making my move, so when the innkeeper was gasping in shocked delight I began to step forward—and discovered that Fallan hadn't counted on my being intimidated by his threats. Three of his men were inches away from me at left, right and back, and the disguised captain himself was right in front of me. I took no more than that one short step before finding myself in a box of hefty male bodies, and seconds later our party had separated, the redhead and Ralnor being led to a table, Fallan and six of his men, the three girls and I all moving toward a door in the far wall. With all eyes in the place on the "princess," no one noticed that one of the peasant girls wasn't moving entirely on her own. I noticed it, of course, but there wasn't much I could do and still stay in character. Shouting over wide shoulders or past thick arms wouldn't be very effective, but that was the only option Fallan had left open to me.

The door in the far wall let us into a big, stuffy room filled with the odor of cooking food. Four women in peasant dress hurried from pot to pan to preparation table to fire, sweat on their faces and boredom in their eyes. Five girls hurried around filling wine jugs and collecting goblets, three male slaves in chains lugged heavy sacks or carried armloads of wood, and two men wearing yellow and white neck scarves and very obvious swords stood and watched the hurry all around them without sharing in it. The two armed men were house guards, and when they saw Fallan and his huskies they straigthened and came away from the wall they'd been leaning on.

"Calmly," Fallan called, holding one hand up, palm outward, toward the two men. "Our Company rides in the service of the Princess Bellna, who now pauses for refreshment in your house. We, ourselves, are here to assist you in guarding the pots—as well as help to ourselves to a bit of the best of them. Are there any about it would be wise to look upon with suspicion?"

"None save yourselves," answered one of the men, a dark-haired, dark-eyed, almost-match to Fallan. He was grinning faintly to show he might be joking, but he and the other man kept their backs to the wall and their hands not far from their hilts.

"Well spoken," Fallan nodded, clearly in approval. "To accept my word would be foolishness on your part. It would undoubtedly be best if you were to. . . ."

"Why do you all stand about gawping?" a sudden voice demanded, and we turned to see the innkeeper in the doorway. "The Princess Bellna honors my house with her presence, and those in my service take their ease while my wine sours and my food burns! To your work, all of you, and that as quickly as you value your freedom—or skins!"

The women and girls, who had obviously been watching the exchange between Fallan and the house guards, paled at the snap in the innkeeper's voice and immediately turned back to what they'd been doing. The three slaves, dressed in filthy rags tied around their middles, short, heavy chains, and a good selection of whip marks, also worked at looking busy, two of them shuffling out of the room on some errand or other. The only ones not upset by the innkeeper's threat were the house guards, who finally relaxed from the stiffened, ready position they'd been in, and sauntered over closer to be heard over the unending flow of commands coming out of their employer.

"Were you about to suggest that we await the arrival of the innkeeper, the suggestion was sound," the dark-haired guard told Fallan with a grin. "It is now clear that you are honored guests, and may be offered a cup or two—when the hubbub has finally quieted."

"A cup or two would be well received," Fallan said with an amiable nod, turning his head to watch the frantically hurrying girls and women, who were being commanded to even greater speed by the innkeeper. "A pity this hubbub will be awhile in quieting."

The guard raised his brows in doubt before also looking at the goings-on, but Fallan turned out to be right. The hurrying back and forth took forever to be over, and once it was, half the contents of the kitchen was gone. I remembered all the courses I'd been offered at the last inn, and hoped the redhead was hungry. If it had still been me in her place, I couldn't have eaten a thing.

"You wenches may now serve us and take your own fare," Fallan announced in the sudden peace and quiet, stretching where he stood near the house guards. "I will have a bowl of that root soup and a cut of light bread, but first of all a cup of wine."

"Bring wine for all, including us," the dark-haired house guard amended, looking over at the three girls near me and then, last of all, me. Bellna gasped and backed trembling into her corner at that look, and the guard showed a faint grin. "With your permission, Lieutenant, I would have that red-haired one serve me," he said to Fallan without looking at him. "Is she yours or your captain's?"

"Neither," Fallan answered, putting his hand on the man's shoulder while joining his stare. "Her service belongs to the Princess, a fact she is well aware of. By cause of that fact, her actions when out of sight of the Princess are much like those of the Princess herself. Her service to us is clumsy, reluctant and far from pleasing, for she believes the Princess will protect her from our wrath. For the sake of your temper, you would be wise to choose another."

"For the sake of my eyesight, however, there *is* no other choice," the man laughed in answer, still watching me. "Have her fetch our wine."

"As you please," Fallan agreed with a shrug in his voice, but his eyes were a lot less unconcerned. "Fetch two cups of wine, wench, and see that you do so in an acceptable manner. Should you be beaten the Princess may well be furious, yet will you still have received the beating."

I tossed my head and turned away from them, annoyed as all hell that Fallan had boxed me up so neatly. If I refused to serve them, Fallan would *have* to beat me, or the house guards would surely get suspicious. The role I was committed to would let me do not a single thing to stop him, which meant that if I didn't want to be beaten, I'd have to avoid it rather than stop it. I stalked over to the three peasant girls already working on getting wine and food together for Fallan and his men, ignored their smirks, and appropriated two goblets of wine. Since the goblets had been poured for and by someone else that took care of the smirks, but I didn't care if the girls *were* displeased with me. If they didn't like what I was doing, they could complain to the "princess."

I carried the two goblets of wine over to Fallan and his new friend, not paying any attention to how much was spilling onto the floor as I moved briskly along. Fallan had laid down the parameters of my new role, and the character he had drawn wouldn't have cared if all of the wine had ended up on the floor. The two men watched me approach, Fallan annoyed but the house guard grinning, and I toyed briefly with the idea of seeing how well the two of them would look *wearing* the wine. It seemed like a dandy idea to me—just an accident, of course—but I suddenly became aware of the fact that my mind guest didn't agree. Somehow, the Bellna presence had picked up the thought I'd been toying with and had nearly gone into shock over it, then had begun pouring out flash after flash of nearly pure panic. Her attention was focused more on the house guard than on Fallan, and I was reluctantly forced to agree with her conviction that he would not find having wine spilled all over him at all amusing. As soon as I decided against the accident Bellna's panic calmed a good deal, proving that she *was* picking up my intentions. I would have enjoyed looking a little further into the new development, but Fallan and the guard were stepping forward and reaching for the goblets.

"Clumsy, as you said, yet commendably swift," the guard remarked, still grinning as he sipped at the wine he'd taken from me. "A wench clearly trainable by one who is willing to spend the time. Does the Princess mean to pass the darkness with us?"

"No," Fallan answered after taking a good swallow from his own goblet. "We depart as soon as her meal is done."

"A pity," the house guard murmured, half his face hidden behind his goblet as he drank. Only his eyes remained visible, and the look in them sent a shudder through Bellna, which she helpfully passed on to me. I didn't much care for the house guard either, but Bellna seemed really afraid of him. I faded back as the two men began discussing employment opportunities available to mercenaries in Narella, and was rewarded with Bellna's sigh of relief. She would have enjoyed staying near Fallan, but with the house guard there, she was happier being a good distance away.

The thought of distance brought back my previous thoughts of separating myself from Fallan and his game, which was still a point well worth considering. I stood to one side of the big kitchen watching the three peasant girls hurrying back and forth with wine and food for Fallan and his men, wondering if the damage had already been done. At that point I couldn't very well go back to the first inn we'd stopped at, but the present inn would do just as well if I could have access to it without Fallan and and his group being there. I wasn't worried about the innkeeper believing my story—there was a great deal of difference between peasant and princess on that world, and a few minutes of conversation with the man would prove everything I said. No, the biggest problem was the question of which of us Clero's men would find and zero in on, me or the coach and the redhead. I was more than well aware of the fact that Dameron's project would be a success whichever way the choice went, but being that practical was beyond me just then. If Clero's men attacked the coach the redhead and the other three girls would die, right along

with Fallan and any of his men who tried to stop them.
I was the only one who knew how well-mounted that
attack was sure to be, but I couldn't tell anyone, least of
all Fallan. Making a fuss at the inn was the only chance
I had of drawing the heat away from the others and
back to someone who had a chance of surviving it;
letting it go on the easy way was something I couldn't
live with.

As soon as all the men were served, my three ex-
servants began putting together their own meal. I'd
been drifting aimlessly around the edges of the kitchen,
passing every doorway in it and trying to decide which
of them led outside. Two of them did without a doubt,
but Fallan's eyes had been on me the whole time I'd
been near them, showing he didn't intend to be caught
asleep at the switch. I could have beat out Fallan in any
footrace ever proposed, but our little to-do in the tent a
short while earlier had shown me I would need overland travel mode to do a real job of it. Overland travel
mode lets an agent draw on his or her *entire* bodily
resources, which makes it very draining even when used
for only a short while. During that short while, however,
speed and endurance are improved by a minimum fac-
tor of five, which makes for one hell of a spectacular
show. I could put on that show in the middle of a
forest, with no one but insects, birds, and animals
watching, but not in the close environs of that inn.
Near the inn I'd have to use normal speed, and Fallan
had shown me just how fast he could be. If I didn't
want to take the chance of being run down I'd have to
find another way out of that kitchen, one that would
keep Fallan unsuspicious until I had a good enough
lead. It took two circuits of the kitchen and five minutes'
worth of should-I-shouldn't-I, but I finally settled on
the doorway the slaves had been using.

A doorway was just what it was, doorless and dim and undoubtedly the access to an attached storeroom. Most storerooms had doors leading to the outside, but even if they didn't they usually had windows. Fallan had ignored me when I'd passed that doorway, which made it a good bet even if I had to loosen a couple of boards in the wall at the back. When I neared it the third time, no one in the room was looking my way, not even the three slaves, which made it definitely the time to go. I took two more steps, then slipped through into the dimness.

Wooden crates, kegs, and sacks almost filled the room, leaving no more than a couple of narrow aisles with which to reach the back. I slipped through the congestion to the second aisle, the one farthest from the doorway, and headed back to see what there was to see. There were large stacks of firewood, sacks of vegetables, boxes of salted meat, cases of wine, kegs of ale, stands of goblets, racks of bone plates—but no doors or windows. I worked my way all the way back, using the glow of two small lamps on the wall to keep from tripping and killing myself, but it was a waste of time. No doors, no windows, and heavy wooden logs for walls rather than kickable slats. The semi-darkness wasn't even a cool darkness, and when I saw three piles of ragged bedding below three metal rings set into the walls, I pitied the slaves. In full summer that storage room would be an oven, in winter a true refrigerator, but that was where they were probably chained every night. If I could have broken out and left the way open for them I would have done it, but breaking out of a room like that was beyond the resources then at my command. I moved the top of my blouse down a little against the closeness, then turned to retrace my steps out of that dead end.

"An excellent beginning," he said in a very soft voice

as I stopped short with a gasp. "I will be pleased to assist with the removal of the entire bodice, therefore you need concern yourself no further. The pleasure will be entirely mine."

"You may not touch me!" I said in an overshrill voice, that and the heavy fear turning my heartbeat into a thud all through the courtesy of Bellna. The man was the dark-haired house guard, of course, and it was clear that not everyone had been looking the other way when I'd entered the storeroom.

"May I not?" he grinned, moving forward slowly and making me back away. "There are many things one may not do, yet are they done over and again. The Princess, I understand, would pout and protest if her favored wench were to be put beneath a man, yet such protest would not occur if she was unaware of the doing. You will give me service on your back, pretty wench, and afterward say nothing of that service, else shall those who count themselves friend to me see that you are taken from your place and sold as a slave. Do you understand?"

"No," I moaned, trembling with Bellna's terror and nearly out of control. There was no need to look around for a way out because there was none; the only way out lay past the man who continued to advance on me. I also continued backing, shaking my head numbly, and then I struck the wall. The contact seemed to be the final shock, and my mouth flew open, ready to release the scream of abject terror in my throat, yet the mercenary before me was prepared. As quickly as my mouth opened, so quickly was a cloth thrust in, and then was I taken by the arms and lowered to the filthy rags piled upon the floor.

"Silence is best when engaged in an activity of this sort," he chuckled, lowering himself to one knee above me. "Your moans of pleasure will be lost to me I know, yet one must make sacrifices in such instances. My, my, what have we here?"

His hands had gone into the top of my bodice, and the touch of them upon my breasts was an even greater spur to my terror. He was clearly the sort I had been warned of, the sort who would take my use without leave merely because he thought me a peasant. I reached for the cloth to pull it from my mouth, yet he took my wrists and held them in one large, merciless hand.

"Ah, no, my pretty, you must recall the need for silence," he whispered, grinning well at the fear he was able to see in my eyes. "Far better that we seek what other treasures lie beneath this cloth."

His free hand touched my leg, rose upon it beneath the thin skirt, and then I was back again, Bellna gibbering in fear in her favorite corner. Her panic was still racing through me, sapping my strength and reason, and her relinquishment of control was almost too late. The house guard slid his hand onto my thigh, making my head ring with Bellna's screams, and I just couldn't help myself. I *had* to do something to make him let me go, even if it blew my role straight out of existence. The bastard had my wrists pinned, but that still left me free to raise both legs and kick him in his face and chest. He released my wrists as he went over sideways at the blow, cursing in surprise as he hit the dirty floor. I scrambled to my feet and pulled the wad of cloth out of my mouth, intending to go over him before he could recover, but the man was no lily with a glass jaw. He pulled himself to his feet almost as fast as I had done, blocking me in with his body again, wiping his mouth with the back of his hand.

"So, you would strike at me when my attention was elsewhere, eh, slut?" he snarled, well beyond finding the situation as amusing as he had. "Let us see what you may do with my eyes full upon you—and my hands, as well!"

He came for me then with those hands outstretched, ready to close the distance between us in three or four fast steps. Never in my life had I had trouble making decisions, but right then I didn't know what the hell to *do!* If I stopped him—which I could do very easily—there would be no accusations of hitting him when he wasn't looking. He'd know a better fighter had settled his hash, and on that planet fifteen-year-old girls just didn't do that to trained mercenaries. I had enough control back from Bellna to just stand there and let him do whatever he pleased, but playing patsy was almost guaranteed to do more than protect my role. As mad as he was it would also probably get me good and knocked around, possibly to the point of broken bones. I know I'm better than most, but instant healing isn't among my store of talents. Even a bad sprain would likely mean the game for me with Clero's men, but if I put the clown away Clero's men could hear about it and know something was wrong. Whatever I did would turn out to be the wrong move, and as he closed with me I still couldn't decide which way to go.

The first slap told me which way I *wanted* to go, but an open hand isn't a fist, and I've lived through a lot worse. I stumbled sideways with the force of the blow, gasping involuntarily at the ache in my teeth and the pain in my head and shoulder as they hit the wall. The room swung around for a crazy minute, dark shadows and smudges of light mixing together in a swirl, and then there was a ripping sound as the house guard's hands came together on my blouse then pulled violently apart. The spinning of the room stopped when a big hand closed hard on my breast, deliberately hard, mak-

ing me grunt with the pain. I was pulled close to the
guard's now-sweating body, his pleasure at hurting me
almost thick enough to feel, Bellna's hysterical screaming tearing at the inside of my head. I fought no harder
than Bellna would have to get myself free, but holding
back was getting more and more difficult to do. The
man pulled my head back by the hair and forced his lips
onto mine, smothering the scream he expected when his
squeezing fingers closed on the nipple of the breast he
held. The fear raced through me, as did my rage,
exploding then coalescing, when—

"Get of a scrofulous muck slave!" came a snarl, and
the guard was pulled away from me so suddenly that I
dropped to the slave rags on the floor. It was Fallan
who had pulled the slob off me, and I sat and panted in
an effort to reestablish control while the big mercenary
did what I'd almost been unable to keep from doing.
He'd pulled the guard around to face him, blocked a
wild roundhouse aimed at his head, then threw one of
his own into the guard's middle. The guard grunted at
the strength of the blow, doubled over, then went to
one knee with his arms wrapped around himself. I
expected Fallan to finish him off, but he turned to me
instead, which was a mistake. Fallan took no more than
a single step before the guard came up with one that
started at the floor, trying to unman his opponent with
the blow. It would have done a lot of damage if it had
landed, but he didn't know how fast Fallan could move
when he wanted to. Fallan jumped back as the house
guard brought himself up from the floor with the missed
foul, but the mercenary captain had had to move too
fast to keep his guard up. The other man was able to
shoot a fast, hard left right into his middle, harder than
the one he'd taken.

The fact that I was starting to get to my feet showed

that I'd underestimated Fallan as badly as the house guard had. We both expected to see him fold from the punch he'd taken, but it didn't happen. He grunted to show that the try wasn't everyone's imagination, then came back with one of those measured throws from two feet behind him, right into the house guard's face. The solid, meaty "thwak" sent the house guard straight back and down, to land unconscious even as his hand was starting to reach for his sword. I had time to stare down for a brief moment at the motionless form at my feet and wonder why he hadn't drawn his sword to begin with, and then Fallan was gently turning me to face him.

"How badly are you hurt?" he asked at once, carefully brushing my hair back so that he could look at my face. "How many times were you struck?"

I tried to answer him, to tell him that I wasn't hurt, but the Bellna presence had been through too much as well as having just been saved by her idol. I began shuddering with reaction as if *I* were the one feeling it, and Fallan quickly wrapped his arms around me and held me to him. It was a strange sensation, being held by him like that, feeling Bellna's delirious joy overlapping her narrow-escape hysterics and realizing that he'd saved *me* as well as her. Truthfully he'd saved me twice, once from the possibility of being badly hurt by the house guard, and once from defending myself against the attack and thereby blowing my role. Bellna was terribly aware of his broad chest against my cheek, his powerful arms holding me gently, and when I raised my head and looked up into his face, I could feel how desperately she wanted him to kiss me. I felt exactly the same, couldn't help but feel exactly the same, but at the same time I didn't want his kiss. None of that assignment was over with, not really, and I couldn't afford to

want to kiss him. As if he were reading the thoughts of
the Bellna mind, Fallan's head began to lower to mine,
to take a small part of the victory winnings he'd earned,
and that was when I pushed out of his arms.

"I am not hurt badly at all, Captain," I said with a
good deal of tremor left in my voice. "You have my
thanks, and will surely have the thanks of my father and
my husband-to-be. It would not be presumptuous of
you to also expect a rew-ward."

Considering the way he was looking at me, I couldn't
help stumbling over the word "reward," and that seemed
to amuse him. Laughter touched his eyes very briefly,
wiping away the sharpness of desire, and then he took a
step backward to give me an up and down.

"I have your permission to expect a reward?" he
asked, folding his arms as he stared at me. "I consider
that extremely kind of you, wench, yet would know
what you believe *you* may expect."

"I?" I echoed, wondering what he was talking about.
"What might there be which *I* would expect?"

"A good deal," he answered, the amusement gone
from him. "Were you not told to remain near to me, so
that you might be properly protected? Were you not
told what would befall you if you were to disobey? Had
you not taken yourself off, this would not have happened,
nor the possibility of worse, had I not noticed your
absence. Are you prepared for the reckoning?"

"Should you wish to see the matter in that light,
Captain, there is surely another more deserving of a
reckoning with than I," I came back stiffly, finally
remembering to make a stab at pulling the tatters of my
blouse back together the way Bellna would have. "When
I walked about in the kitchens, I made certain that your
attention was with me; had I thought it would wander,
as though I were of no consequence, I would certainly

not have allowed my curiosity to bring me in here. It seems, then, that my lack of protection is the fault of another rather than mine."

He stared at me in silence for a minute, the flickering lamplight showing nothing in the way of an expression on his face. Because of that, it was hard to tell what he thought of my counterattack, especially since it was pure hogwash. I didn't know if he'd realized yet that I was trying to slip the leash, but if he hadn't, I certainly wasn't about to tell him.

"So once again is it circumstance rather than yourself who may be given the blame," Fallan said at last, a slight nod accompanying the observation. "I would venture to assume that my reward is soon to be turned to a reprimand, therefore shall I dismiss all thoughts of reward and inform you that no longer will circumstances be held at fault. You, wench, will reap the consequences of your actions, and that as quickly as we have reached our night's lodgings. Wrap your shawl about yourself so that we may depart."

"I shall reap nothing of the sort," I huffed, reaching for the shawl I'd forgotten all about. "Had I remained in my proper position, such an outrageous attack would not have occurred. Need I remind you, Captain, at whose insistence I did *not* remain in my proper place?"

"All points of the disagreement will be clarified when we have reached our night's lodgings," Fallan said, dismissing my arguments by refusing to discuss them. The hard decision in his voice was turning Bellna wide-eyed again, but I refused to believe the man would cut his own throat by beating me. He might decide to lecture me for an hour, but lectures were easy to turn off, especially when you had experience at it, the way I did. It might not be a bad idea to pretend to be browbeaten at the end of the lecture, which could take Fallan's eyes off me long enough for me to do a fast fade. Even though Clero's men weren't in sight yet, I knew I was running out of time. If I didn't separate myself from Fallan soon, the entire question would become academic.

Fallan took my arm in one of his now-familiar firm grips, and began hustling me out of the storeroom. He seemed to have overlooked the fact that I didn't yet have the shawl tied around me, and his hand on my arm wasn't helping matters any. The closer we got to the door out of the storeroom, the more heat I could feel in my cheeks from Bellna's wailing embarrassment, and the more frantically my hands fought to tie the green wool-like material around me. *Back off and let me do it!* I ordered the presence in my mind, silently cursing her too-deep sense of modesty and lack of control, but I could feel I wasn't getting through. My breasts were bouncing with the pace Fallan was forcing on me, and the feel of the rough shawl against my skin was adding to Bellna's agitation. She was about to be dragged naked in front of *peasants*, and the humiliation was killing her.

Fallan reached the end of the aisle and turned without even slowing down, taking me with him, seemingly oblivious to the fact that I was tripping over every third thing sticking out of the stacked items to the left of the aisle. His hand on my arm kept me from going down, but my own efforts to stay on my feet and avoid more bruised shins, toes and feet bottoms were destroying Bellna's fumblings with the shawl. We were back in the kitchen before Bellna—or I—realized we were being punished after all, and by then it was too late. Every male eye in the room was on me, staring hard as I frantically closed the shawl and *held* it in place, their eyes taking in the inner burn of embarrassment I was helpless to stop. Fallan finally let go of my arm to look at my face again in the better light, and one of his men came up to him.

"Was the wench harmed, Lieutenant?" the man asked as Fallan put his hand on my face under the chin to keep me from squirming away from him. "What of the one who followed her?"

"The one who followed her is now asleep," Fallan replied, frowning only slightly at the spot where the house guard's slap had caught me. "She will not be much bruised, a fact he may thank as the reason for his continuing to live. I also choose to ignore his having reached for his weapon."

"In opposition to the codes?" the other man asked, sounding shocked, echoing the sounds of shock from the other mercenaries in the room, including the other house guard. "When not engaged to fight for opposing sides, we are forbidden to draw weapons against one another!"

"Perhaps he was taken by forgetfulness," Fallan suggested, a dismissal in the tone he used, finally letting my face go. "Go and inform the captain that we shall await the Princess in her carriage, so that we may depart as soon as she has ended her meal."

"As you say, Ca— Lieutenant," the man responded, giving me a last glance before turning and heading out of the kitchen. I was still holding the shawl, knowing damned well Bellna would have a fit if I tried tying it in front of all those people. Once it was closed it would cover me more completely, but the process of tying would just about strip me again. Fallan put a hand in my back and pushed me toward one of the two doors leading directly outside, and the rest of our party hurried to join us.

The coach stood waiting for us in the afternoon sunshine, the harnessed vair looking peaceful and satisfied. Fallan made me stand and wait while the other girls climbed in, then put his head in the door after I'd reclaimed my seat on the far side of the coach.

"Should I feel you sufficiently remorseful for your unthinking willfulness, girl, I will obtain a new bodice for you," he told me, letting his glance slide over the shawl. "Until that time, however, you will cover yourself as best you may with that which you have. When the new bodice is brought, I will also expect an apology for your past behavior."

Don't hold your breath unless you look good in blue, I commented to myself as he closed the door and walked away. I didn't need his generosity, and especially wouldn't need it when I managed to take off in my own direction. The man may have helped me out of a tight spot, but he was still a royal pain in the backside.

"Should the Captain see such an expression upon your face, he will punish you to an even greater extent than he now intends," a whispered voice came, and I looked up to see the brown-haired girl who had told me how unhappy Fallan was with me that morning. "Should you give him the apology he wishes, he will surely be more lenient with you."

The other two nodded their agreement to the sentiment, all three of them looking extremely uncomfortable, and I didn't have to wonder why. In my place they *would* have been punished, and undoubtedly knew what it was like.

"There will be neither apology nor punishment," I assured them, taking the opportunity to quickly tie the shawl before Bellna could squawk. "Though the beast has forced me to dress as a peasant, never would he dare to treat me as one to so great an extent. I will arrive at my destination as I was at my departure, totally untouched by the beast Fallan."

"Perhaps, Princess, you are correct," said one of the others, the oldest of the three, her expression serious. "Perhaps your true station will indeed keep you safe

from the Captain's displeasure. It will be well to hope
that this shall be so, for if it is not, there are none to
protect you from him. This, above all other things,
must be remembered."

They broke off the conversation then out of respect
for the "princess," who had finished her meal and was
being escorted back to the coach. Considering it just as
well, I let it drop, too, working to keep the pity off my
face. Those girls really did have no one to protect them
from the men around them, and they were trying to
make a sheltered young girl aware of the real world, to
keep her safer than her ignorance was likely to keep her.
It didn't matter that I didn't need anyone to protect me;
they didn't know that, and they were trying to help. I
damned Fallan for risking their lives so casually, then
slumped back and waited for the coach to get moving
again.

The only thing more boring than a slow, primitive
trip is a monologue by a small-town bumpkin on the
wonders of big city life, and once we were on the road
again we had both. The redhead chattered away about
the fantastic meal and service she'd been given, her
previous silence disappearing behind the flood of words
like shadows in a rainstorm. The three girls listened
with a good deal of interest, but I sent my attention out
the window and turned my hearing off, spending my
time praying for the attack that should have already
come. The redhead hadn't noticed that her blouse was
hanging on me in tatters, so taken was she with her new
life. She seemed to have forgotten that her life—both
new and old—could disapper at any time, but I hadn't.
I had decided that I had to force Fallan to let me play
princess again, but the one thing I couldn't decide on
was how.

The afternoon disappeared behind one disgarded plan

after another, and nightfall found me empty of ideas and in a really lousy mood. The woods were dark blobs on either side of the road, a breeze moved in against the warmth of the day, and I was beginning to think about being hungry. I was just wondering how far ahead the next inn was when the coach turned off the road into the trees, making me sit up with abrupt suspicion. Both of the previous inns we had stopped at had been built right at the side of the road, and there seemed to be no reason for the unannounced side trip.

"A pity we left the last inn too late to reach the next at a comfortable time," the redhead observed, looking casually out of the window on her side of the coach. "We now must take lodging in a woodsman's house, a location far inferior to an inn, yet the Captain feels it best that we travel as short a distance as possible in the dark."

"A woodsman's house," mused the girl who was oldest, staring at me through the darkness. "A place with a house, a stable—and perhaps a woodshed. My father's house had no more than a small woodshed, yet that was where my sisters and brothers and I were taken, to be punished. The polished switch stung more greatly there than any other place, and this, I think, is true of all woodsheds."

Again there was agreement from the other girls, echoed even by the redhead. The oldest girl was trying to tell me to watch my step, but her estimation of my biggest problem didn't come anywhere near my own estimation. I had been looking forward to the next inn to see if I couldn't pull some swindle even with Fallan there, but we weren't going to be *at* an inn. Woodsmen's houses were located all over Narella, funded by the Princes at the orders of the King. Too many of the people of Narella couldn't afford to stop at an inn, so when they traveled they were forced to camp out, making themselves targets for slavers and outlaws. The woodsmen, employed by the Princes to control overpoaching in their territories, enlarged their houses and larders, then made travelers welcome. If the travelers were poor they ate and slept for free, but if they weren't they were expected to pay for what they consumed. It was a system that worked well in Narella, but it wasn't likely to work well for *me*. An innkeeper could be expected to know the difference between a princess and a peasant, but how many nobles did a woodsman get to see? If it came down to a choice between believing me or Fallan, did I stand even the slightest chance? I pulled the shawl more tightly about me and growled under my breath, knowing damned well that I didn't stand the chance of a feather in a windstorm. The woodsman would back Fallan, and I'd be left with the pleasant job of explaining what I was up to without admitting anything damaging. And I didn't even have the option of walking away any longer! Once we stopped, slipping off into the darkened woods would be child's play, but what good would it do? I wasn't likely to run into Clero's men that way, and even if I did they wouldn't know who I was. They would still go after the redhead, take her out, then continue merrily on their way. For the hundredth time I didn't know what to *do*, and so just brooded.

It took longer than I expected to get to the woodsman's house, and the lighted windows hanging in the blackness were a warming, welcoming sight despite everything. My feet were cold and my hands were cold, and the damp of the forest night was even beginning to work its way under the cheap green shawl. The only one of us who was comfortably warm was the redhead; it was probably the first time all day she hadn't been sweltering. The coach pulled up and stopped in front of the wide, two-storyed house, the mercenaries dismounted, and "Captain" Ralnor came to hand the "princess" out. With that done the other girls climbed out and I followed, all of us finding Fallan waiting to escort us inside. At that point it didn't matter much one way or the other, so I did as the others did and went along quietly.

The inside of the woodsman's large house was warm, but it was also the scene of throttled-down bedlam. Kids ran in all dirrections for goblets and pitchers of wine, for chairs with cushions, for hastily made snacks. Three older women stood at the big fireplace where they were cooking, but their eyes were shining when they glanced over their shoulders at the redhead. The grand announcement had obviously already been made, and I was glad I'd missed it. Even the woodsman himself, a shortish, stocky man with brown hair and eyes and rough, home-made clothes, seemed impressed, a depressing observation to my mood of the moment. Fallan's men filed into the room behind us, closed the door, then stood around with arms folded, watching the excitement and eyeing the food and drink. Curious about how many men had been left outside I turned toward one of the front windows, but Fallan caught my arm before I was able to take the first step, and took me with him over to the woodsman.

"A good evening to you, Lieutenant," the man greeted Fallan, raising his goblet to him. "Will you join us in a cup of my best ale?"

"With pleasure," Fallan answered, responding to the woodsman's gesture with a friendly nod. "First, however, I must attend to a matter too long unseen to. I have a girl to be punished, and would ask the use of your stables."

"Why, certainly, Lieutenant," the woodsman agreed with a chuckle while Ralnor, the redhead—and I—stared at Fallan in disbelief. "My stable is yours, for however long you require its use. You will find it through there."

The woodsman nodded toward a bolt-adorned door in the far wall to the right of the fireplace, and Fallan nodded again.

"My thanks, Woodsman," he said, tightening his grip on my arm. "This matter will not take long, and then we may drink to one another's fortune."

The woodsman returned Fallan's nod as the big mercenary pulled me away from him, heading us both toward the door that had been pointed out. I struggled against Fallan's hold in the sort of lame way that had long since begun to be very frustrating, and got exactly as far as you would expect.

"You may not do this to me!" I hissed at Fallan, seriously wondering if I had the patience left to just stand there and let him do as he pleased. "I refuse to accept this! I will not accept it!"

"You will accept all I give and more," Fallan muttered back, not even looking at me. "The time has come for a true understanding between us, one too long in the coming. I cannot keep you safe without your complete cooperation, and this I will have when we return from the stables. I am now able to see that this should have been done much the sooner, as Grigon recommended."

Grigon? What the hell did Grigon have to do with this? I glanced at Fallan's determined profile as I asked the question silently, immediately deciding that I'd ask it again aloud as soon as Fallan and I were alone. I couldn't see Grigon telling Fallan to beat me, even if the Absari agent hadn't been all that pleased with my obedience quotient. It didn't make any sense, not any of it, but we were only three steps away from the door that would open on some answers and I could afford to wait that long. Fallan reached the door, pulled it open to reveal a large, dimly lit stable that was closed tight from the inside, and then—

"Attack!" shouted one of the mercenaries near a front window, peering out at the darkness and what it held. We could all hear the sound of swords clashing now, the thud of arrows into the house, the cursing of men hard-pressed. Clero's force had finally made it, and I couldn't have been happier. If I let them see me, I might be able to lure them into the woods after me— and then take care of them one or two at a time. They were committed to me now, and that was what we'd been trying to accomplish. Bellna and her King's Escort would find nothing they couldn't handle in their way, and I was all through with having to stand around being helpless. I took a half step back toward the front door, forgetting all about Fallan—which turned out to be a mistake.

"That direction is not for you," he growled, pulling me off balance by the hold he had on my arm and pushing hard enough to send me stumbling through the doorway. "*That* is the place for you, wench, and as you value your life you will remain there."

I opened my mouth to tell him what to do with himself, but the bastard slammed the door in my face before I had a single word out. Raving furious was a good description of what I felt then, and I moved fast to the door to shove on it—only to find that the bolt had been thrown.

"Cross-eyed, impotent son of a beslimed street stroller!" I snarled, pounding on the unmoving door. "Gelded crawler in and eater of offal! Open this door, else I shall. . . ."

I was so wild I was ready to *break* the door, which turned out to be my second mistake in as many minutes. Getting mad in a dangerous situation is as stupid and potentially fatal as walking blindfolded through racing ground traffic. All the shouting I was doing covered whatever noise they made coming up behind me, and my ranting was abruptly cut off by the presence of a wet cloth pressed fast to my nose and mouth. I suddenly knew they'd been hiding in the stable, waiting for the attack to start, waiting to do whatever they planned on doing. I tried to stop my breathing as I brought an elbow back hard into the ribs of whoever was holding that cloth, but before the blow landed his free arm had already brought a fist back into my middle with a goodly amount of force, causing me to gasp in two complete lungfuls of the flat, strangling vapors coming out of the cloth. The cloth-holder did some gasping himself as he let me go, but my head was already spinning too fast for me to take advantage of the freedom. I tried to move away from the door and farther into the stable, to find some place to hole up until my head cleared, but it was simply no use. Instead of walking I slipped down to the floor, stretched out on my left side and well along in floating away.

"The slut!" said a choked voice from somewhere above me, pain and anger clear in the words. "I will have the skin off her in strips for daring to strike me!"

"The Prince means to do other with her than have her life," came another voice, a somehow familiar one with a chuckle in it. "She will regret having struck at the both of us, more so than if we were to take vengeance ourselves. Her life might have been taken easily enough at the inn."

"Aye, and a good thing it was that the Prince had the foresight to place you at that inn," said the first voice, grimly pleased. "Had you not been there, we might well have taken the wrong wench."

"This one would be worth the taking in any event,"

the second answered, and a booted foot came to push me flat on my back. The foot belonged to the house guard from the last inn, and through billowing clouds of dizziness I could see him grinning down at me. "Had she been unspoken for, *I* would have claimed her, to repay some part of the humiliation I was forced to accept in uncovering her true identity. Did they think me so foolish as to be unable to recognize Fallan, a long-time Captain of his Company? Was I to believe that this same Fallan would be concerned over the brief use of a mere serving wench? They are the fools, not I."

"And double the fools for having sent her out here, alone, at the first outward sign of our attack," agreed the first man. "It was clear they would be unable to reach the next inn at a reasonable time and would therefore stop here, yet I doubted when you insisted she would be sent into our hands in such a manner as this. Your words have now been proven correct, and we are now able to take her to those who wait."

"As the Prince also anxiously awaits her preparation, we shall do that very thing," the ex-house guard said with a grin, slowly going down to one knee. "It will, however, be considerably more difficult for her to awaken to her predicament; therefore—"

His words broke off as his arm moved through the clouds with the cloth he'd retrieved, and there was no avoiding it. Two more breaths and I was gone fishing.

CHAPTER 5

I awoke to the awareness of a faint headache behind my eyes, a dulled pulse that was already beginning to fade away even as I became aware of it. I took a deep breath and my senses flowed out to a greater distance from my body, no longer wrapped up under a blanket of unconsciousness. I could hear the sounds of movement and life a short distance away, people going about their business. Closer up there was a clean, faintly perfumed smell, feminine without a doubt and somehow dainty and delicate. Whatever I lay on was hard and not very comfortable, rough and scratchy to my fingertips, somehow adding to the dryness in my mouth. My eyes blinked open to get a look at it and—

Damn! I sat up so fast that my stomach twisted with nausea, and thick dizziness swirled my eyesight for a minute. I ignored it all and brought my right wrist up to get a closer look at the shackle closed around it, all at once remembering what had happened just before I'd gone beddy-bye. Fallan and I had both been suckered, but he was still back in the woodsman's house, at worst feeling foolish, while I had more immediate problems.

Two of them were the two-inch wide metal cuffs closed around my wrists, another the foot-and-a-half length of chain holding those cuffs together, the fourth, fifth and sixth the same cuff and chain setup on my ankles. I twisted the right wrist cuff around to get a better view of the lock that kept it closed, and immediately felt a little better. The lock was simple and obvious, one I could have opened in no time as soon as I found a pick, so I wasn't quite as securely chained up as those who had put me there wanted me to be. Even so, I didn't like the looks of the rig I had been closed into, a sentiment shakily echoed by the Bellna presence, who peeked nervously out from her favorite corner.

The torn blouse, green shawl and print skirt I had been wearing were all gone, replaced in part by a very short, poncho-like piece of sheer white material. The thing went over my head to hang down front and back, was completely open at the sides, and was slit wide enough and deeply enough in front to reach my waist and then some. Holding it tight to my body was a slender belt of chain, delicate-looking but locked on as securely as the wrist cuffs, two smallish rings and a short metal tongue attached to the front. The chain linking my wrists ran through the two rings, but the purpose of the slim metal tongue was a mystery, one I had no real interest in poking at. What I did want to poke at was a way out, but the place I sat in didn't offer many options.

The room was clearly part of a tent, but floored as it was and as well staked down, even an outer wall would have probably been useless. I heard a tinkle of chain and looked at the girl who had turned in her sleep, a young girl, one of two others who were in the tent room with me. Four lamps, one on each wall, let me see around the room, but there wasn't much to see; tan tent

walls, a hard, scratchy mat of a floor, a series of carved
wooden chests along the walls, three young, attractive
females chained and half-dressed in translucent white.
Not a hell of a lot to work with, and nothing at all to set
the mind at ease. I hadn't been brought wherever it was
for *my* benefit, and I couldn't afford to forget that "the
Prince" was "anxiously awaiting" my "preparation." If
it wasn't Clero they'd been talking about I'd demote
myself to cadet status, but nothing that drastic would
be necessary. Clero was waiting for me, all right, and
the best thing I could do would be to disappoint him.

I struggled to my feet with a light tinkling of chain
which was answered by the movement of the second
girl, stirring slightly as the first girl had. The first one
was dark-haired and slender, the second chestnut-haired
and smaller, neither one looking older than Bellna's
fifteen, the brunette possibly younger. Both girls moved
a second time, fitfully, as though they were beginning
to come out of the same unconsciousness that had held
me, showing me it was more than time to move on. Or
mince on. The chain stretched between my ankles was
too short to allow a decent stride, which meant I had to
flounce along almost on my toes. That, together with
the length of the skimpy poncho—a quarter of an inch
less and it would no longer be able to be called a
"covering"—must have made me a sight to behold, but
looking foolish wasn't my major concern. With my ankles
chained, the only kicks I'd be able to execute would be
two-footed blasts, and I'd never be able to land upright
after one of them. If I ran into anyone standing in my
way, I'd have to sneak up on him and use the wrist
chain as a strangle cord. One-handed. I felt like cursing
but sighed instead, knowing it could have been a hell of
a lot worse. The chains I wore could have been bolted
to a wall, or there could have been watchdogs posted

right inside the room. Knowing how lucky I was I
turned away from the two sleeping girls toward the tan
hanging covering the room entrance—just as it was
pushed aside by the two men coming in.

The two men were far from small, both dark-haired
and dark-eyed, dressed in black pants and boots and
golden yellow shirts, typical heavies and looking the
part. Bellna squeaked inside my head and scooted back
into her corner, leaving me all alone in the middle of the
floor, caught in the act, so to speak. It wasn't the first
time I'd been caught like that, but Bellna's fluster and
my own idiot reflexes almost did me in. Automatically I
started to go into standard attack-defense position, which
was not meant to be taken when ankle-chained. Rather
than looking dangerous and ready I managed to trip
myself, which ended me up on the hard floor-covering
belly down, looking up at two faintly amused men.

"Where did you think to go, slave?" the one on the
left asked, letting his eyes move over me. "It was not
expected that you would be awake as yet."

"For what reason would I not be awake?" I countered,
playing dumb as I usually did. Special Agents were
harder than normal to put out, and had a faster snapback when wake-up time came. Survival is made up of
edges like that, but it hadn't been too helpful that time.
"And I am not a slave! I am free, and therefore should
not be chained in such a manner! I must be released
immediately!"

I knew I was pushing it by making inane demands,
but it was the sort of thing an innocent like Bellna
would have done, and these people should have had
some idea as to who I was supposed to be. I held my
mental breath as the two men stared down at me, and
then the one who had spoken a minute earlier laughed.

"It has never failed to amuse me to see wenches in

chains declare themselves free," he said, drawing another smile from the man beside him. "Best you prepare yourself, wench, for you will soon learn better. Also will you learn to respond quickly and completely to questions put to you. Those who brought you here spoke of having given you twice the vapors usually given a captured vessel, and yet are you awake before those others. For what reason are you awake, and where did you think to go?"

"I am awake from having awakened, and thought to take myself from this tasteless room!" I snapped, cursing his persistence as I began to get to my feet. I didn't want him to think there was anything special about me, but I wasn't getting much of what I wanted just then. He moved forward a fast two steps to bend and get a fistful of my hair, then knocked my head into the hard, scratchy floor.

"A slave is not permitted to take such a tone with anyone at all, not to speak of a free man," he said in a level voice after I had cried out at the double pain of the knock and the grip on my hair. "You will remain on the floor, face down, until you have my permission to rise. And I will recall this matter of early awakening, and will speak to our records keeper of it. It is a thing your future master will need to know."

He waited a few seconds to see if I would have anything else to say, but with the damage already done the effort wasn't worth it. Bellna was sending waves of shivering disbelief through me, making my body tremble with her fear, and I let it happen to cover the almost-snarl I felt in my own right. Big, brave men who abused chained women were a special love of mine, and all I wanted to do was get my hands on the clown—with or without being chained. But I wasn't likely to get my hands on him, and even if I did it wasn't likely to do much good with the second man there. Survival right then meant being a helpless, frightened little girl, and that's what I'd have to be. We'd all thought that Clero wanted Bellna's life, but we'd been wrong; if I'd known he wanted her as a slave instead, I'd never have gotten involved. I'm not what would be considered good slave material, not even under the best of circumstances. Right then, with the main attack drawn away from its legitimate target, all I wanted was out of there.

Once my hair was released, my new friend and his companion moved past me, and moments later I heard groaning protests in female voices, telling me that my two roommates were being roused. I continued to lie face down where I'd been left, the chains and rings digging into me, my nose on the scratchy surface of the flooring. The part of my mind that was me rumbled uselessly with dark thoughts, and the part that was Bellna sniffled and blubbered in fright. It was a good opportunity to see if I could reach the Bellna presence to calm her, but after ten minutes of trying I gave it up. Nothing seemed to reach the Bellna presence but spiteful intentions, which could not be considered communication of the reliable sort. If I started out with the idea of doing some damage, I got either protest or silence, putting me in the driver's seat; if I let things ride to see how they would go, Bellna's feelings crowded mine aside. It looked as though I was too well controlled and Bellna not controlled enough, and that would be another problem to face in those chains. As if there weren't enough without that.

The two newly awakened girls went through exclamations of disbelief and protest much in the same way that I had, but only one of them tried to insist. She was laughed at and roughed up in a small way the same as I had been, and then there was movement at the door flap to interrupt any further messing around. Another heavy in black pants and golden yellow shirt entered, but he just stood there holding the flap. The next man in was of slighter build, wearing a pale yellow shirt, moving with a polished grace, light brown hair and gray eyes adding to his air of superior breeding. Behind him came a pretty blond female slave, wearing the same sort of outfit and wrist chains that the rest of us wore, carrying a small package wrapped in cloth. The girl hurried through the opening and moved quickly to one side, keeping as much distance as possible between herself and the male slave who entered slowly behind her. The man was big by almost any standard you care to use, and his chains were a lot heavier and wider than the ones used on females. He was followed by two whip-carrying, armed men in dark gold, and he'd been given nothing but a faded green loin wrap to wear, a green that matched the color of the very brief cloth poncho his female counterpart was wearing. The other two girls and I were wearing white, but this girl and the man both wore faded green. The concept of color-coding is a lot older and more universal than most people know, but before I could think about what the differences might be, the newcomer in the light yellow shirt got the show on the road.

"I see they are all awake and aware," he said to the two men who had entered earlier. "A prompt beginning is ever a good sign. Arrange them now, and prepare to take your own places."

The man in pale yellow walked to a wooden chest, pulled out a thick, wool-like mat and several yellow pillows, then sat down on the mat and made himself comfortable against the pillows. By the time he was ready, the other two girls and I had been put into a row halfway across the room from the man, all of us on our feet and facing the man, all of us tinged with the flush of embarrassment. Being displayed like that was as horrible for Bellna as it was for the other two girls, but the grin the man wore showed he was enjoying the sight.

"You are each of you quite lovely, slaves," he said, examining us one at a time in frank approval. "Your future masters will be pleased, most especially after you have completed your training. You will learn quickly and obey completely, else will you be punished as you have never before experienced."

"You cannot treat me so!" blurted the girl on the extreme left, her voice quivering with emotion. The third girl stood between us, smaller than either of us, frightened from the roots of her hair to the tips of her toes. "When my father has discovered where I have been taken, he will bring his guard and destroy this evil place!"

"There will be neither discovery nor destruction, slave," the man answered without anger, locking eyes with the pretty brunette. "Best you know that it was your father himself who allowed your capture, to provide a gift for his good friend who desires you in slavery. Your second eldest brother is now pledged in marriage to the daughter of this friend, an arrangement which will bring considerable benefits to your father. Your enslavement was but a small part of the bride price."

The man's tone was so matter-of-fact that the girl just stared at him open-mouthed, knowing the truth when she heard it. Even if she managed to escape the chains she wore, she no longer had a home to return to. The man in yellow smiled faintly when he saw the point hit home, then he turned his eyes to the next girl in line.

"You, slave, were foolish enough to be rude to a man of considerable position," he told her, watching as her trembling increased. "The haughtiness of your family place is to be made into slave obedience and a desire to please, and then you will be his. Your family now believes you to be dead, therefore may you also consider the matter of search and discovery closed."

The small girl just stood there shaking, not even bowing her chestnut-haired head, probably due to being deeply in shock or as forced to believe the bitter truth as the first girl. The man in yellow let his eyes move over her small but lush curves another minute, and then it was my turn.

"As for the last of our newest slaves, the matter is somewhat different," he said, smiling faintly as he met my eyes. "Your father dared to attempt elevating you to a position which was not meant to be yours, therefore must another position be given you. In your instance discovery is, to a small extent, possible, and yet for you discovery would undoubtedly mean ultimate destruction. One who was enslaved, even for a brief time, would be totally unacceptable for the marriage you were pledged to, and the insult of your presence might well bring about war between your father and the father of your intended husband. Your father, surely as well aware of the point as any, would either have your life taken as quickly as you were found, else would you be sent to a far-distant retreat, there to live out your life in unrelieved solitude. As a slave, you will be spared both of those consequences."

The shock Bellna was feeling brought a shudder to me, silencing me as effectively as the other two girls had been silenced. Everything the man in yellow had said to the girl he thought of as the Princess Bellna was true, and the cruelty of that truth was worse than a flogging. I felt abandoned and alone and helpless and betrayed and completely destroyed, all of it at once and all of it overwhelming. "I" was lost beneath the onslaught, and

I sank to a sitting position on the floor, only peripherally aware of the fact that the other two girls had done the same thing before me.

"And now it is time to truly begin," the man in yellow announced briskly, as though he were getting more than dull, uncomprehending attention from his three victims. "Two of you are as yet virginly untouched, the third used so little that there is scarcely a difference. We will begin by teaching you the truth concerning your bodies, yet first must another matter be seen to."

He gestured in the direction of the slave female he had brought with him, and she immediately hurried with the package she carried to the two men in golden yellow shirts, who had been standing behind the line formed by the other two girls and myself. The third man in golden yellow, the one who had held the flap open for the man in light yellow, followed the slave to join the other two behind us, but Bellna's upset left me nothing in the way of curiosity as to what they were doing. I sat in an envelope of misery, one palm against the scatchy mat to lean on, both legs and their ankle chain to the other side, beyond even the thought of trying to escape. Because of that, I found myself crying out in pained surprise with the other two girls when a big hand tangled in my hair and forced me to my knees.

"Slaves are not permitted a sitting position save they be ordered to it by their master," the man in light yellow said mildly, looking from one to the other of us. "You will now be fitted with a device to remind you of this stricture, and also to remind you of the matter of punishment. You may proceed."

The last was for the men around us, and proceed they did. One of the armed, whip-carrying men circled the male slave, crossed to the girl on the far left, then took a fistful of her hair when the man behind her released his grip. The whip man waited while the other took the girl's wrist chain, pulled it out between the two rings, wrapped it several times around the two rings, then used the metal tongue on her chain belt to hold the whole arrangement in place. The girl's wrists were then tight to her waist, having no motion-room at all, and the girl was even more frightened than she had been. She struggled in an attempt to free her wrists, getting nowhere of course, and then the whip man bent her low to the floor mat, her forehead not far from her knees. She was ready to be done, and it didn't take long.

The man from behind her had thrust something into his belt while he was securing her wrist chain, and once he was through and behind her again he pulled it out. The something was T shaped and about two and a half or three inches long, of polished wood, as thick around as my little finger, and tapering slightly toward the uncrossed end. The cross-bar itself was less than an inch in length, and had a thin strip of leather running through a small hole in the center of the bar, where it met the body of the T. The man went down to one knee behind the girl, pushed the six inches of her poncho-skirt out of his way, then brought the wooden something to her bottom. She screamed at the first touch of it, a lot more fear than pain in the sound, and again tried to struggle, but it was still a waste of time. The thing was slowly forced into her to the cross-bar, and then one end of the leather strip was tied to a similar thin strip already knotted around her waist under the cloth poncho. At a nod from the man behind the girl, the armed man straightened her to kneeling again so that the other end of the leather strip could be tied snugly in front. The girl was wild with fright and panting hard just short of hysterics, but she wasn't struggling any longer. The man in the golden-yellow shirt brushed her tiny skirt back down, the armed man released her hair, and then the two of them came toward the second girl and me.

At that point struggling was no more than strength-wasting, but I couldn't tell the Bellna presence that. Because of her I struggled to keep my wrists from being secured to my waist, struggled to keep from being bent forward, and struggled and screamed when that wooden thing was pushed inside me. It was one of the most uncomfortable things ever done to me, but Bellna felt shattered by it. I was able to get most of the way back to control then, but I wasn't entirely sure that I wanted control. Every one of us had screamed and struggled, and slaves weren't usually allowed the luxury of emot-ing as they pleased. The man behind me was the one who had spoken to me when he and the second had first arrived, and he smoothed my skirt down once the front leather tie had been secured, and then looked at me with a faint grin. None of us would be getting away with anything, that grin said, and Bellna's tremor of fear sent a shiver through me.

"You will now give me your attention, slaves," the man in the light yellow shirt said, drawing our eyes to him. The men who had put those wooden things in us continued to stand right next to us as we knelt on the floor mat, but we were no longer supposed to pay attention to them. "The devices placed within you are for the dual purpose of teaching and punishment, and will be withdrawn when your lessons have been ade-quately learned. Should those devices be allowed to slip from your body before that time, you will be beaten and the device will be reinserted, to be kept within you for many, many more days. Therefore are you to be alert, for there will be no exceptions to the additional punishment."

The man paused to let his threat sink in, and the small girl next to me whimpered in misery, voicing what all three of us felt. The—*device* we'd been fitted with was allowed some small degree of movement despite the leather holding it in place, only we didn't know how far it could go before it slipped out altogether. Under those circumstances the only thing we could do was use our legs or heels to push it back in, even though all we wanted was to be rid of the filthy things. We'd been put in the position of having to make sure our own punishment continued.

"Now to the matter of your bodies," the man went on, gesturing at the same time. The pretty blonde slave hurried to him and knelt where he indicated, showing nothing but absolute obedience and an eagerness to please. The men tugged her green poncho loose and pulled it off over her head, then smiled faintly at the gasps of embarrassment from his captive audience.

"As you see, a slave shift is easily removed from a slave, allowing her master access to her body," he lectured, running his hands lightly over the girl's body. "The body of a slave is the property of her master, his to do with as he wishes, just as he wishes. The slave may not deny him, just as you will not deny the men who own you—or any man who stands as master to you. You are no longer high born and untouchable, no longer the owners of your own bodies. The sooner you accept this, the less punishment you will find."

There were gasps again as the man in the yellow shirt began to deliberately arouse the slave under his hands, making her writhe and moan where she knelt. Her chains clinked faintly as she moved involuntarily, her eyes closed and her head went back, her nipples hardened and her knees spread wide, his hands taking the very soul from her. In no more than a minute or two she was more than ready to do anything asked of her, but the man wasn't there to ask.

"Slave arousal is easily achieved by a master," the man said in his casual way, ignoring the sobs coming from the slave he gave no rest to. "Are you able to feel the touches on your own body, the warmth beginning deep in the center of you? Do your breasts tighten with the desire to be touched as I touch this one? Heed the voices of the stirrings within you, for you, too, will be required to respond in such a way."

I could hear the heavier breathing of the girls to my left, knowing they were beginning to be aroused just as Bellna was. I tried to fight the feelings but it was impossible, and moving in discomfort did not more than shift that device around. It was starting to make me feel strange, somehow, and that was helping to distract me from control.

"Now you must see one of those things designed to give you relief," the man said, still working the girl as he turned his head to nod at the two armed men. One of them drew his sword and placed it in the middle of the male slave's back while the other gave his attention to the faded green cloth around the man's loins. One short tug, one strong pull, and the cloth was gone to another, deeper set of grasps. The slave was hung like a vair stallion, and even I found myself impressed.

"This slave is well equipped to use any female given him, yet he, himself, is not aroused," the man said, finally taking his hands away from the girl. "Should this slave wish to be given that which she so desperately needs, she must give that one whatever pleasure he desires. Slave, go to the other slave and beg to please him."

The girl whimpered at the command, clearly afraid of the big male slave, but she was too far gone in need and also even more afraid of disobeying. She struggled to her feet with difficulty, hurried to the male slave, put her arms around his body, then moved against him.

"Master, I beg to be allowed to please you," she whispered, kissing at the hard male body she rubbed against. "Ask me anything, anything! so long as I am allowed to serve you."

"You may assume that he has commanded you to waken his body," the man in the light yellow shirt told her. "Accompany him to the mat, and then obey his command."

The male slave didn't seem to be in a very cooperative mood, but he couldn't have had access to women in his state of confinement, and the pretty blonde slave was *very* eager to please him. He hesitated a long minute, but finally put himself down on the floor mat. The girl followed him down, moved to his far side so as not to block our view, then went to work on him with hands, lips and mouth.

"Oh, look!" gasped the small girl to my left, horror and fascination in her tone. "He grows larger yet! Never have I seen such a thing!"

"Rest assured that it is a thing you will see much of from now on," chuckled the man in the light yellow shirt, watching us rather than the two slaves. "You will come to think of the sight as the most glorious thing you are able to accomplish, and will strive with all of your being to accomplish it as often as possible. In no other way will you find any measure of happiness."

What a great life, I thought as I watched the girl slave work on her chain brother. Live and work for no other purpose than to be thrown to your back and raped. The slave propaganda made it sound like the ultimate aim of the universe, but in order to believe it you had to be a slave. Or maybe a slave had to believe it to survive, which seemed to be the name of the game no matter what position you held in life.

Not long after the girl started on the male slave, the man in the golden-yellow shirt who had been standing next to me walked away for a minute, then came back with a thick mat and fat pillows like the ones the man in the light yellow shirt used. The mat and pillows were put down next to me, to my left, and then the man was next to me, making himself comfortable. My knees and legs hurt from kneeling, my arms were beginning to numb up from being chained in one place, and my bottom was still protesting the invasion, but the man who had done it all was making himself comfortable. He leaned on one arm facing me, the back of his head toward the two performing slaves, the look in his eyes too direct to meet. He wasn't there by accident, I knew, and I wasn't overly anxious to learn the reason for it.

"I think it would be best if you now learned more of the feelings of a female slave," the man in light yellow told us, drawing our attention to him again. "You will then understand the slave's eagerness to please, and may then imagine the priceless gift she is given."

A hand came to slide along my thigh, and then it moved around to my buttocks, stroking briefly before patting twice. I gasped and rose up off my heels to escape the sensations brought about by being patted on that device, but golden-shirt's hand followed after me and touched me again. Bellna flared inside my mind and her lack of control with her, responding to what was being done to me with bewildered desperation. A burning had begun between my thighs, deep in that place which was my womanhood, a burning more intense than any I had ever experienced. The brute beside me touched the device which had been inserted within my body and caused it to vibrate softly but terribly, and though I strained away from him, I could not escape the intrusion of his touch. Farther and farther I strained away, the burning growing higher and more intense—and then his other hand was at my thighs, his fingers touching my womanhood!

"To *serve!*" said the one of higher breeding who sat before us, as my body was caught in the indescribable sensations of that touch. "You will live to serve and serve well, you will beg to serve and serve well, you will fall into a frenzy of need if you are not allowed to serve! Down to your heels now, and do not rise from them again. Merely look upon the ecstasy you may be given."

The touch which had sent flares through my body was suddenly gone, leaving the burning and desire unrelieved. With a whimper I lowered myself to my heels, fearful that disobedience would bring me—I knew not what. For me there would be no rescue, no return to the life I had known. I, of higher birth than any of these others, was now no more than the lowest of slaves, captured and chained and touched as none before them had dared. Oh, how unfair to do me so, as though I were of no worth whatsoever! To leave me so terribly aburn! Were I free of those chains, I would happily take the lives of all of them, for daring to do such things to me! I hated them all, fiercely, and yet— what would be done to me if I were to disobey?

"See how the slave is urged on to greater effort," said the high-born one, indicating the manner in which the male slave touched the female tending him. His hand moved between her thighs as she moaned over his manhood, the burning in her clear to one who burned as she did. And yet she was touched while I was not, which brought involuntary movement to my hips—which in turn brought new awareness of that device and of my burning need. They were sure to take my use; why had they not yet done so?

"You may now take the slave who has aroused you," said the high-born one to the male slave. "Take her fully, yet must you take her slowly. You may begin."

The hands of the male slave went to the waist of the female, lifted her across his body, then put her to her back beside him upon the mat. She lay trembling as he rose up above her, so deeply in need that she seemed to have no fear of that terrible weapon of his body. Her breathing quickened as he spread her thighs and approached her more closely, and clearly could we see her greater agitation when his manhood merely touched her womanhood.

"Please, master, enter me now!" she begged in a hoarse whisper, twisting about and attempting to draw him to her. "I must serve you, else I shall die!"

"Slowly," cautioned the high-born one, speaking to the male slave. "She has not yet reached a true frenzy. The longer you delay, the greater will be your pleasure— and hers."

"Should I delay too long, she will lose a good measure of arousal," growled the male slave, speaking for the first time. His manhood touched the woman beneath him more deeply yet, and the woman screamed and attempted to impale herself.

"Take me now!" she screamed, struggling against the large hands on her thighs which held her in place upon the mat. "Now, now, you must take me now, and quickly!"

"Slowly," repeated the other, and the male slave, with a glance for those who wore swords and carried whips, obeyed the command of the high-born one. Slowly, slowly, did his manhood enter her, she screaming and thrashing about, and when at last he was fully within and began using her, I thought it likely that I would soon be senseless. My head whirled dizzily to the throbbing burn of my body, and I yearned desperately for my wrists to be freed. As though from a distance I heard the whimpers and moans from those who stood in capture with me, and knew that they, too, were taken as I.

"Should you wish to be touched, you must beg it," came a soft voice from beside me, the brute who had touched me earlier speaking so that only I might hear. "Beg that I give you that which only a master might give."

I turned my head to look upon him, seeing the amusement in his eyes, yet also suddenly seized by the knowledge that my torment might be ended. My body flamed high with the realization that his touch might be forthcoming, and I could not halt the sudden trembling which took me.

"Touch me," I whispered so that only he might hear such terrible words. "I beg that you touch me! Please! Quickly!"

"There is scarcely so great a rush, slave child," the brute chuckled, placing one large hand upon my thigh. "Your knees must be more widely separated, else I shall be unable to reach you."

The embarrassment of doing such a thing was great, yet what else was I to do? In dire haste I opened my knees as widely as I was able, and again the brute chuckled.

"You are truly well made for a child of your years," said he, raising one hand to the cloth which covered my breasts. The cloth upon my left breast was moved aside with the smallest of efforts, yet he did no more than gaze upon the breast.

"Please!" I whispered, slowly growing frantic. "I have begged for the touch, and you must give it to me!"

"You are mistaken," the brute said, laughing softly. "You must beg, yet I need not heed your begging. The choice of whether or not I shall touch you is mine alone."

"Oh, no," I whimpered, devastated by his cruelty. "You *must* touch me, you *must*! I beg to be touched, do you hear, I beg to be touched! Please, I beg it!"

"Perhaps I shall touch you," mused the brute, sending his gaze to my thighs. "Are you unable to open yourself any farther?"

The slave female screamed in delight at the pummeling being given her body, and with a shudder I strove to open my thighs even farther. The device touched my heels in such a position, yet when I attempted to straighten against the pressure, the brute's hand was quickly upon my arm.

"You were forbidden to rise from your heels," he said, all amusement gone. "Do you mean to disobey?"

"No, I will not disobey!" I whispered, frightened at the thought of what would be done to me. "Please! I will not disobey!"

"Very well," came his gruff agreement, filling me with relief that I would not be harmed—yet also increasing my misery. The feel of the device as it touched my heels was fuel to the flames consuming my body, yet he would not allow me to escape the sensation.

"I must see that the device yet remains within you," he said, putting his hand behind me. "Do not rise from your heels, else shall you be punished."

"Please!" I begged as his hand touched me. "Please make the choice that I be touched! Please, I beg it!"

"Ah, how quickly you have learned," he chuckled, continuing to toy with the device. "You beg that I *choose* to ease you, rather than believing that I am bound to do so. Am I bound to ease you?"

"No!" I wept, beside myself at what he did to me. "You may choose whether I am to be touched, and I beg that you do!"

"A slave touched is a slave given a great gift," he said, taking his hand from the device. "The slave may earn such a gift in only one way, and that is to obey without question and serve eagerly. This is what you will learn."

No longer was I able to respond to him, for with the last of his words did he touch me, fully, strongly, and with great knowledge of my need. I, too, screamed as the female slave did, touched again and again so deeply that consciousness was soon lost to me.

When I came out of it Bellna was still in a daze, so the turn was mine again. I lay on my side on the rough mat, aware of all the people around me, aware of everything Bellna had gone through. For once I had to admit it was a damned good thing she'd been there to take over, even though it was my body being put over the hurdles. These slavers were obviously trying to condition their three victims, and the purposes they had in mind clearly called for a type of conditioning beyond the usual fear-of-a-whip sort. Bellna had reacted properly to the conditioning, whereas I, aware of it, probably wouldn't have done such a thorough job. I needed to be thought of as nothing out of the ordinary, so they'd turn their backs on me without a second thought. As soon as that happened I'd be gone, and they could take their conditioning and—use it on themselves.

A couple of minutes later I was slapped "awake," and a minute after that I was back on my knees, right in the same spot I'd been in earlier. The other two girls on line were crying, and had obviously been given the same treatment Bellna had been put through. Their golden-shirts didn't look as pleased as mine, though, and I wondered what sort of test Bellna had passed that the others hadn't. It felt as though I'd been out for some time, but that wasn't possible; the male slave was still at it with the girl slave, and they both seemed to be enjoying the rapid movement. A second go-around would have been more leisurely and undemanding, so they still had to be at it from the first time. My knees began aching again almost immediately, and that device was more uncomfortable than it had been earlier; I listened to the other girls crying and watched the two slaves enjoying themselves, and thought about how nice the deep, empty woods would be right then.

My mind wandered a short distance, but it was brought back rather quickly when the male slave was commanded to finish his fun. Very reluctantly he did so, emptying his played out need into the girl who was also reluctant to let him go, and then he leaned down and kissed her briefly, something he hadn't done even when he was using her. The girl seemed touched by the kiss, but she was given no more than a matter of seconds to enjoy the gesture. As soon as the male slave had withdrawn from her and stood, one of the armed men took her by the hair and dragged her in front of light-shirt.

"I seem to recall, slave, that you attempted to counter a command of mine," he drawled, looking at her with an unblinking stare. "Could such a thing be possible?"

"Master, forgive me!" she whispered, beginning to tremble violently despite the fist in her hair. "I had no knowledge of what I said! Never would I have. . . ."

"Enough," he interrupted mildly, cutting off her out-pouring with the single word. "There are no excuses and there are no exceptions. Punish her."

The girl fell apart into absolute hysteria, but that

didn't keep her from being dragged farther into the space between our line and the seated man in the light yellow shirt. She was forced to a kneeling position with her head to her knees, a position that her extreme terror kept her rigidly locked into. No one said anything about what would happen if she broke the position, but no one had to. It might have helped the girl a little to know that the male slave stood with his feet spread and hands curled into fists, a furious expression in his eyes and the point of the sword of the second armed man in his back, but only on a moral-support level. Physically nothing was going to help her, and when the first armed man, who had dragged her to where she knelt, opened his swordbelt and slipped the scabbard off, even the sniffles of the two little girls to my left died to silence.

The beating was pretty bad, especially since it was given so matter-of-factly. There was no anger on the part of anyone, but the poor girl was beaten until her body was covered with welts, until too many of those welts were split open, until the blood covered all of her back like oozing paint. Toward the end of it she didn't even twitch, showing she was unconscious, but knowing that even that hadn't stopped the beating made the whole thing much more chilling. The trembling I was taken with wasn't all Bellna's doing, and there was no dispute as to who was in control. The Bellna presence was able to pick up the tenor of my deepest feelings, and they frightened her even more than the beating.

When it was all over, men were called in to carry the unconscious girl out, and then we were back to lesson time. Or, rather, specific training time. The girl's beating had been a lesson for the three new slaves, and that lesson wasn't lost on any of us. I trembled and cowered just as much as the other two girls, but only because

I'm a professional and therefore able to force the necessary self-control.

Light-shirt had the male slave chained down tight on his back, and then we were set to practicing on him, touching, caressing, arousing. His obvious displeasure at the girl's beating hadn't been missed, and he was next in line as an object lesson, his lot only a little less painful than the girl's. We took turns at the various tasks, practicing until we got some response out of the slave, all the time being urged on, directed, and aroused ourselves by our individual golden-shirts. The key word for the conditioning turned out to be "serve," and the conditioned reflex itself was arousal. Given enough time, the slavers could have had almost anyone writhing just about instantly, and that became a considerable worry for me. I can fake interest and desire better than most, but true arousal involves bodily reactions that simply aren't on my instantaneous list. The golden-shirts were arousing us slowly and checking those bodily reactions on a casual basis just then, but the longer that training went on, the faster they'd expect a reaction and the closer they'd be checking. I had to be out of there before that happened, or else allow myself to be really conditioned. Anything in between would be a dead give-away, of my differences if nothing else. The male slave strained at the chains that held him, gritting his teeth at the way we were being taught how not to allow release in order to increase pleasure, his suffering getting my full sympathy. We three girls were too clumsy to suit our golden-shirts, so we weren't being allowed release either.

The training seemed to go on for days before we were allowed a break. We three and the male slave were covered with sweat, aching all over and with no strength left, but the training didn't stop until the slavers decided it was time. We girls were each sent to a separate wall of the room to lie down near, but our guinea pig was left where he'd been chained. I lay on my side beside the wall I'd been given, my eyes closed, but there was nothing I could even try to do about how hot I was. My golden-shirt was very thorough when it came to women's bodies, and he'd been trying to see how eager he could make me and how long he could keep me that way. I'd stayed in character and had begged him to decide to touch me, but that hadn't been part of the training program, so he hadn't. We were up to having to earn our caresses of release, but as clumsy and inexperienced as we were that was just about impossible. I'd cried the way the other girls had, and had gotten patted on the bottom as punishment like them, and then I'd gone back to practicing as they had done. The only thing I hadn't done was show how practiced I already was at those lessons, and even as strung out as I felt, the omission wasn't hard. I don't believe in cooperating with the enemy unless forced to it, and I'd taken a lot worse in my time.

I was left alone for about twenty minutes, long enough for the sweat to dry and some measure of strength to return, but not long enough to be over squirming uncomfortably where I lay. The worst thing about those devices that had been put in us seemed to be the way they continued arousal and made it worse, an on-going feedback from one set of sensations to the next. The absolute worst was when they were patted or deliberately moved around, and the sadistic sons had done a lot of that during the hours just past. Bellna was beaten down and miserable in her hidden corner, well into the need for tears, so I had taken my cue and let the tears roll silently down my cheeks to keep me in character. I didn't know what was on the schedule to be done to us

next, but when footsteps came up to me and stopped, I
knew it was about to happen.

"Do you weep, little slave?" came the voice of my
golden-shirt, sounding smugly superior. "Are you harmed
in some way?"

"I am not harmed," I sniffled in answer, opening my
eyes to look up at him. He stood above me holding a
wooden bowl, and looked as distantly amused as he
sounded.

"For what reason, then, do you weep, little slave?" he
asked, folding down to sit cross-legged at my side.

"I am—in great discomfort," I got out, coloring with
embarrassment as I said it. "Never have I been given
such discomfort before, and I dislike it a great deal."

"Your discomfort comes from the fact that you have
not been pleasing," he told me pointedly, with an air of
mentioning something I knew as well as he, but just
wouldn't yet admit. "Slaves who are displeasing are
often left in discomfort for days, despite the fact that
they dislike the state. Would it not be better to serve
properly?"

I gasped at the twinge and rush of heat I felt at the
use of the key word and immediately closed my eyes
again, pretending to feel more of the reaction than I
really did. The conditioning had gotten a weak hold on
me after all—since I was human, it would have been
surprising if it hadn't—but I was still well in control
when wanted to be. Right then I couldn't afford to be in
control at all, and the tears welled up in my eyes even
more.

"I have not refused to do as I was told," I sniffed, just
short of sobbing. "I have tried and tried, and still am I
left in terrible discomfort. I have not refused!"

"You have not been permitted to refuse," he answered,
still in that same tone. "Nor *shall* you be permitted to

refuse. It is true you have attempted to obey, yet you have not succeeded. Rewards are given for obedience alone, the mere attempt being insufficient. When you have succeeded in being truly pleasing and obedient, the reward will be yours. For failure you may expect no more than punishment."

I opened my eyes fast to look at him through a film of tears, seeing what I hoped I wouldn't see. He was trying to look solemn and stern out of necessity, but his eyes said he was about to have some fun.

"No," I begged, shaking my head against the rough floor mat. "Do not punish me, I beg of you!"

"Punishment is the manner in which young slaves are taught," he chided, sticking to his decision. "The sooner you are able to be totally pleasing, the sooner will true ecstasy be yours. Were I to withhold punishment from you, so would I be withholding your ecstasy. Do you wish to reach perfection?" I had no choice but to nod miserably as I cried, but all he acknowledged seeing was the nod. "Very well, then. Ask that I punish you."

"I—ask that you punish me," I sobbed, silently damning him for his sadism. He smiled in full approval, put down the bowl he was holding, then moved me to my back. It didn't take long before I was kicking and screaming from his ministrations, but I was just led up to the threshold, not allowed to cross. He seemed to know exactly when to stop what he was doing, when to keep it going, and when to increase the rhythm. Every once in a while he moved his hand beneath me to play with the device, and that made it all terribly worse. My whole body screamed with need, but all I was given was punishment.

When he finally took his hands away, I lay crying for some time before I was able to control it and then I was given some help. I was told to calm myself, and when I couldn't I was touched again, lightly, enough to know that the longer I kept it up, the more I would be touched. Out of desperation I swallowed down the sobs and half-screams, dimly realizing that I wouldn't be allowed to cry at all pretty soon. They would tighten the chains slowly, slowly, until nothing was left but those actions demanded of a slave.

The bowl he had brought over was filled with pieces of soup-soaked dark bread, and I was forced to my belly and made to eat what he put in my mouth. The mess was unbelievably tasteless, but I needed the moisture content desperately. As far as hunger went I didn't have much of an appetite, but Bellna was starving so I had to be the same. I had to lick his fingers clean when I'd had all he wanted to give me, and that *really* put my self-control to the test. If I'd had any fast way out of there, he would have had one or two fingers less.

As soon as my meal was done, I was put back to practicing on the male slave. He hadn't been given anything but a couple of swallows of water, and despite the savagely determined look in his eyes, he was really suffering. Once the other two girls had been punished and fed the way I had been, they were sent to join me in working on the slave while our golden-shirts and light-shirt had a meal served them. The meal was an elaborate multi-course thing served by slave females in faded green, and it wasn't long before it became clear that that meal would be used as another training device. The slaves in green were treated as so much furniture, but we three in white were under constant observation. They waited until we'd begun casting covert glances at the food and were nearly drooling, and then we were offered bits of it as a reward for setting the male slave to moaning. The offer seemed to be totally on the up-and-square and completely logical in a slave-training sense, but something bothered me about it right from the beginning. Our training had been different from the slave-training procedures usually used by slavers, but I couldn't see where the kicker could be. The dark-haired girl was the first to earn her reward, and although she was required to crawl on her belly to her golden-shirt, she got it without more than a little "good-natured" teasing. The small, auburn-haired girl was next, and she, too, got a mouthful of juicy, nicely roasted fowl. I was the only one who hadn't been rewarded, and I couldn't afford not to earn what the others did, so I cheated a little and got my squirming howl out of the male slave, then turned anxious eyes on my golden-shirt. He smiled in approval and gestured me to him, and once I had wiggled and crawled my way over, he held out a good, dripping chunk of roast.

"Complete obedience is rewarded," he said, almost word for word what had been said to the other two girls. "As you have been obedient, you may now claim your reward."

It seemed as though I was expected to take the food, but the nagging doubt I'd had earlier hadn't left me. I hesitated as I looked up at him, trying to ignore how unbelievable the device in me had made the crawl, and suddenly, just that easily, everything fell into place.

"I was—was told that my dis-discomfort would be seen to if I were obedient," I stumbled, humiliated, embarrassed—but desperate. "Must I have the food instead?"

"Did I not tell you she would be the first to respond properly?" my golden-shirt said to the other three men with a laugh of triumph. "A body such as hers must of necessity be responsive."

"Ours remain virgin and therefore ignorant," grumbled one of the other golden-shirts while light-shirt laughed. "Yours has had a taste of what a man might do, and is therefore more eager. The wager should not have been made."

"And yet the wager *was* made," my golden-shirt laughed again, tossing away the piece of fowl and wiping his hands on a cloth. "Mine has won and yours have lost. Which is to come first, the punishment or the reward?"

The question was addressed to light-shirt, who looked between me and the now-trembling other girls with lighthearted amusement. He made a show of thinking the question over, probably to increase the girls' torment, and then he looked back at my golden-shirt.

"The punishment will be given first, I think," he drawled, completely aware of the terrible disappointment he thought he was causing in me. "Rewards are given when the master considers it appropriate for them to be given; punishments are given as quickly as they are earned. Also, the loss of reward will be more keenly felt after punishment."

"I do not understand what I have done to be punished!" the small, auburn-haired girl wailed, trying to shrink back even as she spoke. "I was completely obedient!"

"Obedient, perhaps," light-shirt nodded, looking at her soberly. "As to pleasing, however, the answer is not the same. Is your master to be pleased when you have chosen another thing above his caress? The highest obedience you may give is to consider his pleasure above all else. This is a lesson you must learn before you are fit to serve him."

The key word again. I heard the other girls choke as the heat flashed through me, and knew their punishment had just been added to. The fact that I was punished right along with them made absolutely no difference to light-shirt, of course; I was nothing but a slave under his training, and the little bit of extra would surely do me good.

"We will also see how truly obedient *your* slave is," light-shirt went on to my golden-shirt. "Unbind the chain between her wrists, and we will give her the position she must maintain till the time of her reward."

I gave them the look of frightened anticipation they expected, and my golden-shirt chuckled as he reached down to my waist. I had to lie on my side until the chain was unwound, and then light-shirt rose and gestured me to my feet.

"You will observe your sisters' punishment from here," he said, leading me over to the male slave, who was still in a state of intense excitement. I followed with the small, mincing steps forced on me by the ankle chain, and couldn't help whimpering from Bellna's worry over what was going to happen. "Go to your hands and knees beside this slave, and then I will direct you further."

I got down to my hands and knees as quickly as possible, afraid to ask myself what that chief sadist was up to, and then didn't have to ask. He walked behind me, put an arm around my waist, then lifted me up and put me face down on the male slave's legs. I gasped and grabbed those legs to keep from falling off, but light-shirt wasn't finished with placing me. I was tugged backward by the ankles until my arms were just about around the slave's knees, my own knees were spread by the simple expedient of pushing my ankles closer to me, and then I felt the touch of something being put just inside the furnace that had once been a part of my body. Reason began leaving me when I realized it was the male slave who had been started into me just when I needed him so badly, but a heavy hand kept me from inching backward until I had all of him.

"You may not allow him more deeply within you,"

light-shirt ordered as I whimpered again and squirmed hard enough to drive myself even crazier. "Nor may you release him from where he was placed. Also are you forbidden to touch yourself in any manner, for that is a doing reserved to your master alone. You will do no more than watch your sisters' punishment, and then you will perhaps be given your reward."

Perhaps. The bastard laughed softly as I began to cry, even more when I cut off the crying fast in response to being touched in warning. No more crying without permission, especially no crying which would distract me from the way I felt—and the way the male slave felt. His leg muscles strained under my arms as he gruntingly tried to drive himself into me, over and over again, as though he really had a chance of accomplishing it. I wanted him inside me, just as desperately as he wanted it, but I'd been ordered not to let it happen. Bellna screamed inside my head and tried to take over, but my mind was so full of hatred that she couldn't do it. A golden haze formed in front of my eyes, making me look longingly at the swords the armed men wore, but I knew I had no chance of taking them. Another time, something inside me seemed to say. Soon another opportunity will present itself and then the sword will be yours. I settled down behind the golden haze, burning all over, and just waited.

The other two girls were punished again with arousal without relief, but one at a time. The golden haze intensified when I realized they were dragging it out to make it worse for *me*, but by the time it was all done the haze was gone, Bellna was practically comatose, and I was trying not to move even to breathe. The male slave underneath me was making noises that said he would kill everyone with his bare hands if he ever got loose; I empathized more than he would ever know. At long last I was allowed to crawl away from the slave to my golden-shirt, was ordered to beg to be touched, and then was taken into my golden-shirt's lap for my reward. He bent me backward over one knee before throwing the tiny skirt out of his way, buried his fist in my hair with a really painful grip, then finally got down to giving me relief. As hot as I was it didn't take long, and as soon as I had what I'd been promised, I was dumped back on the floor mat to recover. I lay unmoving with my eyes closed, hearing the muffled sobs of the two punished girls, feeling as though I'd been working out a sentence at hard labor. My body was exhausted but my mind slowly grew clear, and then some interesting questions occurred to me.

I'd been too busy to notice it earlier, but I had finally gotten around to wondering what light-shirt and the three golden-shirts were made of. Nothing that had been done to us, neither pleasure nor pain, had aroused them in the slightest. They had enjoyed the times they were putting us through hell, but they hadn't enjoyed it to the point of arousal. The two armed men, I had half-noticed, had been replaced three times since the first pair had brought the male slave, and even so the latest ones had been shifting from foot to foot, growing hot despite being on duty. The other four men had been here right from the start, were intimately involved, and—nothing. What made them so different? And what was the main object of the way we were being treated? The golden-shirts and light-shirt called me and the others slave and referred to themselves as masters, but neither I nor the other girls had been ordered to call them that. All three of us had spoken without specific permission, but we hadn't been punished for it and our questions had been answered promptly and seriously.

Slaves weren't usually given that much freedom, and the reason for it became a gnawing, twisting worry.

I was given a generous five minutes to recover, and then all three of us were ordered to our feet. My two fellow victims were so badly in need they could barely walk, but that's what we were all made to do. My wrists were left with the relative freedom of having their chain undone, but I was reminded by light-shirt that I was forbidden to touch myself. All seven of us, we three girls, the three golden-shirts, and light-shirt then left the room, light-shirt leading; I was first with the other girls in their line positions, a golden-shirt behind each of us.

Outside the room was a tent corridor with other tent rooms leading off it, and all of those rooms were open. Most of the rooms were empty, but a few of them had occupants, mostly doing things I didn't understand. One naked young girl in slave chains lay alone in a room on a large fur piece, her eyes closed, her body twisting and squirming on the fur, a low, constant moan coming from her throat. As I stared at her it suddenly came to me that her body was covered with faint welts, as though she'd been beaten a little before being put in there, but she didn't seem to be in pain from that. Her squirming said she was badly in need and quickly growing hotter, and the last glimpse I had of her showed the thin leather strip tied around her waist and one of the thin strips tied to it leading up from between her legs. Her wrists had been as free as the wrist chain let them be, but despite her being alone, her hands had been nowhere near her body. I didn't know if she was being punished or trained, and if trained, to what purpose?

Another room had two girls in white slave ponchos being rewarded the way I had been rewarded, and their sobs of pleasure and relief seemed to take no notice of the way they were being hurt at the same time. One of them was bent forward by the armlock her golden-shirt held her in while he gave her secondary relief, and the other was bent backward by a tight fistful of hair in the same way I'd been held. The two girls behind me whimpered at the sight, but the next room held a sight that made them whimper even more. A pretty girl in slave green was being used by a dark gold-shirted guard who had dropped his pants for the occasion, and her moan-filled writhings were so intense that they reached out to me as well. It would have been a lot worse, though, if the sight hadn't brought up a very disturbing question: we three and the two girls being rewarded were given hand relief and nothing more; we were even being trained to beg to be touched rather than used. It was possible that they wanted the other two to remain virgins, but Bellna wasn't a virgin. The girls in green were used normally even though it was still rape; what the hell did they have in mind for *us*?

I could have spent a lot of time prodding at the questions I had, but the walk didn't talk long enough. The second room down from the guard and his slave was our destination, and we were led into it. The front of it was nothing more than a narrow corridor formed by heavy hide partitions making up separate, small rooms, and three older women stepped out of three of those rooms. All three of the women were beautiful, all three of them wore slave chains and green cloth ponchos, and all three of them immediately knelt to light-shirt.

"Slaves, there are new slaves here for you to assist," light-shirt told them, giving them the same sort of pleased inspection he seemed to give all slave females. "Have them seen to by our return."

"Yes, master," the three women murmured together,

then rose gracefully to smile at us newcomers. The one on the right came over to me, touched my face gently with a long-fingered hand, then put her arm around my shoulders and led me to the right, toward the small room she'd come out of. She lifted the leather flap, urged me in first, followed and dropped the flap, then put her arms around me and hugged me.

"Dear sister, I am so pleased for you," she said in a low, throaty voice, patting my back. "You have already learned to give pleasure to our masters, I see, and have clearly been given pleasure in turn. How I wish *I* had been so quick to learn! The ecstasy I was unable to receive, merely because of my own slowness! Ah, me. I joy that you need not wait as long as I."

She patted my shoulder again and let me go, then smiled at the confusion she could see on my face. I was still pretending to feel what the Bellna presence really *was* feeling, and my confusion amused her.

"I am able to know of your success through two things," she said, patting my cheek again. "Although you are clearly in discomfort from the device you wear, you are scarcely in such discomfort as the others, showing that you have been eased. Also have you been allowed the full grace and attractiveness of your chains, a further reward for one who has earned approval. You are now able to move and gesture as a woman, rather than be restrained as a child."

"I am now—womanly?" I asked, looking down at the chains and then back to my new friend as though I really believed her. "I am no longer to be burdened with the look of a mere girl?"

"No, you are no longer a mere girl," she laughed in good-natured amusement, looking me over with a light-hearted indulgence I was sure she didn't really feel. "It is for that reason that you must *pretend* to childlike qualities, so that you may give further pleasure to our masters—and thereby reach your ultimate reward the sooner."

"I cannot understand what you speak of," I protested in Bellna-innocence, but I was very much afraid that I *did* understand. "For what reason must I pretend to childishness, and what ultimate reward do you speak of?"

"Perhaps it would be best if I were to explain *all* things to you," she mused, one slim finger tapping her lips as she considered the idea. "Yes, I *shall* give you what explanations you require, yet must I minister to you the while. Should the necessary be left undone when the masters return, we will both be punished. Come here."

She gestured me over to the back of the tiny room, where buckets of water, piles of soft clothes, jars and bottles and all sorts of paraphernalia stood. When we got there she stopped and reached out to the poncho I wore, beginning to tug it off me.

"I must see to the freshening of your body," she explained, having more trouble undressing me than light-shirt had had with the blonde slave. She would have had an easier time of it if she'd been bigger, but she was the biggest of the three who had been waiting for us and she still didn't make my height. My golden-shirt had called me "little slave" and other ickiness of the same sort, all despite the fact that the names didn't fit. I might not have had his shoulder width, but he didn't have more than a couple of inches on me.

"You must be clean and sweet-smelling, else our masters will not be pleased," she said, taking the worn, sweat-stained poncho away. She stopped to look closely at my now bare body, then smiled a sweet smile of remembrance. "How well I recall my own time of beginning," she sighed, glorying in the memory. "My body was as young and innocent as yours, and when I was given reward by our masters, I imagined the pleasure to be the most a woman was capable of experiencing. How foolishly, happily wrong I was! Are you unbroached?"

"No," I answered, already blushing as I was expected to do. "My—engagement was formally announced and consummated."

"Swiftly and with singular lack of skill," she nodded, clearly dismissing the point. "Your first experience would be even greater if you had not been opened, yet will you nevertheless find it unforgottable. Kneel down and I will remove the device from you, and then you may relieve yourself."

Bellna was awed by the beautiful older woman and would have obeyed without question, so I had no choice but to do the same. Once I was on my knees she unknotted the leather both front and back, drew out the device more slowly than I liked, then directed me to the more distant bucket that was half full of water. I let Bellna's distress keep the blush on my skin, but I didn't let her repugnance keep me from using that bucket every way I could. The woman bustled around in a graceful way until I'd finished, and then she directed me to the other bucket.

"I will speak as I bathe you, and you have naught to do save listen," she said, gesturing that I was to kneel again. She knelt too, right near me, and I decided it was time for a legitimate question.

"For what reason am I not to freshen my own body?" I asked, watching as she took a soft, clean cloth from the pile and dipped it in a bucket of clean water.

"In future you will be required to do so," she answered, paying attention to squeezing out the cloth. "For this one time I am commanded to bathe you, and we may not question the will of masters. Lean a bit more toward me."

I leaned toward her, and had my face, neck and ears washed; with that done she wet the cloth again and smiled her lovely smile.

"You are among those who are incredibly fortunate, sister and child of chain," she murmured, moving the cloth over me. "Not many are chosen for our lot, for we are those who are allowed the blessings of ecstasy. Merely by obeying without question and thinking of no other thing than giving pleasure, we are given ecstasy beyond the knowledge of any other woman. Our masters will punish failure, yet even with punishment do they bring us to our ultimate goal. You must strive ever harder to be perfect in your obedience, for in such a way will reward be constantly yours. And when you are at last allowed the ultimate ecstasy, you will know that you must continue striving so that it will be yours forever.

"Earlier we spoke of pretending to childishness, and you were unable to understand the need for this. The answer lies in pleasing our masters, of course, for this is the sole road to our ultimate goal. Our masters are pleased to be given service by the very young and innocent, therefore do we perform the acts which please them. When you are permitted to beg for a thing, do so as though you were a small girl asking a thing of her father. You are even permitted to pout and wheedle to some extent. Do so, and your rewards will be richer beyond even your own expectations, and will quickly lead to your ultimate reward.

"The ultimate reward! Ah, how I wish you might truly know of it before it is given you! Although you have experienced the presence of a man within you, the ultimate reward is so far beyond that small, abortive experience that there is no comparison. You will be used as a slave, will know yourself a slave, and will know that no free woman will experience the ecstasy that you do. You must be fully a slave before this is given you, therefore must you strive with all your might to achieve perfect obedience and the giving of pleasure. I am filled with great joy that you have already come so far along the road, and will surely advance even more rapidly now. Lie on your belly now so that I may wash the back of you."

I flattened out face down as she asked, glad that I had absolute control over my expression. The propaganda she'd fed me made me want to look around for a shovel or hip boots, but the part about pretending to be a child made me want to throw up. Those sadists calling themselves masters liked the idea of messing around with little girls, but they also wanted women's bodies. Catch a girl young enough, train her to continue acting like a child, and when her body matures make sure that her mind doesn't. Perpetual little girls to tickle the perverted pleasure of so-called men, helped along in their training by female slaves ordered to act the part of mother figures. That was what that bathing routine was all about, a young girl being told the facts of life by a helpful, sympathetic, approving mother who has already gone through the same herself and wants nothing less for her beloved daughter. More conditioning of a particularly vicious sort, the sort that took advantage of peoples' basic natures. I despised those slavers for what they were doing, but all they would see was that I was going along with it. Maybe, if I got very lucky, one or two of them would try getting in my way when I was ready to leave that place.

The propaganda lecture went on as long as the washing did, and all of me was washed except my hair. My scalp was rubbed with a cloth and then allowed to dry, and while it was doing so some of those bottles and jars were used. The bottles held unscented body lotions, unscented so that the odors of desire coming from me would be clear to "our" masters and add to their pleasure. I was nothing if not ardently eager to get on with pleasing everyone in sight, but the contents of one of the jars put a strain on the authenticity of my eagerness. I was told it was a salve designed to ease the irritation in my private parts caused by the device and all the handling I'd had, and that part of it wasn't a lie. The salve *did* ease me, but a little gentle rubbing by the woman after it was put on me showed that the salve was also a sensitizer, designed to make my flesh even more sensitive to caresses than it had been. I was made to bend over on my knees so that my bottom could be taken care of, and it was all I could do to follow instructions with the trust of innocence. Bellna wouldn't have known what the salve was doing so I couldn't know; I just had to bend over and take it. After that my hair was brushed out, and then I was told I could rest until the masters came for me. I lay down on the spot indicated and closed my eyes, but the woman knew damned well I wouldn't rest. I'd been faintly aroused again, but all I could do about it was wait for the man who could choose to make it go away—if he was pleased enough to do so.

A good twenty or twenty-five minutes passed before anyone showed up, during which time the salve took my faint arousal and slowly increased it to squirming level. Every minute that passed made Bellna more and more anxious, a clear indication of what my own actions had to be. I was being forced to think of nothing but the arrival of the masters, and also what I could do to please them enough to ease me. Everything done in that place was an aspect of conditioning, a conditioning that would probably have broken down even *my* defenses if it had been kept up long enough. Some people, like me, are trained to take high levels of pain, but no one, trained or not, can avoid being affected by constant positive and negative reinforcement of the pleasure reflex. The human mind is made to resist pain whenever it can, but pleasure? Hell, that's what we're built to try for!

When my golden-shirt finally showed up, the woman went to her knees to him and I wasn't far behind her. I made a real production out of it, sitting up fast in relief, ready to blurt out my need, suddenly seeing what my "mother" was doing, then quickly doing the same. My eagerness to please had been increased as much as they'd wanted it to be, and the indulgent smile on my golden-shirt's face was covering a good deal of satisfaction.

"How refreshed and lovely you look, little slave," he said, stopping a few steps into the room. "Rise to your feet so that I might see all of you."

The blush covering me as I stood up made him chuckle, and that naturally increased Bellna's blush output. Having her there was becoming handier and handier; I can blush on demand, but not from head to foot. I turned slowly at his gesture, making an inexperienced stab at moving as gracefully as the woman had, and when I turned to face him again there was real amusement in his expression.

"Your eagerness pleases me, slave," he said, and so help me my body reacted to that verbal stroking in a way that was horrifying. "Go and fetch your device now, and I will reinsert it."

Morale dropped down to the floor at that, but I felt no urge to argue him out of his decision. Instead I hurried over to where the woman had put the device and quickly brought it to him, desperate to do everything he asked and please him again. If he wasn't pleased I wouldn't be rewarded, so I had to do all I could to please him. The reactions and straight-line logic were all Bellna's, who would have been three-quarters of the way into full slavery if she'd really been there. I handed over the device with a small and fear-filled pout, and my golden-shirt chuckled even more.

"You dislike this device and yet you obey," he said with such obvious approval that Bellna nearly purred. "Your obedience will be remembered. Down to your knees now and brow to the floor."

I knelt and bent over as ordered, trembling with anticipation at the thought of being touched by him. The situation was as frightening as it was infuriating, but I couldn't do anything about either emotion except thrust them away. I was being conditioned more than I wanted to be, and that was the danger; my only edge was that I was aware of it and therefore in a position to negate the worst parts of the condition. Or I'd damned well better be able to negate most of it. I intended going for the break as soon as it got dark; I'd find out then how good a job I was doing.

The golden-shirt took his time putting the device back in, playing around until I'd moaned and squirmed enough to suit him. The Bellna part of my mind found the torture highly arousing; it had come to her that the man was getting pleasure from what he was doing, and she very much wanted to give him pleasure. She was sure he would decide to reward her after that, but once the device had been inched in as deep as it could go and had been tied in back, I was ordered to my feet again.

"Your lessons will continue immediately," golden-shirt said as he tied the leather in front, somewhat tighter than it had originally been. "I feel certain that you wish to achieve the highest level of obedience and skill as soon as you possibly may."

"Oh, yes!" I breathed, looking into his face with all the ardor I could muster. "I feel a—a *need* to obey that I have never before felt."

"Excellent," he nodded, showing only a small smile of satisfaction. "You will be given ample opportunity for obedience. Your slave-shift may be left here, for you will not require the use of it for a time. Precede me out of the room."

I gave my poncho one agonizing glance, then turned immediately toward the room's exit. Bellna was mortified at the thought of walking around naked, but she didn't want to disobey. After all, there were very few people in the tent complex, so it shouldn't be *too* embarrassing . . .

No one was in the small room-corridor or in the between-rooms corridor, but when I followed directions into the room directly across the way, Bellna's shock stopped me short with a gasp two steps through the doorway. There were more than a dozen green-clad slave females, all in their twenties, three dark-gold-shirted men with swords and whips, and a naked, staked-down male slave. The slave females giggled when they saw me even as they got to their knees to the golden-shirt behind me, and all Bellna wanted to do was run and hide. She was absolutely crushed at being the only naked female in the room, but when I took one involuntary step backward, I bumped into my golden-shirt.

"You must move forward, not backward, little slave," he said, putting his hand to me. I gasped again and found myself doing as I'd been told to do, but I couldn't escape his hand guiding me across the floor. The female slaves were giggling almost nonstop, and Bellna would have been happy to curl up and die.

"You will use this slave to show me the extent of what you have learned," golden-shirt told me when we'd reached the staked-down male slave. "Should your obedience and learning prove sufficient, you may be rewarded."

"I am to do this before *them*?" I whispered back, indicating the female slaves with a desperate glance. "And what of those others who were with me? Are we not to await their arrival?"

"You will no longer be training with those others," he said, again highly amused. "Their progress will be slower, and need not hold you back in yours. Also is your training to be somewhat different from theirs. Are you prepared to begin?"

I opened my mouth to answer him, but nothing came out. I was being ordered to arouse the male slave, a strange male slave, in front of an audience that was horribly and embarrassingly intimidating for the Bellna presence. She was an awkward little girl being commanded to perform naked in front of other females older than she, commanded to an act she had never even conceived of before that morning. The agony of wanting to obey but fearing failure and ridicule was terrible for her, but thanks to our link-up it was almost as bad for me. The tears formed in my eyes as I began trembling, but my golden-shirt didn't let me go all the way to hysteria.

"It seems you will require a small amount of encouragement before you begin," he drawled, then pointed to the floor and snapped, "Kneel!"

His tone stopped Bellna short in her misery and sent her cringing back, giving me enough breathing room to kneel before I was accused of disobedience. I had enough time to notice that the floor mat in that room was a good deal softer than the one in the first room, and then golden-shirt had me by the hair. The encouragement he gave was of the expected sort, the key word "serve" being used at the same time to reinforce it, and it wasn't long before I was writhing and begging to obey the orders I'd been given. He let me beg for some time before he magnanimously allowed it, and then he stayed close and started up the encouragement again any time he thought I needed it. It was able to stay just unrattled enough to remember what I was and wasn't supposed to know, but it was a close thing.

When I had the male slave shouting and cursing, I was finally allowed to stop. I was trembling and covered with sweat and had my teeth clenched against Bellna's screaming in my skull, but some cooler, more rational part of me had decided that my reward would for some reason be put off again. I didn't want to hear that any more than Bellna did, but I was very much afraid it would turn out to be true. When my golden-shirt announced that I'd earned my reward after all, I felt a relief and gratitude that was sickening. I was disgusted with myself for reacting that way, but there was nothing I could do to stop it—and then the kicker came. I could have my reward then and there, in front of everyone including all those very amused female slaves, or I could wait and have it later, at some unspecified time, but in private. The choice was given to *me* to make; I was almost too strung out to be suspicious, but suspicion is a disease I've had a lot of years, and it's saved me pain and kept me alive more often than sweet trust ever could. Bellna wanted to wait, and so did I, but for some vague reason that choice didn't *feel* right. The last thing I wanted was to be humiliated in front of a totally unsympathetic audience, but that was the way I would have to go. I hesitated no more than an instant, then looked up at golden-shirt.

"I—beg that you choose to reward me now," I whispered, blushing furiously but still squirming where I knelt. "I—feel great discomfort—and—and—cannot wait."

"You cannot wait," he repeated in a voice loud enough to reach everyone in the room, satisfaction shining from his eyes to keep his chuckle company. "As you cannot wait, I shall give you the reward you have earned upon the moment."

Again Bellna was shattered by the announcement and following laughter, but there was no longer any way out of the mess. Golden-shirt sat down next to me, took me in his lap and bent me backward, then began giving me my reward. I was so deeply lost to the sensations that every other consideration faded away—including the fact that the fingers of his free hand closed even more tightly on one of my nipples as he worked me. The pain was there but so was release, and once again I was thrown to the floor mat to recover.

I don't know when the dirty suspicion came to me, but after an uncounted time of lying in a heap, I suddenly knew another facet of the conditioning I was being put through—and the difference between my training and that of the others. All the hints and unexplained happenings—the bastards were building a link between pain and sexual arousal and satisfaction. Taken one way to its ultimate conclusion, the infliction of pain would bring immediate, uncontrollable arousal; taken the other way, the infliction of that same pain would bring orgasmic release—or make release impossible without it. The set-up was right out of a sadist's wet dreams, and I couldn't help wondering what I'd bought myself with the response my golden-shirt had been looking for. His satisfaction at the choice I'd made had certainly been clear enough, as clear as the retrospectively seen fact that the

deck had been stacked against that choice. A girl Bellna's
age and with her background should have been mortified
at the thought of being done in front of so many snickering strangers, especially as most of them were women
older than herself—unless she had been made so uncontrollably sensual that she couldn't help herself. They'd
wanted Bellna to react that way, and the next step could
very well be what that solitary girl on the furs had been
given. I'd noticed that she'd been beaten, but I'd also
noticed that she was more worked up sexually than
hurting from the beating. I lay on the floor mat of the
room feeling physically exhausted, but my mind was
darting around at light speed. I'd made the right choice
but it had turned out wrong for *me*, which was the way
the game went sometimes. If I wanted to avoid what the
girl on the furs had gotten, I'd have to backpedal a little.

Sometimes making a decision doesn't mean you'll get
to put it into practice, but that time I got lucky. When
my rest time was over and I was ordered to my feet, it
was to be taken to another, smaller room which contained all males. There were half a dozen slave males
and two armed guards, the slaves only lightly chained
and the guards casual and unconcerned. The slaves
were obviously no worry, which told me that the training given the girls was also used to train the men. Male
slaves who gave trouble were punished by being used as
subjects for the girls to work on; those who cooperated
were rewarded by being allowed to help in the training,
probably also being allowed the use of ordinary slave
females afterward. I was pushed into the middle of
them, had one pointed out as my subject, and was told
to *serve* that one no matter what the others did to me.

Use of the key word affected me less strongly than it
was supposed to, but it still affected me. The reward I'd
been given was largely negated, and the men around me

laughed softly when I closed my eyes and squeezed my thighs together with a gasp. They all wore the faded green of slaves while I stood naked among them, and they obviously enjoyed the sight of me. Their hungry reactions were very unsettling, and then I was told to undress my subject in the proper way, the way I'd been told to do earlier. A well-trained slave kissed her master's body when she undressed him, and the slave who had been appointed my master licked his lips in anticipation, eager to get on with it.

I'd decided to make it very clear right from the start that being among all those men made me nervous. I used an anxious expression when I reached out a tentative hand to my "master," then jumped with a loud squeal when I was touched from behind by someone else. I whirled in the direction of the touch, gasped when two more of the slaves touched me, then began to cry.

"You fail to serve your master, slave," my golden-shirt admonished, punishing me lightly by using the key word again. "Were you not told to ignore all others and attend him alone?"

"I cannot!" I blubbered, looking at him piteously over the shoulders of two of the slaves. "I have never been alone among so many men, not to speak of being—unclothed among them! And they all—oh!—touch me! I b-beg to be allowed to attend him in private."

"You have already learned to attend a master in private," he said with a frown, a lot less satisfied than he'd been till them. His brown eyes studied me in silence for a moment, and then he nodded his head. "This was, perhaps, to be expected. The distraction of the highly unusual is enough to overcome the recently learned. You must clearly be first accustomed to that which is strange to you, and then we may proceed. You all may toy with her a short time."

The last was for the male slaves, of course, and they entered the game with a zeal I would have found commendable—under other circumstances. After throwing me to the wolves, my golden-shirt turned and left the tent room, but the three armed guards were still there to laugh their heads off while I screamed and tried uselessly to protect myself. The six slaves moved in as close as they could and began touching me all over, having no trouble getting past my flailing arms, driving me crazy and enjoying my near-hysteria. After a couple of minutes someone took my arms from behind and held them out and away from my sides, forcing the front of my body forward. So many hands touched me in so many places that I nearly lost control and defended myself, which would have scattered and smeared those six like so much firewood or so many rag dolls. I panted more with the effort to hold myself back than with what was being done to me, but that doesn't mean I wasn't suffering. Bellna blubbered in the back of my mind and screamed for permission to obey, but I couldn't allow that any more than I could allow what *I* wanted to do. Now that I'd broken the pattern of training, I had to keep it broken.

When my golden-shirt finally came back, I was down on my knees with my forehead pressed to the mat, one of the slaves kneeling on my hair. I was screaming almost nonstop from the way they were stabbing at me with their bodies without having removed their loincloths, teasing me with what they'd made me want so desperately. Hands fondled my breasts and toyed with the device, different hands taking turns doing different things while I was poked at and stroked and denied what I ached for. I screamed and struggled, trying to get loose to reach one of them—and then all of them were gone, out of reach and through with the game. I pushed myself up on all fours and raised my head, the tears streaming down my cheeks and my body flaming, just in time to see the gesture from my golden-shirt that I was to get to my feet. It was something of a struggle but I managed it, and once I was erect the golden-shirt stepped closer to me, took my wrist chain between my left wrist and the belt loop, turned, and dragged me behind him out of the room.

To be entirely accurate, I was dragged down to the end of the corridor, through a room that looked just like all the others, but which led outside. It was an hour or so past noon of another pretty day, but neither Bellna nor I were in any condition to appreciate it. Bellna was having hysterics over the number of people stopping or turning around to stare at my naked, sweat-covered body, and I was mewling helplessly at the pace the golden-shirt was forcing me to. When I could force myself to speak I begged mindlessly to be touched, but it wasn't rewarding I'd set myself up for. The thin grass and stones and dirt I minced over barely entered my awareness, no more than the wide city of tents stretching in all directions throughout the large forest clearing. We crossed an open space, circled a dark green tent, then made for a large brown, yellow and white tent with flaps thrown back.

The large tent was too well lit with lamps for it to be dim even after the brightness of the day. It was filled with row after row and aisle after aisle of what had to be display platforms, five inches high for male slaves, three or four feet high for female slaves. The male slaves stood with wrists shackled to either side of their heads, their ankles held tight by manacles set in the platform floors, three platforms of females and one of

males, then another three of females and another one of
males. There was an open space on the female platform
directly opposite the tent entrance, and that was where
my golden-shirt dragged me.

When I was lifted up to kneel on the platform, it
came through the cloud of mindlessness I was wrapped
in that this particular platform was covered with silky,
long-haired furs, and that although the other slaves on
display wore their green slave shifts, the three on my
platform were as naked as I. Golden-shirt took out a
key, unlocked the two rings holding my wrist chain to
the chain around my waist, unlocked the right wrist-
cuff, then lifted the chain and my left arm to a thick
wooden bar above my head. The chain was wrapped
around the bar above and somewhat behind me, my
right arm was raised and the wrist relocked in the cuff,
and then golden-shirt turned and left the tent.

It took a couple of minutes to fight my way through
Bellna's constant howling and the clinging aftermath of
what I'd gone through, but once I'd done it, all I could
do was wonder how smart I'd been. I'd been trying to
buy some time away from the slavers' conditioning
program, but all I seemed to have managed was to find
another phase of it. A large number of people were
strolling around through the tent, mostly male people
with less than a handful of females, and all of them
were there to look at slaves. Golden-shirt had decided to
get me used to being "unclothed" in front of large
numbers of men, and putting me on display was the
way he was doing it. The other females on my platform
had struck me as being as beautiful as Bellna during the
few seconds I'd been able to see them, and that was
probably why we were on the furred platform right in
front of the entrance. Draw the suckers in and get them
to look, and even if they can't afford the best there's

always second or third best. I was being used as bait even while I was being trained.

I took a deep breath and moved my head around a little to loosen the knots in the back of my neck, but the effort didn't do much; being comfortable in the position I'd been chained was just about impossible. Not only were my wrists tight to the bar above and behind my head, the bar itself was in exactly the wrong position in relation to the platform: too high to let me sit back on my heels, too low to let me kneel straight without bending. It took a minute or two of still befuddled thinking to decide that I would be better off if my wrists were directly over my head or in front of me, but I'd waited too long for the decision to do any good. A guard in a dark gold shirt stopped next to me, moved aside the furs right under my feet, then rattled briefly. When the rattling was over, the cuffs around my ankles were attached to what was probably a single, very short chain set in the platform, giving me no movement room at all. I was set in place, chained facing the entrance at a three-quarter angle, and that's the way I would stay for a while.

"Pretty little slave," the guard murmured with a half-distracted sound to his voice as his hands pushed my thighs apart. "You are to keep your knees wide at all times. It matters not whether you weep or smile; your knees must remain apart. Should you fail to keep them so, there is a device to see to it."

His message delivered, he went on his way, not caring whether or not I wanted to say anything. If I didn't obey there would be another "device" to take care of the problem, so there was nothing *to* say. Bellna whimpered miserably in my head, burning so urgently that it made me squirm, which in turn set me to cursing silently. I didn't know how long I'd be there, but the past five minutes had already been too long.

Another five minutes passed, during which time I asked myself why I'd been stupid enough to decide to wait until dark to make a run for it, and then another group of buyers came through the tent entrance. There were five of them, and from their clothes they must have been well-to-do merchants or very minor nobility, and they didn't even pause to look around. Just as if they'd done it many times before, they came straight over to my platform and began examining each of us in turn, two of them listing our major sales points, the other three listening carefully and occasionally asking questions. I gathered that we four were a yardstick to measure the other female slaves by, and we had to be gone over carefully so that nothing important would be missed. Every one of those sons found it necessary to touch me, not once but any number of times, and once they were gone I trembled as much as the only one of the other three girls I could see. Bellna wanted to jump screaming out of my skin, and there was nothing I could do to calm her. Hell, there was nothing I could do to calm *me*, and I supposedly had a lot more control over me.

Not only did almost every new arrival visit our platform, lots of those who had been wandering the aisles stopped on their way out to examine the newly added main platform slave. Some few did nothing but look, but those were very few indeed. It didn't take long before I was physically hurting and mentally exhausted, and if I'd really needed to get used to being surrounded and touched by men in large numbers, that little interlude would have done it for me. I had followed one of Bellna's urges and had taken to begging every passing guard to tell someone I would obey any order given me if only I were taken back to the training tents, but the guards ignored me and continued on their rounds. I was still able to think clearly enough to know they were probably waiting for me to beg them to *choose* to send me back, but it was really too soon for me to resort to that. If I used it immediately they'd either think it was a con, or decide I was far enough along for them to get to the fancy training. I kept picturing the welts on the body of the girl on the furs, and from my reactions knew I'd better put that off as long as humanly possible.

At least two or three hours went by before there was a real lull in arrivals. The slavers were doing a thriving business, but none of the sold slaves were taken out the patrons' entrance. The buyers left that way, but the slaves were taken out the back way, to be brought around and delivered to their new owners. A number of offers were made for me, but the light-yellow-shirted overseers refused all of them in some way that left the customers resigned rather than angry. Right then it wouldn't have bothered me a bit to be sold; it would have gotten me off that platform and given me a chance to unlock all those chains on me. I was stiff and tired and uncomfortable and in need, but without those chains I would have been heading south, *over* obstacles if necessary. I wanted out of there so badly I could feel the tendency toward irrationality growing inside me, a tendency that could get me hurt or killed if I stuck around long enough for it to grow stronger.

I closed my eyes for a minute or two during that lull, and when I opened them again the shock Bellna felt was so great that I was nearly knocked out of control. The newest arrival, standing just inside the entrance and looking casually around, was Fallan, someone I'd been hoping I'd never see again. He wore the same black pants and boots, swordbelt and sword at his side, but his shirt was no longer mercenary red. His profession was disguised behind a shirt of dark green with no neck scarf, and after he'd had his casual look around, he ambled over to my platform and stopped in front of the girl to my left, the one I could see.

"You are indeed a lovely slave, girl," he said to her, clearly enjoying the sight of her long black hair and nicely rounded figure. "Are you well trained?"

"I am trained to give a master pleasure beyond any he has dreamed of, master," she answered in a low, throaty, throbbing voice, moving her body for him. "Should master choose to try me, he will not find himself disappointed. I have not yet been used this afternoon, master. A slave begs to be used!"

She moved her body again as far as she could, showing with words and motion how badly in need she was. I'd heard clinking noises behind me a few times during the hours I'd been there, as though the girls I couldn't see were being taken from the platform and then put back in place, but I hadn't known what was happening to them. If I understood the black-haired girl correctly, the main platform girls were available for being rented out. Discovering that led me to wonder if they were for sale at any but a ridiculously high price. Few men would have been able to afford to own a really beautiful, high-priced slave, but using one now and then shouldn't have been beyond them. The girls would bring the slavers more money that way than through any sale price, unless the buyer was really wealthy, influential, and a very good customer. Exceptions would be made for that sort, but not for anyone else. It finally came through to me that the offers made for *me* hadn't been offers to buy, and I wondered why the ones making the offers had been turned down. The others on the plat-

form were certainly available, and Fallan smiled indulgently at the dark-haired girl's begging request.

"I may, perhaps, choose you for use," he allowed,
looking her over one last time. "However, I must first
see what else there is being offered here."

He patted her round, bare bottom, then left her to
come over to me. His eyes worked their way up from
my body to my face, and then he showed a vast, entirely phony surprise.

"Why, you are a mere child, slave," he said, dark
eyebrows high. "I do not recall ever having seen a child
on this platform. Are you, too, trained to give a master
delight and pleasure?"

"I am entirely untrained," I told him in a low, growly
voice I couldn't control, annoyed almost beyond bearing.
Bellna was mewling and fluttering around in my head,
desperate to serve him and feel his hands on her body,
but she had no body. The body was mine, and Fallan
had already touched it more than I cared for.

"As I am such a child," I continued, "you may dismiss the thought of me completely, and find another to
see to your needs. I, in any event, have no interest in
one such as you."

I didn't know what Fallan had in mind by showing
up there, but his invaluable help had already screwed
things up for me and I didn't want any more of it. I was
hoping he'd take the hint and get out of my life, but
instead he got annoyed.

"So you have no interest in one such as I, eh, child?"
he asked in the same low voice that I had used, even
more of a growl in it. "You seem rather high and
mighty for a slave, and badly trained indeed. Have you
not been given punishment for failing to please?"

My body blazed hot at his words and heavy need
flashed through me, reactions triggered by his obvious

disapproval. I'd been conditioned to react like that by what I'd gone through, and Bellna's added reactions made mine impossibly worse. I was being forced into wanting to please him, and a grin touched his ugly face when he saw me squirm.

"So you *have* been trained to some extent," he murmured, reaching a hand out to touch his palm to one of my hardened nipples. "Have they used you harshly?"

"I have not been used at all," I gasped, really suffering from that single, casual touch. "Do not touch me so! Do not . . ."

"You have not been used at all, and that is both punishment and training," he said, a musing tone to his voice as he looked down into my eyes. "Have you acknowledged yourself a slave as yet, or addressed those about you as master?"

"No," I whispered, feeling my control losing its grip against Bellna's frenzied attack for the upper hand. She had *Fallan* there, and she wanted him so badly that I couldn't fight hard enough against her.

"I have come just barely in time, then," the mercenary captain said, his voice still in the low murmur he had been using. "I will free you as soon as I may, yet till then must you behave properly and become an obedient slave. You must address the free men about you as master, and refer to yourself as a slave, else shall they punish you terribly before I am able to take you to safety. Do you understand what I say?"

My head was whirling so fast I barely knew where I was, but one thing I did know was that Fallan was wrong as usual. I could see that the slavers had been trying to make me acknowledge myself a slave without forcing me to do it: if and when I did, I would be one step farther along the road they had me headed up. But doing that would take me even closer to that room with the furs and the beating that preceded it, and that was a way I didn't want to go.

"I am not—a slave—and shall not—call myself one," I got out, using the last of my strength. "I am—I am—"

"You are a spoiled, disobedient child!" he growled, his dark eyes blazing with an anger that kindled Bellna even more. "A foolish, thoughtless wench who has not the wit to know that stubbornness at the wrong time may cost her life! You think to refuse to obey me; I shall prove that you may not."

Both of his hands touched my body then, the hands of a man used to touching women and used to enjoying what he touched. I tried to hold back the moan, but it slipped from my throat as he moved even closer. "I see you have been punished for taking liberties," he said, then chuckled as I gasped at the way he touched the device. "I wonder if you have as yet had it used properly upon you."

His words came to me as if they were being filtered through a long tube, telling me Bellna had grabbed most of the control she wanted. My lips parted, ready to speak words I didn't want spoken, but this time the timing went wrong for *her*. As Fallan's left hand toyed behind me his right hand moved in front, reaching me as I strained away from the device. His touch was more gentle than anything I'd had from the slavers, but it forced me back against the device in his left hand with something like an electric shock. Again I strained forward and again I was forced back, and my mouth hung open like that of an idiot, empty of any and all words of sense. The back and forth motion was immediately overwhelming and Bellna, in control of my body, was completely caught up in it.

"You have said you are not a slave," Fallan murmured,

slowly increasing the speed of the motion he forced on me. "I believe you *are* a slave, and I would hear the words from you. Tell me you are a slave."

"I am—a slave," I whispered, eager to say any words he wished of me.

"Louder," Fallan commanded, so near that the heat of his body was evident above my own.

"I am a slave!" I shouted, lost to the touch of his hands. "I am a slave who is *your* slave! I am your slave!"

"Excellent, slave," he chuckled, again forcing a more frenzied movement upon me. "And how do you address the man whose slave you are?"

"Master!" I screamed, knowing release would be withheld from me till I acknowledged him so. "I am your slave, master! I am yours, master!"

"How obedient and pleasing a slave you are," my master chuckled, the movement of his hands never ceasing. "Now you may dance for me, slave, till your soul cries out the same."

My body flew back and forth in perfect obedience to his demands, and although I wished to scream, I no longer had the breath for it. I panted harder and harder, feeling as though my lungs would burst, and then release was mine, the likes of which I had never before felt. Again and again my body spasmed, obeying the continuing demands of my master, and when it was done I hung upon the bar, my chains enfolded, mindless from the experience—

And I was able to take over again, but not completely. I'd closed my mental eyes the way Bellna had closed my physical ones, but it was still *my* body that had been put through all that. I think I was still in shock over what Fallan had done—damn, but that man knew his way around a woman's body! I shuddered as I tried to stop my heart from racing around so fast, wishing I could lie

stretched out flat and dead somewhere instead of hanging by my wrists, and the sound of approaching footsteps caught my attention.

"My congratulations, sir," came a voice I recognized
as belonging to the man in light yellow who had directed the training I'd been put through. "You have
helped this slave to know herself, and have taken her a
good deal closer to the goal she desires—and that we
desire for her."

"I am fond of pretty little slaves," Fallan answered, a
dryness to his tone. "How much for this one?"

"Alas, but she has already been sold," light-shirt said,
professionally commiserating. "A high noble has reserved her for himself, at a price we lesser mortals
cannot even approach. She is here for training purposes
only, and yet—her training has progressed well in your
hands. Should you wish her use you may have it—if
you are willing to curtail that use in accordance with
her level of training. That she may not be fully used
should not interfere too greatly with your pleasure—
there are always alternate methods."

"I dislike being limited in my use of a slave," Fallan
answered, sounding bored with the whole thing. "I
believe I have had enough of this slave. What of that
black-haired one?"

"That one you may enjoy as you wish," light-shirt
said, professional friendliness now heavy in his voice.
"The use rooms are to your left, and you may also see
to the fees there. I wish you a pleasant time."

There were sounds of movement all around me, bringing Bellna partway out of her stupor with whimpering
protests, but this time she didn't have a chance of taking
over and wouldn't have been able to change the situation even if she had. I opened my eyes to see the
black-haired girl being released from the bar and the

ankle chain restraint, her whole body quivering with anticipation. I didn't have the strength to quiver with anticipation, even when light-shirt began unlocking my own chains. When my wrists were released from the bar I sprawled face down in the furs of the platform, and light-shirt chuckled and patted my bottom.

"You have come a far distance this day, little slave," he said, working on whatever held my ankles in place. "You have earned a time of rest before your lessons continue. You may thank me."

"Thank you—master," I whispered, silently cursing the now disappearing Fallan for having put me in a position where I had to say that. I didn't know what would happen next, but my mouth was dry and swallowing was difficult.

Light-shirt closed the cuff around my right wrist again, locked the chain under the two rings at my waist, then stepped back. My golden-shirt, whom I hadn't seen, was behind him, and he was the one who lifted me off the platform. I felt completely surrounded and out-numbered, which had to be the way I was supposed to feel—according to my training program. My golden-shirt steadied me on my feet, pulled my wrist-chain out the way he had earlier, then led me out of the tent.

We moved through the late afternoon sunshine at a slower pace than we had on the way there, and although I knew there had to be a specific reason for it, I didn't care. The cooling air was like a—a breath of fresh air after the closeness of the tent, and I wished I had the strength to appreciate it. I stumbled along in my chains after my golden-shirt, feeling my mind uncurl and spread out to the openness above. It's almost dark, I thought, relishing the words. Just a little while longer, and then you can go. I looked at the crowds of men we moved through, feeling their eyes on me as a physical thing,

and knew I *had* to get out of there soon. If I were ever
trapped in that place permanently, my life span could
be measured in minutes. Slavers don't like victims who
refuse to be good, obedient slaves, and usually don't
waste much time on them.

I was taken back to the tent I had originally come
from, but the room was somewhat different from the
others I had seen. It was small and dim, covered completely with thick luxurious fur, and held a couple of
odd-shaped somethings made of wood and fur that I
didn't like the looks of. There was also a small table
holding a familiar bowl, but I wasn't given a chance to
get more than a single glance at it.

"Kneel," my golden-shirt said as soon as we were
inside, and his slave obeyed him immediately. The fur
felt strange to my bare legs even after the fur I'd been
kneeling on on the platform, but I didn't have time to
think about that, either. The golden-shirt pulled his
boots off, got out of his clothes, then made himself
comfortable on the fur.

"Crawl to me, slave," he ordered, and when I reached
him he leaned up on one elbow and took my face in his
hand. "You are incredibly fortunate in that you have
already declared yourself slave," he said, looking down
into my eyes. "Had you not, this next lesson would
have been a good deal more painful for you. Are you
prepared for your next lesson?"

"I—was told I might have a time of rest," I whispered,
shaken by what he had said. So Fallan had been right
after all—and the dance he'd put me through had saved
me from something that would have been a lot worse.

"You have already had your time of rest," golden-
shirt answered, still holding my face. "Our return here
was leisurely, and you were to have rested then." Suddenly his hand released my face, and I was slapped hard

enough to bring tears to my eyes. "You must also learn that you are never to question a master. You were asked, slave: are you prepared for your next lesson?"

"Yes, master!" I gasped out at once, trembling and letting the tears roll down my cheeks—and making sure my hands didn't curl into fists. "I am prepared, master!"

"Excellent," he said, leaning back from me somewhat. "Go and fetch your bowl, for it is time that you be fed."

"Yes, master," I sniffled, then crawled after the bowl standing on the small wooden table. The bowl held the same soup-soaked bread I'd been fed earlier in the day, and when I brought it back I was put to my belly again before it was fed to me. I'd said I was ready for the next lesson, but the only thing I was really ready for was about twelve hours of uninterrupted sleep. I felt as close to the end of the line as I'd ever been, and that had to be why the lessons were continuing. Conditioning works best on an undefended mind, and it's hard to defend your inner self when your eyes are closing in exhaustion. I was so tired I could even feel myself reacting to the nearness of a naked male body, and that despite the release I'd so recently had. By the time my "meal" was done and I had licked golden-shirt's fingers clean, I was almost to the point of squirming.

"And now that you are fed, we may continue," golden-shirt said, tossing away the empty bowl. "Tell me what you are, slave."

"I am a slave, master," I whispered, making sure I didn't meet his eyes. "I am your slave."

"You are the slave of any free man who commands you," golden-shirt corrected. "Raise yourself to kneeling beside me, slave."

"Yes, master," I acknowledged, pulling myself to my knees with some difficulty. The device gave me its usual trouble, and golden-shirt chuckled.

"You appear to be in discomfort, slave," he said, reaching around to touch me. "Do you wish this removed?"

"Yes, master," I gasped, finding it impossible to hold still against his toying fingers.

"Then you have my permission to beg me to remove it," he said, laying himself farther back in the furs. "And, as the potion which turned me uninterested has for the most part worn off, you may also, at the same time, serve me."

I gasped at the flaring of heat all through me at the key word, finding it considerably worse than it had been. I was too tired to fight the conditioning, and Bellna was no help at all. She lay cowering in her corner of my mind, sick with fear over the thought of serving the man who had done so much to me that day. She was triggered into *wanting* to please him, but she was so afraid of him that she was frozen in place. It was all up to me again, and I had absolutely no choice.

"Oh, master, please remove the device," I wheedled, remembering the advice of the woman who had washed me. At the same time I put my hands on his body, and began gently kissing him all over. There was dark hair all over him, his body mostly hard but beginning to turn soft from easy living. I worked my way up to his throat with kisses, then licked my way slowly back down, all the while wheedling and pleading and begging in true slave style. His interest was only beginning to stir, and I found that I had no choice at all about encouraging it. I *wanted* to encourage his interest, and when his hands came to me, I *had* to. I did to him what I'd been taught to do, and I could no longer remember when I'd been taught it or by whom. When he moaned and twisted under my hands and lips the faintly disturbing thought came that I might have gone too far, but I was in no condition to worry about it. It might have been something to worry about if golden-shirt had still been in the grip of that potion and watching, but as the victim of my ministrations, he was in no condition to be cooly observant.

"Stop, s-stop," he said at last, pulling me away from him by the hair. "You have—learned your lessons—well, slave, and I am—no longer able to—bear it. Tell me again—what you would have me do."

"Master, I beg you to remove the device," I panted, breathing almost as hard as my victim. I reached my hands out to touch him, but the distance he held me away from him by the hair was too far for the chain linking my wrists. "Also do I beg for use, master. Please, master, please!"

The words I blurted out were a shock to me, but golden-shirt must have been expecting them. He laughed softly in satisfaction, then shook his head.

"The use you beg for you may not have," he said, reaching a hand out to tickle a moan out of me. "You have not yet earned the ultimate satisfaction, and will not till you have pleased the master you are meant for. There is another means by which you may give satisfaction, however, and it is for this reason that I am here. Now that your lessons have prepared me, we are able to continue on to it."

He let go of my hair and reached down to untie the front leather strip of the device, then had me put my forehead to the floor while he untied the back strip. The removal of the device itself was unbelievable relief, but that only solved half my problem. I still needed what that man was nicely prepared to give me, and I was seriously considering raping him when his hand came back to my hair and pulled me painfully to my feet. I mewled in protest, just about all I was capable of in

the way of protest just then, but I was still dragged to
one of those wood and fur contraptions and pushed face
down across it. Before I could blink away the sleepiness
clouding my thinking and stressing how much in need I
was, my wrists had been pushed through holes to either
side of the thing I lay on and clamped tight in place.
Then wheels were turned on the thing, and I lay head
down and bottom up.

"This device will hold you as I wish you to be,"
golden-shirt said as he fiddled with something between
my legs. "Tomorrow, after your lessons, I will return
for the same, and will then expect to have no need of
the device. Should I find a need for it, you will not be
released from it before you have been beaten. Am I
mistaken in believing that you will be pleasing?"

"I will be pleasing, master," I babbled, feeling a
desperate need to *be* pleasing. "I beg you to use me,
master! Please, master, please!"

"I *mean* to use you, little slave," he chuckled, moving
around the room somewhere behind me. "Not in the
manner you beg for, yet will you be used. I must,
however, first prepare myself a bit further."

I knew that what he said should have made me
suspicious, but I couldn't think clearly. A good part of
the begging and groveling I'd done had been because of
Bellna, but some of it was caused by the conditioning I
couldn't seem to hold off. I was so *tired*, and so much in
need, and my body quivered at the thought that he was
going to take care of me.

"I am now prepared for you," he said from directly
behind me, snapping me out of a half-doze and making
my body burn even more. Groggily I tried raising myself to receive him—then was roused to the point of
lifting my head.

"No, master, no!" I whimpered, feebly trying to

escape, but there was no escape. His manhood was taking the place of the device, and he'd greased himself for the purpose. I tried pulling away from the penetration that was beginning to excite me terribly, knowing it wasn't what I really wanted and wouldn't satisfy me nearly as well, but I struck something scratchy and irritating on the device that made me jerk back. I immediately cried out, simultaneously with his grunt of satisfaction; I'd lost and he had won.

I'd begged for use, but not the kind of use I was given. I couldn't think clearly, but bodily sensations came through clear as the chime of perfect crystal. I was battered at over and over again, forced against the scratchy, irritating part of the device until I began using it to satisfy the screams of my body, accepting the pain in my desperate need for release. Eventually I found the release, just before golden-shirt found his own, and I was limp when he unlocked me from the device and dumped me on the floor.

"The potion given you in your food has done well," he said, looking down at me where I lay curled up on the furs. "It will now make you sleep till the time comes for your lessons to continue. Sleep well, little slave, for the next lessons bring learning in earnest."

No, I thought as I blurrily watched him walk to his clothes. I can't sleep and wake up still here, still chained as a slave. I can't. I can't.

But my eyes were closing even then, proving that I sure as hell could.

CHAPTER 6

I awoke with a start, my heart racing and my mouth dry. I jerked my head up and looked around the dim, fur-decorated room without recognizing it, not knowing where I was or what was happening. I started to get to my feet but the tinkle of chain caught my attention—and then the memory of everything that had happened came flooding back.

I sank back down on the floor, took a deep breath, then lowered my head to my hands. My system was still twanging from the emergency wake-up I'd gone through, but being awake was more than worth it. There are a lot of drugs that have little or no effect on me, but of the ones that do, some are able to trigger emergency wake-up. The light opiate sort, mild sleeping draughts and the like, begin to break down in the body rather quickly. As soon as that breaking down starts, my nervous system triggers the release of adrenalin, which gets me up and moving even sooner than my usual fast snapback. It's a rubbing-bare-nerves-with-a-file kind of feeling to go through, but I'll take that any day as opposed to staying cozily asleep.

I took another deep breath then raised my head, still feeling the urge to stretch out and close my eyes, but not about to give in to it. I moved over to the device I'd been used on, keeping the chain-tinkling to a minimum, then began poking around the underside of the thing. I needed something to use as a lock pick, and I was hoping that that device wasn't as neat and clean-lined underneath as it was above. The Lord of Luck must have come back from the lunch break he'd been on so long; the underside of the device had all sorts of thin protrusions of metal, undoubtedly the Narellan equivalent of nails. I chose one, got a good grip on it, then started working it back and forth.

Cursing under my breath did no good whatsoever; the damned thing took its own sweet time breaking free, and time was the biggest unknown I had to work with right then. By the time I had the piece of metal in my hand I was sweating, and I went to work with it without wasting another minute. I tossed my head to get the hair out of my face and eyes then began probing the lock on my right wrist, trying to figure out how a key worked on it. The locking mechanism wasn't only primitive it was alien, and if you think all locks work on the same principle, then you've never opened one with anything but a key or a palm.

As I probed the lock I couldn't count the minutes ticking past without screwing up, but it took all the control I have to keep myself patient and attentive. I knew the slavers weren't going to let their red-haired slave sleep until she was all rested, but I didn't know how long they *would* give her. Conditioning works best on an exhausted mind, but a little too much push and the mind breaks, leaving you with nothing to show for your efforts but an empty husk. I was sure they had enough experience with twisting little girls to know how

long to give it, but *I* didn't know how long to give it. It
was surely night outside, but that wasn't likely to mean
anything to the slavers' plans, especially with the way
they were training me. I'd had to accept pain in order to
get release again, and the thought of continuing on
further with that put a tremor in my hands that I
couldn't quite ignore. If I didn't get out of there soon,
I'd be bouncing off the walls.

When the break came, I almost missed it. You can't
hear the twang of a release catch in a lock mechanism,
but with enough practice you can feel it. If I hadn't
been working left-handed I would have felt the twang
sooner, but having my right hand free first would speed
things up more after the first cuff was open than working left-handed slowed them down before that. I caught
the twang, lost it, then found it again and held it—and
the cuff flipped open at my pull. Only then did I
remember that light-shirt had used his key to lock me
up again as well as release me, which meant that the
mechanism was a variety of dead-bolt. Things might
have gone faster if I'd remembered that sooner, but
there was no sense in beating my breast over it. There
were still the other locks to take care of.

Both ankle cuffs went first, and only then did I do
the left wrist cuff. After that the only thing left was the
chain around my waist, and when I dumped the whole
rig in a heap I unknotted the thin piece of leather as
well and flung it away from me as hard as I could. The
feeling of freedom was like laughter bubbling up inside
me, making me want to shout and jump around; instead
of shouting or jumping I bent and retrieved the lock
pick I'd dropped, then spent a minute or two tying it
into my hair where it wouldn't be seen. I would keep it
until I was off that planet, and maybe even longer. A
good lock pick is hard to find, a lucky one even harder.

A quick look around the tent room showed me nothing I could use, not even a piece of cloth for clothing. Aside from the cool of the night the thought of walking around bare didn't bother me, but it would make me somewhat conspicuous. I'd intended going after one of those guards for his sword, but now it looked like I'd need his clothes, too. It would take more time than I really wanted to spend, but there was no help for it. I couldn't run around the woods of Narella bare, not when there was no telling when that scout ship would pick me—

"What have you done, slave?" came the demanding voice from behind me, causing me to turn my head in that direction. My golden-shirt stood there, something that looked like a thin, rattan cane in his hand, a frown of disbelief on his face. Bellna shivered in fear in the corner she crouched in, but all I did was smile faintly. I'd done a stupid thing not leaving that room as soon as the chains were off, but I knew I'd done it deliberately. I'd been hoping to run into my golden-shirt again—and now I had.

"You mistake me, man," I said as I stepped farther into the center of the room. "I am no slave, and therefore did as I wished to do."

"You believe you are no longer a slave due to someone's having taken the chains from you?" he asked, that superior amusement clear on his face. "The absence of chains does not make one free. Kneel!"

The snap of command in his voice made Bellna blubber in my head and try to obey, but I was riding a high too far above her to feel the same myself. Revenge is usually a pastime for the immature, but that slob had done more than just put his hands on me. You have to be a damned fool or suicidal to treat a Special Agent the way he had treated me, and I was in no mood to be forgiving or generous.

"You are correct in believing that the absence of chains does not make one free," I agreed, enjoying the frown he'd grown when I didn't fall quivering to my knees. "I am prepared to leave this place now, and will give you the opportunity to step out of my way."

"Will you indeed," he said, the superiority back again. "How very thoughtful of a slave to give her master such an opportunity. The master, however, does not choose to accept the generosity of his slave. He will, instead, choose to give his slave a sounder whipping than she was to have received. The choice is ever the master's, a thing you will now learn beyond all doubt."

He took a firmer grip on the cane he held and started toward me, his arm half raised and ready to strike. He took his time coming forward, giving me the chance to understand just how bad a mistake I'd made before getting on with the beating. There was faint disturbance in his eyes over the fact that I just stood there waiting for him, but I doubt whether he was capable of understanding that I didn't intend allowing myself to be beaten. Being very used to dealing with slaves is more dangerous than slavers seem to realize; it makes prime victims of them if they happen to tangle with a non-slave.

The golden-shirt reached me and raised his arm higher, then brought the cane whistling down toward my bare body. It would have struck my shoulder if I'd stayed where I was, but I stepped forward instead and brought up a left-handed block against his forearm. Most people think of blocks as being strictly defensive maneuvers— that is, if they've never had one used on them. The force of the block knocked the cane out of my opponent's hand; as it hit I was already going to one knee and launching a right from belt level directly into his groin, then moving fast to get out of the way. It wasn't retaliation I was expecting but reaction, and that came so fast it might have been programmed. The blood left golden-shirt's face, and even as he began folding up he was already vomiting, spasming out the terrible pain he felt. I straightened up beside him, stiffened my right hand, then clipped him good at the base of the skull, sending him sprawling into the pool of vomit he'd made. I took a split second to consider whether or not to finish him permanently, then turned away and headed for the room exit when I decided against it. It would be a long time before the man was able to function again, not to mention chasing after me. If I wasn't gone out of there before then, his being up and around would not make the difference.

I slid out into the empty corridor between rooms and moved without sound, checking each room before I passed it. Muffled sounds came from a room down at the far end, but aside from that everything was quiet. A couple of the rooms held sleeping female forms, but the rest were empty. I became aware of Bellna as I moved down the corridor, and I had to chuckle softly. The intruder in my mind was still in shock, trying to figure out what had happened. She had been so terribly afraid of the golden-shirt that she would have done anything to appease him, but three simple blows had taken him out of the picture more effectively than Fallan's fistfight had done with the house guard at the inn. She knew nothing about self defense and offense, considering the entire area reserved to those with big, bulging muscles or superior weapons. She couldn't get over the fact that *she* had done something like that, and so simply. She was beginning to think of that store of extra knowledge as magic, the store she couldn't always reach; I thought about all the hard work I'd put in acquiring it, but chuckled anyway. It *was* magic to someone who didn't know about it, and the hard work part of it just didn't enter into it.

When I reached the end of the corridor, I found that the muffled sounds were screams that were coming from the room opposite the one that led out of that section of tents. The room out was dim and deserted, and no one would have seen me go that way; all I had to do was step into the room and cross it, then melt into the darkness outside. There had to be armed guards moving around out there, and jumping one from behind would be a piece of cake. I didn't know what was causing those muffled screams across the way, and in any event it was none of my business. Getting out of there was my business, that and dressing and arming myself, and heading off south into the woods. I took a step into the room, and then a second—and then turned and ghosted fast across the corridor.

From right outside the flap separating the corridor from the room I could hear sounds other than the muffled screaming; grunting and heavy breathing came through, as well as a faint creaking. I moved the flap over a very little bit and slipped inside, but I could have made considerably more noise and still wouldn't have been noticed. A female slave with scraps of green on her was chained to a wooden contraption that bent her backward and spread her wide, an open invitation without need of a sign. A thick length of yellow cloth blindfolded her, and a fat wad of yellow cloth was stuffed in her mouth, gagging her effectively yet allowing those muffled screams to escape. The dark-gold-shirted guard stood with his sword on the floor beside him and his pants down around his knees, bracing himself with one hand on the wooden frame while he thrust down at the chained woman with his body, ramming her deep and increasing the sound of her muffled screams. His other hand was closed painfully tight on one of her breasts, and as I dropped the door flap he grunted one last time with attained release.

"You provided a barely adequate ride, slave," he muttered, resting a minute against the woman's body. "It matters not how many were before me; the ride should have been fully satisfying. Though you were placed here due to your lacks in pleasing your masters, you have apparently learned nothing. It seems I must recommend that you be kept here another day, so that the lesson might be effective. Your pain is of no consequence whatsoever; your master's pleasure is all. As I have received little pleasure, you will also be beaten. Though there is little likelihood of your attaining perfection, the beating will assist you in approaching it more closely."

The guard withdrew from the woman then, not giving a damn that she was now crying behind her blindfold and gag. He turned half away from her and reached down for his pants, saw me standing there, and straightened with a frown.

"What do you do in here, slave?" he demanded, then narrowed his eyes. "Who has removed the chains from you without ordering you to remain where you were? Or for what reason have they ordered you here?"

He really didn't understand what was going on, and the provocative smile I gave him didn't help any. I began moving toward him in a slow, deliberately sexy way, my hips swinging and my breasts thrust out, and the confusion on his face suddenly became a leer.

"You have been sent to give me a proper ride!" he said in a pouncing tone, sure he'd solved the mystery. "I know not which of my brothers sees so carefully to my needs, yet I shall learn his identity from you and give him proper thanks. You will first reawaken me, and then will I make full use of you. The gods themselves would condemn me, were I to do less."

From the way his eyes moved over me, I was surprised he wasn't standing in slobber clear up to his neck. Bellna felt a sharp stab of desire when he used the words "full use," and her passing it on to me nearly threw my timing off. I'd been waiting for him to bend toward his pants again, if only in order to get them out of the way so he could close the gap between us faster, but he started to bend while my muscles were still tightening in protest. It was pure luck that he kept his head up to watch me as he bent, and I couldn't afford to throw that luck away. Despite the throbbing in my loins I forced myself to run three steps and then jump-kick for power, the ball of my right foot striking the son just under his chin. His head snapped back even harder than his body did, the crack! coming before he slammed into the wooden contraption the woman was chained to. He bounced off, fell to the floor, then lay there in a very still, angular way.

I moved up to him fast and bent to check for a pulse, but that was just part of my habit of always making sure. I knew I'd broken his neck with the kick, and he hadn't survived as a fluke in spite of it. The woman on the frame was stirring in her chains and making gabbling noises around her gag, but I'd done all I could for her. The guard would never make another sadistic recommendation, and leaving her chained up would guarantee that she would not be blamed for his death. If freeing her had meant that she would escape to freedom I would have taken the time to unchain her, but despite all wishful thinking it would have meant nothing of the kind. She wouldn't have been able to get herself away and I couldn't take her with me, but all the same I kept my eyes away from her as I worked the dead guard free of his clothes.

I kept expecting to be interrupted, but I got the shirt and pants on and buckled on the swordbelt, and no one came in. The clothes fit as well as a man's clothes will fit on a woman just about his size, but the boots had proved impossible. They were much too big to be of use, and would have been more of a hazard than going bare-foot would be. I resettled the swordbelt around my hips, took one last glance around the room, and then walked out. Usual good-byes are fatuous; in that instance they would have been insane.

The corridor and exit room were still both empty, but I didn't understand why until I'd moved through the dark toward the main exhibition tent. The noise coming from that tent and two others of a similar size near it was incredible in the midst of the forest quiet, speaking of crowds much larger than those that had been present while I was on a platform. I still made sure to move silently through the chilly darkness, staying out of the wide pools of light thrown by the big, flickering torches set all around the three main tents. Armed guards moved around and through the streams of people going in and out of the tents, watching, directing, and generally being very visible. The slavers had a booming business going, larger than one princedom could account for. It was a safe bet that people were coming from all over, making however long a trip was necessary to check out what was being offered. As I stood behind a tree watching, one round-bellied man with three burly assistants took possession of a group of eight slave fe-males and two slave males, his brusque, businesslike manner showing that he was probably replenishing his own stock. The retailer buying from the wholesaler, so to speak, calculating his future profit even as his mer-chandise was growled and prodded into motion. When I discovered that my left hand gripped so tightly the hilt of the sword I wore that my fingernails were digging into my palm, I knew it was time to get moving—before

I did something stupid. You can't change a world all by yourself, no matter how much you'd like to give it a whirl.

I faded back from the tree and moved around some tall bushes, heading toward the outlying tents of the widespread camp, trying to be careful of where I stepped. Small twigs and branches had already gotten me a couple of times, making me decide to keep alert for any vair that might have been left standing around. Traveling by vair-back would be faster and easier than going on foot, especially on bare foot. Being free and on the move felt good, despite the direction the Bellna presence's thoughts had taken. The first sight of the display tent had brought back memory of Fallan to her, and the little girl in my head was trying to decide how she felt about him. It wasn't that she no longer had the raging hots for him; what he'd done to me in the display tent had, if anything, intensified her feelings. What bothered her was the fact that Fallan had chosen the black-haired girl instead of me to use, the idea sending jealous, flaring anger through my head. She chewed at the thought for a couple of minutes, spoiled-brat resentment boiling around, and then she remembered that light-shirt hadn't *let* Fallan use me. The interpretation wasn't strictly true, but Bellna wasn't looking for truth, only a reason to forgive Fallan. When she found one she began humming happily to herself, more than ready to fantasize about what it would have been like with Fallan if light-shirt hadn't interfered. I ignored the fantasizing and paid attention to where I was going, looking for something speedier to ride than the dashing Captain Fallan.

There were considerably fewer people around the outskirts of the camp, but most of them were guards and armed. The breeze tossed the flames of their torches around, but the illumination did nothing to pinpoint the guards without torches of their own. I could see their darker shadows moving around and looking as though they were keeping a sharp eye open, but I couldn't tell how many of them there were. I'd have to get through their line without alerting the whole pack of them, which would have been easier if I'd had a few more hours of sleep behind me. I wasn't quite at the stumbling stage yet, but if I'd been fresher I could have taken a string of vair through their line, not just the one I was thinking about.

Three vair stood tied in front of a small, dark-colored tent, all saddled and probably fresh enough to keep going most of the night. I hadn't tried for one of them yet even though I'd been close enough to make the try for a couple of minutes; those vair looked *too* handy, and I was wondering if they were there to attract any slave who managed to break loose. Walking into a trap isn't smart unless you know you can spring it without getting your foot caught, and something about the vair just didn't seem right. I stirred impatiently where I crouched behind some bushes, knowing it would be stupid not to take the time to figure out exactly what was wrong, but also knowing that I didn't have the time to spend on something like that. I either had to try for the vair or go through the line on foot, but whichever I did, it would have to be done fast.

I had just about decided to try for the vair anyway when I suddenly realized that the perimeter was under attack. Without undue noise a large group of men were suddenly appearing beside and behind the guards, and I wasn't the only one slow on the uptake. The newcomers had been so casual about their approach that the guards didn't know they were being attacked until the bodies started hitting the ground. It would have been nice if it could have kept on until all the guards were done, but professionals don't stay frozen in shock very long. Someone yelled, swords scraped hastily from scabbards, emergency torches flared, and the fight was on.

I watched swords swinging back and forth for a minute, then rose slowly to my feet behind the bush I'd crouched near. The added torchlight showed that the attackers were wearing bright red shirts and light-blue neck scarves, and once I'd seen that, picking Fallan out wasn't hard. The idiot had brought his company to free the Princess Bellna, the charge they were sworn to protect, not knowing their charge had already managed to free herself. It was bad luck of the worst sort that they had chosen to break in on the very spot I'd chosen to break out, but that just proved I wasn't the only one to see the possibilities of the place. I could have used the distraction to get clear without worrying about anyone seeing me—except for the fact that those men were there to rescue *me*. If I simply walked away they would be throwing away their lives to no purpose, especially when they tried plowing through the center of the camp. I wanted to be out of there, damn it, but now I had something else to do.

I unsheathed my sword and walked out of the shadows toward the fracas, heading in the general direction of Fallan. Bellna was wild with the thought of being near him again, but my mood was too foul for her to have a chance at taking over. I would show Fallan I was free and *then* take off, and lord help anyone who tried to get in my way that time. Some idiot guardsman backed from a mercenary he and two of his friends were trying to take out, glanced at me, then did a double-take. The dark gold shirt I wore would have been enough to make him ignore me, except that the added torchlight also showed him my long red hair and bare feet. It took him only seconds to realize that I had to be an escaping slave, and then he came at me as though I were completely unarmed.

Slaver mentality being what it is, I didn't bother warning my abrupt opponent. If the weapon I carried didn't impress him, maybe what I did with it would. As soon as he got close enough he swung his blade at mine with a good deal of muscle backing the swing, obviously intending to disarm me before we went any farther. I flicked my blade up and then down fast, missing the strike he'd planned but not missing his wrist. He howled as the point of my sword released a thick line of blood just above the back of his hand, but he wasn't bright enough to realize that the wound he'd taken had just lost him the fight. He slashed hard in the backswing, his flaring temper making him forget that he had set out to disarm me, and it wasn't hard ringing his blade with .nine and helping the attack past me.

Anger brought three more fast attacks that I either slipped or blocked, and then the guard became aware of how much pain he was in. We weren't fencing with small, nearly weightless foils, we were using the double-edged and pointed Narellan blades that demand a strong wrist and arm. The guard's arm was fine, but the nick I'd given his wrist not only drained his strength, it also gave him considerable pain every time he tried to move that brand around. His face was pale and sweat-covered in the glaring, jumping torchlight, and he cast a quick glance toward the center of the camp, but didn't see what he was hoping for. The clash of blades and cursing of men was noisy enough under most circumstances, but with the uproar being made by the customers in the main tents, it wasn't likely that reinforcements would notice the attack soon enough to come running with support. The guard's jaw tightened with grim decision, his fist tightened on his hilt despite the pain, and he came at me with a last, all-out attack that was the only hope he had.

Of course, the poor fool didn't stand a chance of reaching me. He had the brawny build that slash-and-stab fighting requires, but I was faster and had the benefit of a superior technique to back up that speed. I dodged his first two attacks, parried his next three, then beat his blade aside and buried mine in his middle.

In spite of everything he still looked stunned, and then he was sliding to his knees, on his way to the ground. I pulled my blade free, swiped it nearly clean on the back of his shirt, then continued on in the direction I'd been going.

I had to fight three or four more times before I reached Fallan, the last time more or less taking over someone else's fight. I turned from spitting my own final opponent to see Ralnor, Fallan's lieutenant, gawping at me with his mouth open and his point down. His incredulous expression said he was sure he was dreaming but didn't know how to wake up, and the guard with the bloody sword coming at him from behind just about guaranteed he never would wake up again. I jumped past Ralnor, parried the guard's strike and wiped him fast, then turned to the shaken lieutenant.

"Only a fool allows himself to be distracted during battle, Lieutenant," I purred, glancing away from him only long enough to wipe my blade. "Has something disturbed you?"

"No more than the truth that we are all fools," Ralnor muttered, wiping at his face with his free hand. "We come to rescue one who fights like the goddess of death, and end being rescued by her for whom we came. The situation is somewhat demoralizing, yet do I thank you for my life."

"You are quite welcome, Lieutenant," I answered soberly, letting my eyes continue to move all around.

"Ever have I considered the thought more commendable than the deed, and the thought evinced by you and these others has earned my gratitude. I shall not forget."

Ralnor opened his mouth to say something else, an oddly friendly expression on his face, but the words never got said. The mighty Fallan, terror of brigands and slavers, finally got himself free long enough to notice who was standing near him.

"What do you do *here*, in the midst of battle, girl?" he suddenly demanded, shouldering Ralnor aside so that he could glare down at me with his dripping sword in his hand. "Do you seek an end to your life? Do you not know that these are *men* you raise weapon to? Take yourself to a place behind me and remain there, else I shall. . . ."

"Captain!" Ralnor screamed, and Fallan whirled around and brought his sword up fast enough to keep his backbone from being separated. Three guards had attacked at once, and Ralnor moved fast to draw away at least one of the blades from his captain. I'd seen the three attackers a few seconds before Ralnor had, but Fallan's lecture had convinced me that I had no business interfering. After all, those were *men*, and I was nothing but a little girl who needed to be protected from them. I watched the fight for about five seconds, then I decided that my duty was done and turned away and headed for those vair.

I had to stop for two brief encounters before I reached the vair, and by that time I'd decided against them. The guards were taking a lot of losses, but not one of them had tried for a vair to take him out of the slaughter and away for help. There was also a dim light burning inside the tent the vair stood in front of, but no one had come out even after the battle had gotten into full swing. The whole set-up screamed trap, and I'd rather be afoot and safely clear than mounted and in trouble. I was more than willing to skirt the entire area, but pausing to help out one of the mercenaries who faced two opponents put me right near the tent, and when I stepped away from the now equalized fight, I suddenly found myself in an unequal fight of my own. Two golden-shirts jumped out of the tent with swords in their hands, their bulk blocking my path around it.

"See the silly little slave," said one to the other, gesturing toward me with his blade. "She takes the trappings of one slain in battle, and foolishly thinks herself free—and a warrior queen. Did I not say we would be best off avoiding the battle, so that we might recapture the object of this attack?"

"You did indeed say that very thing," agreed the second, showing a grin. "And now that we have her, we must return her."

The last words spoken must have been a signal; the two came at me together, swords swinging in the sort of silliness that most people consider swashbuckling sword-play. If there had been only one of them he would have been dead before he finished the swash, but with two swinging away like that I needed more room; it's down-right demeaning to get killed by that sort of charge. I jumped back to give myself counterattack room, not realizing the vair were that close—and crashed right into one of them. My back and shoulder hit the stirrup and pad and I staggered, but even the sharp stab I felt in my shoulder didn't make me go down. I tightened my grip on my hilt and started my counterattack, silently thanking the Lord of Luck, but he'd left for another lunch break and I hadn't even noticed. A leaden-ness flared into being in my shoulder and spread like an oil fire all through me, and the last thing I knew was dropping my sword and falling toward my two erst-while opponents.

CHAPTER 7

It took a long time to figure out I'd been drugged; understanding how was completely beyond me. They never let me come all the way out of it, so all I got was bits and snatches of reality all wrapped around with floating gray unconsciousness. The first bit after my almost-fight with the golden-shirts was lying in the darkness, chained again and wearing one of those slave shifts. I stirred as my body began fighting off the effects of the drug, and then there was an arm around my shoulders. I was raised up, and a metal cup was put to my lips. I had enough time to realize that the darkness came from the cloth around my eyes, and then I was swallowing the sweet liquid being poured in my mouth. Two swallows, three—and then nothing. The next time I was aware of motion, and three or four times after that as well, and then came a time when the motion stopped. I was given no more than a single swallow of the sweet liquid, and though my head whirled I didn't fall back into a world of gray. I felt myself being lifted down from something and carried, and then transferred to another pair of arms.

"She is now the property of your master," came a voice I didn't know, and hands fumbled at the cloth over my eyes, then pulled it away. "As you see, she is the one contracted for."

The small stone room we stood in was dim compared to the bright day-glow coming in through the still-open door. I tried to turn my head away from the glow, but a big hand came to my face and turned it back again.

"She is indeed the one," said a voice I might have heard once or twice before. "Why does she seem so strange?"

"It is merely the travel potion given her," said the first voice. "She is aware of that which occurs about her, yet is she beyond being upset by it. The potion also raises her receptivity, therefore are there few of our clients who object to its use."

"Indeed?" said the second voice, and the hand left my face to move under the slave shift. Waves of fire flashed through my body at the brief probing touch, and I moaned and writhed in the arms that held me. "Excellent!" the voice laughed. "Truly excellent! I must have some of that potion."

"What is here is yours, Lord," said the first voice, oily with satisfaction. "She must be given it each time she appears to be rallying from the previous dose, else it will lose its effectiveness."

"Your instructions will be followed," the second voice said. "You may now take your leave."

I heard a rattle and a very pleased, "Thank you, Lord!" but I was already being carried away. The stone room had winding stone steps, and I was carried up and up in a circle until we reached the top and a door. The door was opened and I was carried inside, then through room after room of beautiful furnishings and a vast display of wealth. A small, distant voice inside my head was beginning to cry hysterically, but nothing meant anything to me, nothing mattered. The only thing that seemed to matter was the way the second voice had touched me; I wanted more, a lot more, but whimpering and squirming weren't getting it for me.

"Is this she, master?" a female voice asked, and I realized that we'd come to a stop.

"Yes, this is she," said the second voice, still with us even though I'd thought we'd left him behind somewhere. "The master means to visit with her as soon as he may, therefore is she to be prepared against his arrival."

"It appears her preparation has already been begun," said the female voice. "See how she moves."

"She has been given a potion," said the second voice. "Should she do well under this potion, the master may give it to any slave who does not please him as she is. Are there slaves about who require such a potion?"

"No, master!" came a chorus of female answers, all sounding eager to please.

"Very well, then," said the second voice. "See to this slave."

I was put down on something very soft, and it seemed as though a number of presences left. I couldn't seem to focus on the faces of anyone around me, and even the walls and furniture turned wavery when I tried to concentrate on them. None of that bothered me, of course, only my need to be seen to. My body moved of its own accord on whatever I lay on, and I whimpered again.

"The slave child asks to be touched," came a sleek, superior-sounding female voice. "I believe I will be the one to touch her."

"Now?" asked another, sounding a good deal younger. "The master may not arrive for some time, and the child is already in need."

"When the master arrives, she will be screaming to

please him," the sleek voice answered. "The master will be pleased, and it will have been I who assured his pleasure. Take yourself elsewhere, slaves, and seek in vain to please him as much as I will have done."

Sleek-voice laughed then, and after a minute I knew she had moved nearer to me. I had no idea what would happen until she touched me, and then I gasped and nearly choked.

"All slaves know that the master's touch is ever most welcome," sleek-voice purred in my ear. "And yet it needs a woman to know best the weaknesses of another woman. To be touched in this manner is more than I am able to bear, slave child. How do *you* find it?"

If I'd been able to speak, I wouldn't have been able to speak; the woman's logic was faultless. I spent a time-less time writhing and trying to escape, helpless to help myself, and then a new voice interrupted.

"What do you do here, slave?" the male voice demanded, a voice I seemed to know. "For what reason do you concern yourself with the new slave?"

"Master, I am merely engaged in preparing her for you," sleek-voice answered, sounding a good deal less self-satisfied. "She will beg for the least attention from you, the smallest glance, the briefest touch."

"This was not the reason for her purchase," the male voice answered, sounding annoyed. "Those fools at the slave market tell me they are unable to train her as I wish her trained, and have sent her sooner than she was to have come. They gave no reason for such hasty delivery, yet the reason is clear enough: they fear to face what for them would be failure. I, myself, will not allow such failure." The voice paused for a second and then said, "She seems unaware of my presence. What has been done to her?"

"Master, she has been given a potion," sleek voice

quavered, for some reason more frightened than she had been. "We are to continue with the potion, so that she will be. . . ."

"Unaware of her true fate!" the male voice snapped, wild with rage. "My enemies seek to take my victory from me, to turn its sweetness bitter! How is she to be properly trained if she is unaware of my existence? The potion is not to be given to her again, and I am to be informed when its hold begins to loosen upon her. See to it, slave."

"Yes, master," sleek-voice whispered, and then I was alone in my wavery, need-filled world. It seemed to take a very long while, but slowly I began to be aware of the fur I lay on, the furniture and decorations around me, and occasionally passing people, a lessening in the need forced on me. I lay still with my eyes unfocused, resisting the urge to take a deep breath, coaxing my mind into working again. The thought that I'd been drugged came through for the second time, but now I thought I knew how it had been done. That sticking pain I'd felt in my shoulder when I'd struck the vair's saddle; a needle set into the stirrup pad could have done the work, and would have been in the perfect position to down anyone foolish enough to climb into the saddle. In order to put your foot into the stirrup you'd have to set your leg against the pad, and that would be it as far as staying conscious went. I'd been right in thinking there was a trap and in deciding against the vair; I just should have stayed farther away from them.

My mind wandered for the next couple of minutes, and then it came back to something the male voice had said. Those slavers hadn't told anyone about what I'd done to their people, and they hadn't kept me for further training. I had a funny feeling that it was the golden-shirt I hadn't killed who had gotten me out of that training program. The dead guard could have been killed by accident as far as anyone knew, but there was no doubt about what had happened to the golden-shirt. The slavers wanted nothing more to do with me, but they didn't have the stomach to tell my present owner what I was really like. As paranoid as he was, he'd be sure they were lying in some sort of attempt to trick him out of what was his—and then he'd take steps to get even. No, the slavers couldn't tell their good patron Prince Clero the unlikely truth, and if I had any luck at all, that omission would be my ticket out of there.

Good old Prince Clero. My memory told me that it was his voice I'd tagged as the male voice; I'd just been in no shape to identify it sooner. He'd stopped his sleek-voice female slave from continuing to torture me, but I knew damned well that he hadn't done it out of the goodness of his heart. He had something special in mind for me—or for the Princess Bellna—and knowing approximately where the slavers' training program had been going gave me some idea as to his bottom-line expectations. It wasn't a pleasant thought, especially when you added in the hinting Dameron had done. The room I lay in was somewhat on the warm side, but I still felt a shiver touch me.

"So you have come back to yourself at last," a female voice said from behind me, the woman I thought of as sleek-voice. I'd been aware of *someone* sitting behind me, and there was no sense in trying to pretend I was still under. I still felt sluggish, but hoped the feeling would pass quickly enough to keep from being a problem. I pushed myself into sitting with a small amount of difficulty, then turned to look at the woman.

"I am indeed recovered," I answered, making sure I sounded frightened and uncertain, then spent a minute or two staring at the woman. She was a very beautiful blonde with gray eyes—and she wore the clothing of a woman of the upper classes. No chains, no skimpy little slave shift; a real, dark red dress and shoes, with plain jewelry and her hair put up. I let my expression show the confusion I felt and added, "What is this place? What is to be done with me?"

"You will learn that in due time," the woman answered, rising gracefully to her feet. "For the moment you will do more than obey without question. . . .she is prepared to depart, master."

The last was directed to the man who was approaching us, a man dressed in thigh-length red tunic, heavy, lace-up sandals, thick leather wrist bracers and a sheathed sword. I might have considered his get-up laughable if he hadn't also worn the casually uncaring look of a paid sword and bully. It seemed highly probable that he was a guard, and when he reached down and hauled me to my feet by one arm, the probability became a certainty.

"The Prince awaits this one with impatience," the man growled, looking me over with what seemed to be a practiced eye. "There are guests, therefore are you to follow as well."

"Yes, master," the woman responded in a low, unhappy voice as the guard began hauling me along. The room we were in was relatively small, but it was also paneled in dark wood with touches of silver decoration and silk-seated items of furniture. The carpeting on the floor was thick and soft, and it led through a doorway to another room of about the same size which was decorated just as richly. We passed through three or four rooms of that sort, but I didn't have the time for sightseeing—the guard was in a hurry, and if he hadn't been holding my arm I would have been flat on my face any number of times. We finally reached a room smaller and barer than the rest, with two beautifully carved

wooden doors standing closed in front of us, another
armed, tunic-dressed guard standing in front of the
doors. The guard gripping my arm pulled me to a halt,
then nodded to the other guard.

"The Prince awaits this one, Ryskor," he said, raising
my arm a couple of inches. "The other has been sum-
moned for the guests."

"Then she must be prepared," the guard called Ryskor
answered, showing a faint grin as he looked at the
blonde behind us. "Come to me quickly, little one. The
Prince's guests must not be kept waiting."

"Master, I am already prepared," the blonde quavered,
fingers tugging nervously at each other as her eyes
pleaded with the guard. "Rarely is a latecomer chosen
to tend a guest, yet should I be chosen despite this, I
will give such pleasure as has never. . . ."

"Ah, ah, ah," Ryskor interrupted with a wider grin,
waving a finger at her as he walked toward a heavy
wooden chair. "The Prince has decreed that no slave
shall pass those doors without first having been prepared.
You will then strive that much harder for the privilege
of giving pleasure. Come here!"

The snap in the last two words made the woman
jump, then started her toward the guard, who was
sitting himself in the chair. When she reached him he
took her by the waist and sat her down on his left knee,
then put his left arm around her waist. One of her
hands went to his shoulder and the other to the arm
around her, but bracing herself did no good at all. As
soon as his free and began rising under her long skirts, she
shut her eyes and threw her head back.

"Master, I beg pity!" she whimpered, moving slightly
against the restraining arm around her. "I have not been
used since last I was prepared, and I cannot resist your
touch! Please do not— Oh! Oh, no!"

I turned my head away so as not to have to watch the woman being "prepared," but I couldn't keep from hearing her pleading, gasping and struggling. They wanted her hot for the Prince's guests and hot she was made, none of them giving a damn how much she would suffer until she was taken care of—*if* she was taken care of. The guard holding my arm watched the proceedings with a faintly amused look on his face, which was a damned good thing for me; my hands had curled into fists below the wrist cuffs, and if he hadn't been watching the show he would have seen it. I just stood there staring at the beautifully carved doors, fighting to calm down enough to open my hands, aware of the trembling silence coming from the Bellna presence. She knew where we were as well as I did and the thought frightened her, but she could feel the fury inside me and was somehow comforted by it. If she'd had any sense, comfort would have been the last thing she felt; losing your temper in a dangerous situation is a good way of getting yourself killed, but I wasn't far from doing exactly that. I was out of patience with these big, strong manly men, and was waiting for nothing more than a couple of minutes alone to dump those chains. After that we'd see how big and strong they were.

It didn't take long to get the blonde woman properly primed; the harder part was getting her calmed down enough to pretend that nothing had been done to her. It seemed to be part of the twisted game that she show nothing of the need forced on her, but it took both of the guard males to hold her until she stopped trying to reach herself. The thing that really bothered me was the fact that she hadn't once screamed or raised her voice to a shout during the entire incident, even though she had panted, mewled, struggled and sobbed without tears. Quiet hysterics were fine, but noise was out. That high a degree of conditioning made me sick, but it also began to disturb me. If that was what Clero did to female slaves as a matter of course, what did he have in mind for *me*?

I was willing to consider the question academically on a cold winter's night some place far from there, but that sort of willingness didn't help me much. I tried fading past the guards while they were involved with the blonde, but they weren't involved enough to have forgotten about me. I was just beginning to believe it might be clear when a sandaled foot hooked the chain between my ankles and pulled hard, sending me down to the floor with a crash and a clank of chain. I broke the fall with my hands to keep anything else from breaking, but it still hurt to land on the wrist chains with my body. My guard came over and hauled me to my feet again, pushed me back toward the doors with a shove, then laughed when I tripped and went down again. I was pulled to my feet and then shoved two more times, finally being allowed to just lie there while the blonde straightened her clothing and hair so that she would be presentable. The carpeting was soft but the flooring under it was hard, and I'd been shown what trying to slip away had bought me. I hurt where the chains had repeatedly slammed into me, but that wasn't the reason I kept my head down. I felt so close to snarling it frightened me; what the hell had happened to the self-control I had started out with?

I winced inwardly when I was pulled erect for the last time, then went along quietly in the grip of the guard. The second guard opened one of the doors for us and the blonde followed, walking stiffly with a ghastly smile on her face. She hurried as fast as she could, peering anxiously ahead to get a glimpse of the guest situation, then choked softly when she saw. There were

four men with Clero—and seven women dressed the
way she was.

If I hadn't been in the middle of that insane situation,
the scene would have looked normal if not downright
dull. Prince Clero stood in the center of the group,
dressed in dark red and white, his sword and swordbelt
and those of his guests clearly expensive and made for
the upper classes. They spoke in light tones to each
other and the women, who laughed appreciatively at the
jokes and urged the men to try the dozens of dishes
standing on a side table. Sight of all that food made me
realize how hungry I was, but I was also able to see that
none of the women were eating unless they were fed
something by one of the men. Clero turned away from
the others to see me, and his face suddenly creased into a
warm, beautiful smile that made him look even more
friendly and trustworthy than he normally looked. He
continued smiling beatifically while I was dragged right
up to him, then he half-turned and gestured for the
attention of the others.

"Come, my friends, and give me your opinion of my
newest acquisition," he said in a smugly pleased voice,
his eyes still on me. "Is she not worth the price I paid?"

The other four men left the circle of women to join
Clero, and then five pairs of eyes glittered at me. I
stood in the grip of the guard, trying to look suitably
beaten down, but somehow I didn't think I was making
it. I don't like being looked at like that, and my normal
self-control was still misplaced.

"For one so young she is truly remarkable," one of
the men commented, letting his eyes move all over me
as he sipped from the goblet he was holding. "She also
bears a striking resemblance to a certain high-born young
lady of our acquaintance, and yet this cannot be she.
That particular young lady would not have fallen slave."

"Which is a fortunate thing," said another, a stout man with a slobbering leer. "Were she that particular young lady, it would be necessary for us to remove her from among the living, to spare her poor father the shame of knowing his daughter lived as a slave."

Bellna began trembling at their thinly veiled threat, struck by the horror of her predicament all over again, and I showed everything she felt, making the men around me laugh in amusement. It was suddenly easier to act the way a helplessly trapped young girl should be acting, and that told me my previous trouble with controlling myself had been Bellna again. I stood with eyes downcast, trembling in the grip of the guard next to me, trying to figure out how Bellna had gotten to me without my knowing it, but I wasn't given the time I needed to understand what had happened. The men were enjoying their laugh at my expense, but the round and leering fellow had something else to say.

"How gratifying that the slave makes no attempt to claim a falsely elevated status," he drawled, moving slowly closer until he was no more than inches away from me. "And how generous of you, my lord, to offer her use to us."

All four of the men were suddenly closer, their drooling approval of that idea thick enough to feel, none of them aware of the stricken looks covering the faces of the eight slave women. Bellna's panic made me cringe back wide-eyed against the guard holding me, and Clero chuckled indulgently.

"Your interest frightens the child, my friends," he drawled, getting a good deal of pleasure out of the flinching fear I was showing. "I may perhaps grant you her use later this day, should her training advance in a satisfactory manner. By then, however, you may no longer wish her use."

The men's leers froze, and without their taking a single step they were no longer as close as they had been. A chill descended on the group as a whole, but Clero never noticed it.

"She will, of course, be one of my special prizes," he said, his eyes still glued to me. "She will be taught to hate and fear sexual congress, and to find exquisite release only in the pain of the knife. Her lovely body will be made even lovelier by the scars of the patterns of pleasure—will it not?"

He turned to look at his guests then, and they hastened to assure him that everything he said was true. The man beamed with pleasure at their agreement, never seeing that their blood was probably running almost as cold as mine. The sort of conditioning Clero intended was more than possible; with the right preparation and enough repetition, almost any woman could be taught to respond to a blade the way others responded to men. Sight of the knife hilt would bring on the stirrings of desire, unsheathing the blade would build uncontrollable arousal; the need to be touched by that sharpened edge would grow and grow—until the first, light stroke came to approximate penetration. Abandoned frenzy would grow as the pain grew and then, at the height of agony, release would finally come. It could be done, I knew it could be done, and as I stared at Clero's happily smiling face I shook with the revulsion I felt. I didn't know how many little girls he'd laughingly cut to pieces while they begged for more, and I didn't care. I just knew I wouldn't let him make me one of them.

"Now that we have seen her, you may begin with her," Clero said to the guard holding my arm, the warmth of his expression and tone suitable for offering cookies and milk. "Take her to the holding room beside

the punishment cells, remove those chains and replace
them with the usual coarse-fiber rope, and then use her.
See that at least another ten of my tower guard also use
her, but take care that no permanent injury is given her.
Do not allow her to become aroused, and do not allow
her to feel pleasure. Others will make her feel those
things."

Clero's pleasant chuckle turned his guests pale and
made a couple of them swallow hard, but all the guard
did was nod wordlessly and begin to hustle me out of
the room. Bellna was crouched in a far corner of my
mind, pulsing out whimpering terror, and more than
one tendril of that terror was beginning to wrap itself
around me. Clero had told the guard to take the chains I
wore and replace them with rope, which would make
the lock pick I had hidden absolutely worthless. The
number of dates he had lined up for me would also go a
far piece toward ruining the day, and I could feel
desperation tightening the muscles of my body. Whatever I did in the way of escaping would have to be done
before the line started to form; after the kind of rape
Clero had prescribed for me, I'd be in no condition to
do anything but lie there and moan.

The guard dragged me out of the great presence and
through the doors, and then we went back the way we
had come. We continued on past the spot I had started
from, went through four or five more rooms, then came
to a bare-stoned stair area, beyond which was a door.
Another guard lounged against a wall in the stair area,
but the guard holding my arm did no more than nod to
him before opening the door, shoving me through, then
closing it behind us. I'd been too preoccupied to notice
it sooner, but my guard was angry; when the door was
closed behind us, I found out why.

"Princess," he muttered under his breath, shoving me

again toward a low wooden table which was, along with a matching bench, the only furniture in the bare stone room. There was also a pile of rope in one corner, but rope didn't usually count as furnishings. "They waste what other men would kill to possess. A slave such as this one—to be put beyond the reach of men!"

The idea made him furious, and he pushed me so hard that I stumbled two steps and landed belly-down on the low table, the wrist chain digging into my body again and the ring knocking the wind out of me. I lay there with my teeth clenched, sucking air back into my lungs, suddenly as furious as the righteously indignant guard. He wasn't bothered because of what would be done to me—he was bothered by the fact that I would no longer be available for him to do what *he* wanted to do to me. He was a junior grade sadist too limited to make the big time, and the lack grated. I started to push myself off the wooden table, nearly trembling with a rage that waited for nothing more than the chains to be unlocked, but a big hand in the middle of my back pushed me flat again.

"A slave does not stir from where she is placed," I was informed by a cold voice, the hand holding me down to the table. "You will be informed when you have my permission to move about—else you will find what punishment you did earlier. Do you wish to be punished?"

"No, master," I forced myself to say in a meek whisper. Just unlock those chains, master, and then we'll talk about movement and punishment.

"A pity," he commented, bringing a key to my left wrist cuff and opening it. "A body such as yours is made for no other thing than punishment. I may perhaps fetch a whip before I am done with you."

And I may perhaps shove that whip clear up to your

putrid heart, I growled to myself, then gasped as my left arm was twisted hard behind my back. A second later a rope was being tied around my wrist, and I found out what Clero had meant by coarse-fibered; the damned thing felt like barbed wire digging into my skin. I gasped again and jumped involuntarily, but all that got me was a knee in the back and an amused chuckle.

"After my first use of you, I shall use a length or two of this rope as a seat upon which you may be ridden," the bastard said, reaching over my right shoulder to unlock the right wrist cuff. "When the ride is done, you will find arousal and pleasure completely beyond you— just as the Prince wishes. For your first use, however, you will respond as *I* wish. Another moment and we may have a closer look at you."

The extra moment was used up tying my right wrist to my left, an action I found as painful as you would expect with rope like that. It hurt even though I didn't struggle at all, and then I was turned roughly on my back.

"That slave rag will hamper my enjoyment of you," the man remarked, bringing his key to the chain around my waist and unlocking it, then pulling it free of my body and throwing it aside. "You will have little further need of it, therefore . . ."

The sound his hands made ripping the slave shift open ended his sentence, and then he tossed the torn pieces of cloth to either side of me, the look in his eyes heating up as he took me in. The small table was so low and narrow that he was able to straddle me across my thighs and still stay on his feet, and as I looked up at him he reached down and stroked his fingers across my stomach.

"I am familiar with the slave market you come from,"

he said, grinning faintly as he watched my face. "At one time I was employed there, before I accepted employment with the Prince. You had best be prepared to serve me."

His grin stretched as he watched me choke, the strength of the heat flashing through me widening my eyes in disbelief. My body was writhing uncontrollably on the narrow table, suddenly in the grip of a horrible, crippling need. He'd keyed me with the conditioning word "serve," but worse than that he'd keyed Bellna. It was mostly *her* lack of control that was doing me in, but there was no way for me to stop it. I moaned and struggled to reach the burning that was destroying me, and to my horror the pain I felt in my wrists from pulling at the rope actively increased my need. I was responding all at once to every bit of conditioning I'd been subjected to, and the guard laughed as he put his hand between my thighs.

"I do believe you are already prepared," he said, enjoying the way I gurgled and bumped at the toying motion of his fingers. I needed him in me so badly I thought I would die, but he was in no hurry. "It pleases me to see you so eager to serve, slave," he added with another laugh.

I screamed. Total insanity took me so completely that I remember nothing of what happened immediately after the scream, not until the swirling golden mists faded to the point where I could fight my way out of them. The guard was deep inside me, jolting me into the table with the force of pure abandonment, his swordbelt and sword gone, the ankle chain gone from my ankles. I became aware of the Bellna presence in my head, mindless with released need and simply floating, drinking in the sensations being forced on my body. She was actually enjoying being raped, but it was still my body and

I still didn't. My arms, wrists and hands hurt, and so did my back, but none of that mattered. What did matter was that the guard was jolting me harder and harder, nearing release, and that meant it would soon be over. Right after that, if I could still move, it would be my turn.

The guard held back longer than I thought he could, but every man has his limit. He held tight to my thighs when he reached his, enjoying it to the end, and then he reached over to squeeze one of my breasts.

"Should the Prince wish to see a child put upon you, it may already be done," he panted with a chuckle. "Once, a number of us were set the task of filling the belly of a pain slave. She screamed and fought each time one of us entered her, unable to feel pleasure in the absence of a knife edge. We plumbed her well, we did, pleasuring ourselves in the tightness of her even as we were forced to look away from the scars which covered her. It was her time when she was given to us, therefore did she soon begin to swell, and yet the effort was all for naught. The brat she dropped was male, therefore was its throat quickly cut. Had it been a girl child, the Prince would have had it raised in his own way."

He laughed as he withdrew from me, but I couldn't help shuddering. Clero had surrounded himself with men as twisted as he was, and just being there made me sick to my stomach. There was no doubt that I had to get out of there, and no room for doubt in my mind that I would. I forced myself to sitting on the narrow table, ignoring all pain and weariness, and turned my head to see the guard crouched near a wall, measuring out two more lengths of the rope already on my wrists. My insides tightened at the sight, and I backed up away from the table to the far wall.

"Do you seek to escape, slave?" the man asked, a

chuckle accompanying his glance as his hands kept
working. "There will be no escape for you, and now
there must be additional punishment as well. First you
will ride the rope, and then you will wear it as I drive
you about the room. Afterward, you will no longer
consider moving about without permission."

The idea gave him such a kick that his chuckle grew
to a laugh, and I just couldn't stand any more. If I
didn't get out of there right then, the game would be
permanently over for me. The stone floor didn't look
very appealing, but there was no choice at all. I ran two
quick steps forward, ducked my head as I dived for the
stones, flipped over smoothly despite what my body felt
like, and came up out of the roll with my bound arms in
front of me rather than behind. It had taken me a long
time to perfect that manuever, and I'd bothered with it
only because of the shock value it produced. My shoulders blazed with pain as I came erect in front of the
gawking guard, but pain didn't matter next to the grim
pleasure I felt. I took one more step forward and kicked
the crouching guard right in the face, hearing his nose
and some of his teeth break as he shot back against the
wall. He hit with a heavy thwak and slid down to lie
motionless on his side, but right then that wasn't good
enough for me. I moved over to him, pulled him flat by
one arm, gauged distances quickly, then axe-kicked him
right in the throat. The downward arc of the kick
caught him in the windpipe, and that was the end of
fun-and-games time for him for keeps.

I stepped back from the body and found that I was
trembling, but more with enjoyment than from reaction.
The thought of enjoying that sort of killing shocked me,
and I turned fast to find the sword the guard had taken
off. That world was beginning to get to me, and the
best thing I could do was get off it as soon as possible.

It took me a few minutes to set up the guard's sword in a position where I could use its edge, and another few minutes to saw through the ropes on my wrists. With the rope gone I could move my arms more freely, but my wrists felt as though they'd been dragged through miles of wire studs. The skin was rubbed raw in spots and a few of those spots had bled, but the wrists themselves should still be strong enough to do what had to be done. Hell, they *would* be strong enough; I was in no mood for throwing in the towel.

I'd been considering my plan of action while I was working on the ropes, and it had become clear that I couldn't just walk out of that place. I needed clothes and something to eat, and then I could be on my way. A small window high up in one of the walls showed that it was getting dark outside, so the delay of hunting up clothes and food would work out rather well. It was easier losing pursuit in the dark, and there would probably be pursuit to lose. Clero's guard setup would have very few holes, even from the inside out.

With my arms free and working again, I took the dead guard's sword and simply walked out of the room. The stairs guard wasn't so startled that he didn't draw his own weapon when he saw me, but it didn't do him much good. I held the sword sheath in my left hand, and used it as a combination shield and main gauche; three passes and the stairs guard was done, crumpling to the floor with blood running out of him in a steady stream. I wiped off the worst of the mess on my blade onto his shoulder, then moved more cautiously as I reentered the first of the tower rooms. There hadn't been many people around the last time I'd been through them, but there was no sense in taking any unnecessary chances.

The first room was nothing but a sitting room with

padded benches, and the second was almost the same but with floor cushions as well. The third had everything I was looking for, which was a damned good thing; the deeper I went into that tower the more trapped I felt, and I wouldn't have been able to go on very far. A table against the side wall held half-a-dozen dishes of food, and a prettily carved panel slid aside to show a wide selection of women's clothing. I had an idea that Clero and his closest cronies made a habit of sitting in the comfortable chairs in that room and nibbling at the food while they played dress-up with their living toys. I could only guess at how stimulating it was for those men, to have what looked to be high-born women in front of them and be able to do anything they pleased with them. To order them to strip naked, and then watch as they put on what they were told to put on. Or have one put on nothing at all while the others dressed to the teeth. I shook my head as I helped myself to a side of cold roast fowl, then carried the food to the closet. I usually try not to make value judgments on what other people consider fun, but the men of that planet were just too much.

It didn't take long to make my choice among the clothing, and it was perfect for my needs. The thing looked like a regular dress but it was a riding dress, the two legs of the pants-equivalent flowing together to disguise its nature. It would give me as much moving room as I needed without being obvious about it, and there was even a cape and a pair of boots that fit reasonably well. I pulled out the items I needed, took another bite of the roast whatever, then began getting dressed.

By the time the dress and boots were on and closed, there wasn't much left of the roast. I chewed the last of the meat off the bones, tossed away the half skeleton

and wiped my hands on a delicately embroidered cloth,
then wasted another couple of seconds looking for something to drink. There was nothing on the table but a
thick, heavy wine, and I wanted nothing to do with it.
Water would have been perfect, but water was much
too common for the people who used that room. I made
a small sound of disgust, turned away from the table—
then stood very still.

"I do hope you are not thinking of leaving us, my
dear," Prince Clero said smoothly, that beautiful smile
aimed directly at me as he looked me over. "You would
surely wound my self-conception as a host—in addition
to disappointing my other guests."

"Allow me to suggest that you entertain your other
guests personally," I said, cursing the fact that he'd felt
the urge to take a walk, but relieved to see that he was
alone. If he'd had a bunch of guards with him, it might
have gotten sticky. "They would surely enjoy the opportunity of doing to you what you so often do to others."

"I do not allow impertinence to my slaves!" he snapped,
taking one angry step toward me. "Nor do I allow
certain of them clothing! You may now remove those
things and put yourself at my feet for the beating you
have earned! You have my word that you will be well
punished before you are again allowed to serve!"

I gasped and doubled over as he hit me with the
keying word, finding it impossible to touch myself despite the screaming flames racing through me. I'd been
conditioned against touching myself at a time like that,
and I went to my knees with the effort of trying to fight
back. And then I felt myself pushed flat to the carpeting,
and a hand moved deliberately under one leg of the
riding dress and all the way up to its target.

"You are helpless to do other than obey me, slave,"
Clero gloated as I cried out against the way his hand

began to control me. "You may struggle and cry and dream of disobedience, and yet you will not disobey. Your master will not allow you to disobey. He will allow you no more than a taste of the whip."

I lay face down on the carpeting, leaning on the top of my forehead, my hands clawing at the nap for the double grip I needed so badly, my body twisting and writhing to Clero's merciless urgings. I'd been conditioned as a slave and I was reacting like one, but I wasn't a slave. I was free, damn it, and no one could touch me like that or whip me and get away with it! No one! I tried to break loose from what Clero was doing, moaned when I couldn't, and then felt the fear. If I didn't get loose he would have me to whip forever, and the rage and terror of that thought rose up so strongly that I was able to feel nothing else. The strength of panic let me push myself into a sideways roll, and as I rolled I brought my feet up and hit Clero right in the face. There was no skill or damaging strength in that double desperation kick, but it was enough to knock the man away from me. I rolled two more times, threw myself to my feet with the last roll, then grabbed the sword I'd taken from the first guard and turned to face Clero. The Prince was rising slowly to his feet, one hand to the bleeding cut on his lip, his insane eyes seeing nothing of the way I struggled to calm my breathing. He lowered his hand and saw the blood on it, raised those eyes to me again, and a blood-chilling growl escaped his throat.

"You would dare!" he hissed, all rationality gone as he held his hand out toward me, his very round eyes blazing. "I will one day be king, and yet you dared to strike at me! At *me!* For that I will mark you so that no one will ever again look upon you without the need to shudder! You will live on and on, suffering the most horrible tortures I am able to devise! You will regret many times over the sin you have committed, yet there will be no surcease! None! You have the word of a king!"

He drew his sword slowly and began to advance on me, and I wondered if he realized that I stood there with my own sword. He was so far out of it that all he wanted to do was carve me up, but his ranting had given me the time I needed to steady down. My nerves still felt raw and bloody, but at least my hand was steady as I stepped out a short way to meet him. Clero closed the distance between us and swung at my face with his point, his intention obvious and easy to parry. I ducked his backswing and parried four more wild tries at my face, and then a few more threads in his mind snapped. He voiced a terrible scream and attacked without any attempt at defending himself, a sudden all-out rush that usually demoralizes an opponent enough to let your point reach his middle. Clero seemed to have given up on his previous ideas and was now trying to put an end to me, and my arm felt the jarring shock every time our blades met. I backed a couple of steps against the onslaught, knowing I couldn't stand long against his hysterical strength, but I couldn't disengage and I was running out of backing room. I could feel the sweat on my forehead—and the way my whole body ached—and then all of that was gone from my awareness. For a split second there was an opening through Clero's wild swings, and instinct took over. I beat his blade aside and lunged for him with every ounce of speed I possessed—and only just made it. My blade sunk deep into the middle of his chest, but his gouged along my ribs, no more than an inch away from doing some real damage. Pain flared wildly in my side as I yanked my blade free, but at least I was still in a condition to notice pain. Prince Clero was beyond that, his mad eyes glazing over even as he crumpled to the carpeting at my feet. I watched him all the way down before grabbing my cape and putting it on, then, with sword held somewhat firmly ahead of me, got the hell out of there.

There was a guard at the bottom of the spiraling stone staircase, but unfortunately for him he was taking a stretch with his back to the stairs when I reached bottom. I don't think I killed him, but if the hilt of my sword didn't give him a skull fracture, the Lord of Luck was guarding him. I stepped over his body and eased my way outside, then dived into the deepening shadows around the tower's base. The thing stood a good distance from Clero's keep, but it still took some skill and effort to cross the open space without being seen, even with twilight and a dark cape both doing their bit to help. I was prepared to walk away from that place if I had to, but one of Clero's mounted guards spotted me once I made the woods. He came galloping up with the clear intention of making a fight of it, but then he saw I was female. There was just enough light to make out his grin, and then he resheathed his sword and started to dismount. I felt absolutely no hesitation about putting my point in his back, and then stepping on his body to reach his vair's saddle; playing fair when your life is at stake is a pastime for professional suicides. I turned the vair in the direction that should have been south, and dug my heels in.

I was able to put a decent number of miles behind me before I absolutely had to stop. The pain in my side was sharp enough to let me know it was there, but that wasn't the main problem. I knew the wound was still bleeding, because the entire left side of my riding dress was warm and soggy and slowly getting soggier. The night was dark now, but a single moon shone brightly almost directly over my head, and I wondered if Dameron was looking down at me while I was looking up at him. The air smelled woodsy-fresh and damp, with a light breeze blowing enough to feather my hair, but I could still smell vair sweat from the way I'd pushed my mount, and the leather smell of the saddle added itself to the rest until I began feeling queasy. I drew rein beside a small stand of thin trees, dismounted and tied the vair, then walked a few steps away before beginning to tear up my cape lining. The makeshift bandages should take care of the bleeding, but I needed a few lungsful of clean air to settle my stomach. I had no idea how much farther I would have to go before I was picked up, and nausea has never been my favorite riding companion.

I gave myself no more than ten minutes before moving on again. The chirping, creaking quiet of the woods was reassuring, and I rode quietly enough so as not to disturb the denizens around and about me. My vair moved at the slow pace without fighting it, his head nodding up and down in the rhythm of his gait, his breath coming out softly explosive when the scent of something he didn't like came to him. I patted his soft neck and spoke quietly but reassuringly, and he let the scent of whatever it had been pass by with nothing more than a slight shiver.

Another couple of hours went by, and I was trying to decide whether or not to give myself a short break when the vair found a stream. I didn't know if he was thirsty, but my mouth felt like a sandstorm in a desert, and the calm gurgling in the quiet of the night was pure magnet to the iron in my blood—or what there was left of it. I rode close to the stream and dismounted stiffly, holding the vair's rein as I knelt down and bent forward. My lips appreciated the ice-cold water more than my palm

did, and there was a satisfied stirring in my mind as I
drank, reminding me for the first time in hours that
Bellna was still around. There seemed to be a faint hint
of fear left around her thoughts, and she was steadfastly
refusing to think about what had happened in Clero's
tower. All she knew was that she had gotten herself out
of the mess without help from anyone, and if I'd had
the strength I would have been furious. She was nothing but a parasite, and if I could have gotten rid of her
in any way short of half killing myself, I would have
done it on the spot.

The vair next to me was standing with his head up,
sniffing the air, making no attempt to drink from the
stream. He seemed to be nervous about something, but
he'd shown himself to be a sensible beast, alert but not
skittish, and I knew he would drink when he felt it safe
to do so. I leaned forward again, to scoop up more of
that sparkling water, and the scream came so loud and
close that my blood temperature dropped ten degrees
below that of the stream water. The vair went flying off
in three directions at once, sounding a fear-filled echo to
the original scream, but I was still holding onto his rein.
When he found he couldn't take off horizontally, he
opted for vertical hysteria and reared straight up, pawing the air. I had a fast, confused picture of hooves
rising above me, and then I was flying into the stream,
no longer holding onto a rein. The ice cold water closed
over my head, but I clawed my way back up to the
surface, fighting the faint stream current and my suddenly steel-heavy clothes. The pain in my side seemed
frozen in shock, so I took advantage of the fact to pull
myself back to the bank and up onto it, where I lay still
long enough to restore my heart's natural beat.

When I finally sat up, achingly aware of Bellna's
blubbering inside my head, the first sight that met my

eyes was that of the vair, standing no more than ten feet away, calmly chewing at the grass in the moonlight. Whatever that original scream had meant, whatever had scared the living hell out of the beast, it was obviously long gone and no longer worth worrying about. My side stabbed harder than it had originally; I was sure it was bleeding again—if not still—my head ached, my lungs ached, and I was soaked head-to-toe all the way down to my skin, but there was nothing to worry about. I climbed to my feet muttering a few comments about how good vair steaks would probably be, then went to reclaim my transportation. At least with all the water I'd swallowed I wasn't thirsty anymore.

I continued on through the dark woods, but the simple presence of water added a large, messy complication to the trip. The night had been cool but bearable before my stop at the stream, but the presence of sopping wet clothes and hair changed cool and bearable to cold and shiver-making. The riding dress clung to me all over, the cape weighed an ice cold ton, and my feet squished in the boots that had once protected them from the damp. Just to make things even better, the breeze had stiffened enough to be noticeable, pulling at the wet strands of my hair with cold, invisible fingers. It took almost no time before I was shuddering violently, having trouble with even so simple a thing as holding onto the reins. The vair snorted and danced, wondering what was going on, and I tried talking myself into taking the wet clothes off, knowing I'd dry out quicker without them, but I couldn't do it. I was already so cold that I couldn't stand the thought of being bare in that wind, having nothing to keep its full breath from me. I shivered and shook, and wished to hell that I had even a thin green shawl that was dry and warm.

After a long time the shivering subsided, but I almost

didn't notice that it had stopped. My entire body had begun to ache, I was having trouble sitting straight in the saddle, and my face felt as though it were burning up. I saw the moon again and remembered all the innoculations I'd been given up there, wondered why the hell they had bothered, then gave up on wondering. I had a bad fever, probably an infection to go along with it, and I didn't even know where it had come from.

Not long after that, the moonlight took to rippling. It danced all around me, making the dark ripple with it, and my head pounded with thunder that had come out of nowhere. I was riding something, going somewhere, but I couldn't remember what or where. There seemed to be trees all around, waving tall and dark through the night, getting in my way, stopping me, making me turn back. A faint, faraway voice screamed through the thunder, but I couldn't make out what it was saying, and didn't really care. A heavy weight hung at my waist and I almost took it off and threw it away, but my left arm wasn't moving well and I couldn't fumble the buckle open.

Then I was riding through a cleared area between the trees, an area the trees had left clear, a broad, dirt and stone emptiness that I could ride on. It went on for a long while, the moonlight rippling, the thunder pounding, and then the moonlight fell from the sky and stuck to the dark in front of me, lighting up part of it in funny-looking squares. I peered at the squares as whatever I rode moved closer, and finally decided that the odd-looking squares were the windows of a house, a three-story house. I leaned heavily on my mount's neck and stared at the house, and after a while realized that it wasn't getting any closer. My mount had stopped almost directly in front of the house, and maybe the house was where I had been going. I slid off its back, nearly going all the way down to the ground, but my feet stayed under me and my knees firmed up a little, so I left whatever I'd been riding and made for a lopsided door. The door swayed back and forth, shimmering the way the dark had shimmered, but I grabbed for the doorknob to hold it still and it finally settled down enough so I could open it.

Inside was nothing I knew, nothing that had been expecting me. My eyes slitted against the bright lamp-light as I moved forward, looking at strangers seated at long tables whose conversation didn't quite penetrate the thunder in my head. I suddenly realized how warm it was in the room with heat pouring out of the fireplace, and fought with the catch that held my cape closed until it clicked open and let the cape fall to the floor behind me. Some of the strangers in the wavering room had been staring at me, but once the cape was gone one of them suddenly appeared in front of me. He wasn't very tall, but he was very fat, and his fat face frowned as his piggy eyes looked me up and down.

"Who are you, wench?" he demanded, his words and accent strange and harsh against the pounding in my ears. "How dare you enter my house so covered with wet and filth, and how dare you wear a man's weapon?"

It took a minute before I understood what he was saying, and then I started getting mad. Nobody talks to a Special Agent like that unless they're tired of living. Ringer would be mad as hell if I killed the jerk and caused an Incident, but Ringer wasn't there just then and I couldn't even remember what my assignment was. Getting mad had made my head hurt worse, and that stupid fat man was to blame. If I killed him, maybe Ringer would never know. I moved my hand to the back of my neck, looking for the knife that was usually

sheathed there, but it was gone. I didn't remember
taking it off, and the fat man was shouting at me again,
and my left hand brushed up against the weight hanging at my left side. I reached for it right-handed and
found a sword in my grip, noticing the dry, red-brown
stains with disapproval. You never leave blood on a
weapon you've used, not unless you expect to use it
again very soon. I looked up from the blood to the
shouting fat man, and felt the disapproval vanish. I'd
used the weapon and bloodied it, and now was about to
use it again. I'd clean it right as soon as I was through
using it.

Walking was hard on the tilted wooden floor of the
house, but I had to walk on it to reach the fat man. He
saw me coming and his face paled as his hands rose
protectively in front of him, but that wouldn't do him
any good. He'd find out what it meant to challenge a
Special Agent, but the knowledge wouldn't do him
much good either. Cold-blooded killers, some people
called us, and saviors of the Federation, said others, and
the hell of it was they were all right—and all wrong.

I moved another step closer to the quivering fat man,
the blade in my hand ready to do its work, and then my
hand began trembling, unequal to lifting the full weight
of the blade. My point fell to the floor, and my breath
came faster as I tried to lift the sword, tried to replace
my guard. I had fought the point up a foot or two when
a steel-hard hand grabbed my arm, and then the sword
was gone from my fist.

"No," a deep voice came, and I swung my eyes
around to see a face I knew. The face had a name,
Fallan, and I knew he was no friend.

"I'll kill you," I whispered, not knowing whether any
sound came along with the words. He held my sword
and I reached for it, but his hand refused to let go of my

arm. He looked mad as hell, his once-bright shirt dirt-ied and ringed here and there with sweat, and he wouldn't let me take my sword back.

"Sh-she would have attacked me!" the fat man quavered, sweat running down his bloated face and ridged neck. "Who is she, and what does she do here?"

"She is in my charge," Fallan said hoarsely, his eyes hard as he kept me from my weapon. "We were at-tacked by bandits and after my men and I had driven them off I discovered that she had taken a weapon and fled. She must surely be deranged from fear."

"Remove her at once!" the fat man squeaked, one trembling hand pointing behind us while I fought to keep him in focus.

"She and I are both weary," Fallan began, closing his hand tighter as I tried to pull loose. "I would have a room so . . ."

"Remove her!" the fat man repeated in a scream, his face going redder than before. "I will not have her sort in my house! Away with her, and yourself as well!"

Fallan looked ready to argue the point, but when two armed men appeared from the kitchen area he reswal-lowed the words without saying anything further. He nodded curtly, a gesture which wasn't as reassuring to the fat man as it should have been, then he turned to me. The entire room was spinning slowly around me, only a small distraction from the pain in my side, and Fallan's face blurred even as I looked at it. I knew he was no friend, knew I couldn't trust him, but it hap-pened too fast. One minute he was hazily before me, and the next he was bent forward and reaching, lifting me to his shoulder without the least effort. I cried out hoarsely and struggled, fighting to loosen his arm around my legs, but that was the wrong thing to do. The pain in my side screamed louder as the room whirled faster, and then the light and I spun away together.

CHAPTER 8

I woke up slowly, with a great deal of effort, fighting my way up out of the mists. There was daylight pouring through the window into the room I lay in, but I was too busy sorting out the dreams I'd been having to pay much attention to it.

I remembered the fight with Clero, remembered getting wounded, remembered being dumped in a stream, but after that things got hazy. I vaguely recalled riding through the woods and stopping at what must have been an inn, but nothing that happened was at all clear—and then I remembered how I'd gotten to the room I was in. Fallan. Go old Captain Fallan, leader of mercenaries and royal pain in the backside.

I moved one arm out from under the old blanket I was covered with, feeling the annoyance at Fallan rise up all over again. That he had somehow found me at the inn was obvious, as obvious as the fact that I had left there with him. I remembered coming to just as he was carrying me into a small wooden house. We passed a dingy lamp-lit room with a fireplace and ended up in a smaller room with a bed, where Fallan deposited me,

not too gently, on the bed and left me just long enough
to light a second lamp. He was back immediately and
bending over me with a frown, his big hands going to
the wound in my left side, and I hadn't had the strength
to fight him the way I'd wanted to. He'd muttered
something under his breath, almost in a snarl, and then
I was being stripped of the wet, filthy clothes and soggy
boots. The swordbelt was gone, a faint memory saying
that it had been taken back at the inn, with the sword,
so it wasn't long before Fallan had an unobstructed view
of the results of my brush with Clero. His jaw tightened as he examined the wound more closely, then he
strode out of the room altogether. I lay still, my head
pounding and all of me burning up with the roaring fire
inside me, and then Fallan was back, depositing an
armload of things on a small wooden table standing next
to the bed. The first thing he did was smear a jelly-like
substance on the gash in my ribs, and then he went on
to bandaging. The bandage was wide and much too hot,
but Fallan refused to let me pull it off. He knocked my
hands away as he reached for a large, metal cup, and
then the cup was at my lips and Fallan was forcing its
contents down my throat. I'd choked and struggled,
more than ready to throw up from the taste of the stuff,
but Fallan hadn't leaned back till the cup was empty. I
didn't know what the cup contained, but before I knew
it everything had gone black.

I moved my free arm to my face, but I really didn't
have to bother. The fever wasn't raging as high as it had
been, but it was still there, something I could feel all
over my body. I ached as though I'd exercised for hours
after not having bothered for a year, and even moving
my head around on what passed there for a pillow was
an effort. I dropped my arm back onto the bed, not
having the strength to hold it up any longer, then

cursed under my breath with a lot of feeling. I hadn't noticed it sooner, but someone—probably Fallan—had put me into an oversized nightshirt of sorts, and I felt as though I were tied tight under the blanket. I squirmed around, trying to loosen the nightshirt's hold, and my resentment against Fallan grew stronger with each useless movement. I knew the man thought he was protecting my modesty, but I'd really had more of him than I'd ever been interested in.

"So you have awakened," a voice came, and I turned my head a little to see Fallan standing in the doorway to my room. He'd changed his shirt again from the bright red of a mercenary back to the anonymous dark green, but he still wore the same black pants and boots. He looked at me with as neutral an expression as he'd ever managed, but that didn't go very far toward endearing him to me. Inside my head, the presence I'd forgotten about again came to life, stirring in eagerness at Fallan's nearness. She wanted him more than ever now, but it was her tough luck I was in no shape to accommodate either of them. If I'd tried, it probably would have killed me.

Fallan was holding a cheap, earthenware pitcher in his hand, and he left the doorway to bring it over to the small wooden table next to the bed. Once he'd put it down he turned toward me to put his hand on my forehead, and I, annoyed, reached up and knocked it away without thinking. The mercenary grabbed my wrist and held it above my head.

"Though your body has been injured, the sweetness of your nature remains intact, I see," he drawled, keeping his eyes directly on me. "It causes me great suffering to refuse your ladylike wishes, and yet the state of your health demands that I accept the painful burden. You will remain abed and under my care till you have

recovered, Missy, else shall there be harsh words between us."

He let go of my wrist and put his hand back on my
forehead, and all I wanted to do was cut that hand off at
the shoulder. I'd thought I was all through with Fallan,
finished with having to let him push me around, but
he'd barged into my life again. I was in no shape to do
anything about it then, but I tend to heal faster than
most and the job I'd had was over.

Fallan kept his hand on my forehead a good deal
longer than was necessary, then took it away with an
almost-pleased nod. He walked away from the bed
toward the window, and when he came back he was
carrying an old but beautifully carved straight-backed
chair which he deposited in the spot where he's been
standing. Once this was done he sat down as though he
were really tired, and stuck his legs out straight in front
of him with a sigh.

"Now," he pronounced, bringing his eyes to my face.
"You have a disturbing yet hopefully not serious wound,
and a high, though lessened fever. I believe I know how
you received the wound, yet the fever remains unac-
counted for. I would know how you came to acquire
it."

His tone was too dry and superior for my liking, but
I was glad to see he'd jumped to the wrong conclusion
about the wound: he thought I'd gotten it at the slave
market. It would have been too much trouble to correct
him, so I pushed the neck of the nightshirt down to get
it out of my way and returned the calm, dark gaze I was
getting.

"Do you think I acquired the fever to heat the cool of
the night?" I asked sarcastically. "The illness came out
of nothing, as though sent by the dark gods. Perhaps
you would do well to question them on the matter."

"A fever such as yours does not appear from nothing," he snorted, unsatisfied with my answer. "It may have come about as a result of the wound, yet I do not believe this the case. That you were filthy when I found you I can well understand, yet you were wet to the skin as well. What caused that?"

"I—was thrown into a stream," I muttered, wishing I didn't have to admit it. "A beast of the forest frightened my vair, and it pitched me headlong into the water. The vair was male and stupid."

Fallan ignored my half-hearted attempt at insult and frowned in thought, looking down at his knees, then brought his gaze back up.

"This stream," he mused. "Was it one from which your vair was willing to drink?"

I didn't know what he was getting at, but instead of snapping an answer I stopped to think about it, remembering how the vair had stood with his head high in the air and his nostrils flaring. I'd thought at the time that he smelled an enemy, but he just might have been getting something from the water that I couldn't detect. Fallan was watching me closely, and when I shook my head he nodded with another snort.

"Just as I suspected," he congratulated himself. "The stream you stopped at must have been visited first by barbarians. They know of ways to foul a stream for days, and do so in the hopes of catching the unwary. Had you drunk from the stream rather than bathed in it, you would surely be dead by now. Undoubtedly you were infected through your wound—it was badly inflamed when I first looked upon it. This should teach you that the woods are no place for a female alone."

He was looking so damned smug and superior that I felt like loosening his teeth. He was probably right about the barbarians having gotten to the water, but I couldn't very well call him on the part he'd missed. I *had* drunk the water, but if I admitted it I'd also have to come up with a reason why I wasn't dead. It looked like the base inoculations had been good for something after all, but I could hardly cite them as the reason for my continued existence.

Fallan sat straighter in the chair again and reached for the earthenware pitcher, then poured what looked like water into a battered metal cup that also stood on the small table. The sight and sound of that water made me immediately aware of how thick and furry my tongue was, overcoming the weakness that made me want to do nothing more than just lie still. Fallan saw me struggling to sit up so I could get at the water, and moved closer to put an arm under my shoulders to hold my head up. I took the cup with both hands, still needing the mercenary's free hand to steady it, and tried to drown myself in it all at once.

"Slowly," Fallan cautioned, not letting the cup tilt as far as I wanted it to. "You may have the water, but you must drink it slowly. It is far colder than it would be at an inn, for I drew it myself from a well just a few moments ago."

The water *was* cold, fresh and cold and gloriously satisfying. I could feel it rolling all the way down to my stomach, tracing a cool path through the heat of my body. Even Fallan's arm and hand felt cool through the nightshirt, and I knew the water would help my body fight off the fever. I finished all of it, down to the last sparkling drop, and didn't pick up on Fallan's comment until he had lowered me to the pillow again.

"I remember now," I said, pushing more of the blanket off me. "We had to leave the inn. But if we could not remain there, where are we now?"

Fallan took the blanket I'd pushed away and resettled it over me, then got to his feet.

"We are now in a Paldovar Village," he informed me. "I had little choice, yet perhaps it will prove to be for the best."

He turned and walked out of the room then, but I barely noticed it. His use of the phrase, "Paldovar Village" had triggered all sorts of informational memories from Bellna, and although she accepted the location without as much as an eye-blink, to me it was pure revelation.

Paldovar Villages were spread out all over the area and were easy to get to, but usually were never found closer to one another than twenty-five or thirty miles. Just as inns and woodsmen's houses were places for travelers to stay, Paldovar Villages always had some number of empty houses which were for the use of temporary visitors, but the difference between the Villages and the other two places of rest had nothing to do with price. Inns had paid guards to insure the safety of their guests, woodsmen's houses had the woodsman himself and the men of his family, but Paldovar Villages had nothing comparable—and didn't need it. In Paldovar Village, no one could harm anyone else!

I moved the blanket down again and squirmed around a little, trying to see all of the possibilities. I knew from Bellna's memories that it was possible to house blood enemies next door to one another in one of those villages, and each of the parties concerned would leave just as healthy as they'd come, but no one knew how they did it. The Paldovar couldn't be "questioned" in their own villages, but a few of them had been grabbed now and then when they left the vicinity of their village. Interest and curiosity had been intense, conscience and mercy nonexistent, but the Paldovar had proven themselves willing to die rather than speak a single word about how they managed their tricks. It had become an accepted fact on Tildor, no one who stayed in a Paldovar Village would be hurt, and no one had tried to find out why in a surprising number of years. I could finally understand why Dameron and his people were so frantic about the big secret, and why they refused to discuss it with strangers.

I had just enough time for a few brief thoughts on my current whereabouts before Fallan came back, carrying another metal cup. He was moving more carefully than he usually did, as though the cup held something spillable, and a horrible smell came in with him. I narrowed my eyes at the cup, suddenly remembering the battery acid he'd forced down my throat the night before, and he glanced up from putting the cup on the small table and grinned at my expression.

"As the fever is still with you, you will require further of this herb mixture," he announced pleasantly. "You will continue to have it till the fever is gone."

He was getting a big kick out of the thought of pouring that stuff down my throat again, but I wasn't about to sit still for a sadist.

"I shall require nothing of the sort," I answered as firmly as you can answer while flat on your back. "I have no desire for peasantish concoctions, nor do I have the need for them. Those of my family are well known for their powers of recuperation—*without* so-called medication."

The speech would have gone over better if I'd been on my feet, but I didn't think it was as comical as Fallan took it. His grin turned wider as he chuckled his amusement, and his head shook back and forth as he folded his arms across his chest.

"You are indeed amusing, Missy," he chuckled, "indeed

amusing. Despite the 'recuperative powers' of your family, there is little difference between peasant girl and princess. Each must be put to bed with a fever, and each must have the fever tended. Should either, in her illness, refuse to do that which is necessary, she must be made to obey. Princess or peasant, Missy, you shall obey me."

I don't always find it necessary to rise to a challenge, but there are times when nothing else will do. Sick or not, I growled low in my throat and tried to claw my way to a sitting position, but Fallan wasn't asleep. He jumped for me as soon as I began moving, and forced me down flat again with no effort whatsoever. I squirmed and fought as my arms were pushed under me and held down by the weight of his body and mine, but it was wasted effort. Bellna was mewling and trying to get me to bring him closer and somehow arouse him, and that was all I needed: someone else to fight. When I ignored her she began raving, but when I saw Fallan's hand reaching for the cup of battery acid, I did some raving of my own.

"You misbegotten lowlife!" I screamed, tossing my head back and forth. "Had I my sword in my hand your blood would be upon the ground where it belongs!"

"Then I am fortunate that you have no sword," he murmured, carefully moving the cup closer. "Will you drink or must I do the thing myself?"

At that point in time I would have died rather than give him the least amount of cooperation, but he didn't need my cooperation. When it became obvious even to him that I wasn't going to be drinking that swill on my own, he held my nose and waited until lack of air forced my mouth open, then began pouring the mixture down my throat. Amid choking and coughing I tried spitting it out again, but he was wise to that trick and held my jaw shut until I absolutely had to swallow. He emptied that damned cup to the very last drop before letting go of me, and by then it was too late. Wrapped in nausea, flattened and battered, I didn't even stay conscious long enough to see him leave the room.

The next time the mists rolled out it was daylight again, but a late-afternoon daylight. I moved around on the ancient linen, stretching my muscles and testing them, then decided to see what sort of shape I was in. Sitting up wasn't impossible, but my hand still shook when I reached for the metal cup on the little table to see if there was any water in it. The cup turned out to be half full, so I drained it without spilling too much in my lap, then took a good look around at the room.

The door to the other room was to the left of the bed I sat in and it was closed, leaving no way of telling whether or not Fallan was around. Since I heard nothing, there was a chance that he might have gone out. To the right of the bed, against the wall, stood a large wooden wardrobe, as old and as scratched as the small table directly next to the bed, but as beautifully carved as the one I'd seen in Prince Havro's lodge. The window, uncurtained and overbright with the sun's last efforts, was directly opposite the bed, and the carved, straight-backed chair had been returned to its place in front of it. Aside from these few things and the bed I was in, the room was totally bare.

As I looked around my mind was working, and it didn't take long to come to a decision. I'd been on my way to pick-up when the fever had hit, and there was no reason not to take up where I'd left off. Granted I wasn't feeling any too steady, and my strength seemed to have drained out of my toenails, but I'd continued on in worse shape in my life. I threw the old blanket into a

heap and swung my legs over the side of the bed, then
waited a minute for the dizziness to go away. The fever
was almost completely gone, the wound in my side was
barely more than tender, and if I ignored the weakness I
should be able to do what had to be done. When the
room settled down I put my feet on the bare wooden
floor and stood up, wavered a little, then decided to
hold onto the bed for support. My ears were ringing
faintly and Bellna was getting upset, but I still managed
to walk to the foot of the bed without falling all over my
own feet. Once there I took a deep breath and straightened up, then ran my fingers through my knotted hair.
It wouldn't be a snap but I would make it, and as soon
as darkness fell my trail would be obscured. The next
step was finding out if my clothes were anywhere around.

I had just let go of the footboard of the bed and had
taken a step or two toward the wardrobe on the far side
of the bed when the door behind me swung open.
Fallan started into the room with his usual broad stride,
but stopped short and stared when he saw me standing
in the middle of the room. He looked tired, as though
he'd been working hard at something, and I cursed
under my breath and wished he'd kept at it a little while
longer.

"You are awake sooner than I—" he began, obviously
surprised at seeing me, and then he realized just where
he was seeing me. "And you have left the bed. With
whose permission did you leave that bed?"

"With my own permission," I answered, ignoring the
growing annoyance in his eyes. "I dislike this place and
shall now leave it. You, of course, may stay as long as
you wish."

"How kind and generous of you." He nodded, folding his arms as he stared down at me. "And where, may
I ask, do you think to go?"

"You may *not* ask," I retorted, looking up to meet his eyes. "What destination I have in mind is none of your concern. And you need no longer waste your valuable time on me, Captain. You will receive no reward for the doing, nor even recognition. I do not return from whence I came."

A statement which, I hoped, was a lie. I'd come from Dameron's base and I wanted to get back there, but I was quickly running out of strength. My knees were vibrating when I turned away from Fallan toward the wardrobe, but his hand came to my shoulder before I could move toward it.

"You believe I care for you for no other reason than reward or recognition?" he asked, his tone unexpectedly quiet. "Is it not possible that I merely care for one who is in need of such care?"

"It may perhaps be possible." I shrugged, too tired to wonder why he wasn't feeling insulted. "After my recent experiences with the men of this area, however, I prefer to disbelieve the possibility. And I prefer, as well, to continue on alone. The presence of one of the male persuasion makes me uneasy."

"An understandable attitude," he said, still sounding unreasonably reasonable, still holding my shoulder. "You, however, must understand a thing as well. Though I am a man and therefore suspect in your eyes, you must continue to remain with me till you are well. At that time I will see you safely to wherever you wish to go. Is it agreed?"

Oh, sure, all the way back to base. Dameron would just love that, and I'd be guaranteed first prize in any unusual souvenirs contest they might have.

"No, it is not agreed," I said, turning back to look at him and knocking his hand from my shoulder. "I do not wish to remain here and I shall not. I do not care to have your company upon my journey, and I shall *not* have it. Is it so supremely difficult for you to understand that I wish to be alone?"

I wasn't feeling too well and was therefore in a lousy mood, but Fallan didn't come up with the fight I was looking for. Anger flashed briefly in his eyes when I knocked his hand away, but by the time I asked my question the anger was gone.

"The language *is*, I fear, a trifle too difficult for me," he agreed with a sigh, then moved forward fast and scooped me up off the floor into his arms. "It will be best, I think, if I return you to your bed till I am able to puzzle out your meaning. You require rest and I mean to see you have it."

I had the strength and the time to pound at him only once before I was back in that bed, flat on my back with the old blanket pulled over me. I struggled up to one elbow and glared at his grin, but all he did was pat me on the head.

"It pleases a simple man such as I to see acceptable obedience in a girl child such as you," he said with a good deal of amusement. "Your departure now would be beyond reason, and although you seem to have grown to your present size without acquiring a drop of reason, you shall not continue further without it. I will be pleased to teach you reason in our time together—during which time you will also mend and be restored to full health. I go now to fetch a bowl of the thin gruel I have prepared for you. Your body requires the moisture and nourishment. Do not stir again from that bed."

He gave me a hard-eyed look to go with the order, then turned and walked out of the room. If I'd had the strength I would have been furious, but all I was up to was a glare at his departing back. He thought I was being unreasonable by insisting on leaving right then, but I didn't give a damn. I could damned well be as unreasonable as I felt like being. He was nothing but a cheap, for-hire mercenary, and had no business ordering me around. He probably would have been damned good in bed, but his constant crowding was beginning to turn me off. I wanted out of there and I would *get* out of there, and nothing he said would stop me.

I pushed the blanket away and got to my feet again, then headed for the window. Passing the open doorway I could see Fallan bending over the hearth, messing with a pot and a bowl. I wasn't in the least hungry, and wouldn't have wanted anything made by a low-born like him even if I were. I reached through the dusty sunlight to the side of the window, opened the latch, then pushed the window wide against a small amount of resistance. My clothes in the wardrobe were probably still wet, so I'd be better off forgetting about them. The nightshirt covered me well enough, and would certainly do until I got where I was going. I leaned out the window to see how far it was to the ground, pulled my head back in and hiked up the nightshirt, then—

"There is clearly *one* of us who is incapable of understanding simple speech," Fallan growled from behind me, all traces of patience gone. "Take yourself from that window and do so *now*!"

I glanced back over my shoulder to see him standing there with a full bowl in his hands, his dark eyes flashing with such strength and dominance that my body attempted to respond. I had, however, already decided to leave the good Captain Fallan, and right then, when his sexiness couldn't reach me, was the best time. I turned back to the window and threw a leg over the very narrow sill, started to swing out—but was caught before I could free my second leg. Fallan pulled me back in with very little effort, his arm wrapped tight around my waist. I screamed and kicked, but he still reached out and pulled the window shut.

"In all fairness, you should be taught a good lesson for such foolishness," he growled, fighting to hold me still. "Were you not hurt and ill, I would—uhh!"

He grunted with the pain of my elbow into his middle, a blow I remembered just in time. His arm loosened enough from around me that I was able to put my leg behind his before pushing with my hip, and he actually went down! I couldn't help giggling as he sprawled flat on his back, but I didn't have time to giggle long. The door to the room was standing open and that would be the easiest way to go, so I started toward it—just as Fallan reared up, threw an arm around me, and pulled me down to the floor on top of him.

"No!" I screamed, furious that he refused to acknowledge the way I'd defeated him by staying down the way the others had. "Release me at once!"

"I am to release you so that the long series of accidental mishaps which have descended upon me since first we met might continue?" he demanded, forcing me face down across his folded legs. "I knew well enough that they were no such thing, yet chose not to press the matter. It is now time to cause a mishap of my own, one that has been much too long in the coming."

He held me across his knees and pulled the bottom of the nightshirt up, and I didn't know what the hell he was doing. I struggled and fought to get loose—and then howled with the first swat from his big hand on my bottom. It stung less than the second smack, and the second less than the third, and after that I lost count. I couldn't believe he would dare do that to me, that he would dare spank me, but that's exactly what he was doing. It began to really hurt and I began to cry, but that didn't stop him. He continued to hold me

down across his lap and spank me, and I couldn't stand
any more. I had to get away—and then everything
suddenly changed, but only inwardly. Outwardly Fallan
was still spanking away, but inside nothing I'd done
seemed all that right any longer. Somehow the Bellna
presence had gotten the upper hand without my realizing it, and this time I was really stuck with the
consequences. I'd never been spanked before, not even
as a child, but it was much too late to stop it. All I
could do was squirm against his leg as I stared at the
dirty wooden floor, while Fallan paid me back for everything I'd ever done to him—and what Bellna had done
as well. I really felt it every time his big hand reached
my bottom, and it didn't stop reaching my bottom for
what seemed like a very long time.

When the bastard finally let me go, I crawled off his
lap and knelt there with my hands behind me, the tears
streaming down my face. Bellna had started the crying
but I couldn't seem to stop it, not with the way my
backside stung. It wasn't that the pain was so terrible—it
was nothing compared to the way I usually got hurt on
the job—but the humiliation was more than I could
stand. If I could have stood straight right then I would
have broken Fallan into small pieces—but I couldn't
stand straight. Fallan did the standing instead, and then
looked down at me.

"You may now return to your bed," he said, sounding all through with playing games. "Should I find you out
of it again without permission—*my* permission—you
will find sitting a vair even more difficult than it currently is for you. Now, go."

I swiped at my eyes with the back of my hand and
then tried standing up, but I still couldn't do it. Somehow Bellna had used my body as though there were
nothing wrong with it, and with her out of control I had

nothing left. Walking wouldn't have been very comfortable after that spanking Fallan had given me, but in order to walk I first had to stand up. I couldn't stand up, I couldn't walk, and it slowly became harder even to kneel. The things in the room started swirling around gently, and suddenly I was heading face down for the floor. A big arm caught me just before I hit, and then it and another arm lifted me into the air.

"You would indeed have done well on your own," Fallan's voice came, the dryness impossible to miss. "After a few brief moments of activity, you seem near to a faint."

He put me into the bed and covered me with the blanket again, and although my head was already beginning to clear, he wasn't far wrong. I did feel as though I were about to pass out, with or without the dizziness. I'd been more than eager to be on my way to rendezvous, but I really hadn't intended killing myself doing it. Insisting so stubbornly had been Bellna's idea, that and getting so rough with Fallan. She'd managed to pry loose a couple of simple techniques, and hadn't realized how stupid using them on someone like Fallan was. After watching him fight that house guard, she should have had *some* idea as to what it would take to put him away. She was huddled in her usual corner of my mind, sniffling and hurting from the spanking we'd gotten, nicely intimidated but almost as aroused as she'd been during training with the slavers. She wanted Fallan more than ever, but I wanted him less than ever. He'd had every right to get even for what I'd done to him, but not by humiliating me like that. I would have faced him if that was what he wanted, with or without weapons, but he wasn't interested in facing me. All he was interested in doing was humiliating me, and I'd get him for that.

"You will eat some of this, and then you will sleep," Fallan's voice came, and then his arm was under my shoulders and raising me up. "We must strengthen you if you are to journey alone."

"I cannot sit so!" I yelped, trying to twist away from his arm. "The sting—I cannot sit so!"

"Then you had best swallow this quickly, so that you may lie down again," he said, making sure I couldn't slip free. "Or do you mean to disobey me?"

I looked up into his eyes as he said that, and what I saw there made me stop struggling even as feebly as I'd been doing. He raised the wooden spoon sticking out of the bowl and put it to my lips, and with a vast amount of reluctance but absolutely no hesitation, I swallowed every drop. I'd get him for what he'd done to me that day—but some other time.

CHAPTER 9

That first meal didn't last as long as Fallan thought it would. I continued swallowing until half of the soupy, watery gruel was gone, and then, between one spoonful and the next, *I* was gone. I either fell asleep or passed out, but I didn't know I had until I woke up again. By that time it was well into the night, but Fallan was still awake and waiting for me with a present. The fever was still faintly with me, so it was battery acid time again. I really wanted to tell him what to do with that swill, but all I did was take it and drink it down. For some reason I felt—intimidated—by Fallan, but that had to be because of the weakness that continued to hold me. Once I was back to my old self, I'd find some way to get even with him.

The next day I felt considerably better, but even with the fever gone, Fallan refused to let me out of bed. In the afternoon he changed the bandage on my ribs after reapplying the jelly-like glop to the raw-looking wound, but what pain I felt during the process had nothing to do with Clero's handiwork. Bellna was back to actively panting after Fallan, and what her yen did to me with

339

the mercenary Captain so close to my naked body is best left undescribed. If he had finished the bandaging and then had dropped his pants and raped me, Bellna would have been in soft-headed heaven. Fortunately or unfortunately, he did nothing of the kind. He finished the bangaging, put the nightshirt back on me, and then left without a word. I spent the next couple of hours twisting around in the bed, wishing to hell that planet had cold showers.

Just at darkness Fallan brought me the meal he'd cooked, and after I ate it he took the plates away and blew out the lamp. I was annoyed as all hell that he didn't even give me a chance to discuss the matter, but after only a few minutes of bad-tempered tossing I fell asleep. Not much time could have gone by before I was awakened by the sound of soft voices from the next room, and at first I was more sleepy than curious. After a couple of minutes of hearing the voices, curious got the better of sleepy, so I eased out of bed and moved silently to the door. Opening it just as silently was not as easy, but after another minute I had it done. I had a nice, wide three-inch opening to look through, and what I saw made me feel like a peeping Tom. Fallan was entertaining, and he and his lady friend were lying on a comfortable-looking pile of blankets in front of the fire. Neither of them were wearing anything, and whereas I couldn't help but be impressed by how well-endowed Fallan was, his companion seemed more nervous than eager. She lay there trembling, just short of flinching, and when Fallan began to reach out a hand to her, she screwed her eyes shut and clenched her teeth and fists.

"Believe me, girl, I shall bring you no hurt," Fallan whispered, but he sounded as if he'd said the same thing a dozen times before and the girl still wasn't believing. He shook his head with very faint annoyance,

then began working on her as if he were also trying to
work himself up. Someone would have had to have
been blind to miss how ready he was, but he took his
time with the girl as if she were the only one who
mattered. It didn't take all that along before he reached
her, but he kept at it until she was not only aroused but
as eager as he was. She lifted herself to him when he
moved over her, her moans low but intense, and when
he took her in his arms and entered her she welcomed
him with her entire self. After that she made nothing
but sounds of pleasure, and I closed the door on their
enjoyment feeling more confused than I had in a long
while. I'd had a good deal of personal if not intimate
contact with the men of that world, but none of them
had acted the way Fallan did—either in bed or out. And
mercenaries were supposed to be worse than the general,
run-of-the-mill population. If that was so, then why—

Suddenly all thoughts were driven out of my head by
the screaming that filled it, the screaming produced by
Bellna. I'd forgotten all about my unwelcome guest
again, but she hadn't missed paying close attention to
what was going on in the other room. She hadn't been
quiet while watching she'd been speechless, and now
her rage was filling me the way spring storms fill an
arroyo. When Fallan had chosen the black-haired slave
over me in the slave market Bellna had excused away
his rejection, but she was totally beyond looking for
excuses now. She hated him for not taking her when
she wanted him so badly, and she hated him even more
for bringing another woman to his blankets when she
was just in the next room. I climbed back into bed fairly
resonating with her fury, but there was nothing I could
do to stop it. The little girl in my head was feeling
betrayed and vengeful, and I'd just have to wait until
she got over it. I did wait, but I had the makings of a

really good headache before the frozen, still-offended silence finally descended. If not for that hovering headache I would have gone back to my own thinking, but the threat *was* there and I was also tired. When the peace and quiet came I closed my eyes, and before the noise could start again I was asleep.

When Fallan woke me in the morning, the first thing I remembered was how much I hated him. He was in a great mood, undoubtedly due to the fun and games of the previous night, and that made me hate him even more. He'd dared to punish me and humiliate me, and then he'd given me the ultimate insult. I'd never forget, not any of it, and the first chance I got I'd fix him good.

Fallan took a nap later that day, and I spent the time exercising hard. My strength was quickly coming back and the stiffness was leaving me, and as soon as I could I'd be out of there and on my way to where I had to go. I hated it there with Fallan as much as I hated *him*, and I had to get out of there before I went crazy. He continued to insist that I stay in bed, and even went so far as to start toward me when I told him that I didn't want to. I jumped down under the blanket and pulled it over my head, and after a few minutes when I took the blanket away he was gone. I was furious then at the way he'd bluffed me, making me think he was going to spank me again, and after that I worked even harder to get back into shape.

It was late in the afternoon of the third day after that when Fallan left the house. I didn't know where he was going, but I waited a minute after I heard the door close, then hurried to the window of my room. Fallan was walking away from our house farther into the village, and it didn't much matter where he was going. He would surely be gone long enough for me to get dressed and get out of there, and that was all that did matter.

I went to the wardrobe and opened it wide, hearing the loud screech of protesting parts that had kept me away from it sooner, and was pleased to see my clothes draped over wooden pegs. They were really a mess, filthy, mud-covered and stiff with dried blood, but they had the benefit of being much less conspicuous than a nightshirt. I pulled them off their pegs and bent to the bottom of the wardrobe to look for my boots—and stopped still just to stare for a minute. On the floor of the wardrobe, just behind my boots and almost invisible, lay the sword I'd found so much use for, sheath and all. I'd never expected to see it again, and I suddenly remembered that I hadn't cleaned it properly. I stared for another moment, then abruptly pulled out the boots and sword and carried all I'd found to the bed so I could dress.

With my boots tied and the sword belted around my middle, I left the bedroom to do a little exploring. The other room of the house turned out to be surprisingly neat over the layers of ancient dirt and use. Aside from the hearth and fire, there was a plain wooden table and four straight-backed chairs, a couple of familiar blankets spread on the floor not far from the fire, and a paired set of leather pouches near the blankets. A piece of bright red stuck out from the top of one of the pouches, showing what had happened to Fallan's uniform shirt. It wasn't far from being full dark out, and I intended using the door to the outside, but not as quickly as I'd first thought. Finding my sword had changed things, and I would have some words with Fallan before I left. The thought added pleasure to the sudden golden haze around me, and I smiled as I went back into the bedroom, closed the door, and sat down on the bed to wait.

Fallan took his time getting back, but eventually I heard the sound of the front door opening. I sat up on

the bed then got to my feet, and the small wall lamp let
me reach the door before my shadow. I grasped the
doorknob firmly, intending to yank it open—but it refused to move! The door that had opened so easily just
a short time earlier now felt nailed shut, but it wasn't
stuck. I used two hands on the knob, trying to rattle it,
trying to shake the door in its frame, but nothing moved.
It was like trying to rattle or shake a tree, and in fury I
raised my fist to bang on the door—then stopped short
of hitting it as a cold thought came to me. That was a
Paldovar Village, a place where no one could harm
anyone else. What would the Paldovar do if I continued
to try reaching Fallan? The golden haze had thinned to
flickering around me, and I wanted to get to Fallan so
badly I could feel it as a hunger, but I was in no
position to play deep games with the natives of that
village. It was hard leaving Fallan to the arrogance of
his ways, but it was better than getting more deeply
involved in a place well left far behind me. As I moved
to the window and threw it open, I almost had myself
believing that.

The nigth was cool but without wind, and I took my
time saddling my vair, hoping I might be discovered. It
was a small surprise that my vair stood right next to
Fallan's in the lean-to, but he must have found it near
the inn after finding me inside the inn. My vair snorted
softly as I mounted, and I looked at the small house one
last time before riding away toward the south. I knew
there was a reason why I had to ride south, but it took a
minute before I remembered it. Pick-up, I was riding to
pick-up, and after I made pick-up I could relax.

I rode through the woods all night, changing the
vair's pace now and then to give us both a rest, and
made sure to stay away from any bodies of water. The
night was relaxed and quiet, and I rode on in the middle

of chirping and occasional roars, bathed by the light of the larger moon. Dameron's hidey-hole was floating above me again, and sight of it forced me to ask the question I'd been avoiding so long. I was alone and heading south and had been doing it for hours; why the hell hadn't a scout ship come for me?

Dawn was already streaking the sky with gorgeous colors when I finally decided to stop for a rest. I was no more tired than I expected to be, but I'd been ignoring a headache for hours, and I didn't want it to start pounding on my eyeballs for attention. I dismounted stiffly and tied the vair where he could reach some grass, then sat down a short distance away with my back to a tree. I'd stopped at the edge of a small clearing, and although it was damp with dew it was also pretty and quiet. I closed my eyes and relaxed all over, emptying my mind of all thought. The headache throbbed with my pulse, but the more I relaxed and regulated my breathing, the more it eased and faded, becoming lighter and fainter with every indrawn breath. It was just about all gone when a snapping twig and high-pitched whicker brought me abruptly back to myself, and I was on my feet with sword in hand before I really knew which direction the sound had come from. Talk about your bad pennies! There, not five feet away from me, Fallan sat on his vair, still wearing that green shirt, still giving me that dark-eyed stare I'd had so much of in the past few days. There was a great surge of elation in me, accompanied by the sudden presence of the golden haze, and I grinned as I tightened my grip on the sword. We weren't in a Paldovar Village any longer!

Fallan looked me over carefully, then rested his arm on the pommel of his saddle.

"You seem pleased with some matter," he observed,

keeping his tone neutral. "Might I know the reason for your pleasure?"

"Certainly," I answered, not even trying to keep the delight out of my voice. "I have just been given a gift I had thought beyond my reach forever."

"In all modesty, I presume you mean me," he murmured with a nod, dismounting and letting go of his vair's reins. "However, before you begin something we will both undoubtedly regret, I suggest you listen to what I have to say."

There was something strange about the way he was speaking, but the golden haze convinced me that it wasn't worth noticing. I shook my head, still wrapped up in the pleasure of a grin.

"I will listen to no more of the Fallan Beliefs on proper obedience," I told him, then felt the grin slipping away from me as the sword flicked around in my hand. "Defend yourself or be cut down where you stand!"

The mercenary continued to stare for a moment, but I was already moving toward him, giving him no choice but to face me. He left his vair and moved farther into the clearing, then slowly drew his sword. He didn't seem to want to face me, but he showed no fear and no doubt, undoubtedly thinking that a man of his size and training would have no trouble at all with a young female like me. I couldn't wait to show him how wrong he was.

Fallan held his sword at the ready, but it was hardly a decent en garde position. He was prepared to counter the swipes and round-house swings Tildorani seemed so partial to, but he was wide open to a slip and glide. I feinted toward him in a backswing, curious to see if he would notice the opening, but he never even twitched in my direction. He brought his weapon up to meet the move, obviously intending to stop it with sheer muscle,

and blinked off balance when our blades didn't meet.
I'd switched fast to slide under his blade, and my point
was right near his ribs, well past his guard. I'd wanted
to show him how open and vulnerable he was when he
faced me with weapons, that and nothing more, but the
golden haze glittered around me, whispering a reminder
of what he'd done to me, how terribly he'd humiliated
me. The hatred I felt for him pounded in my head and
made it whirl, and then I had pushed my point a full
inch into his side, pulling it free covered with the blood
that was meant to be spilled. The mercenary's face
twisted as the pain came to him, but I was well pleased
with what I had done, and was already out of reach of
the fool's blade.

The sight that greeted the sun's full light was one that
really pleased me. Fallan stumbled around the clearing,
touched dozens of places with streaks and smears of his
own blood, his arm tired from the wasted effort toward
defense, his face a mask of silent agony. Over and over
again he'd tried for a better defense and had even tried
attack, but his attacks had found me already moved
elsewhere and his defense had shown itself to be a mass
of gaping holes. I hadn't taken his life yet, and wouldn't
until he threw down his blade and begged for his life.
Then I'd show him the exact same mercy he'd shown to
me!

I was so intent on the target I was playing with that I
heard nothing of the forest noises around us. Fallan's
sweating face swam before me, his eyes locked to my
arm and blade, and then his gaze went up and past me,
widening at whatever he saw behing my back. Or was
trying to make me think he saw. That trick was so old I
would have been an idiot to fall for it, but as I raised
my point again I saw that he had dropped his guard
entirely and was still staring behind me. He had also

stopped backing away, and then he did something that shocked me. He twisted the blade in his hand, holding it as though it were a spear, then hurled it past me with a shout of, "Look out, Diana!"

The golden haze flickered and died as I whirled around, having no time at all to see the barbarian with Fallan's sword in him go down—there were too many other barbarians still on their feet to worry about. Lord only knows where they'd come from, but they were suddenly all around, screaming and swinging away with an abandon that made everyone else I'd seen look reserved and dignified. I defended myself for the first few seconds of adjustment, then began eliminating opponents before I was eliminated.

I'd accounted for a respectable number of barbarians before it came to me that I wasn't fighting alone. Strangely enough, some of the barbarians seemed to be fighting on my side. I'd just come to the conclusion that I'd blundered into the middle of some intertribal rivalry when I spotted something that cleared away the strangeness. Over the heads of the screaming, sweating barbarians nearest me, I saw the familiar features of the giant Leandor, head of Dameron's special section. I blocked a thrust from a determined barbarian and riposted cleanly, then paid attention to staying alive now that I'd finally reached my contact back to where I'd come from.

It took many more frantic minutes before Leandor and his people were able to push the real barbarians farther away into the trees. I took a deep breath of relief at finally being in the clear, stretched my aching arm and back muscles, then turned to look at "the mercenary Fallan." One of the barbarians had opened his thigh with a quick jab before I'd finished her, and the wound had obviously been the last of too many. The man lay sprawled on the ground unconscious, still alive but not doing very well. I felt the very long night and morning in every muscle and bone of my body, and squatted down close to stare at the face I'd learned too know so well. He'd shouted my name just before the barbarians had hit, and there was only one way for him to have known my name. I stared at the pale, drawn face that was still covered with the sweat of pain, and wondered which of Dameron's people he was.

Five minutes later there was the sound of hurrying footsteps and I stood straight fast, glad I hadn't resheathed my sword, but it was only Leandor, coming back alone. He still had his reddened sword in his fist, but I was suddenly too tired to hang onto mine, so I wiped most of the blood off on the skirt of my riding dress and resheathed the blade before walking a few steps in his direction.

"Girl, am I glad to see you!" he called as he got closer. "Up to a few minutes ago, we all thought you'd had it permanently!"

"Why would you think that?" I frowned, looking up at him as he stopped in front of me.

"When somebody's beacon goes off, it usually means they've gone with it," he grinned, his eyes moving all over me. "You seem to be one of the few exceptions to the rule. What did you run into?"

"Nothing much to speak of," I muttered, holding down the rage that wanted to flame out at anything handy. If my beacon had gone out as Leandor said, it was a fairly safe bet it had been planted in my side, in the spot I currently had a half-healed gouge. If Leandor hadn't come along, I would have waited for a pick-up till I died of old age! I picked out a few choice words to say to Dameron's medics and put them aside, then looked back up at Leandor. "How are you fixed for a first-aid kit?" I asked, moving my head around to nod at

Fallan. Leandor followed my gaze and lost his grin, then moved past me to the unconscious ex-mercenary.

"How bad is he?" he asked, bending down to see for himself without waiting for an answer. It was obvious Fallan wasn't good, so I shrugged at Leandor's back.

"If he's faking, he's doing a good job of it," I commented. "He's lost enough blood to put him on anyone's critical list, and I'm fresh out of bandages. How fast can you get him back to base?"

"We can't get either one of you back before dark," Leandor said without looking up, "but I can give him a transfusion at my camp. It isn't far and it'll give us all the privacy we need."

He wrestled Fallan off the ground and over his shoulder, then started off in the direction all the barbarians seemed to have come from. I collected my vair and Fallan's and followed, but it wasn't long before I mounted my vair, finding it easier following Leandor when I didn't have to match his stride. Leandor continued on through the trees, and before long we came to a larger clearing than the one I'd stopped at. There were tents pitched all over the clearing, and some of Leandor's team was still there, relaxing only a little when Leandor nodded at them before disappearing inside one of the tents. I just sat on my vair and slumped over its neck, feeling the soreness in my left side for the first time in days. I'd probably still be there if one of Leandor's team men hadn't come over to offer me a place to wait and something to eat. I half fell off the vair and plodded after the team member, and the tent I was led to was more inviting than many palaces I'd seen.

Once inside the tent, I was able to collapse in peace. The thing was surprisingly spacious, with blanketlike hangings on the skin walls, furs on the floor as carpeting, and a large fire burning in a deep hole in the middle of the floor, all of it fitting in very well with the "barbarian's" clothing. The men were wearing long, loose trousers in assorted colors, the legs of the trousers being tied tight around their ankles with leather, and the women had brief, vest-like halters to add to that. Both wore knives and sword-belts around their waists, and both were barefoot, not needing boots for their saddleless vair. I picked a spot on the furs near the fire and stretched out, and didn't move until the food came. The meal was no more than grilled steak from some animal or other and a bowl of barbarian beer called gannas, but to me it tasted like the next thing to ambrosia. I swallowed it all, then leaned back to relax again.

I was happily digesting what had gone down my throat when Leandor came in. He was carrying his own bowl of gannas, but waited until he was sitting near me before swallowing at it.

"Just what I needed," he commented after lowering the bowl. "Sometimes this stuff is better for what ails you than anything the clinicians have."

"How's your patient?" I asked, rolling onto my side in order to see him more easily. He swallowed at the gannas again, and waved a hand around.

"Oh, he'll be fine," he assured me. "Nothing too badly wrong with him, and the transfusion will do the job until we can get him back to base."

"Glad to hear that," I nodded, keeping my eyes on him. "Now for the next question: who the hell *is* he?"

Leandor's eyebrows rose, and he forgot about the bowl in his hands.

"What do you mean, who is he?" he demanded. "Didn't he tell you? And what kind of game were you two playing when we got there?"

"He didn't tell me anything, and it was no game," I growled, holding his gaze. "And if you start beating around the bush, we'll see how long it takes me to pull this tent down around your ears."

I hadn't raised my voice, but there was no longer a reason to swallow whatever annoyance I felt. Leandor looked surprised again, then raised a hand in a calming gesture.

"Just take it easy," he soothed, a frown beginning to crease his forehead. "Nobody's beating around the bush. I don't know why he didn't tell you, but there's nothing secret involved. Granted, Valdon hasn't been in the field for a while. . . ."

"Valdon!" I exploded, sitting up straight. "The man's a damned fool! How could Dameron send him?"

"There wasn't much choice." Leandor shrugged, not very pleased with my reaction. "We got the chance to substitute one of our own for the real Fallan at the last minute, and Valdon grabbed the privilege. He *is* second in command, and doesn't usually abuse the position. When he insisted, Dameron gave in. I got back yesterday, and we were following his beacon for a pick-up when that tribe of barbarians jumped us. We didn't mean to drive them straight toward you, but we didn't have much choice about it."

"Choices," I muttered, as if it were a swear word, as I leaned back again, then I thought of something else. "Every time I turned around I found myself tripping over that man. If my beacon was knocked out, how did he keep finding me?"

"He must have been attuned to you," Leandor answered in an "everyone knows *that*" tone of voice. "Beacons are for long-range pick-ups and emergency spotting. Attuning is for close-up work, when your target might take off in any direction at any time. The base has your pattern, so attuning would be a snap."

I shook my head sourly at his idea of a snap, then brought my eyes back to his.

"If you knew someone was in that Paldovar Village because of Valdon's beacon, why didn't you show up there for a pick-up?"

"You've got to be kidding!" he snorted, looking outraged at the idea. "We stay away from those places except in absolute emergencies." Then he eyed me curiously. "How did you two happen to end up there?"

"It's a long story," I sighed, settling down flat in the furs. "If we ever get drunk together, I might let you in on it. Right now I'd appreciate a spare corner to sleep in. Does your hospitality extend that far?"

"At least that far," he chuckled, moving slightly where he sat. "You can use the spot you're on, and forget about keeping one eye open. We'll look after you for a while."

"Gee, thanks," I murmured, turning over to bury my face in the soft, warm fur. "But where were you when I needed you?"

Leandor chuckled again but didn't say anything, and it must have been a good ten seconds before I conked out cold.

Getting back to base was as eventful and complicated as leaving it had been. Fallan—Valdon, I mean—was hustled off to the hospital area, still unconscious from a shot Leandor had given him. After stepping out of the scouter into the docking area, I had just enough time to stretch once before an escort showed up to guide me through the base proper. I thought I was being taken to Dameron's office for their version of debriefing, but instead found myself being awaited by a hungry group of medics who were dying to get their hands on me. I enjoy popularity, but not of the medical variety, and politely declined their offer of attention. They took to insisting; I suggested what they might do with their spare time; they turned red then threatened to use restraints, and I rested my hand on the hilt of the sword I was still wearing. Just before the real bloodshed started, Dameron walked in.

"I thought hospitals were supposed to be quiet," he commented, stationing himself between me and my admirers. "I could hear the bunch of you back in the residential wing."

The stars of the medical profession knew as well as I did that Dameron was exaggerating, but they flushed anyway at the implied criticism. Then my most ardent admirer, the same little man I'd met when I'd first opened my eyes in the base, detached himself from the rest and faced Dameron.

"Commander, it is our considered opinion that this young woman is badly in need of treatment and bed rest," he announced in that fussy way of his. "We will defer to others in any area but medicine. If we do not have the final word there, we can be of no further use to you. It is, of course, your decision."

I snorted an estimate of his considered opinion, a reaction he chose to ignore as he folded his arms and stared at Dameron, but the base commander didn't share my estimation. He seemed to be thoughtfully considering the little man's words, and when he moved his dark eyes over to me, my headache started coming back.

"Dameron," I began, intending to make my position very, very clear, but Dameron wasn't waiting to hear what I had to say.

"You've got to cooperate, girl," he rumbled, holding up a conciliatory hand. "They're only trying to help you."

"I've had enough of people trying to help me!" I snapped, noticing that the golden haze was beginning to form again. "For a change, I'm damned well going to see a little disinterested neutrality!"

My hand was at the sword hilt again, the golden haze thickening by the second, but that didn't keep me from hearing the hiss behind my back. I whirled around on the frightened medic who still held the pressure hypo and began drawing on him, but never got the chance to clear the scabbard. Dameron jumped me from behind, wrapping those oversized arms around me, holding me until the shot could take effect. I struggled to get free, intent on killing everyone in the room, but the dark took over before I could.

CHAPTER 10

A small click woke me first, intruding on a deep, dreamless sleep that seemed to have been a part of me for some time. I was lying on my side, all curled up, so I rolled over onto my back to stare at a flat gold ceiling. My eyes stayed with the ceiling for a while, moved slowly down blank gold walls, then settled on the soft yellow cover over me before I reached the point of wondering where I was. By that time I knew I was back in the base, knew where the base was, and knew that the gold walls meant the hospital area, but I wasn't quite up to remembering why I had to be in the hospital area. My head felt as though it should hurt—though it didn't—and I was bothered by an annoying disorientation.

I was still trying to sort things out when there was another click, this time accompanied by the door sliding open. Dameron came in, his steps over-quiet, his face preoccupied, and the door closed behind him again as he walked to a mound chair not far from my bed. I watched him sit down with more weariness than I'd come to expect from him, wondered what sort of a problem he had this time, and then saw his eyes come to me. He started when he saw me watching him, and leaned forward anxiously in the chair.

"You're not supposed to be awake yet," he rumbled, almost in accusation. "How are you feeling?"

"I've been worse—and better," I admitted, looking him over. "If I'm not supposed to be awake yet, what are you doing here?"

"I've been listing my sins and estimating penalties," he snorted, then leaned even closer. "Are you sure you're all right?"

I took some time to roll myself into a sitting position before answering him. My head felt—tight, I guess you could call it, and the gears of my mind seemed to need a good oiling.

"I'll probably live," I conceded thickly. "What did those fumble-fingered idiots do to me?"

"If you're referring to my medical staff, they probably did the best job of their careers," he chuckled, finally relaxing a little. "You're sounding more familiar by the minute. How anxious are you to get your hands on a sword again?"

I was about to ask him what a sword had to do with anything when the tightness in my mind broke, letting in a flood of memories and associations. The time with Grigon, the time in the slave market, fighting, running, bleeding—and Fallan. The man called Fallan who was really Valdon, a man who had tried to give me a hand, a man who had fought to protect me, a man who had saved my life at least twice. I tangled my fingers in my hair and bent over with a moan when I thought of what I'd done to him.

"Why didn't he say something?" I choked out, not realizing that Dameron shouldn't have known what I was talking about. I kept my head down, rocking back

and forth with the pain, and only vaguely heard Dameron
get out of his chair.

"Considering what went on between you two before
you left, he thought at first that it would be better if
you didn't know who he was," Dameron's voice came,
soft with compassion. "When you reached the woodsman's
house he was about to tell you everything, but that
'bandit' attack came first. The next time you were alone
together, you were in a Paldovar Village. The Paldovar
already know about too many things that should be
secret, so it was no place to go into explanations. But
don't blame yourself for what happened—it wasn't your
fault. You're the first one to react to impressions the
way you did, and it couldn't have been anticipated. It
simply wasn't your fault."

"Then whose fault was it?" I demanded, looking up
at him again. "Who do you think that was, cutting a
man to pieces without giving him a chance? Not a swift,
clean death, but cut by agonizing cut, trying to make
him beg for his life!"

I cut him off, sickened by the memory of how pleased
I'd felt, more ashamed by that than by the actual doing.
Killing a man is sometimes necessary, but it had always
been something that had to be done, not something to
be enjoyed.

"That mind presence was too much for you," Dameron
insisted, crouching down to put a hand on my shoulder.
"We've removed every trace of it we could find, so you
won't be bothered by it again. Your side has been
Healed, Valdon's wounds have been Healed, and you're
both safely back where you belong. Why don't you try
forgetting about the rest of it?"

"Sure, forget," I agreed tonelessly, moving away from
his hand to lie flat again. The plain gold ceiling was
projecting images, so I closed my eyes and added, "There

are some cartons of cigarettes among the stores on my ship. I'd appreciate the favor of having one brought to me."

Dameron sighed without saying anything, then I heard him straighten up and leave the room. I just kept my eyes closed and fought for control.

The carton of cigarettes was brought by an amiable young thing who gave me her best friendly smile along with the carton. I nodded my thanks in a distracted way, unsealed the carton and one of the packs, then lit up and took a deep drag. I like thinking with a cigarette in my hand, and I'd done enough cussing at myself without a blue-gray cloud around to emphasize the points. I was still in bed, still wearing the brief, one-piece garment those medics kept supplying me with, but I'd shifted to a cross-legged sitting position for better leverage on the ideas I'd been tossing around.

It was fairly obvious to anyone with a brain that I'd been a double-damned fool. I should have called a halt to the operation as soon as I found out about my alter ego, but I was too damned stubborn to admit I'd come up against something I might not be able to handle. I'd looked at it as a challenge—a challenge, for Pete's sake! —when my life and a good number of other lives depended on my being rational enough to handle a simple part. Twelve years in the business, and I hadn't even had the sense to realize that it was Bellna growing stronger and more in control and not me. She grew to the point of being able to take over without my even noticing it, and the end result was a murderous, conscienceless little monster with the specialized abilities of a Federation Special Agent. Special Agent! I laughed bitterly. Special idiot was more like it!

No matter how long I thought about it, I still couldn't understand why I hadn't guessed who Fallan was. Look-

ing back at it I could see one clue after another, starting
with the way Grigon had acted. If Fallan had been a
real Tildorani mercenary, Grigon would never have let
him get the last word in about not talking to me before
we left. And that comment Fallan had made in the
woodsman's house, about Grigon having been right.
Grigon had probably urged him to tell me who he really
was, but he hadn't agreed—until it was too late. The
speed the big man had showed, the unusual amount of
patience, the times he hadn't been insulted when he
should have been—hint after hint after hint and none of
it had come through! I hadn't even asked where his
Company was while he was looking after me in the
Paldovar Village—or, more to the point, *why* he was
looking after me. Bellna wasn't bright enough to ask
questions like that—and she'd been the one in control.

"Don't you ever believe in smiling?" a voice asked,
and my head jerked up to see Valdon standing in the
doorway. I didn't know how long he'd been standing
there, and I stared at him for a minute without being
able to say anything, then cleared my throat.

"Don't you ever believe in knocking?" I tried, not at
all sure what else there was to say. He was back to
wearing a blue uniform coverall like Dameron's, and he
was back to having black hair and eyes and a ridiculously good-looking face that looked nothing at all like
Fallan's, but there was something familiar about the
way he stood and moved—and looked at me.

"Attack and counterattack," he grinned, moving out
of the doorway and closer toward my bed. "I think I
recognize the pattern." Then he noticed the cigarette in
my hand and stopped short. "Now what are you doing?"
he asked, studying the pile of ashes I'd accumulated.

"I'm smoking," I supplied, taking a drag to prove the

point before putting the cigarette out. "And what are you doing out of bed?"

"You've got some catching up to do," he commented, still eyeing the ashes and dead cigarette. "I've been out of bed for days. Apparently they found fixing my body easier than fixing your mind."

He was standing no more than four feet away from me, and I couldn't keep my eyes on his face. I looked down into my lap at a pair of hands that suddenly had nothing to do, discovering that my mind was as blank of dialogue as the walls were blank of decoration. Apologizing is a snap when you don't mean a word of what you say, but the real thing tends to be somewhat awkward.

"What's wrong?" he asked, moving closer to the bed so he could sit down at the foot of it. I would have been happier if he'd left the room, but there was no getting out of it.

"Look," I blurted, bringing my eyes back up to his. "I don't really know how to say this, but it's got to be said. I had no right doing what I did to you, and I—apologize."

"Sincere and from the heart," he observed, leaning down on one elbow as he shook his head. "If I hadn't gotten to know you so well, I might have doubted your sincerity."

His sarcastic tone of voice might have begun eating away at my regret if I hadn't remembered that he had the right to be sarcastic—at the very least. I decided it was time for another cigarette, and occupied my hands and mouth that way.

"You're showing admirable restraint these days," he said, still sarcastic. "They must have done a good job on you after all. Is that all there is to it? You 'apologize'?"

I pulled the cigarette out of my mouth, exhaling a thick cloud, and stared at him without much amusement.

"That's a good deal further than I usually go," I remarked. "Were you looking for something written in blood?"

"That would be appropriate," he grinned, making himself more comfortable, "but maybe we can think of something even better." His eyes moved over me where I sat cross-legged at the head of the bed, and his grin grew lazy. "Have any suggestions?"

I wasn't sure I understood what he was getting at—or maybe I didn't want to understand it.

"I'm not feeling particularly swift today," I said, leaning back against the wall. "Why don't you try being more specific?"

"There's not much to be specific about," he shrugged, keeping his eyes on me. "If you've got something you'd like to apologize for, there are more—intimate—and friendly—ways of doing it."

He just sat there watching me, that irritating grin faint but obvious, his longish black hair falling over his forehead, patiently waiting for a more—intimate— apology. I studied him silently for another moment, my thoughts not quite polite enough to describe, my breath filling the space between us with light gray smoke.

"If that's your price, you've got it," I told him after the minute, the decision coming out flat and emotionless, matching a reluctant willingness to pay for my mistakes. I put the cigarette out with three or four stabs at the shallow, square ceramic bowl I'd been given, then got to my feet to remove the short body-suit. The mustard yellow color of the thing was inexplicably annoying, but Valdon wasn't looking annoyed. His eyes moved over me with a good deal of interest, and his grin widened again when I lay down next to him.

"Very nice," he murmured, still absorbed in his inspection. "Very nice indeed."

His approval was obvious, but he wasn't making any attempt to touch me. I looked up at him from where I lay on the soft yellow cover, wondering what he was waiting for. I wasn't enjoying the episode and wanted an end to it as soon as possible, so I moved my hand toward him with the intention of increasing his interest, but never got the chance. His hand shot out to grab my wrist, stopping my arm in mid movement, and the look in his black eyes sharpened.

"As I said, this is all very nice," he repeated, "but what do you expect to gain by it? Do you think I can be bought off with the chance to exercise a few muscles?"

"Bought off?" I choked, gaping at him incredulously. "What do *I* expect to gain—?" I was so mad I totally lost the ability to speak. He was the one who had wanted more than words in apology, and now he was acting as though *I* was the one who—! I growled low in my throat, feeling the rage surge through me, and struggled to get my wrist loose from his grip. His fingers tightened around my wrist, improving his grip instead of loosening it, making me fight harder to get free.

"What's the matter?" he drawled, grinning that infuriating grin. "You can't be thinking of giving up on the apologizing?"

"Apologizing!" I echoed in outrage, trying to calm down enough to remember how to pull loose the right way. "I'll be damned if I'll stand for this any longer! I may not have had the right to do what I did to you, but I sure as hell had the provocation! You might as well get out of here right now, because I have nothing to apologize for!"

As mad as I was, I was totally unprepared for his reaction to that. The grin left him entirely, and his eyes became as serious as his expression.

"That's right, you don't," he agreed, finally letting go

of my wrist. "As a matter of fact, you never did have what to apologize for."

I gaped at him again, mechanically rubbing at my wrist, and his grin was back as suddenly as it had gone.

"You're one hard female to convince of something," he said, reaching over to gently close my mouth. "Dameron told me that you refused to understand about what had happened, so I thought I'd try my hand at reaching you. But first I had to get you mad enough to forget about the guilt you felt."

Well, he had gotten me mad, all right, but I could see he didn't understand what was really involved. I sat up and ran my hands through my hair, shaking my head at him.

"I don't feel guilty, but I do feel stupid," I explained. "Stupid and incompetent. I appreciate your effort, but there's not much anyone can do about it."

"I don't understand what you're talking about," he protested, beginning to sound annoyed. "The way you acted was a direct result of the impression, and couldn't possibly be considered your fault. Bellna's presence was so strong and overpowering that I noticed it as soon as you'd been impressed—that's why I insisted on being the one to take Fallan's place. No one else noticed a damned thing, and wouldn't have believed me if I'd tried warning them about it. It's also why I brought in another 'decoy,' pretending it was all Grigon's idea. I wanted to be prepared if anything went really wrong, and it gave me a good excuse for shoving you out of the center of things, where Bellna would feel at home and therefore be stronger. It wasn't anyone's fault but Clero's that it didn't do much good."

"You're still looking at it backwards," I insisted, rolling over to grab a cigarette. "The whole thing was my fault from beginning to end, and I know it even if you don't."

I got the cigarette lit and was about to move farther away from him with it, but his hand on my arm rolled me back toward him.

"If you know so much, explain it to me," he invited, a stubborn look in those dark black eyes. "Maybe there's something I'm missing."

His expression said he didn't think he was missing anything, but if nothing else, he was entitled to an explanation. I shrugged inwardly as I took a drag on the cigarette, then lay back to make myself comfortable.

"When I first arrived here," I began, "I took great pains to keep you and Dameron from finding out what I was really like. It turned out to be a mistake, because if Dameron had had all the facts he probably wouldn't have gotten involved with me.

"My full designation is, 'Special Agent of the Federation Council,' and doesn't begin to explain the sort of person who carries such a designation. When I first woke up here at the base, I was prepared to kill any or all of you if I found you in my way. I have as small an amount of conscience as is humanly possible, a state which is a prime requirement of my job. I know how to kill and have done so each time it was required of me. I am trained in unarmed combat to an extent that most people find terrifying. The only redeeming feature I possess is judgment, a characteristic which allows me to function as an asset to society rather than a blot on it. With all these things in mind, knowing myself as no one here knows me, I let myself be put into a position where a childish mind presence could impair that judgment—and did. I am a professional in my field, and as such my actions were inexcusable—and stupid. Do you understand now?"

I turned my head to look at him, and saw that he *had* been listening. His head was down and his eyes were on the soft yellow cover, and he seemed to be considering what I'd said. After a minute or two his eyes came up to meet mine and he smiled gently.

"I see your point," he murmured, "but there's something you're not taking into consideration. Dameron *did* know what he had in you, otherwise he never would have sent you. He questioned you thoroughly when we first found you, and when a crisis came up Dameron took advantage of what he'd learned. But as far as I can see, neither one of you is at fault because there was no way of anticipating what the impression would do to you. Even Grigon has admitted that he let you talk him into not reporting what he observed because there was no alternative plan to substitute for what had to be done. Dameron knew it, Grigon knew it, and you knew it. How could any of you be expected to walk away from such a necessity on the outside chance that something might go wrong?"

The sincerity of his spiel was tempting, but single-mindedness is an integral part of my character.

"Stupidity is stupidity," I muttered, taking another drag on the cigarette. "Dameron and Grigon didn't know how hard I had to fight to keep Bellna from taking over. I did. I just refused to admit it."

"If stubbornness was a power source, you could handle a city," Valdon growled, narrowing his eyes and shaking his head at me. "A large city. If you're that dead set on taking the blame, maybe getting punished for it would ease your nonexistent conscience. Suppose I turn you bottom up again and find out?"

He began reaching a hand out toward me, but I knocked it away with a snort.

"That's not funny," I told him, remembering all too

well the first time he'd done it. "I'm used to coupling crime with escape, not with punishment, so don't do me any favors. As a matter of fact, your—interesting—manner of punishment was a prime motivation for what happened later. Was that Fallan's way of doing things or yours?"

"Mine," he admitted with no backwardness or regret, but with a broadening grin. "I'd worked pretty damned hard at pulling you out of that fever, and I was in no mood to see you wandering around. Just being out of bed so soon might have gotten you that whacking, but then you started pulling some of your fancy tricks. I suddenly remembered all the other things you'd done, and that clinched it."

"That particular reminder came from Bellna rather than me," I told him with a grimace. "She started the whole thing, then ran out and left me holding the bag. The only bit of luck in this whole mess was the luck I had when there was enough time to change you to look like Fallan. I doubt if the real Fallan would have gone to the lengths you did to keep me whole."

"The real Fallan would have disappeared as soon as he found out about Clero's plans," Valdon said, but he was again frowning at me. "He liked to think of himself as a practical man. But let's return to what you said about there being enough time to change me. Didn't Dameron tell you that we got our hands on Fallan no more than three hours before he was due to pick you up?"

"No, he didn't," I said, matching Valdon's frown. "But if that's true, how did they manage to change you so fast?"

"That's what I'm trying to tell you," he insisted, raising himself higher on his elbow. "The clinicians *didn't* change me. You may not realize it, but I have original Absari blood. I do my own changing."

It was a distinct temptation to call for the men in the white jackets, but instead I snorted again.

"Is that so?" I challenged, determined to show him how sick he was. "If you can change yourself without any help, prove it by showing me."

I was expecting a lot of hemming and hawing and excuse-making, but all he did was shrug.

"Sure," he answered agreeably, and then his features—*blurred*. Without moving a single muscle I could see, it was suddenly Fallan lying on the bed near me. Brown-haired, brown-eyed Fallan in all his arrogant glory, slightly smaller than Valdon but not much. I heard Fallan's chuckle and saw his grin, and couldn't pull my eyes away from the over-familiar face.

"This is the talent that makes our people such effective Watchers," Valdon told me in Fallan's voice. "It must have started as a simple defense mechanism, but we've learned to put it to good use. Don't you feel uncomfortable with your jaw hanging down like that?"

I closed my mouth with a snap, then controlled the urge to gape again when Valdon turned back to Valdon. Or Fallan turned back to Valdon. Or whatever the hell you want to call it. I'm not easy to shake, but I don't mind admitting that that quick-change act really got to me.

"How do you do that?" I finally managed to demand, looking at him from all angles to see if I could spot hinges or mirrors.

"Just talented, I guess," he grinned, really amused by my reaction. "Want to see it again?"

"No, thanks!" I answered as fast as I could get the words out. "Once will do me for a while!"

Valdon was chuckling in his own voice, something

that would normally have annoyed me, but my mind had begun working too fast for anything as petty as annoyance to have a chance. If looking like Bellna would be an asset in my work, having someone who could look like anything he pleased would be ten times as valuable. No worrying about make-up or false whiskers, no worrying that someone who knew the person who was being impersonated would come by and upset the whole plan. Partnering with someone like that would let me do just about anything I had to, and there was only one thing that might interfere with the plans I was formulating.

"Tell me something," I mused, taking a deep, satisfying drag on the cigarette. "It's fairly obvious that I shouldn't have been as trusting as I was with Dameron, but what sort of man is he basically? If he gives his word about something, is he likely to keep it?"

"Certainly," Valdon nodded, looking somewhat puzzled. "He only forgets about decency and fair play when the project is involved. What have you got in mind?"

"Oh, nothing much," I demurred, lying flat on my back to blow smoke rings at the ceiling. Dameron and I had some bargaining ahead of us, and it might be better if Valdon knew nothing about it—until the proper moment. Interesting times were on their way back again, and it would be fun to see just how interesting they could get.

I would have gone to see Dameron immediately, but the clinicians weren't as through with me as I'd thought. Valdon's visit was interrupted by the appearance of three of the medics, and the base's second-in-command was figuratively thrown out so I could be gone over. I was well rested and in a fairly good mood so I didn't make too much of a fuss, but I couldn't help wondering what would have happened if I'd been in the middle of apologizing to Valdon more intimately when they'd walked in unannounced. The three clinicians were completely red-faced over my having taken off the body suit—if they'd found me comfortably in Valdon's arms as well, they'd probably have blown some fuses. I spent the time of the examination grinning at the thought, and when the clinicians were finished with their chore I sent them to Dameron with the message that I wanted to see him.

Word came back that Dameron would be waiting for me in his office, so I got into my original one-piece jumpsuit after finding it in the closet, brushed my hair a little, then went to keep my appointment. Dameron rose from his terminal seat when I walked in, and came forward to greet me.

"Well, you certainly look better than you did earlier," he said with relief-tinged joviality. "How are you feeling?"

"Not bad at all," I answered with a friendly smile. "A lot better than I thought I'd be feeling."

"You have no idea how pleased I am to hear that," he said with an easier grin, gesturing me toward my old lump chair while he went back to his blocky terminal seat. "I'd never have forgiven myself if something permanently harmful had happened to you."

"Oh, it's the *permanently* harmful you were worrying about," I nodded soberly as I made myself comfortable in the lump chair. "I'm glad to see you weren't worrying about the temporarily harmful—like being captured and slave-trained during a 'simple' decoy operation."

"That was something we couldn't have known about," Dameron protested, looking uncomfortable. "We thought Clero just wanted Bellna dead; we had no idea he wanted her for his collection."

"He wanted her for a pain slave," I corrected with all the brutality I could put into an otherwise neutral tone. "They started training me as a pain slave, and he was going to finish the job. Do you have any idea what's involved in that?"

"Now, yes," he answered, a deep inner illness showing in his eyes. "If you hadn't killed him, I would have set a team on the job with orders to use whatever they had to. Even if I knew I'd be replaced here because of it."

"If I hadn't killed him, I'd volunteer to go back," I said, then made a deliberate effort to reject the memories. "But as it stands, I don't have to volunteer to go back. How are we doing in everything else that matters?"

"Well, Bellna's with her prince, Clero's oldest son is fighting to keep the princedom, we're all back under cover, and your ship is ready for course programming," Dameron summed up, forcing a smile to get rid of the bleakness that had held him. "Have you decided yet about keeping that face you're wearing?"

"Yes, and I've decided I *will* keep it," I said. "You can give me my own voice back, but I think I've earned the face—and possibly a little something extra."

"Name it," Dameron pounced, leaning forward eagerly in his chair, his eyes lighting. "Some piece of Tildorian carving that caught your eye. Name the piece and where it can be found, and I'll have a field team after it before you can blink."

"That wasn't *quite* the souvenir I had in mind," I said, looking vaguely around his office. "It was something I stumbled across in the base, actually . . ."

"Oh, well, that doesn't matter," he said, perking up quickly after looking momentarily crestfallen. "If it belongs to someone else, I'll buy it from them for you. No matter what it costs."

"I'd really hate to put you out," I demurred, still keeping my eyes generally away from him. "I'm not sure how right it would be, and I don't want to put you on a spot."

"You're not putting me on any spot," he said with a good deal of confidence and reassurance. "I *want* to do it for you. I give you my word that I want to do it for you. Anything you choose will be just fine."

"I'm glad you look at it like that," I said, finally bringing my eyes back to look straight at him. "The souvenir I want is Valdon."

"What?" he said, all the confidence and reassurance draining out of his broad face, confusion immediately replacing them. "What did you say?"

"I said I wanted Valdon," I repeated, keeping him pinned with my stare. "Didn't you say anything I chose would be just fine?"

"I was referring to inanimate objects," he said, confusion now fighting with anger in his eyes. "I'd have to check back with Valdon's home world to find out what price to pay for him."

"Then do it," I shrugged, giving him a faint grin. "I don't expect to be unfair about this."

"Unfair!" he echoed, outraged. "Now, you listen to me. . . ."

"Don't get wild, I was just kidding," I soothed him, waving a hand to cut off the tirade. "I don't want Valdon permanently, only for a standard year or so, and I have a fair price already ready."

"Just for the hell of it, I'm going to listen to what you consider a fair price," Dameron growled, his brows down low over his eyes. "This ought to be good."

"It is," I answered with complacency. "For one standard year of his time, I offer one standard year of my own time. I understand you're in a postion to appreciate just how good a price that is."

"People talk too much around this base," he muttered, but his heart wasn't in the complaint. He *did* understand what I was offering, and the horsetrader in him was hooked. I let him think about it in silence for a couple of minutes, and then I rose to my feet.

"I'm sure you'll find the right time to give Valdon the word," I said, turning toward the door. "Right after that we can all pay a visit to my course computer. I'm sure you'll understand if I don't spend too long a time in fond farewells."

"Hold it right there," he growled, stopping me before I took more than a step or two. "This isn't anywhere near as settled as you seem to think it is. You can't simply bargain for a year of a man's life."

"Sure I can," I said, then turned back to really have it out. I'd forced Dameron to the arguing stage, which meant the argument was already half won for me. The poor man didn't have just *me* to argue with; he was still feeling guilty over what had happened to me during the job he'd given me, and he also couldn't stop thinking about the trade I'd offered. It finally came through to him that he was doing no more than giving Valdon an assignment for a year which, as Valdon's superior, he had every right to do. He still wasn't happy, especially when I refused his counteroffer to let me choose someone else with original Absari blood to save him the trouble of training a new second, but he had rationalized the decision to the point where he could accept it. When the last protest was swept under the terminal, I looked down at the mixed emotions on Dameron's face and smiled.

"Now that that's settled, I have one more question," I said. "Is Valdon completely healed, or does he need more looking after? I don't want to take him away before it's good for him."

"It's too bad you're not that concerned about me," he muttered, then got to his feet and straightened his shoulders. "Valdon is Healed all the way through, and doesn't need any looking after—at least as of this moment. What happens after he gets involved with you is another matter entirely."

"Such bitterness!" I laughed, patting his cheek in a comforting way. "Don't worry, Dameron, I'll look after your friend for you. If you like, I'll promise to never let him out of my sight."

"That's what I'm afraid of," he growled, knocking my hand away. "If you keep *your* eye on him, I'll probably never see him again."

He was so upset that all I could do was laugh to myself and get out of his way. Valdon would do fine with me taking care of him, and I hummed a little as I walked back to the hospital section to collect my belongings.

I had just moved my very few things back to the room in the residential section that had originally been mine and was moving around putting them away, when the door slid open to admit Valdon. Dameron's second was not looking pleased, so I assumed that Dameron had passed the word along. I watched my new associate stride across the room toward me, and the thunder in his black eyes was fascinating to behold.

"So that's what you were up to," he growled, stopping in front of me. "And I was feeling sorry for Dameron! Why the hell didn't you say something?"

"I hadn't completed the negotiations," I shrugged, giving him a small, friendly smile. "If it hadn't come through, you would have been ruffled for nothing."

"And this way I'm ruffled for something," he nodded. "What if I refuse to go?"

"You're perfectly free to do so," I agreed, turning the smile a touch solemn. "But if you do, don't make any plans that require good health. Dameron wants this deal so bad he's talking to himself, and if you refuse on your end, all bets are off. I'll be leaving soon, but he'll still be here, remembering what he missed out on because of you."

He growled low in his throat, a frustrated look on his face, and then his big hands were on my arms, pulling me closer to him.

"I don't like being blackmailed," he said, his voice dangerous as his fingers dug into my arms. "Give me one good reason why I shouldn't say to hell with the whole thing."

His fingers were hurting me, but I could understand how he felt. It was time to mend a few fences if the deal wasn't to come apart like rotten cheesecloth. I didn't try pulling away from him, but just looked up into those dark, angry eyes.

"I thought the matter over carefully and found that I needed you," I said, merely stating the reasoning behind my thinking that had made me start the whole thing to begin with. I thought about adding to it, telling him how useful he would be to me on the job, but the single sentence seemed to do the trick. The hardness left his eyes, his fingers loosened on my arms, and a half smile touched his lips.

"I still have the feeling I'm being had, but I can't argue with being needed," he murmured, and just for an instant I had the feeling he was reading something into what I'd said that really hadn't been there. I almost said something, but he was still talking. "Speaking of needs, I think we need to get to know each other's real selves a little better. They're giving me your language in a few minutes so I have to get going, but how about later? Unless you've got someone else to blackmail and con."

At least he was grinning when he said it. I laughed to show I appreciated the comment and said, "No, you're the only mark I'm involved with right now. Later will be fine."

He nodded his agreement, remembered to peel his hands off my arms, then left as abruptly as he'd come. I stood and stared at the closed door for a minute, wondering if I ought to pursue the thoughts I'd had about how he was interpreting things, but then decided against it. If it made Valdon happy it made me happy, and happy people made good workers, which would make the Federation happy. With all that happiness things would roll along just fine, and I turned away from the door to finish putting away my belongings, idly thinking about how nice it would be to get home again.

CHAPTER 11

It didn't take long for Valdon to get the Federation Basic that had been taken from my mind. I spent the time busy myself, getting rid of Bellna's sweet, girlish tones. I was put to sleep and then awakened, and when I opened my eyes I had my own sultry voice back. I went back to my room, and Valdon showed up just as I was thinking about getting something to eat so we went to eat together. The base refectory was a large room in stark, hungry white, with different sized tables scattered here and there in a neat but patternless arrangement. Valdon and I sat down at a small table for two, and he began checking out a box the table held. I looked more closely at the box and saw pictures of various dishes, some of which I thought I recognized. Since all my meals had come on a cart, though, I hadn't known about the box.

"Name your poison," Valdon said with a grin in Federation Basic, gesturing at the box.

"That's not what you'd call up-to-date vernacular," I laughed. "It's supposed to refer only to drinking, and is normally never heard outside of tri-v. You really got everything, didn't you?"

"Only as far as the language goes," he laughed back. "I don't think I'd care to try your *persona*."

"Not many people could handle it," I answered, flicking some imaginary dust from my sleeve. "I tend to be close to one-of-a-kind."

"And modest, too," he snorted. "No wonder you had so much trouble in Tildor."

"Name me a normal woman who wouldn't have trouble on Tildor," I countered, watching him press buttons on the box. "Any woman with an ego bigger than a bird's eye would have trouble *there*."

"No need to tell me the size of *your* ego," he commented, leaning back in his seat to grin at me. "Dameron told me what you're paying for my time with."

"That's not ego, that's fact," I shrugged, answering his grin with one of my own. "I'm good and I know it. False modesty is as stupid as egotism."

"But a little restraint in patting yourself on the back is highly recommended," he rejoindered, his tone dry. "It saves wear and tear on the arm muscles."

"Oh, after a while the muscles get used to it," I said, for some reason enjoying the idea that he seemed to be annoyed. I was willing to bet he'd matched up with Fallan a lot easier than someone else would have.

"You have an answer for everything, don't you?" he asked, leaning forward to put his forearms on the table. "That's one of the things about you that got to Fallan."

"I have to have all the answers," I shrugged again. "I usually work alone, so if an answer doesn't come from me, it doesn't come at all. It's something that's helped me to survive."

"I'd almost forgotten about that," he blinked, sitting

back a little. "The girls here at the base work as part of a team, but you work all alone."

"I've worked with teams," I smiled, "but as a matter of strict fact, I prefer working alone. That way there's less confusion about who the enemy is, and if something goes wrong you also know who to blame."

"That's one way of looking at it," he agreed. "But I don't see how that ties in with your wanting me with you. You can't work alone if I'm there."

"You'd be surprised at what I can do," I laughed. "But there won't be any problem. Your unique—talents—will balance out any petty distractions, and I'll still know whom to blame."

Suddenly he sat up straight, disquieted.

"I don't think I like the sound of that," he said, his eyes going hard. "That sounded like everything that goes wrong will be *my* fault."

"You're awfully touchy, aren't you?" I asked in annoyance, frowning now. "All I meant was that we'll be in my territory and I'll still be responsible no matter who does what. Do you expect to know what's happening right from day one?"

"I'm not an inexperienced amateur," he answered, his entire manner having gone stiff. "I don't have to be led around by the hand, and I'm big enough to be responsible for my own actions. Save the excuses for what you do on your own."

"I don't make excuses," I told him flatly, reacting to his tone. "I do what has to be done and take it from there. If that disagrees with you, maybe I'd do better with someone else."

"Maybe you would," he agreed and got to his feet, his eyes having turned very cold. He walked away from the table and out of the room, the pleasant atmosphere of a few minutes earlier gone to oblivion, and as I watched him disappear I decided it was good riddance with no regrets. I'd look through Dameron's files and find someone with his talents but without his shoulder chip.

Without my noticing it, three dishes had appeared on the table. I recognized two of them so I pulled them closer and started eating. I was too annoyed to finish either of them, but decided that there *was* something I was in the mood for. I left everything where it was on the table, asked a couple of questions of other diners, then found my way to the lounge.

The room was yellow and white, with narrow and wide lump chairs scattered around, plus a glasslike stack of shelves with bottles and the odd-shaped hexagonal glasses on it. The first of the drinkables I poured went down smoother than I thought it would, so I poured a second glass, lit a cigarette, and made myself comfortable in one of the narrower chairs. I had just about decided that the wall hanging directly opposite my chair was a cubist representation of impressionism, when Dameron walked in. His eyebrows rose slightly in surprise, but he nodded anyway.

"I thought you'd be checking on your ship," he commented as he poured something I swear was striped into a glass. "You haven't decided to stay with us instead of going home, have you?"

"Not quite," I answered, looking up at the ceiling. "I'm still anxious to start for home, but I've changed my mind. You can keep Valdon, and I'll take someone else."

"What made you change your mind?" he asked, turning away from the stack of glasses. "Under the circumstances I hate admitting it, but Valdon is the best I have here. If you think he won't measure up, you're not likely to find anyone better."

"I'm not looking for better," I answered and swallowed my drink. "Friendlier, though, is another matter entirely. When can I look through your files?"

He took a chair of his own and got comfortable.

"Barring emergencies, our official work day is now over," he said, staring at me over his stripe-filled glass rim. "As soon as Nelixan is back to work, I'll have her show you who's available."

"And willing," I amended, standing up to replace the glass I'd been drinking from. "Forcing someone into something doesn't pay in the long run. It only turns them resentful. See you around, Dameron."

I could feel his eyes on me as I walked out, and I didn't understand his attitude. I'd expected him to do handsprings over getting his precious assistant back, but instead he seemed almost disappointed. I made my way through the different groups of people going toward the refectory, and went back to my room.

I sat and smoked for a while, but there wasn't even anything to read. I was bored stiff, and too restless to even think about going to bed, but nothing else came to mind. I wondered briefly what the base personnel did for amusement, then decided to find out. I'd been kept isolated before going down to Tildor, but the briefings were over and so was the isolation. I'd see to that.

I got out of the lump chair and started resolutely for the door, but it slid open before I could reach it and I was almost run down by Valdon, who was striding angrily into the room. He was the last one I wanted to see just then, but he stopped short and folded his arms, doing a good job of blocking the doorway.

"What do you mean, friendlier?" he demanded, sending that deep black stare down at me. "What's wrong with my friendliness?"

"Oh, absolutely nothing!" I assured him sincerely. "Your sweetness attracts people by the thousands."

"Damned right it does," he nodded. "There isn't a person in this base who doesn't get along with me."

"Take another look," I suggested, folding my own arms. "If you try real hard, I'm sure you'll be able to find at least one exception to that rule. Now if you don't mind, I was just on my way out."

The ice in my tone seemed to cool him down, and the angry look faded from his black-eyed stare.

"Now, look," he said, taking a deep breath. "I don't know how we got so far off the track, but how about calling a truce? We were supposed to get to know each other a little better, and this isn't the way to do it."

"Even if there was still a reason for us to get to know each other," I informed him, looking him up and down, "I couldn't think of a better way to do it. And you're still in my way."

"I can think of a better way," he murmured, letting those hunter's eyes move over me. I was wearing a one-piece ship's suit, but he was looking at me more with his memory than with his eyesight.

"I'll just bet you can," I drawled. "This is the last time I'm going to say it—get out of my way."

"Let's talk about it," he urged, putting his hand out toward me. "We can always argue tomorrow."

" 'Never put off for tomorrow what you can do today'," I quoted, then knocked his hand aside and sent a fist with all my body weight behind it right into his heart area. He went pale and doubled over with a grunt, but having changed his looks hadn't changed his ability to take a punch. If I'd been right enough to remember that the Valdon in front of me was the Fallan who had been in that fight on Tildor I would have used a kick, but my eyes were playing tricks on my mind and I didn't remember. It only came home to me when I tried to move past him to the door; he straightened up again, threw his arms around me, and pulled me down to the floor with him.

We rolled around panting and struggling, and I was better off than the last time I'd fought with him, but was still at a bad disadvantage. He was too damned big to stop with a casual blow, and he was making sure I didn't get the chance to use anything else. He was good and mad, but he didn't try getting any of his own back, not even the way he had the last time. He kept me down until he could grab my wrists and force them over my head, then used his body to hold mine down.

"Now then," he continued, breathing hard. "Are you ready to talk things over like a real grown-up, or do we have to play more games first?"

"You son of a bitch, let me go!" I snarled, trying to break loose. "There isn't a damned thing you have to say that I want to hear!"

"It's your choice, Missy." He shrugged. "You probably couldn't have handled being partners with me anyway. Have a good trip home."

I thought he was going to let me up, but instead of moving away he grinned slightly then leaned down to kiss me! I squirmed trying to avoid it, but he just tangled his fingers in my hair to hold my head still. I was mad as hell that he would pull something that idiotic, but I still had no trouble noticing that he really gave a kiss his attention.

He took his time with the kiss, but before I realized it I was free and he was gone. I sat up slowly on the floor, disgusted with myself for closing my eyes like a vapid virgin. I decided I really must have been desperate to let him get to me like that, and then I remembered what he'd said. So I probably couldn't handle being partners

with him, huh? That damned egotist! The choice of
who went with me was mine, and I had just changed
my mind again. We'd see how cocky he was after he
had a taste of being a Federation agent!

I thought briefly about going out, then said to hell
with it and stood up to get out of the ship's suit I was
wearing. I was in no mood for amusement, and the real
entertainment would start the next day.

it. Another day or two might show you someone you like better."

"I don't think so," I denied, shaking my head "If what you said was true and Valdon is the best you have, I'd be short-changing my government if I took anyone else."

"I hope you mean it this time," he said, pushing himself away from the table and to his feet. "I get dizzy every time your mind shifts. Maybe you're getting it from eating a dinner dessert for breakfast. Let me give you one word of advice, girl. Valdon isn't a man to appreciate being wanted for what he can do rather than what sort of person he is. Keep it in mind, and you might find getting along with him a little easier."

He waved a hand and left the refectory, giving me a chance to lean back and light a cigarette while I thought about what he'd said. I didn't know how Dameron had found out about it, but I *had* been looking at Valdon as an interesting specimen rather than as a person, and it had obviously come through to the man I'd intended partnering with. That would explain his touchiness, and I had to admit it was my fault. No one wants to be wanted for nothing more than some ability they happen to possess, and something like that would have gotten to me, too. Lack of proper nourishment had obviously given me a bad case of foot-in-mouth disease.

I looked down at what I'd been eating with a grimace, then left the table and asked my way to Nelixan's office. She was an attractive woman in charge of all base files, and she nodded when she heard I wouldn't be needing those files after all, but said she was disappointed: she'd been looking forward to giving me her private opinions of the males who were available. I grinned and made myself comfortable in a chair, then told her to go ahead anyway. Nelixan didn't need much encouragement, and we spent a very entertaining couple of hours.

The work load finally got too high to be ignored, so I left Nelixan to it and went back out into the corridor. She had originally seemed like a quiet gal, but she certainly had gotten around. It would have been fun checking some of her conclusions, though. . . .

"Find anybody yet?" a voice asked in a very neutral way, and I looked up to see Valdon standing in front of me.

I smiled pleasantly and said, "Uh hum. As a matter of fact I *have* made a choice. Nice-looking fellow, and highly thought of by his co-workers."

"A true prince, I'm sure," he said with desert overtones. "Do you think you'll get along any better with him?"

"I'm sure of it," I said in my best solemn voice. "I'll be making every effort to—smooth the way."

"I'll just bet you will," he said in what was nearly a growl. "I wish you two the best. You'll need it."

He stomped off down the corridor, and I turned to watch him until he'd disappeared into a room. Very briefly I considered telling him what I'd meant, but decided quickly against it. He'd find out as soon as Dameron was back among the living, and I couldn't resist twisting the knife in him a little. There was something about Valdon that brought out the worst side of my sense of humor, something that made me want to get even. Even for what I had no idea, but there was no confusion about the feeling. He was one man I had to get even with.

I took a minute to check back with Nelixan, and she gave me a couple of suggestions about what loose ends at the base did with their time. Since relaxing in the solar room held no attraction for me, and rock hunting in a vacuum suit on the surface was just as bad, I went to see if anything was happening in the physical reconditioning chamber. Members of the Tildorian teams who had been hurt and Healed used the room to stay in shape until they could get back to the planet.

There were more than a dozen people in the room, not all of them team members. I watched quietly for a while, then joined a couple of the girls who had been working with the barbarians. We tossed each other around a little, then chose swords and got serious. I took it as easy as I could with them, but they were still outclassed, though through no fault of their own: the sword technique I'd learned in the Federation was clearly superior to anything the Absari Confederacy had developed. When the girls had had more exercise than they really should have tried, three of the men interrupted and threatened to tell the medical staff. Since that would have meant a longer stay in the base the girls quit, but not with very good grace.

The men took over for the girls and bombarded me with questions. I went through stance, balance, and angle of blade, and was just beginning on parries when we were interrupted. Valdon smiled pleasantly at the men, yanked the sword out of my hand, excused the two of us, then hauled me out of the room by one wrist. I didn't know what was going on, but he didn't slow down enough for me to ask any questions until we had reached my room. As the door slid closed behind me, I was finally able to pull my wrist away from him.

"What the hell is the matter with you?" I demanded, rubbing a wrist that felt stretched. "Where do you come off barging in and dragging me around?"

"I wanted to talk about your new partner," he said with a hard look in his eyes as he folded his arms. "You know, the good-looking fellow who's well thought of by his co-workers."

"Oh, him," I muttered, not liking his dark tones of voice. "I didn't know Dameron was awake yet."

"He isn't," Valdon said flatly. "I happened to be talking with Nelixan, and she passed on the word. If you had to change your mind again you might have told me about it! This on-again, off-again business is beginning to get to me!"

"But you didn't ask," I pointed out in a very reasonable way. "If you had asked, I would have been glad to tell you."

"Aren't you generous," he said in a voice that had suddenly turned very soft. "If it's my fault for not asking, let's take care of it right now." He moved closer fast, put his palms to the wall to either side of me, then looked down and locked eyes with me. "I am now formally asking the identity of your new partner. Would you care to tell me who he is?"

"Sure," I answered, looking up at him with a smile. "You're my new partner. And you're also wide open."

He flushed very faintly, but didn't move.

"Then take advantage of it," he offered, still staring down into my eyes. "You might be interested in what happens right after that."

I stared back at him, realizing I had a problem. I knew—without knowing how I knew—that if I started playing rough again he would not retaliate in kind as most men would. For some reason I didn't want to think about how he *would* retaliate, and above that there had already been enough argument between us. The smartest thing would be to drop a subject that never should have been brought up.

"I couldn't do that," I answered, not having hesitated long. "I said I'd be making an effort to get along with my new partner. That isn't my idea of getting along."

"What *is* your idea of getting along?" he asked, the

hard look fading from his eyes. I brought my arms up, put them around his neck, then returned the kiss he'd given me the night before, but with interest.

"That's more in line with my thinking," I said softly when the kiss ended. "Does it disagree with you?"

"I'm willing to suffer," he laughed gently, brushing some hair out of my eyes. "As your new partner, I think I ought to offer my services. Is there—anything else—you might be thinking about that I could help with?"

His faint grin made it plain what sort of anything he was referring to, but I had my own ideas on the subject.

"As a matter of fact there is," I murmured, moving closer to look up at him. "I'm just about starving to death. What are the chances of getting a decent meal around here?"

For a minute he didn't make a sound, then he started laughing. He threw his head back and roared, and I couldn't help grinning as I watched him.

"You are without doubt the craziest woman I've ever met," he said after he'd run down to chuckling. "Working with you will be an experience and a half. Well, come on! We can't have people starving around here."

He took my hand and led the way over to the refectory, then found some real, live meat dishes for me. For some reason most of the dishes looked alike in their pictures, and that's how I'd ended up with a dessert instead of what I'd really wanted. It was obvious that telling them apart took practice.

When I was happily stuffed, Valdon and I went to check on my ship. He and Dameron had done a good job putting it back together, and it seemed to be all ready to go. I poked and puttered for a little while in preparation for the next day, then took Valdon up on his offer of a tour of the base. We covered the entire thing, from the ship's entrance tunnels to the smallest of storage areas, and the base finally settled down into perspective. The people using it were humanoid and therefore had developed a lot of things strange humanoids like me would recognize, but there were enough oddities to remind me that I was a long way from home.

For instance, one of their favorite sports was deep-dropping, and an inner cavern had been prepared especially for its practice. The deep-dropper stepped off the edge of an abyss, free-fell lord-only-knows how far, and was finally caught by a safety field a random number of feet from the bottom. Since the positioning of the safety field was decided by computer, they never knew when their fall would be stopped. Also, since the safety fields had been known to fail occasionally, they never even knew *if* they'd be stopped. It takes more nerve than I have to casually walk into one of the dozens of ten-foot-wide, unlit holes, and I didn't mind saying so. Valdon looked at me less with amusement than with an odd sort of respect, then suggested that we eat again. I wasted no time agreeing with such a sensible suggestion, and we walked into the refectory to see Dameron at a table, watching as three or four dishes were raised to eating height from the center of the table. We were about to choose a place of our own when Dameron spotted us and gestured us over.

"Just the people I want to see," he said, shoveling part of his meal into his mouth. "Sit down and have something to eat."

"Why do I get the feeling I ought to be suspicious?" I asked as Valdon and I sat. "That isn't anything like the tone of voice you used when you told me how easily I could handle that business on Tildor."

"You must come equipped with ultra-sensory gear," Dameron grinned. "Better watch out for her, Valdon.

She's the type to know what you're doing even when you're only thinking about it."

"He can do or think anything he likes," I countered, not willing to be distracted. "I'm his partner, not his mother. Now what was this oh-so-casual thing you wanted to mention to us?"

"It's not exactly casual," Dameron admitted reluctantly, losing his grin. "The truth of the matter is, you can't leave for home yet."

"Why not?" I asked, keeping my eyes on his face.

"Now, don't start looking like that," Dameron protested, clearly uncomfortable. "I didn't say, you couldn't go, I just said you couldn't go *yet*."

"I think you'd better tell her why," Valdon put in quietly, placing his hand on my arm.

"Nelixan woke me for a shift level call," Dameron said, giving a lot of attention to his food. "When I got the transmitter link, I almost had my ears burned off. Seems one of our long-call operators had mentioned to the caller that we had a special visitor here. I'm sorry I ever told them about you."

"And they say only women don't know when to keep quiet," I muttered, remembering my earlier thoughts on not spreading the word. "What happened then?"

"Phalsyn took his turn at me," Dameron said, his face glum. "He and I have been friends for a long time, and that's probably the only thing that saved me. Phalsyn reminded me that little things like contacting members of other civilizations ought to be mentioned to Absar Central, even if only in passing. He also said that if I let you leave before he gets here, I'd better go with you."

"Always room for one more," I said, leaning back a little. "You and Valdon can share a cabin."

"Be reasonable, Diana!" Dameron pleaded, his eyes directly on me. "Phalsyn only wants to talk to you! He may be high in governmental circles, but he's really bright. He won't cause you any trouble."

"So *you* say," I countered, holding his gaze. "What happens if I decide to take off right now?"

"Take off where?" Valdon put in in a calm, gentle way. "We haven't programmed your course computer yet."

"I'd still be better off than when I got here," I said, throwing him a quick glance. "And maybe even better off than waiting around. When things become official, they also tend to become complicated."

"This time it can't be helped," Dameron sighed, pushing his half-eaten food away from him. "I'm sorry, girl, but you'll just have to wait to see Phalsyn. He's already on his way, so it shouldn't be too long." He stood up from the table, turned three-quarters away from me, then added, "Under the circumstances, I think you'd better stay away from your ship—at least until Phalsyn gets here."

He left then, and I watched his broad back disappear while I cursed feelingly under my breath. You can always trust people to come up with more complications than any one particular situation calls for. I started to get up too, but found Valdon in my way, still holding onto my arm.

"We haven't eaten yet," he said in the same calm, gentle voice he'd used a minute earlier. "We can't have people starving around here, remember?"

"I'll eat later," I answered hust as calmly and quietly. "There's something I have to do first."

"Do you mean get to your ship before guards are put on it?" he asked. "And then what? Take off in the first direction that appeals to you? How do you plan on getting through the ship locks? Or evacuating the air from the tunnels?"

"I'm very resourceful," I told him, merely stating a fact. "Want to bet on it?"

"Not after having given you a tour of this place myself," he snorted. "Sit still and behave yourself, or I'll have you confined to your room."

"What, no brig?" I asked with raised brows. "Surely you'd feel safer with me behind bars."

"I'd feel safest with you tied hand and foot!" he answered sharply. "If you don't stop acting like an idiot, that's exactly what will happen to you! Waiting a few days for Phalsyn isn't going to kill you."

"I'm glad you're so sure about that," I muttered, looking away from him. "I wish I could be as sure."

"Hey, nothing's going to happen to you," he protested, putting an arm around my shoulders. "If Dameron or I thought there would be any trouble for you because of this, you would already be on your way. I know Phalsyn too, and I give you my word that everything will be fine."

"Would that come under the heading of famous last words?" I wondered aloud, turning back to him. "Look, Valdon, basically I'm a pessimist. If I expect the worst to happen, I'm prepared when it does. Now, why not be a good boy and turn your head for a few minutes? You can always tell this Phalsyn that I overpowered you."

"Oh, that would solve the problem." He nodded. "He wouldn't even bother bringing me up on charges. He'd just tie a ribbon around me and send me home. You'd better sit back and relax, Diana. When it's time to leave we'll leave together."

His determination wasn't hard to see, and any more words would have been a waste of breath.

"I have very little choice," I shrugged, leaning back as

he'd suggested. "Just bear in mind that if you're wrong, I'm the type to come back and haunt you."

"I'll take my chances." He grinned, then reached past me to press buttons on the box. While we waited for the food, I reflected that "middle-of-the-night" would be as good a time to leave as right then. In a base as quiet as that one, no one would be expecting trouble.

When we finished eating, we went to the lounge and sat around with a number of the base personnel, listening to some very strange music for longer than I would have stayed on my own. When Valdon finally walked me back to my room, I wasn't disappointed over missing the "entertainment." Even if I'd been in the mood for it, I wouldn't have been able to bridge the gap between cultures alien to one another in a single sitting. My new partner followed me inside, then gave me a strong, reassuring smile.

"It shouldn't be too long," he said, referring to the wait he'd mentioned more than I had. "I can't honestly say I know what Phalsyn wants to talk to you about, but he really is the reasonable sort. After we're through with him we'll be on our way, and I *won't* have to share a cabin with Dameron."

"You sound awfully pleased about that," I commented over my shoulder as I reached for a cigarette. "I thought you liked Dameron."

"There's liking and there's liking," he said, coming up behind me to take the cigarette out of my hand and pull me gently to him. "You're a lot more my type, and I'd much rather share a cabin with you."

He looked down into my eyes as he said that, but rather than sending the sort of "let's get to it" signals most men did in a situation like that, he seemed to be searching for something. I couldn't imagine what the something could be, until I suddenly realized that his last statement had been a question. "I'd rather share a cabin with you," he'd said, not, "We *will* be sharing a cabin." He was making no attempt to force me into anything, and from my experience with him on Tildor, I knew it wasn't a put-on. He'd been very much aware of how dippy Bellna had been over him, and if he'd wanted to play twisted bed games he would have done it then. But he also knew how *I* had felt about him, and had brought in a substitute player rather than take the advantage he could have. I also remembered then what Dameron had said about how some women re- acted to him when he showed interest in them, and his lack of aggressive behavior became more understandable. The hunter had gone hungry too many times, and had therefore learned to keep his claws sheathed.

"I think you're making a mistake not wanting to share a cabin with Dameron," I said after the briefest silence, then put my hands to the top of the long stay-tab that closed his uniform and slowly began opening it. "There are men in this universe who would fight fire and flood to get a chance at a man like the commander, and here I offer you the chance and you don't even appreciate i—"

My words cut off as his hands came to my face, and when he raised it to his, the hunter's look was there in his eyes: hunger and unquenchable desire, the intention to take, the intention to continue on until complete satisfaction was attained. It was a statement as raw and direct as a big cat's scream of challenge in the night, and I didn't wonder why so many women had flinched away from it. Most women were smart enough to be wary of hunters like him—but I've never been smart in that particular way. Valdon saw the answer he was looking for when our eyes met, and a very faint smile touched his lips, then he lifted me in his arms and carried me to the bed.

*   *   *

Valdon had fallen asleep on his stomach, and I was careful not to disturb him when I got up to find my ship's suit. Before getting up I had spent some time watching him sleep, silently cursing the fact that I had to leave alone rather than take him with me. The man was absolutely incredible, and I still didn't really understand what had happened between us. I remembered being carried to the bed, remembered having the ship's suit opened and taken slowly from me, remembered the kisses and touches during the lengthy unveiling. Somehow I seemed to have missed seeing Valdon getting out of his own things, but I was very aware of his naked body when it was pressed up against mine. By then my breathing wasn't very steady, and I met his kisses with parted lips, which did even more damage to my breath rate. Somehow his hands and lips had been everywhere, and somehow I had lost all say in what we did when. Once or twice he had whispered to me, and I had done exactly as he had asked. All thought ended when he finally entered me, and didn't begin again until we had both had all we were capable of giving or taking. He had kissed me a final time then, and then had put himself on the bed beside me to sleep, one arm still around me. By the time I was able to get up, he was asleep and his arm was gone.

I turned away from him as I got into the ship's suit, not knowing what made him so different from all the other men I'd ever tried. There had been no resisting him, no ignoring him; he had asked before starting anything, but once he'd gotten his affirmative there had been no stopping him. In a way, sex with Valdon was very demoralizing for a woman, and it might have been a good thing after all that he had to be left behind. He'd made me forget about all sense of dignity and self-esteem when he'd had me in his arms, and that was nothing to make a habit of. I just hoped they wouldn't give him too hard a time when they found me gone; under other circumstances, he probably could have kept me right there. I closed my ship's suit and glanced at him one last time, then left the room.

The corridors were as deserted as I'd expected them to be, but once I'd slouched down to where the ships were and entered the bay, I stopped to frown. There wasn't a guard in sight, and that might not be too good. I could only hope that Dameron had been counting on Valdon to keep me occupied.

I cycled through the lock and headed directly for the control room. If everything was on the green I could worry about evacuating the ship's chamber and exit tunnel later. I reached the control console and started to activate the board—and my hand stopped in mid-motion. There was a thick metal cover over the activating switch, and half a dozen leads stretched from the cover to a small, featureless box that sat on the console itself. I'd never seen the cover or box before, but I knew damned well what they were. The cover kept me from activating the controls, and the box would be an alarm of some sort, set, no doubt, to go off if the cover was touched or the box itself was messed with.

I cursed with feeling for a minute, then tried to decide whether or not to tackle that box. It looked as if it couldn't be approached except from underneath, and moving it was sure to wake it up. I'd be better off diverting the leads, but that presented an entirely different set of problems. Diverting them one at a time would be easier, but there was a greater chance of setting them off that way. And with all my equipment a long way off, what the hell could I use to divert them?

"You can't get around it," a quiet voice said from

behind me. "It's completely tamper-proof, and you don't have a chance."

"I told you before that I'm resourceful, Val," I said as I turned to face him. "It would have been better if you'd stayed asleep."

" 'Val'?" he echoed with raised eyebrows. "That isn't my name."

"It's sort of silly to be formal now." I shrugged, giving him a faint grin. "Not after we've—gotten to know each other so well."

"I can't argue with that," he agreed, laughing softly with his eyes, too. "Let's go back and see if there's anything we missed."

"Maybe some other time," I denied with regret. " 'Business before pleasure' has always been the way I handled things; I'm too old to change now."

"You don't look too old," he said, studying me with his head to one side. "As a matter of fact, you look like you should have been in bed hours ago. Let us return to your accommodations, Missy. It is past time that you retired."

He stood with his arms folded and a grin on his face, and I couldn't help returning the grin. He'd switched to Tildorian speech, but we weren't on Tildor.

"Best that you tend to your own affairs, sir," I countered and folded my own arms. "I am not a child to be ordered about in such a manner."

"I do tend to my own afairs," he assured me. "At this moment *you* are my affair. You may come willingly or you may come with struggles, but accompany me you shall."

"I go my own way," I said and set myself. "No man may interfere with that."

"I must," he said, a sad look in his eyes as he got

ready to move at me. "I cannot allow you to do something wrong."

"The rough stuff won't be necessary," another voice said from behind Val. We both looked over to see Dameron, and he was shaking his head at me.

"I knew you'd probably try, but I didn't think you'd try this soon," he said, leaning against a bulkhead. "Doesn't Val suit you?"

"He isn't bad," I answered with a shrug. "I'm just not as impressionable as the other girls around here. How did you know I was here?"

"If you think I'll tell you that, you're crazy," Dameron snorted. "You're enough trouble just as you are."

"You haven't seen anything yet," I commented, studying them both. I might be able to take them, but only if I was willing to go all the way; they were too big and well-trained to play games with. The only questions was, *could* I kill them? They had saved my life more than once. Could I now justify to myself the taking of theirs?

"This isn't the time or the place to discuss it," Val said, putting his hand out toward me. "Come on, Diana, you look tired. After you've had a good night's rest we can sit around and talk it to death. Or even ignore it. How about it?"

I looked at him for a minute, then looked a Dameron, then finally walked between them and out of the control room. I'd have to take my chances with their friend Phalsyn just as I'd taken my chances with them, but I hurried back to my room so they would not have a chance to catch up to me. I was in no mood for the company of either one of them.

CHAPTER 13

I washed and dressed when I woke up, but didn't leave the room. I wasn't pleased with the thought of Dameron's surveillance system and I wasn't very hungry. I sat and smoked and fretted about things in general.

It didn't take more than a couple of hours before my peace and quiet was disturbed. The door slid aside as if I were open for business, and Valdon breezed his way in. I looked at him sourly from the low comfort of the chair I was stretched out in, and took another drag on my cigarette without saying anything.

"Are you trying to make *me* starve now?" he demanded as he stopped in front of me. "I've been waiting for you in the refectory for hours."

"That's a shame," I murmured, putting the cigarette out. "For some reason I don't remember asking you to wait."

"Asking isn't necessary." He grinned, looking down at me. "I'm a prince of a fellow, remember? Think you'd like to try it on your own this morning? I won't let you poison yourself."

"What thoughtfulness," I murmured, putting the

ashtray aside, then I looked at him again and stood up. "Well, why not? It's getting boring around here."

He stood aside to let me go first, and he looked all too pleased with himself. I'd have to see what I could do about changing that.

As I'd half expected, Dameron was sitting at a table looking somewhat anxious. When he saw me he brightened a little, but only a very little. He didn't know how right he was.

"You look like you had a good sleep," he said heartily as I sat down. "Have you been thinking things over?"

"I certainly have," I agreed with a solemn nod. "And my thinking has led me to notice something very interesting. Have you any idea how many different ways it's possible to put a bomb together from just what you find around you? Not chemically speaking, of course. . . ."

"A bomb?" Dameron yelped, paling a shade or two. "You couldn't have—" He glanced at a stunned Valdon, looked back at my small, satisfied smile, then jumped up and raced from the room, Val hot on his heels. I watched them with clinical interest for a minute, then tried my luck with the food box. When the food was delivered, I are happily in solitude then was able to smoke half a cigarette before Dameron and his trusty second came back. Neither one of them looked very happy, and that was even more satisfying than using the food box right.

"The detectors say there isn't a bomb of any sort in your quarters," Dameron growled as he sat opposite me. "You were lying, weren't you?"

"Not at all!" I protested with injured dignity. "I never said I'd *made* a bomb, I just commented on how easy it would be. If I ever decide to make one, I won't comment on it."

Dameron wearily ran his hand through his hair, and Val leaned back, looking more than annoyed.

"All that trouble for a comment," Val muttered, his black eyes filled with thunder. "Never in my life have I been more tempted to—" He broke it off, but continued to stare at me.

"A whole lot of trouble could be saved all around," I mused, lazily blowing smoke at the ceiling. "If certain people suddenly turned reasonable, they'd never have to find out how bad it can get. And believe me, you ain't seen nothin' yet."

"You are not leaving!" Dameron choked out, his face red with suppressed fury. "I don't care if this entire base is put in jeopardy—you don't budge until Phalsyn gets here! Valdon! Have her get her possessions together and move her in with you! I want her watched *constantly*! If there's any more trouble out of her, I'll hold *you* responsible!"

Dameron poked an emphatic finger at Val, pushed away from the table, then stomped out, leaving Val with a dark expression on his face. I wasn't exactly thrilled with the arrangements either, and I was still in a perverse mood.

"I think I'd prefer your lock-up," I said coldly, beginning to get to my feet. "I'll tell Dameron. . . ."

"You'll tell him nothing," he growled, grabbing my arm and slamming me back down in the seat. "You've done enough doing and telling to last everyone for a while. You'll sit there until I've finished eating, and then we'll get you moved. Not a word out of you until then."

"The *hell* you say!" I snarled, at the same time kicking for his kneecap. I was too fed up with being told where I could and couldn't go and what I could and couldn't do to worry about what damage I did, but the blow didn't land square. He moved his leg at the last instant, catching no more than the painful tail end of the shattering move, then brought his foot down hard right on top of mine. I was wearing rubber-soled deck shoes and he was wearing nothing but that one-piece uniform, but I still gasped and clutched at a mashed foot.

"That's exactly what I do say," he countered, giving me a look containing all the elements of an electrical storm. "If you try that again, you'll be limping for a week. Now, keep quiet."

He reached across me to press buttons on the box, then he leaned back again to wait for the food and stared at me unwaveringly. I turned completely away from him and ignored him totally, then surreptitiously rubbed at my foot.

When he had finished eating, he grabbed my arm and hustled me out of the refectory. I put my few things together without a sound, then was escorted to another room in the residential wing. This room, done in blue-green, brown and white, was considerably bigger, with three low chairs grouped together around a carved, obviously Tildorian table, a long lounge of sorts off to one side by itself, and a larger, more comfortable-looking bed. I dropped my possessions in one corner, walked silently into the very strange but extremely utilitarian bathroom, sat down on the floor, and proceeded to ignore everything.

For the rest of the day, I could occasionally hear Val moving around in the outer room, and he came in every once in a while to check on me. He didn't say a word and neither did I, but when he brought food in to me, I took it and ate it. But I ate just for the hell of it; my appetite had long since disappeared.

It was just about going-to-bed time when Val came in

and bluntly told me that I'd hogged the facilities long enough. I got to my feet and left him to his requirements, and just for curiosity's sake went to the door to the corridor. It was no real surprise to find that it didn't open, but I was still pushed a little deeper into the pit. I turned the room light out, groped my way to the corner where I'd left my things, got out of the ship's suit, and curled up on the floor.

The bathroom door eventually slid open, but the light was partially blocked off by Val's body as he paused in the doorway. He stood without speaking for a minute or two, then he moved farther out into the room.

"You can take the bed," he said, his voice soft in the silence. "I'll make do on the lounge."

"It's your bed and your room," I answered, moving my head around on my arm. "I'm fine where I am."

He came over and sat down on the floor near me before he spoke again.

"Diana, we're not barbarians here," he murmured. "You don't have to sleep on the floor." When I didn't say anything he put his hand on my arm and added, "You're not wearing anything, and you feel cold. Take the bed and don't worry about what will happen. I gave you my word that Phalsyn won't give you trouble, and I'll see that my word is kept."

"How nice that you can speak for Phalsyn," I murmured back. "Where I come from, bigwigs usually speak for themselves."

"I'm speaking only for me," he said, anger in his voice as he pulled me closer to him. "I couldn't keep you from being hurt on Tildor, but this base is another story."

I couldn't see his features in the darkness, but his hand was warm on my arm. I was far away from the

area of space I considered home, and there was only me
against a group of very determined strangers. I still had
no real idea what they were determined about, but it
has been my experience that some of the nicest people
you'd want to know are often ruled by the most ruthless
of governments. If you deal just with the people themselves you're all right, but if you happen to tangle with
their government, it isn't wise to plan on being home
for the holidays. I felt his warm hand on my arm and
didn't say any of that.

"I know how you must feel," he said softly, drawing
me up against him. "But you're not really alone. I'm
here, too." His hand caressed my hair and moved farther down to my back. "I saved you from that fever on
Tildor, and now I feel responsible for you. You don't
think I tended you just to turn you over to Phalsyn for
dissection or something, do you? Besides, Phalsyn isn't
so old that he wouldn't be more interested in your
outsides than your insides. You have mighty attractive
outsides."

I leaned my head on his chest, and couldn't help
grinning while my eyes blinked.

"You're not so bad yourself," I whispered, really
feeling his presence for the first time. "Don't go away
for a while."

He didn't go away, and for a lot longer than a while.
Neither one of us slept in the bed, and the lounge was
ignored, too. I still don't know how they manage to
produce tiles that are so warm and resilient. It's just a
good thing they do.

The next day Val refused to let me sit around in his
room. He dragged me to the refectory against my will,
and then had the nerve to say mixing with other people
would be good for me. When he left our table for a

minute to speak privately with someone, I casually leaned over to the next table and asked the people there if they'd heard anything about the rumor that the base was slowly losing air from an unidentified breach. They hadn't heard a thing, but by the time those particular people had left, everyone else in the room had heard about it. Val looked around at the buzzing knots of conversation, and wondered what was going on.

After we were through eating, Val stopped in to see Dameron, and I waited in Nelixan's office. She'd always been too uncertain to try Val, and was curious to know if I had. She listened carefully to my evaluation of him with a big grin, and when Val came in she looked at him with a good deal of interest.

"All set," Val said to me as he came up. "Dameron thinks that Phalsyn will be here in the next couple of days, so we have some interim time to waste. Is there something in particular you'd like to do?"

"Ah, Valdon," Nelixan interrupted in a very warm voice. "I have no plans at all for my off hours. Why don't you and I spend them together—in my room?"

"In your room?" Val repeated blankly, staring at her. "What would we do in your room?"

"Oh, I'm sure we could find *something*." She grinned, and Val finally understood what she was talking about.

"What brought this on?" he asked, curiosity in the dark gaze he sent to her. "I always had the impression I wasn't your type."

"I thought you weren't, but in the light of the latest reports, I've had to change my mind," she answered, still grinning. "How about it?"

"Sorry, Nelixan, but I'll be busy," he said with a growl, turning to give me that look again. "I have a date to strangle someone."

"What did I do?" I demanded plaintively. "I've been sitting here quietly, not even thinking about my ship . . ."

"Sitting there quietly?" he exploded, taking a step toward me. "You consider discussing me sitting there quietly?"

"Why not?" I shrugged. "Are you ashamed of your abilities?"

The look in his eyes darkened as he stared at me, but he couldn't seem to think of an answer to that one.

"It's hard to remember that some men are shy about such things," Nelixan said with a laugh. "Maybe we shouldn't have mentioned it to him."

"I'll remember that for next time," I said, which for some reason forced a wordless growl from him. He grabbed me by the neck, pushed me out into the corridor, then directed me by hand to the solar room. We sat in artificial sunshine for a couple of hours without talking, and he made sure I stayed away from anyone else who came in. I sat back and relaxed completely, and made sure that no sign showed of the grin I should have sported.

I had almost decided to take off the ship's suit when someone came over saying that Dameron was looking for Val and me. We went back to Dameron's office, noticing the knots of excitedly whispering people on the way, and were gestured right in. I had on my most innocent of expressions, and Val was genuinely in the dark, but Dameron didn't leave him there for long. The rumor about the base's "air loss" had finally reached the base commander, and though no one could actually trace it back to me, Dameron had no doubts. He must have ranted and yelled for an hour, but Val got the brunt of it. Val had been made responsible for me, so anything I did was his fault, and Dameron kept repeating the point so it wouldn't be lost on Val. Val caught on real quick, and spent most of his time just looking at me. After a few minutes, I wanted to scrunch down in my seat.

When the tirade was finally over, Val rose from his chair without a word and stood next to the open door, waiting for me to go through first. I wasn't sure about trusting him behind my back, but I didn't have much choice in the matter. He followed me down the corridor and back to his room, and we spent the rest of the day with Val staring straight at me, not saying a single word. Our food was delivered by cart again, and no one came to call.

By the time I was ready to call it a day, I still hadn't heard anything from tall, dark and awesome, but I was too sleepy to still be bothered by it. I hadn't had much sleep the night before, and the safe passage of time tends to wear off most sharp edges. I used the facilities to wash as best I could—I hadn't found any equivalent of a shower or bath—then got out of the ship's suit and into bed. Val was still staring at me, but I discovered that his stare was on a different level, so I smiled to myself as I got comfortable, wondering if he would forgive me enough to join me in bed. The chances were still 50-50 when he went into the bathroom, but the scales tipped all the way in my favor once he came out. He got into bed next to me, waved the light out, then pulled me to him.

"I thought you were mad at me," I said with a small laugh, rubbing my cheek on his chest.

"No, I was more disgusted with me," he murmured, already touching me with hands and lips. "It was my own fault for taking my eyes off you. It won't happen again."

After that we were too preoccupied to say anything else, but I clearly remember laughing at what he'd said. I hadn't yet learned he was a man of his word.

The next two days started off badly and got steadily worse. When Val had said he would not take his eyes off me again, he hadn't been kidding. We went to the refectory to eat—once. All I did was wonder aloud what the Tildorian barbarians could have put in their herb mixture that was able to get around base inoculations, and pow! Right back to that crummy room. And I hadn't even had the chance to suggest it might be something contagious! We stayed in the room every minute of the two base days and nights, having our meals delivered to us, with no one being allowed to listen or talk to me. I considered getting violent, decided that that would be stupid, then tried it anyway. Even with the limited number of non-lethal things I could do Val ended up bruised, but I ended up flat on the floor, face down, with him sitting on top of me. He refused to let me up unless I gave my word not to make any more trouble, but I'm not often that easy to convince; we stayed that way a ridiculously long time before the delivery of our next meal broke it up. I hadn't given my word, but I needed some help in standing up.

By the time the confinement was over I was nearly insane. Val had ignored all the frozen silence coming from me, and had calmly chattered away almost without stop. I was bored to the point of wanting to start a fight just for something to *do*, but he refused to argue and I was in no mood to spend more time being mashed into the floor. I flatly refused to be friendly in bed, but that didn't bother him either. He just laughed and said he could wait.

When we were finally escorted over to Dameron's office, I was as far from feeling diplomatic as you can get. Dameron was nowhere in sight, but a man sat relaxing in the blocky terminal chair, and I studied him openly. He was a lean, well-preserved man in his apparent sixties, wearing a base uniform in yellow with no insignia, and he had gray hair and sharp, intelligent gray eyes. He moved his head to inspect me as Val and I took seats, but there wasn't a word out of him. I returned the appraising look and just waited, but he kept up the silent treatment for longer than was wise with me just then, so I decided to make the first move.

"Did—you—want—too—see—me—about—something?" I finally asked slowly and clearly, as if he might be hard of hearing—or well into senility. Val made an exasperated sound, but Phalsyn just laughed.

"I see why Dameron was so impressed with you," he said pleasantly. "Many people in your position would be apprehensive, if not down-right frightened. I applaud your self-possession."

"Thanks," I answered, not joining his amusement. "Where I come from, people don't think I'm bright enough to be frightened. Situations have to be spelled out for me. Is there a reason for me to be frightened?"

"Not at all," he assured me, leaning forward to emphasize his words. "On the contrary, we have every reason to be grateful to you."

"Grateful," I repeated. "For barging in and disrupting one of your outposts?"

"Of course not," he smiled. "We're grateful for the help you supplied on Tildor. The planet is of special concern to us, and we like having things go smoothly there. If our—assistance—becomes too noticeable, we may never get to the bottom of the Paldovar Villages question."

"You probably never will anyway," I commented. "I had a taste of their methods, and I couldn't even guess about how they do it."

"That's almost *our* problem," he agreed with a grimace. "Our people have had more than one taste, are willing to speculate endlessly as to the how of it, but the speculation is useless. We want to *know*, but precipitous action won't gain us the knowledge." Then he flashed a quick grin. "Perhaps a fresh outlook is what's needed. When you return to us, you may well find yourself back on Tildor."

"I can live without the honor," I assured him. "Am I supposed to notice that 'when you return to us' phrase, or ignore it and go on discussing Tildor?"

"Notice it, by all means," he laughed, leaning back in his chair. "It's the introduction into the second reason as to why we're so pleased to have you here. We've been hoping for a go-between for some time now."

"And since I'm anything but a private citizen, I'm it," I summed up. "I can understand your pleasure, but I can't understand why you neglected to mention it. It would have made the last few days slightly more enjoyable."

"Call it—an experiment," he said with something of a smile behind his eyes. "We still don't know as much about your people as we would like to, and it was an opportunity for observing you. For someone who handled a weapon on Tildor with such lack of concern, you showed remarkable restraint with our base people. It's an encouraging sign."

"That's me," I muttered, remembering what I'd gone through the last few days. "Encouraging. We're all lucky I happen to be fond of certain of your base personnel. I take it the proposed partnership now has official approval?"

"It certainly does." Phalsyn smiled, picking up a cube marking rod to play with. "It's an excellent chance for one of our people to look around your Federation without causing a stir. When the two of you return here, you'll have a similar opportunity to study our Confederacy. That combined with the formal talks should go far toward establishing an atmosphere for friendly negotiation."

A previously unnoticed tension seemed to have melted out of me by then, so I was able to get more comfortable in my lump chair.

"Formal talks," I mused. "You sound as though you have something specific in mind."

"Something very specific," he nodded. "We would like to have a delegation of your people meet with a delegation of ours—in our sector of space. Do you think they'd be willing to agree to that?"

"I have no idea," I answered honestly. "It all depends on how they take the news of your existence. The only thing I can suggest is that the approach to my government be made through the chief of my department. He has some fairly intelligent contacts who might be able to keep the flap down to a minimum."

Phalsyn considered that for a minute, and then nodded again. "Very well. It would be foolish not to take your advice on the matter. I'll supply you with a set of coordinates and a date far enough in advance so that there will be ample time for adjustment to the situation." He hesitated very briefly, looked at me with casual friendliness, then began, "About the report you'll be making to your people. . . ."

I laughed. I threw my head back and laughed with more sheer enjoyment than I'd felt in too long a time. When I finally ran down, Phalsyn smiled politely.

"You found amusement in something I said?" he inquired.

"You might say so." I grinned. "Are you really that nervous about what my report will contain?"

"I hadn't realized it was all that obvious," he answered wryly.

"To be perfectly frank, I considered bringing Dameron up on charges when I learned what the impression had done to you. His carelessness could have caused a good deal more trouble than it did."

"But it did work out, so there's really nothing to complain about." I shrugged. "My report will include everything that's happened to me here, told as objectively as possible, with no hidden resentments. Don't forget, I accepted the assignment even though I didn't have to."

"That's true," he agreed. "But with an assignment of that sort, you shouldn't have to contend with problems from your own people. If I were in your position, I don't know if I could be as broad-minded as you."

"I'm not broad-minded." I smiled, then glanced at Val. "I simply feel that I've been repaid for any inconveniences I might have suffered."

Val stirred in his lump chair with an annoyed look in his eyes, but I didn't care if he *was* feeling like a joy boy. After the last couple of days, annoyance was the last thing he deserved.

"Your partnership may be even more useful than anyone at first imagined," Phalsyn said with a grin when he saw my glance. "It's occurred to me that if we exchange enough personnel, we may bypass most of the acceptance difficulties inherent in a situation like this one."

The comment made us all laugh, but Val found it necessary to put in, "That would take a lot of personnel. I don't advise starting that project until my final report is in."

I looked at the louse in annoyance, and Phalsyn chuckled.

"I'm glad to see that your partnership isn't based on anything as foolish as romance," he said. "I've always found venal self-interest to be much more reliable. Dameron is waiting for us in the lounge, and I suggest we join him. We have a new partnership to celebrate."

"Celebrate," I snorted, sending a withering glance

toward Val before standing up and turning to the older man. "What's your favorite potion, Phalsyn? If it isn't striped, I'll try it."

"No, my favorite is definitely not striped," Phalsyn answered in amusement and stood out of the chair to take my arm. We left the office companionably, and Val hesitated briefly before following us. Maybe he was thinking about Nelixan—or dissection.

The party was long and friendly, and I made sure to get relaxed without getting looped. Val eventually relaxed too, but Dameron seemed too preoccupied to join in the general conversation and laughter. Phalsyn was nothing but charming and attentive, and that bothered me. I'd expected a few select questions about the Federation, yet he discussed nothing but trivialities. That means he had either gotten what he'd been after, or he knew I couldn't give it to him. I wasn't about to try guessing which, so I just enjoyed the party.

Just as I got the impression that Phalsyn was ready to make a suggestion, Val stepped in smoothly, remarked that we'd be leaving early the next day, and hustled me off to his room. Phalsyn had been amused by the action, but I was more annoyed. I started to tell Val off as soon as we were alone, but he didn't let me get very far, and when he pulled me into his arms I lost all interest in arguing. We had a nice, warm time together, as a kind of farewell to the base; the next day I would be heading home to look up the slaver Radman—which was certain to prove interesting.

DAW

Presenting JOHN NORMAN in DAW editions . . .